to my wife

by Albert Memmi

The Pillar of Salt

BY ALBERT MEMMI

TRANSLATED FROM THE FRENCH BY
EDOUARD RODITI

*"But his wife looked back
from behind him, and she became
a pillar of salt."*
Genesis 19:26

A Howard Greenfeld Book
J. Philip O'Hara, Inc.
Chicago

J. Philip O'Hara, Inc. 20 East Huron, Chicago 60611.
Published simultaneously in Canada by Van Nostrand
Reinhold Ltd., Scarborough, Ontario.

LC: 55-7841
ISBN: 0-87955-907-1 (trade)
ISBN: 0-87955-905-5 (paper)

CONTENTS

PROLOGUE

This morning I got up before the alarm clock rang. I washed my face with cold water, bathed my smarting eyes in my cupped hands, and was out of the house before the first streetcars came by full of sleepy grocers on their way to the central market. As I entered the examination hall, my name was called out, and I felt, as always, my heart beat faster. I took the seat that was marked with my name and made the acquaintance of my neighbors.

We are old hands at the game of being students, and to display any emotion now would be absurd, so much so that we even exhibit our disinterest in the tone of our conversation. My neighbor to the left is small and dark, with somber eyes set deep beneath jutting brows. His name is Bounin. Yes, he's a North African from Constantine, and already a teacher. He is taking the exam now just for sport. The degree might be useful, of course, but he is already too old to be tempted by considerations of vanity. My neighbor to the right is called Ducamps, and he affects an elegant disorder in his dress and manner, with his well cared for hair all rumpled. He is finishing the job of studying if only to have done with it all, and he detests teachers and the whole teaching profession: a fool's job that reveals the nature of the men who choose it. Ducamps leans back in his chair, stares at us as if taunting us, and forces us to concede his complete detachment. In my turn I explain that I come from Tunis. No, Tunis has not been razed to the ground by the Germans. Have I gone through the whole reading list? No, indeed; not even the most important books, the required readings. What do I intend to do after the exams? I don't know. Bounin insists, with all of his anxiety: will I choose journalism or research? Frankly, I don't know, I no longer know.

Silence spreads from the back of the hall, hesitates, then soon dominates the anxious aisles. This is the solemn moment when the anonymous supervisors, their faces like masks, their gestures ritualistic, move in a wave along the rows of students, passing out the examination questions at the end of each table. The hands of the students feel these little squares of yellow paper, their eyes inspect them in flight. They have read the questions, and their heads rise again as they smile anxiously, though their words must remain detached. This easy banter is aimed against the future, the university, our own shameful weaknesses, and the watchful gaze of the supervisors. But we can only whisper, for silence has already triumphed. Silence. The huge hall and its hundreds of students no longer seem even to breathe. Each one of us has now identified himself with his own task, each is alone for the next seven hours.

In that moment, facing my blank sheet of white paper, I suddenly understand that these tasks no longer concern me. The spring that was taut within me is now completely released, my strength and my will power have abandoned me. I am neither surprised nor disappointed. How was I ever able to be interested in these games that now seem so absurdly futile? Today, we are asked the following: "Analyze the influence of Condillac on John Stuart Mill."

I look around me at all my comrades. Their heads bent forward, their faces pale, their hair tangled beneath their nervous fingers, they all know what they want. All of them— the old students whose studies have been delayed by the war, and the younger whose luck has not yet run out—all are jealous of time. To gain time, to waste time. But what have I to lose? There is but one final stake for me to risk, and I have perhaps already lost it.

Bounin looks up, with a movement of his chin towards me, his fountain pen still moving, he asks: "How's it going?" Bounin's eyes are vague, he is already deep in his subject and he scarcely hears my answer. His lips sketch a smile and he bends his head again. Ducamps is examining the ceiling. He is one of those who pretend to reflect before they begin to write. I, too, appear to be thinking, but I'll not be working later. For the first time in my life I'm about to waste the time allotted for an exam. Within a few hours, I'll be wasting a whole year, in fact all of my life. But what have I done with my life up till now? I can no longer play this part that I've been acting.

No one looks up any more, all these backs are bent in the silent struggle. Now, if I don't write, I'll attract the attention given to the defeated or the novice. I've allowed my eyes to wander all over the hall, to the painted panels of the ceiling, along the walls lined with books. I've counted the panes in the windows, the shelves of the bookcases, the aisles and bays of the hall. No, I'm not a novice and I don't want them to think that I am. I still have this absurd sense of shame, so I lower my head and pretend to write. I write anything that comes into my head, and the first hour goes by, as always, quite pleasantly.

This solace is a vice: this forgetting through writing, which is the only thing that gives me some peace of mind and distracts me from my world. I can no longer think of any-thing but myself. Perhaps I should begin by closing my own account. How blind I was to what I really am, how naive it was of me to hope to overcome the fundamental rift in me, the contradiction that is the very basis of my life! Well, I might as well admit it: there's a constant ringing in my ears and a pain in my chest. At first I refused to pay any attention to it, but the ringing in my ears is now like an insistent bell. The truth is that I'm a ruined man, that I ought to declare myself a bankrupt.

To give myself countenance, to escape, I continued writing for seven hours, like all the others. I even made the most of the extra fifteen minutes of grace granted to the stragglers. That is because my whole life was rising up in my throat again, because I was writing without thinking, straight from the heart to the pen.

At the close of this exhausting session, I had some fifty pages to carry away with me. Perhaps, as I now straighten out this narrative, I can manage to see more clearly into my own darkness and to find a way out.

PART ONE

The Blind Alley

1

THE BLIND ALLEY

MY FATHER'S BREATHING, a rapid hissing, punctuated the nighttime silence of our room. The world of my childhood was reassured and protected by this asthmatic breathing that dispelled the terrors of my solitary awakenings. When the moon rose high and plunged its light deep into the narrow blind alley, the anxieties of night stopped at the bars of our window, as their shadows, slowly revolving, cast a pattern of squares on the wall of the room. But I hated to stare at the room that was all sticky with the darkness that seemed to distend the clothes hanging from nails in the wall behind the closed door, that appeared to stifle the mirror of the wardrobe, and then to dissolve itself in a bluish mist by the window. I kept my eyes closed and was soon asleep again. Now, I want to remember all this. My life has known days of innocence when I had only to close my eyes in order not to see.

Regularly, at dawn, I was awakened by the muffled and spasmodic rumbling of the garbage carts. Frightened, I would nestle close to my father in the big family bed, with my legs

3

against his belly. He would then place his heavy hand on my head, with a gesture that had become a ritual. After the resounding crashes of the empty garbage cans being dropped to the ground, the cart would move heavily away, stumbling with all its loosely joined boards over the uneven street-paving. I would then fall asleep again until morning. My mother was always the first to rise, always in a hurry to begin her daily life at once; and soon the odor of Turkish coffee would fill the kitchen and overflow into our room. My mornings of hope are still perfumed with Turkish coffee.

We lived at the bottom of the Impasse Tarfoune, in a little room where I was born one year after my sister Kalla. With the Barouch family we shared the ground floor of a shapeless old building, a sort of two-room apartment. The kitchen, half of it roofed over and the rest an open courtyard, was a long vertical passage toward the light. But before reaching this square of pure blue sky, it received, from a multitude of windows, all the smoke, the smells, and the gossip of our neighbors. At night, each locked himself up in his room; but in the morning, life was always communal, running along the tunnel of a kitchen, mingling the waters from the kitchen sinks, the smells of coffee, and the voices still muffled with sleep.

We took turns with the Barouch family to go into the kitchen to the only washbasin with its single faucet. We came there fully dressed so as not to catch cold while crossing the little yard, and we had to be content with spreading a lather of soap over our faces as far as our ears while taking care not to wet the collars of our shirts. But it was forbidden for us, whether for reasons of self-esteem, hygiene, or religious belief, to sit down to a meal without first washing our faces.

In our alley, the goatherd would announce his impatience with long blows on his horn. My mother would remove the two iron bars that protected our front door against thieves and pogroms. I never dared follow her as she pushed through the compact herd of goats that stared at her without blinking their insolent and surprised eyes. The Maltese goatherd wore a thick red flannel sash around his loins, and he would squat down against the wall, on his patched boots. He would take the brown earthenware pot and grab a goat at random to draw from her the sudden spurts of foaming milk. Angry infants, always numerous in our part of town, cried sourly. The street, seeming to awaken with regret, grumbled from all its open windows, shaking itself free from the sluggishness of a light mist that slowly settled on the damp paving stones. The sun was still benevolent. My mother came back through the herd, pushing aside with her hand the goats that were too obstinate to move and holding her pot of milk safe above any unforeseen or capricious movements of the animals. We then breakfasted in our room that was still full of the odors of sleep, seated at our round table that was our sole heritage from my grandfather, between the walls washed with blue lime and the bed still warm beneath a mound of red and green blankets.

One morning my mother forgot and left the door ajar. I opened it wide and found myself, for the first time in my life, alone facing the goats, those monsters with their long silky hair, black and rust-colored, that stood taller than I by a whole head plus their horns. I hesitated on the threshold, but a plan that had long been maturing within me, though I had always postponed its execution, now pushed me ahead: at last, I had an opportunity to test the world all by myself and, at the same time, to revenge myself on these goats that seemed to challenge me. Without moving, I selected with a glance the most terrifying and most maternal of them all, the one with the most swollen dugs. The beast was turning its head away from me. Softly, I came a few steps closer, stretched out my hand and, suddenly seizing a fistful of the heavy fur of its haunches, pulled as hard as I could. Then something happened that I had not allowed myself to foresee, for courage demands contempt for consequences: the beast did not try to escape, did not utter a cry of anguish, but suddenly turned around, lowered its head, aimed its sharp horns at me, and

charged, the bell at its neck furiously ringing. I uttered a hor-
rifying howl and threw myself toward the door. I no longer
know—indeed, I never knew—whether the horns really grazed
me. But I slammed the door and, still howling with all my
might, propped myself with both hands against the panel,
as if I were holding back the whole of Hell.

Avowing my distress by my cries, I automatically called on
my guardian angels for protection. At once my mother, the
neighbors, and my father, holding up his unbuttoned pants,
rushed to my rescue, while heads appeared at the balconies
and galleries of the upper stories of the house. Someone
caught hold of me, lifted me up, and I closed my eyes,
yielded entirely, my legs suddenly weak, my heart in anguish.
But I was safe, no matter how painfully my heart beat
against my ribs, no matter how weakly my legs failed to
carry me. My mother gave me a glass of sugar and water
and told me to go and urinate.

"But I don't feel like it."

"One always feels like making pee-pee. Go ahead and do
it, or else you'll catch jaundice."

I pissed and didn't catch jaundice. But my mother attrib-
uted to this scare an abscessed gum that I developed later.

In all the history of my early childhood, this incident stands
out as one of the few unpleasant ones that I remember. And
the few small dangers that ever dared disturb my day-to-day
happiness were immediately dispelled by the all-powerful
appearance of my parents.

After breakfast, my father used to slip into his oldest
jacket, his work jacket, then his only overcoat, which he
carefully folded inside out when he reached his shop, and
took his two heavy Arab keys, each of them weighing a full
pound. Before leaving the house, he piously kissed the
mezuzah on our door, which contained the name of God in
a small glass tube, and then he departed, leaving us in peace,
and with his own mind at rest. Once my father had gone to
the store and my mother had settled down to her work in

our kitchen, we children took possession of the alley. Narrow as it was, it seemed huge to me. Closed at one end by the wall of the cemetery, the other opened onto the narrow rue Tarfoune, useless and deserted. This double bottleneck that led into the heart of the noisy and crowded Arab neighborhood followed two sudden turns so that it seemed to be defending a hollow of silence. And we defended it, too, against the few children who ever dared venture there, until the day when a howling gang of rough and nasty boys picked this out-of-the-way place in which to play their forbidden games. We were insulted, pushed around, even beaten; and our dead end, no longer safe for us, ceased to play so important a part in our imagination for it became just another alley in this sordid city. Soon after that, I began to go to school and lost the dead end for good. But before this catastrophe and ever since my birth, my mother's breast and our one room seemed to extend into a soft and unreal world that submitted patiently to our play like a good-natured old dog.

Immediately after breakfast, Mother used to send us out so that she could do her household chores in peace. We would still be acting out our undisturbed dream when the sun, rising straight ahead in the sky, filled the alley to the brim with a blinding light that dispelled every fold of shadow. We used to play at trades, at being doctor, tailor, saddler, above all, grocer. Our plump little fingers transformed old matches, stuck into holes in the wall, into the spigots for drawing olive and peanut oil. We used to mix water with the black earth in order to make sorghum paste, or with yellow sand to make *halva*, or with crushed apricot stones to make milk. In old tin cans in which tobacco was sold we put the semolina we made from chalky plaster we scraped from between loose stones in the walls. Measuring and mixing very seriously, I played the part of the grocer while Kalla was the housewife: as among grown-ups, I benefited from the masculine privileges. We also had seasonal games: fruit pits in summer, buttons in winter, in spring we hunted green caterpillars that were born spontaneously, we thought, of the morning dew. We also believed that they headed for cooking pots in order to poison our food. We used to throw handfuls of coarse salt on the poor things to see them suddenly shrink and then melt, soon leaving but a small spot of yellowish liquid on the cold pavement of the yard.

We even had our secret pleasures, the first expressions of an inner life that was independent of our parents. In winter, once night had fallen, Mother used to light the oil lamp. The flame would hesitate, reddish and exhaling a malodorous black smoke, and the furniture seemed to dance in the struggle of light and shadows. Of this uncertain strife the room as we knew it by night was born, mysterious and welcoming, with planes of yellow light, shadows with hard edges, and impenetrable voids. We then abandoned the passage that had grown too cold, and climbed into bed, to slip as fast as we could beneath the heavy blankets with their warm colors, the red of embers, the green of cactus, the purple of eggplant. We would disappear completely, alone in the heart of the darkness. Whispering and groping, we helped our hands to find each other. Mother, awaiting Father's return, busied herself with some sewing, her head almost touching the lamp. Sometimes, she would ask us:

"What are you up to?"

Half-stifled, raising the blankets with difficulty, we thought that we gave, from the outside, the appearance of a small tent, and announced our alibi:

"We're playing at housekeeping."

I doubt whether she ever suspected what we were actually doing and I do not remember experiencing any deep feelings of shame about it.

One evening, however, the harsh sound of the needle piercing the stuff in the warm silence of the room suddenly stopped. We heard a strange voice speaking. Inquisitive, we stuck our heads out. Catarina, the wife of the Maltese goat-herd, was there to collect for the morning milk. Impru-dently, when she saw us, she exclaimed to my mother:

"Fancy that! You already have two children, and I thought you had only one."

Mother's expression changed, her mouth drawn tight and hostile in the face of this appeal to the Evil Eye. Wild as a female animal that feels its offspring threatened, she came toward us and, pretending to caress us, stroked our bodies with her hand wide-open, all five fingers held straight. I shivered, feeling a mortal cold descend through me. God forbid that the exorcism should fail! To distract attention from what she was doing, Mother asked me:

"But what are you doing there?"

Perhaps because the danger had unnerved me, perhaps also because I wished to take advantage of it in order to betray a secret that was beginning to weigh on my conscience, I exclaimed:

"We're making love!"

After that I covered my face, while Mother and Catarina burst out laughing, both of them believing that I had only repeated some coarse remark overheard in the street.

Of my earliest years, I have no memories other than those of an endless game, played in constant safety in our twice-concealed blind alley.

2

THE SABBATH

At first, I wanted to write a whole book about the even tenor of happiness of my earliest years, but in spite of my nostalgia for this period, I have barely managed to scribble these few pages about it, as though I were trying to avoid its very memory. Still, I would like to add something now about our Friday nights and our Saturday mornings, so wonderfully joyful and peacefully holy.

Friday was always born in an excited dawn, and it blossomed majestically into a triumphant Sabbath that made us stiff and solemn in our holiday attire, all lit up by the solemn candles. Kalla and I had no new duties, but we enjoyed the happy excitement of the household. Mother and Joulie, our neighbor, assisted by the latter's daughter Touira, hurried all day at their chores, with twice as many fires in their earthenware hearths, for they had to set out, all over the rooms, the meals for two whole days. They only just managed to get everything done by the time the first star appeared to announce the Sabbath. At five o'clock, the darkness that was beginning in our room discovered a new order: the laden table spread with an embroidered white cloth, the chest of drawers bearing a bowl of yellow narcisssus, the bed and the sofa covered with white sheets. The great brass candlestick and two Phoenician lamps replaced the oil lamp. The olive oil sizzled as it burned, with an occasional sputter, and cast trembling shadows that were soft and unfamiliar on our walls. For the Sabbath, even the light seemed unusual. Scrubbed in warm water, combed and dressed in our best, we waited for Father to come home earlier than usual. But on his way he had stopped at the barber's so that when he appeared he was well shaven and combed, already Sabbatical in spite of his working clothes. He dropped his heavy keys on the marble top of our chest of drawers and drew oranges, sweet lemons, or dates and nuts from the depths of his coat pockets, or else a big bag of roasted chick-peas and a smaller one of pistachio nuts, all of which he handed to Mother.

One after another, our Friday evening friends then began to arrive: Didakh the cobbler, Hmaïnou the watchmaker, sometimes Joule, the landlady's son who felt happier with us than with his own mother. My father, with everything about him clean, his hair carefully brushed flat, and a sprig of jasmine tucked over his ear, was happy and relaxed, seated Turkish style on the divan as on a throne. The men would then drink their little glasses of *araki* as they ate force-meat balls, chick-peas, and strongly seasoned pickled carrots and squash. As for me, I greedily accepted the little drop of alcohol that they often offered me; and as the feast went on, my eyelids began to grow heavy and I was already slightly drunk by the time we got around to eating dinner. I cannot remember ever having gone to bed on a Friday night; I suppose I used to fall asleep while still at table, as I have often seen Kalla fall asleep, her white face disappearing beneath her beautiful black hair.

Sleep, when one has no worries, tastes like honey. We

woke up without haste, and found ourselves in a morning
filled with an unusual happiness. We stayed longer in bed,
where Father helped us perform complicated acrobatics.
Then, once we had annoyed Father and driven him out of
bed, we stared at the world upside down, with our heads
down and our legs propped against the wall, enjoying the
exquisite vertigo that made us dizzy. Oh, these Saturday
mornings! In our room, through the wide-open window, the
blue stretches of sky with their slow white clouds and the
streaming sunlight, the sun swimming in the limitless universe
as in those dreams where I felt myself rise and rise in the
open sky, my heart and my breast so brimful. . . . So far
away, I still suffer whenever I think of Saturday mornings.
All my life, the bitter and oily odor of the narcissus, their
fresh explosion of gold in the transparent glass of the bowl,
will remain rich with implications of holiday.

My father was in no hurry to finish dressing and took
unusual pains, letting a few drops of eau de Cologne fall on
his shining hair. I always demanded the same ritual for
myself, but immediately protested when the alcohol made
my eyes and my scalp smart. But it was already too late:
"Let it be and don't be silly, it's good for the skin." Mother
would hasten to dress me and always ask my father: "Will
you be taking your son along?" My father would ask me:
"Do you want to come along?" as if it were possible for me
to refuse the greatest joy of the whole week. Then we would
wait for the faithful Joseph. Ten years earlier my father's
only workman had renounced his Italian origin and had
changed his name from Giuseppe to Joseph so as to become
part of our family. My father trusted him fully in the shop
and chose him also as his companion for all holiday pleasures.
When, one day, Joseph talked of getting married, my father
opposed this project so violently that we were all astonished.
Obscurely, my father sensed that Joseph would then belong
to his wife and become Giuseppe again; his opposition was

so successful that Joseph remained an old bachelor. So he still turned up every Saturday, looking ungainly and odd in his best suit—the "Sunday best" of the careful poor—pants and a jacket of fawn-colored cloth and a white artificial silk scarf that bore the marks of having been pressed with too hot an iron. Our housewives, in North Africa, seem to press clothes badly: they are either in a hurry or try to do the job too well, laboring at the iron as if to give what they are pressing a sheen of newness that it has long since lost, as if care could somehow compensate for wear and tear. Whenever Joseph happened to turn up late, my father would be upset, but Joseph allowed him to grumble without answering back, staring at his shoes that were always of a light spring or fall model and well aware of the fact that he was at fault. We had to go to Bodineau's store to choose some leather and to Sarfati's to renew our stock of whip-thongs. Joseph never objected that my father's store did not belong to him or that Saturday was a holiday and he was free to spend his time as best suited him. Like my father, he was part and parcel of the store, and it was the store that kept us all alive.

The street was lazy and relaxed like a young girl's rose-colored vision of dawn. We had long given up going to the synagogue on Saturdays and visited our suppliers instead, but Saturday was still a holy day. We felt pure and clean and had the assurance of the well-dressed who enjoy leisure. Besides, we usually met the faithful on their way back from Temple, walking daintily in the soft sunshine, holding with the tips of their fingers their book and the little bag that contained their *taleth*. Fat and happy, their faces quite unresponsive, they went along unhurriedly, as sure of the absolute harmony of the universe as they were of finding their home full of flowers perfuming the air, with a white cloth on the heavily laden table.

Toward eleven o'clock there would appear, at the end of

our walk and impressing my gaze with their great pomp, the
huge stores of Bodineau. They dominated this whole part of
town, both by their location and their proportions and by
their wealth of window space and nickel fixtures. One
reached the main entrance up a flight of rather high steps
on either side of which a large showcase, each as big as our
room, triumphantly reflected the sunlight on the town. The
showcase on the right was the home of a fabulous beast that
shared the enchantment of Sabbath: a whole horse, all har-
nessed with brand-new leather that was studded with gold,
its eyes blazing, its reddish and white-haired chest borne
proudly aloft. I admired it each time for a long while,
though without coming too close to it and always clutching
my father's hand.

Later, I was surprised to learn that there are people who
dislike the odor of tanner's bark; for me, it remains one of
my basic experiences of smell. Beneath our big family bed
we always had a store of skins of all kinds, and during the
long summer siestas I often slept in our shop on improvised
beds of leather that imposed their character on my dreams.
I can reconstruct the whole world and find my way about it
like a fox, guiding myself by the warm and masculine scent
of the leathers from France, by the tart, heavy and greasy
odor of white skins, the stink of stables that clings to fresh
skins as they rot, the almond bitterness of blackened calfskins.

In the big salesroom, we would meet my father's artisan
colleagues, all just as awkward in their Sunday clothes.
Balancing themselves on the tips of their toes as they crouched
so as not to dirty their clothes by sitting or kneeling, they
felt the skins with their heavy fingers before they selected
those they wanted. They greeted each other cheerlessly.
Nakil, a big fellow with a face that was all hard angles
around his piercing eyes, was the one they all watched most
closely, the one they feared and envied most. Once a year
he went to France to make a few purchases without having

to go through the hands of the wholesalers. "He's a devil," my father always said, and I hated him too, with the hatred that all felt for him. Only later did I understand why he was so relentless in his attempts, in the hard day-to-day struggle for life, to snatch customers of merchandise from his colleagues: he was the father of two invalids, a paraplegic son who, at the age of eighteen, lived in a wheel chair, at the mercy of all the street urchins, and an idiot daughter whose mental development had stopped at the age of four.

My father was more tolerant, however, of Bichik, a fantastic character, and of the terrifying Baba Fredj. The nose, mouth, and eyes of Fredj were normal, but they were all crowded together within a tiny area of his enormous head. Perhaps my childhood has left me a magnified image of them, but I am sure of the extraordinary size of his hands, because I was always surprised to see how small the hammer seemed when he held it. As I was not particularly scared of him, I was quite fond of this lackadaisical and friendly giant, in spite of my father's constant teasing. Bichik was a jack-of-all-trades who always seemed to return from his other loves to the work as a saddler, when all other doors seemed to close before him. His colleagues appeared to like in him their own dreams that had never come true and spoke of him at all times with a mixture of envy and contempt. In my own memory the others have lost their faces, like those ancient statues whose features have been rubbed away by the years. Sebah, the forger, was accused of putting cardboard in the hooks of *araba* cart harnesses and hated because he sold his wares cheaper. Bissoum, a crazy old man, would spend a whole week working on each item, sewing it twice but refusing to add any decorative work, so that he never managed, out of sheer love for his trade, to earn even a meager livelihood.

Among these colleagues, my father would crouch too, joining them in their collective meditations. With the help of

Joseph, he soon pushed aside the rest to select, with an eye that never hesitated or failed him, the four or five skins that he wanted. Then he remained motionless, leaning forward and resting on the palms of his hands that lay flat on the floor while his eyes worked: he was cutting the skins with his mind's eye and calculating how many cuts of his model would be possible. Sometimes, the body's eyes refused to follow those of the mind, and he would then turn the skin to get a better view of it. I admired his knowledge and his ability to think so fruitfully. Joseph was perhaps more husky than Father, but lacked his intelligence and authority as a master craftsman. Whenever his employee would propose a skin, my father would spread it out before him, placing it on an imaginary worktable, then make up his mind and say either "Good," or else "No, take a look at it." His heavy calloused fingers then drew on the dust the one defective cut that would reduce the yield of the skin. Joseph rarely argued, forced to admit his inferiority.

Then the long walk in the sun brought us back to the coffeehouse where we always found the same crowd of Sabbath friends, cheerful and loud, smelling of eau de Cologne and of snuff. How blessed was the Sabbath coffeehouse where we remained pure because there was no cigarette smoke and where our conversation remained courteous because we were forbidden to play cards! In addition, I enjoyed a child's privileges: everyone had a smile for me and welcomed me, making room for me. Seeing myself treated in this manner by grown men, I felt that I assumed a man's dignity. All new members of the group would question my father:

"Is he your son?"

"Yes, he's my son."

In his voice there was pride, I'm sure, and the pleasure of it put me ill at ease.

"May God bless you and protect you," they would then say to my father.

And I would feel that I was powerfully protected.

Above all, I kept watching for Abdesselam, the waiter, in order to perform the little ritual that, each week, confirmed my status. When he finally appeared, slipshod in his heelless Turkish shoes, with his baggy pants hanging loose between his legs like a sheep's tail, I made the most of the few minutes that our friends needed to order their drinks and to tease Abdesselam. The good man had earned himself quite a reputation: as a waiter serving coffee in a native moviehouse, he had howled with terror and dropped his tray when he had seen a railroad engine driving full-speed toward him on the screen. At last he leaned toward me:

"What would you like, my son?"

All the men looked at me with benevolence; so much attention made me feel important. I pretended to hesitate before ordering a grenadine in regal tones. This was the high point of the day, a voluptuous triumph of color and taste. Abdesselam brought me a big glass of a wonderful red; holding it tight with both hands and concentrating my senses of sight and of smell on it, I lost myself in a world of sweetness, all harmony and perfume, which was the very world of my childhood. All around me the grownups were joking, laughing at something or other. I had abandoned the superficial pleasures of society for sublime ecstasies; I had become an exquisite thread in a web of silk, a melting color in a rainbow, a light bubble kissed by the breeze.

As soon as we were hungry we returned home. Here an atmosphere of more concentrated solemnity greeted us. With the afternoon, the holiday burst into bloom. In the room that had been specially prepared, the Bride of Sabbath was awaiting us, with the bed all covered with light-pink spreads, the narcissus flowers drooping in the bowl, and the table ready, covered with a flowered cloth. The women, like Oriental dolls dressed in bright silks, were sagely gossiping in the yard, all in chorus, as excited as little girls. My mother had darkened her eyes with long black lines of kohl and was wearing all her jewelry. As we, the men, now came home, the bride began to show some emotion; my mother and sister abandoned their meditations to busy themselves in the kitchen. The feast of black and oily *Pquela,* of rice-stuffed sausage, of tripe, and of oxtail would last for two hours. Then we generally entrusted our heavy digestion to sleep, and we concluded our Sabbath at the movies.

3

OLD CLOTHES

MEMORY TENDS PERHAPS to exaggerate the length of this happy period when I was an innocent in a world that I still believed to be innocent. I belonged to my family and to our alley, I lived according to the laws of this world and joyfully accepted its sanctions. Once, because I had cursed the Name of God, I was severely whipped with a belt on the soles of my feet. For three days I was unable to walk, but I felt that my punishment was just and had even saved me from worse when I learned about the danger I had faced: in Hell, I would have had my eyelids torn off and would have been forced to stare without blinking at the midday sun. The mere thought of this otherworldly punishment made me imagine the sufferings so vividly that tears came to my eyes to protect them from so much light. But my easy happiness could not last very long, this life ruled by respect that was also confidence and by fears of punishments that were felt to be just. Very soon, some serious hints began to upset the established order, in spite of the uninterrupted presence of my parents and of the community.

I was not born in the ghetto. Our alley was at the frontier of the Jewish quarter of Tunis, but this was enough to satisfy my father's pride. In the cool twilight of summer days the heat often drove us out of our rooms, and we made ourselves comfortable in chairs leaned against the wall and cushioned with pillows. The men wore their long white underpants, the women their housecoats of printed cotton, and the blind alley took on the air of a common living-room. My father was a better talker than Barouch, so that everybody listened to him. He liked to contrast the dreamy silence of our alley, cool from having recently been watered, with the offensive stink of the ghetto alleys. He would describe the foul fluids of the gutters as they filled the air with the fetid stink of the butcher-shops, the greasy and sickly odor of dishwater from the houses, and the acrid vapors of chlorinated water from the laundries. He spoke of the mountains of garbage where the sunlight hatched swarms of green and black flies, and of the roaches that emerged from them, so well fed that they could scarcely crawl along on their thin legs. In a tone of condescension he deplored the common lavatory that several families must share. We might well have but one room, but we were only two families to share our kitchen and our toilet. Besides, we had the privilege of running water and were not obliged to fetch it, at the risk of freezing our fingers till they were blue, from the fountain in the street.

Meanwhile, I was being spared the extreme poverty of the ghetto. Often, on Saturday evenings, I went to see my aunt Abbou, who lived in one of the sixteen rooms of the poorhouse called Oukala of the Birds. In the morning my cousins and I used to race each other to the toilet. The walls of the tiny closet were as sticky as a slug's hole, the ceiling so low that one couldn't stand upright. I shall never forget the heat, experienced nowhere else, of that hive, with its stairs of rotting wood. How can wood be so warm, so brotherly? I loved those rooms that seemed to trespass on each other, all built to a man's size, with no preconceived plan but the eye's desires and the limits of an arm's reach. One of the rooms was halfway up the stairs. To economize on kerosene, all doors were closed as soon as it was dark, and we all woke up together, with the same lisping voices. The Oukala of the Birds lived according to the rhythm of the world.

But I believed in some social distinction between its inhabitants and ourselves, since we lived a good five hundred meters from the nearest Jewish home. Besides, my father owned a store and was an employer. Once the crops have been harvested, the Bedouin has a little cash on hand and comes down to the city to buy a new halter for his horse, and this makes him feel important. Crossing the threshold of the narrow store where two men, as poorly dressed as he, are both busy at their tasks, he proudly proclaims:

"I want to speak to the boss."

Without interrupting his work, my father would then raise his head and invite the customer to be seated on a stool. I would put aside my toy whips, made of threads of leather and matches, to concentrate on the serious business that was at hand. I was proud of my father's nod of assurance, of being the son of the boss. Ours was a dignity of an entirely different sort, superior indeed to that of the street hucksters who are always being told by the cops to move on, or of the workers in a tailor's shop, shaken by spasms from dawn to nightfall.

One evening, as it was getting dark, Kalla and I were busy, without being unduly hurried, putting the four chairs with which we had been playing at trains back where they belonged. We were tired of traveling around the world, with my sister as the only tourist while I alone drove the engine. Besides, the tiled floor of the yard was cold and our legs were frozen. So we then played at being bakers: we were kneading our painless legs, laughing at their being so strangely numb and threatening to put them in the oven to bake. My mother came out of the dark room and, as the light outside still allowed her to see a bit, set about checking the wick of her lamp. The twilight comes late in our country, but night then falls suddenly, and Mother, as always, was in a hurry.

Two discreet knocks were heard, barely touching the wood of the street door. So as to avoid giving me any excuse to go out, I was forbidden ever to open the door. Kalla was more obedient than I and was therefore allowed to open it, which humiliated me, but gave her no particular pleasure. Her large dark eyes and her shoulders apologized to me as she went to open the door. It was Fraji, the son of Choulam: puny, with his scared, wide-open eyes like those of a bat, his sickly hair that grew in greasy tufts on a scalp like a barren moor.

"Is your mother at home," he asked Kalla.

Dancing shadows suddenly appeared on the walls that seemed to stare as Fraji's dark double arose at his feet, crawled from the ground up to the door, and then spread huge across the ceiling. My mother was on her way, holding the lamp at arm's length before her. She saw the visitor:

"Oh, yes, I know what you want. Wait a moment."

She went into the room and the light vanished, drawing the shadows away in its wake. We followed her, wondering what she was up to. She pulled back the mattress of the bed-chest where my sister slept, and propped the top open while she rummaged inside. A sharp odor of mildew invaded the whole room. Her arms went deep into the chest and she drew forth the dirty linen, a handful at a time, and then began to sort it out methodically. She would bring the clothes close to the lamp to examine them before deciding. One of my sweaters, two pairs of pants, and a shirt were chosen, with a dress, a sweater and two pairs of drawers of my sister. Lastly, she removed all the buttons of imitation mother-of-pearl, leaving only the tailor's buttons, which could all be replaced easily from my uncle's stock. We were at last witnessing the mysterious operation that regularly deprived us of our old clothes. Fraji didn't seem to notice our hostile glances, but continued to stare intently with his big protuberant eyes at the pile of clothes that was beginning to assume some importance. Then my mother sent me to borrow ten cents from Joulie Barouch. When I came back, I found on the table a bundle wrapped in newspaper and a thick slice of bread. Fraji hastened to bury the money deep in his pocket, grasped the parcel and the piece of bread in his arms and, without uttering a word, made a dash for the door. Then, at last, we exploded with anger:

"Why do you give him our clothes?"

Mother, in a dreamy mood, answered briefly, but in a decisive tone:

"Because they are poor."

But this explanation didn't satisfy us. Our life of confinement in our blind alley had scarcely prepared us to understand the world, and we resented Fraji, who was filthy and aroused our disgust, as well as all the poor who helped dispossess us. Gravely, we concluded that our dignity must truly be very considerable, our own and that of our father, the Saddler.

An hour later my father sent me back to repay Joulie her ten cents and I did the errand without more ado. When we were sent to bed, my sister to the bed-chest and I to the far side of the big family bed, right up against the blue distempered wall, I began to project upon the uneven surface of the masonry the images that my imagination always discovered there.

Two days later, while the women were all away at the public bath, I was left at home, under the none too careful supervision of Imiliou, the eldest of the Barouch children. It did not take me long to cross the forbidden threshold and to find myself in the deserted alley, where I could perceive the unfamiliar noises from Tarfoune Street. Soon, I had ventured even further afield, as far as the source of the disturbance: the neighborhood kids were playing the game

that was called "apricot kernels," behind the handcarts and
close to the garbage cart. Their ears were red with excitement,
their knees already covered with mud, and they threw themselves suddenly onto the ground and then jumped up again
like devils, pulling frightful faces behind the backs of the foe
and stressing every gesture with a howl of rage or of triumph.
At once, I recognized on the back of Fraji, the son of
Choulam, my own sweater.

As I had never played except with my sister, I stayed
away from the others, feeling vaguely ill at ease and hostile.
All around these savage trespassers, the whole street remained
silent and deserted, expressing its disapproval of their strange
liveliness in the heart of my own kingdom. Suddenly, the
game stopped because of a *nigat,* a draw. All the players
uttered one single yell in a single clear-cut peal, after which
they relaxed, joking and jeering before deciding to play
another game. Chouchane, the tailor, and Fraji were both
considered too weak and were refused by both teams, ruth-
lessly sacrificed. As for myself, I approved this decision.
Without wasting time, the game began again, a bit further
away from the garbage cart. Chouchane and Fraji, both disappointed, continued to gravitate around the stakes of the
players, although the latter kept a watchful eye on them,
and had to content themselves with kibitzing and giving
advice that nobody followed. Fraji finally lost interest in the
battle and, having nothing better to do, became aware of
the presence of the garbage cart, pushed it forward with one
hand, and then took hold of the two shafts. The mountain
of refuse began to tremble, with avalanches of green and red
vegetable peel rolling down its sides. Fraji then discovered
the real use of this godsend: he set his right foot on the hub
of one wheel, grasped the rail of the cart with the palms of
his hands, and began to climb the whole edifice. Scarcely
hesitating, he dug his little legs deep into the rotting garbage
and stood up, staring all around and quite surprised at what
he saw: himself towering above us all, above the whole world,

on a many-colored throne made of butcher's wrapping paper, egg shells, and vegetable peelings. The meat flies, all green and gold as they rose disturbed, made a moving halo around him, glistening in the sun. Then he raised his hands to the sky and exclaimed, proud as a crowing cock and convinced of the truth of his claim:

"I'm the king of the castle, I'm the king of the castle!"

The other urchins paid little attention to this claim, all of them tense in the moment of silence that comes before the apricot kernels are thrown. Only Chouchane was watching him and exclaimed:

"Yes, you're king of the outhouse!"

As for me, I was furious at hearing this dirty little rascal, to whom we actually gave food and who wore my old clothes, utter such impertinences. I was indeed the only uncontested king of the whole alley, and Kalla would have been able to testify to the validity of my claim had she not been away at the bath house. So I approached him, full of noble anger, and placed my hand, the heavy hand of the owner, on his sleeve, on the sleeve of my own sweater:

"No, you're not the king, because you're wearing *my* sweater, and it's *my* mother who gave it to you only the day before yesterday."

Chouchane was staring at us, and the game was again in its moment of tense silence, so that my remark sounded loud as the proclamation of a herald. Fraji's terrified batlike eyes became even wider as he stared at me before casting a single glance, as fleeting as the signal of a lighthouse, on Chouchane and all the others. Finally, Fraji climbed painfully down from his crumbling pedestal and went off without uttering a single word in reply, without looking at any of us, as though he were alone in a deserted street.

My pride and my justifiable anger suddenly fell flat and I felt a lump in my throat. By that time the other boys had decided to play another game and offered me a small part in it. In all the excitement and shouting I forgot the incident and became lighthearted again. When the violet-colored twilight began to fill our street, it seemed to me that the afternoon had been very short. Soon my mother appeared at the end of our alley, heavily veiled, as is proper for a woman returning from the bath house. Although she rarely wore a veil, I recognized her at once by her hurried gait and rushed to greet her. A minute later, Kalla and Joulie were there too, and my sister began to tell me about her interesting afternoon at the Turkish bath. That night I slept very quietly.

It was only the next day, when my mother returned from her marketing, that I was punished. Oh, it all happened without any insults, without any blows. How much would I have preferred a good thrashing! A spanking delivered with the hard and horny hand of my father, or even a whipping, with his belt, on the soles of my feet. I would then have howled, swallowed my tears for a good quarter of an hour, and been able to publicize my suffering; after which my conscience would have been appeased and I would have played out of doors until I had forgotten my crime. Instead, a vague anxiety already began to pervade me when my mother refused me the privilege, granted to me twice a week, of awaiting her return from the market at the opening of Tarfoune Street. As soon as we saw her, we always rushed toward her from there and seized her heavy basket that my sister and I would then drag as far as our kitchen. Seated side by side on the brick-red tiled floor that was never cold, we played a wonderful game of fishing in it, punctuating our fun with loud cries of joy. Mother always left us in peace, our excuse being that we put the vegetables away in the kitchen closet and the fruit in the room. We always put all the yellow lemons together, so vividly bright and rich in aroma that I never wearied of breathing their scent deep in my lungs, as if I wanted to absorb their contents through my sense of smell, and then the eggplants, dark purple with mysterious lighter spots that turned to red, the tender green artichokes that seemed to paraffin the whole mouth and to coat the palate with rubber, lastly the heavy watermelon that was so heavy we had to roll it along the floor to the room. Each time we discovered a little surprise, some peanut butter, a piece of *halva,* a sesame cake. But we always tasted everything: a fresh mouthful of fennel, a lick of sugar, a bite into a carrot. Mother knew our joy and didn't constrain it with useless nagging. To prevent any damage was her only concern:

"Be careful with the eggs! Don't get all dirty from the fish!"

On this particular morning that I remember so bitterly, she wouldn't let us take hold of her basket. I knew the meaning of her tight lips. Her fine Berber face was drawn taut over the jaws and the hard peaks of her cheekbones. A painful anxiety began to pervade me, all the more disturbing because its cause was unknown. Desperately I searched my conscience and discovered several grave sins, but I was still afraid that some terrible and odious crime might rise to the surface of my memory. It did indeed come to the surface, and I felt no sense of relief at all when she said to me:

"I've just seen little Fraji's mother. . . ."

She hadn't raised her voice, she didn't promise me any spanking to be administered by my father, she didn't even strike me, hurting her own hands, as she generally did, and suffering more than I. She was a primitive and unsophisticated woman who had never learned to count or to speak a word that was foreign to her native dialect; but she knew quite miraculously that she had to make me understand a drama of which I too was destined to be a victim—the very drama of Fraji's life. My wickedness was caused by my ignorance: instead of scolding me, she explained my mistake to me.

"There's nothing degrading about wearing someone else's old clothes. Nearly all your shirts and pants belonged to the son of Uncle Binhas before belonging to you. Look at this one, for instance: I made it out of an old one that came from Uncle Elias. You too, Kalla, and even I, we all wear old clothes."

Unhappy and estranged, I tried for a while to find my footing again:

"But the son of Uncle Binhas is my cousin, and. . . ."

Why didn't she stop at that? Instead, she grew impatient, felt that too much kindness might fail to have the right effect, and added:

"Would you be pleased if, one day, in front of everybody, Uncle Elias asked you to give back his pants that you're wearing? Or if Uncle Binhas pointed out to all the urchins in the street that you're wearing his son's shirt?"

"He'll never say it, they'll never say it," I stammered. "They're my uncle and my cousin. . . ."

"But it's the same thing," she concluded, "We're poor too, we're all like Fraji Choulam!"

So I was poor, like Fraji Choulam! But Mother already regretted what she said and wanted to draw a moral conclusion. She now added, clumsily and contradicting herself:

"There's no reason to be ashamed of being poor and it's a sin to make fun of the poor."

Oh yes, poverty is something to be ashamed of, and this was clear to me from the mutterings of my own parents, from their remarks about the Oukala of the Birds and their pity for the Choulam family. As for me, I despised the poor. Fraji had to pay with shame the price of his poverty and I too, if we were poor, would have to pay with my own shame. In the disorder of my awareness, I made that day a great and unhappy step forward. I noted that I too wore new clothes only rarely and was forced to receive, like Fraji, bundles that stank of mildew and dirty linen and from which all the expensive buttons had been removed. I now understood his suffering fully, the shame that I had poured forth upon him in the presence of Chouchane and the other kids.

His suffering and shame were my own too; on my own shoulders I now felt the burden of the same contempt, as if I had his hair, all clammy with filth, and his eyes like the headlights of a car. I felt that I had become Fraji.

Since that day, I have slowly acquired the uneasiness about my clothes that characterizes the poor who are ashamed. I was no longer at my ease in any suit: I felt that I was badly dressed and that I attracted the attention of all. I feared, even when wearing a new suit, the mockery of others at my unsuccessful attempts. That is how I became what is known as careful of my clothes. Before going to bed, I folded my suit with care and set it tidily on the back of a chair. To avoid dirt-stains, I examined each chair before sitting on it, and I often preferred to keep my annual new suit in the closet rather than face the wearisome responsibility of wearing it with the respect that it deserved.

4

THE TWO PENNIES

THE VERY EXISTENCE of kindergarten was unknown in Tarfoune Street, and school, as a whole, did not assume there, as in middle-class homes, the character of an absolute necessity. I was already quite a grown boy, seven years old, I think, when my parents decided to send me to school. Whereas school seems mere play to most young children, the news of this decision made me cry. My mother tongue is the Tunisian dialect, which I speak with the proper accent of the young Moslem kids of our part of town and of the drivers of horse-trucks who were customers of our shop. The Jews of Tunis are to the Moslems what the Viennese are to other Germans: they drag out their syllables in a singsong voice and soften and make insipid the guttural speech of their Mohammedan fellow-citizens. The relatively correct intonations of my speech earned me the mockery of all: the Jews disliked my strange speech and suspected me of affectation, while the Moslems thought that I was mimicking them. But when I entered school, it was no longer a matter of shades of pronunciation but of a total break.

30

"How shall I manage to understand the instructor? I've never learned French!"

"Well, he'll teach it to you," my father concluded.

"But how shall I answer his questions *before* he has taught me to speak it?"

I faced an abyss, without any means of communicating with the far side of it. The instructor spoke only French and I spoke only dialect: how would we ever be able to meet?

These childish anxieties may now seem futile and my position is surely not unique. Millions of men have had to lose their basic unity, no longer recognizing themselves and still seeking in vain their identity. But I also say to myself that this confrontation has nothing reassuring about it; that others try to reassemble, without ever managing it, their scattered limbs. This mere fact confirms me in my awareness of the split in myself. All my life I have forced my friendships and my acquisitions to readjust continually to whatever I happened to be.

The first day of school came too soon for my fears. Thanks to remnants from my uncle the tailor, my mother was able to outfit me with a pair of brown pants and an overall apron of black poplin, a material the mere smell of which can still remind me of elementary school. My father had been able to get from Bodineau, his supplier, a fine calfskin school satchel. This was my only scholar's luxury. I was allowed to wear my Saturday jockey cap, which added considerably to my awe and to the solemnity of the occasion. Still, nothing much happened. There was too much confusion, during those first few days of the school year, to allow much attention to be lavished on us, so that I had time to become accustomed to my new surroundings. Without any serious shocks, my sense of alienation was overcome by my curiosity. The school was situated in some old stables of the Bey's palace which had been purchased advantageously by the Alliance Israélite and subjected to minimal alterations; to me, it all seemed most beautiful. Except on a few Saturday walks, I had never had

a chance to see any trees or greenery, and our schoolyard
had two tall rows of eucalyptus trees that seemed huge to me
and elicited my constant admiration. All the classrooms were
small, with narrow windows that were closed with dirty
gratings; I soon found them warmly intimate. My schoolmates impressed me less favorably, all of them being too
noisy and brutal for my liking.

Every morning, before leaving home with my fine satchel
slung from my shoulder and my cap pushed down over my
eyebrows, I marked time, on our doorstep, with my shoes. I
insisted that my mother say, before I leave:

"Peace be with you!"

Only then did I set forth confidently. But sometimes my
mother was still angry from some outburst and would utter
a curse:

"Go away! May death carry you off!"

Then I would immediately feel a shudder go right through
me, and all day I would fear some dreadful event.

Never have I been able to rid myself of this magic spell
of language. Whenever a colleague curses me, "May you
perish," I feel cold at the back of my neck and foresee the
horrors of death. Whenever anyone says "Drop dead!" I can
already feel myself begin to fail. It is as if language, far
from being a transparent tool, really shares some of the
nature of the things it designates as well as some of their
weight.

For my ten o'clock snack, my mother always gave me two
pennies and a big piece of bread crust, of the bread that she
kneaded herself and took to the Arab oven to bake. With
my two pennies, I could buy myself a piece of chocolate or
the makings of a sandwich. Chaoul, the school janitor, did
sell whole sandwiches made of exquisite small loaves of white
bread, but these cost ten pennies. So Chaoul would dig with
his agile finger into my piece of bread to bury in it a couple
of green olives, as many black olives, a sliver of anchovy, a
few crumbs of tuna fish, and a bit of boiled vegetable, all

of which he then seasoned with olive oil. I watched this carefully to make sure that he gave me all the tuna I was entitled to and that he refrained from giving me any *arissa,* the strange sauce of fire-red peppers that all my compatriots carry with them wherever they travel, for fear of ever running out of it. *Arissa* always burned my palate and gave me a cold sweat.

Generally, we reached the old gateway long before schooltime. We enjoyed the freedom of chatting together before being locked up for three hours within those mouse-grey walls. Besides, we met there all the quick-getaway hucksters who offered us all sorts of cheap dainties. They had learned, from long experience, to classify schools according to the purchasing power of the pupils. We certainly came last but one on their list, only just ahead of the other school of the Alliance that was situated in the heart of the ghetto and where the midday meal and even the clothes of the pupils were distributed free. That is why all these little tradesmen used to bring us whatever they had failed to sell at the gates of the other schools. In October, for instance, the small green apples that had fallen too soon from the tree and had been dipped in a sugar solution with red coloring. We licked the taffy crust until we reached the actual fruit, ate the fruit too, but pulled hideous faces as we did it, with our teeth on edge and our eyes grown dim. I had discovered that if one bit the taffy apple without first licking it the bitterness of the fruit was reduced by the sugar. But then I ate it all so fast that the pleasure was over before I had really experienced it. In spring, the fruit that was sold to us was already full of sunlight: yellow arbutus berries, the less expensive ones still greenish, big as marbles and all kernel, sharp to the taste and giving us belly-aches; the better fruit was of a fine golden yellow or bright red and tasted and smelled exquisitely sweet. Under the pressure of necessity, some of us had even learned to like the cheaper arbutus berries and to claim that they preferred them to the riper ones. To my great surprise, they chose those that were most green and most acid. But I never reached that stage, though some of my schoolmates may actually have been fortunate enough to like the green berries. Toward the same time of year, we were also offered the jujube fruits, small wild berries that were shiny as beads of brown marble or all wrinkled like the cheeks of an old woman, and much more attractive to look at than good to eat. Later, there were also oranges and dates, especially the big yellow dates that have an astringent effect on the mouth, leaving it all dry and resistant to any liquid.

Of all the hucksters, only "Birdie" managed, in all seasons, to achieve the miracle of bringing us real goodies at a reasonable price. He was a tiny man of no specific age, who had adopted as his dress for all times an ancient pair of tuxedo pants, a jacket that had a patch over the left elbow, and a cap of Persian lamb that seemed to overwhelm his birdlike head. He owed his nickname to the sweets of the "Bird" brand that he sold in a biscuit box. This tin box could easily be concealed whenever the cops turned up, as the police, God alone knows why, seemed to be intent on mercilessly pursuing all the little hucksters; so Birdie's biscuit box was his stroke of genius, his secret weapon of defense that allowed him to remain invulnerable, whereas all his colleagues were sooner or later arrested. This miracle box always contained a few defective candies from one or the other of the better makers, some excellent pastries that had been spoiled in the process of baking, or some candied almonds that had failed to acquire the right color while cooking, all of this stock having been sold to Birdie for next to nothing. Even if we failed to get any of these treats, we found at least some cakes made of heavy semolina that were full of bits of straw and somehow numbed our stomachs that were always underfed.

For some time Birdie had been offering us flat Nestlé chocolate bars, together with a colored card. The Nestlé firm was launching a very successful commercial campaign: in the wrapping of each bar they put one or two of these picture cards of which a complete set would fill an album. The prize, for whoever turned in a full album by a certain deadline, was something pretty serious: a bicycle, if I remember right. Each one of these chocolate bars cost seven pennies, but since I had only two pennies a day to spend, I was disqualified from the start. However, I was not aware of this handicap and, as the Nestlé firm gave its albums away free, I went to collect one too.

Every Friday, on the morning before Sabbath, classes began and finished an hour earlier, which seemed to us to be a considerable gain. For this reason, among others, I particularly enjoyed my Fridays, whereas my mother could never get accustomed to this interruption of our daily routine. Harried by her responsibilities in preparing the three Sabbath meals, she never made a success of the first one, actually the least important one.

This particular day, it was the bread that was lacking when I sat down for breakfast, so she asked me to go and fetch it at the baker's oven, which was in the Street of the Sparrows, a blind alley fairly far from our home. As I was not very hungry, this unexpected chore annoyed me and I grumbled, pretended it was already too late, and made up my mind to go off without breakfasting. With the vast selfishness of a child, I guessed quite rightly that this would upset my mother and punish her for her forgetfulness. Finally, she lost her temper and, running short of other arguments, called upon heaven as a witness to curse me. But I was stubborn, slung my school satchel over my shoulder, and left the house. When I reached the end of the street, I heard her calling me, so I turned back with some ill will, dragging my feet, to receive from her my two pennies and an unexpected piece of bread crust. She had certainly borrowed it from Joulie, and this gesture made my vague remorse weigh all

the more heavily on my conscience. The day had been
spoiled for me, by my empty stomach and my confused
conscience.

I reached the old iron gate of the school, of course, too
early. Birdie's head, with his humble expression, his heavy
eyelids that were always lowered, scarcely rose above a compact group of school children, while the other hucksters
managed to attract only a few customers. One of them, a
new trader, was giving us the old blarney to build up his
trade. I noticed Saul as he detached himself from Birdie's
group: he was my rival and had thus come to be my first
comrade. Our teacher in the first grade used to make us sit
in the classroom by order of merit, so that Saul and I occupied
the first row almost all year round. Comrades in the front
row, we soon became friends by force of habit, though there
was some irony to this as Saul was the son of a rich merchant
in the covered bazaar, a fact that was each day more notice-
able to me. Beneath his black apron that always seemed
new, he wore fine cloth pants with mother-of-pearl buttons
on the side, which had long aroused my curiosity: what
could possibly be the use of buttons without any buttonholes?
I had often made fun of them and Saul never knew what
to answer. One day, as I repeated my taunts, he took on a
superior manner: his mother had explained to him certain
facts that he could not reveal to me. In spite of my exasperation and insistence, he absolutely refused to speak. In addition, he always smelled good, every day of the week, which
impressed me very much.

I went toward Saul, this particular morning, and greeted
him. He smiled amiably, but seemed preoccupied. The news
was indeed serious: one of the older boys, the elder of the
Garsia brothers, claimed that the Nestlé firm had set the end
of the month as the deadline for the set of pictures to be
completed, and that a new album was being launched for
the following month. Saul was furious for he would never
be able to complete his set in time. I watched the whole

excited crowd like a spectator who is not involved in what is happening on the race track. The younger Garsia bought two chocolate bars at once and tore one wrapping open: all heads were bent over the card, a bird. That one belonged to a set already completed by all true collectors! He tore the second wrapping: a machine tool, which was better, but still failed to satisfy him.

"I already have it. Who wants to swap it?"

I would willingly have accepted it, but I had no card to give in exchange. Garsia put the pictures carefully away in his wallet, then offered the chocolate bars to Birdie:

"Will you buy them back from me?"

Birdie counted out two pennies twice and took the bars back without their red wrappings. The sons of rich parents, with Birdie's help, had surely worked out that deal among themselves. Too well fed to eat all the chocolate bars that they bought, they sold them back to Birdie for two pennies, and he then sold them to us for three. That way, everyone was satisfied. I could now afford a chocolate bar every other day, if I wanted, as I needed to spend only one of my pennies on the intervening day and could save the second for the morrow. It was difficult to breakfast off bread and a single penny, but I had found a compromise: I bought a chocolate-flavored candy that I placed between my cheek and my lower jaw. I bit into my bread without touching the candy, which then melted slowly, giving me the impression that I was eating my bread with chocolate. I repeated this experiment several times and, for the days of celebration when I could afford a Nestlé bar, I also had a technique of my own for consuming my treat just as I had a plan for purchasing it. First, I economized carefully, eating my bread in large mouthfuls with as little chocolate as possible. Once I had swallowed my bread and assuaged my hunger, I then hesitated a while before suddenly gulping down all the chocolate that was left, I mean more than half the bar. All my mouth would then participate in this orgasm, with chocolate all over my gums, the lining of my cheeks, and my palate. This lasted thirty seconds, but thirty seconds of total bliss, almost making me feel nausea.

But today, I had not yet had any morning breakfast, so that there could be no question of saving. The sandwich that Chaoul, the janitor, prepared for me would scarcely be enough.

Saul felt reassured and went ahead, buying his daily ration of Nestlé. Unlike Garsia, he bought his bars one by one and tore the wrappings slowly, like one of those gamblers who uncover their cards one at a time, a millimeter at a time. He kept all of us on tenterhooks, crowding round him in silence. But he too had no luck. One after the other, he drew a bird, then a second bird, and a fish, all of them run-of-the-mill cards of which he already owned several copies. Saul had thus spent twenty-one pennies and now searched the pockets of his pants and of his overall apron, to find there only a top, some marbles, a piece of string, a two-penny piece, and a single penny, and that was all. On his face there began to appear the signs of a spoiled child's tantrum, and he almost made me pity him. He shook out his crumpled handkerchief: another coin fell out of it. We all rushed to pick it up, another two-penny piece. We were interested in watching the last efforts of the luckless gambler, and only Birdie seemed to remain impassive, watching it all with a kind and paternal look in his eyes.

Graziani, the gateman, then appeared in the entrance, clapped his hands and began to push open the heavy door. The group around Birdie slowly dispersed. Out of a feeling of friendship, I waited for Saul who was now fumbling in his satchel. He finally spoke to me, asking me with great affability:

"Can you lend me two pennies?"

I was his last chance, and I didn't hesitate long. To be sure, I didn't have much time to think it over and the whole situation was too new for me. Poor little rich boy

Saul needed my money, my two pennies. I was vaguely and stupidly proud of this. Perhaps, too, I would have been ashamed to say no, and I later felt more resentful toward him because of this feeling of shame than of anything else. Saul had offered me, from time to time, chocolate or candy, but I had never offered him anything.

I knew exactly where my own money was tucked away. But as I always hid it in a tobacco tin, well concealed beneath my apron, in the breast pocket of my shirt, and as Saul was now in a hurry, I fumbled around with my fingers in the pleats of the shirt and Saul became impatient.

"Hurry up!" he exclaimed.

I hastened to open the tin that was rattling with the only sound of my single coin and handed him the two-penny piece that was intended for my sandwich. Saul was thus able to complete the required sum, bought the last Nestlé bar, tore the wrapping, and exclaimed to me, in disgust:

"What? Another fish? Well, I have no luck today."

It seemed to me that nobody had any luck at all that day.

The street was deserted and Graziani was shaking his head with a sad expression, acting as if he were about to close the gate. We rushed in through the opening that was scarcely wide enough to allow a cat to pass.

"*Ragazzi! Ragazzi!*" the old Italian grumbled affectionately.

The massive door shut loudly behind us. We went to our seats in the first-year class and sat still. The crowd was now transmuted into an organized little society that respected order, and silence followed the earlier clamor. It was then that my stomach chose to rumble loud and long as I realized that I would get no breakfast.

I felt that I had been imposed upon. Up till then, I had never experienced the revelation of jealousy and envy. I had envied Saul his fine clothes and his pocket money, but it had been without any true bitterness or animosity. Later, I began to hate the Sauls of life, but the power of the rich, at that time, still inspired in me some respect, as if I were witnessing a constant and almost magical run of luck. I still saw no relationship between their riches and my own poverty, but Saul's self-centered lack of any awareness established the first link between the two. He could take away from me the two pennies for my breakfast in order to purchase himself an unnecessary Nestlé bar, and then was able to throw away the chocolate that I could not afford.

Saul never remembered to repay me my two pennies, which was quite natural, for it was such a small sum. . . .

5

THE SUMMER CAMP

I FELT FOR my father a kind of admiration that included respect and some fear. His big and heavy hands were, in my eyes, the symbol of strength and skill. On one of our wonderful Saturdays I was running along beside him, with my tiny fist deep in his big hand where I could feel the horny skin and the scars. I wanted to dispose of some last doubt in my mind and asked:

"Who is the more powerful, the saddler or the policeman?"

The policeman with his uniform and his pistol was an arbitrary and mysterious power in our eyes. All the street vendors, so loud and vulgar in their arguments with house-wives, suddenly became polite and quiet as soon as a cop appeared on his shining bicycle. The silence of a polite gathering then settled down on the street: they all wished the cop a good day in sweet tones and handed him little parcels that had been waiting, ready for him to come by. He accepted all this with a negligent contempt, without any thanks, and nevertheless, every once in a while, drove all the vendors off to the city pound.

My father guessed at once whom I admired most, but he thought of my education as a good citizen and sacrificed himself to a proper respect for the established powers:

"The policeman is the more powerful, my son," he answered.

I didn't believe him and thought, for a while, that he had lied out of modesty.

Later, in the midst of all my conflicts, we dealt each other wounds that would never heal. After having long remained silent and reserved, suddenly overwhelmed, we would explode one day in anger that had lost all control and burst out. After that, we avoided each other's eyes and re-established some distance between us. Actually, there never was any real familiarity between us, and I was never able to rid myself of my respect for him, no matter how great my disappointments.

He was assuredly intelligent, more intelligent than any of the others around me during my early childhood. As a matter of fact, my father had a story of his own that had determined the character of his whole life. When he was still a boy, in the early years of the European occupation of Tunisia, children were only just beginning to be sent to school. He was one of those who benefited by this innovation, in spite of his jealous older brother who insisted on taking him on as an apprentice. But one day, he broke a leg and the bonesetter fixed it wrong, so that it had to be fractured twice again. As a result of all this, he missed two whole school years and, in spite of all his protests, finally landed in the shop of his brother who was a saddler. At once, the older one made clear to him what he was to expect:

"Well, now I'll see to it that your bones don't stay stiff."

My father thus abandoned his early ambitions and acquired his muscles, his brooding silence, and his surprisingly expressive eyes. But among all the limited and rough craftsmen around him, he soon discovered his own real superiority: while his colleagues wore themselves out on day-to-day problems, he would wait and finally show them the most economical solution. Whenever he wanted to congratulate me on anything, he would gravely say to me:

"You're no fool, I can see that."

I was finally convinced of it myself, and intelligence gave me too much pleasure, pride and desire for power, until the day when, at last more lucid than my father, I rejected even this modest ambition.

I must have been about ten years old and already in the fourth grade when I suddenly ceased to believe in my father.

Toward the end of a warm spring morning, our sleepy attention was suddenly revived by an announcement made by our instructor, Mr. Chouk, whose voice always became ceremonious on such occasions. The army was organizing a free holiday camp for the following summer. I had heard something about it through the schoolyard grapevine: it was rumored that one returned from this camp with healthy red cheeks. Most of us, in the schools of the Alliance Israélite, were somewhat puny, with yellowish or grayish complexions, as a consequence of malnutrition and lack of fresh air. Red cheeks were something that characterized an ideal child, the average notion of the well-fed high-school kid, of the young French boy returning from his vacation in France, of the model child in handbooks on hygiene and the huge Nestlé baby advertisements that were placarded all over the city's walls. In addition, we all thought, though we may not have said it, that what was now offered us was free, wonderfully free. One cannot hesitate to take what is free and all profit.

I was getting ready to raise my hand as soon as Monsieur Chouk finished his speech. Of course, he added rather clumsily, only those children would be acceptable whose parents could not afford any other vacation for them. My hand then seemed to become paralyzed. In any case, only three or four pupils proposed themselves as candidates: on the whole, we didn't like living among non-Jews.

"Is that all?" our instructor insisted, with his overemphatic voice. "It would do you a lot of good. Come, Lussato, Lévi, Spinoza. . . ."

His eyes wandered over the whole class and his chin pointed in turn at each one of the more puny or poorer pupils. I lowered my head and tried to make myself very small, as I always did when I wanted to avoid being questioned.

"Talk to your parents about it," he concluded. "I'll turn in the list tomorrow evening. All those of you who decide that they want to go can come and see me after class."

Now that it was no longer necessary to confess one's status as a pauper in public, I allowed myself to hope again. At noon I asked for permission to put my name down for the summer camp. My mother angrily refused. Was I undernourished? Did I find fault with the quality of my bed? Nowhere can one be happier than at home! The mere thought of wanting to leave my parents proved that I was a selfish son. This accusation of selfishness—I'll hear it from my mother's lips until her dying day, and always as a comment on actions that seemed to me to be legitimate enough, in fact necessary as far as my own life is concerned. For all petty crimes, careless hurts, expressions of self-centered forgetfulness, all the peccadillos that weigh on my conscience, she was nevertheless indulgent enough. Here too, her primitive Bedouin mind and heart had unerringly distinguished what was essential from what was accessory.

My father didn't come home at noon for lunch. So we waited until the evening, sulking at each other, my mother as childish about it as I. But my father immediately hit upon the essential argument: it cost nothing. He calculated the price of such a vacation in the mountains if one had to pay for it. The total amount was too big for us to be able to refuse, which would be sheer waste. He probably reckoned also how much he would save while I was away. Anyhow, he decided that I could go there, and my mother, having nothing more to say, began to prepare my kit. It was all

quite expensive: I was expected to take with me a number
of things we didn't own, a toothbrush, tooth paste, pajamas,
and other items of which we had only a single sample for
the whole family: a comb, a towel, a shoeshine kit.

The whole adventure began very badly. It was the first
time in my life that I was going away so far and for so long
from my family and the blind alley. At the collecting point,
I found none of my classmates. We were alone in a crowd
of Europeans who were waiting in the shade of the trees and
joyously shouting remarks from group to group. The loneliness of my parents, silent and scared, moved me even more
deeply than my own. I was seeing them, for the first time,
uneasy and ashamed, with all their prestige left behind them
in our blind alley. They spoke in muffled tones, probably
ashamed of their dialect, which, to me, now seemed vulgar
and out of place. As a precaution, we had been asked to turn
up much too early and now we had to wait for quite a while.
The last cool morning breeze vanished and a humid heat
began to weigh on us while the flies buzzed ever more insistently. People who had to go in the sunlight ran from one
patch of shade to the next. My father no longer uttered a
word. I felt that he was exasperated by weariness, heat, the
flies, and a sense of alienation. My mother's face betrayed,
by its softness, that she was on the verge of tears, and her
lips were beginning to relax when, at long last, the signal
for our departure came. We were then loaded in closed
military trucks. I found myself cornered at the back of a
truck, no longer able to see my parents for a last farewell.
Later, I often experienced this strange feeling of being quite
close to them and at the same time kept irremediably apart
from them. Only then did the tears at last come to my eyes.

The trip was very unpleasant. We had to stand for five
hours, our fifty breaths flowing together as we almost stifled
beneath the painted tarpaulin of the truck. In near-darkness
we were brutally jostled against each other at every bump in
the road, while the vibration of the truck made the soles of

our feet tingle and made me sick at my stomach. I reached our destination in such a state of exhaustion that I fell asleep at once, barely glancing at the impersonal dormitory in which I had been assigned a bed.

I was ten years old, as I've said, and an only son. I indeed had my sister Kalla, but in our families the son, especially an only son, is truly a privileged being. For a long while, I actually expected to hear God speak to me personally, and my heart often beat faster if I thought that I could distinguish a voice speaking in the rustling of tree leaves. Always encouraged and confirmed in my awareness of superiority, I was convinced that an extraordinary destiny awaited me.

In the summer camp, this feeling of being unique was badly shattered the very first day. We were awakened too early, when our limbs were still numb, by the gruff voice of a soldier. I was terrified not to find myself in my accustomed bed and my gaze sought in vain the green bars of our window, which seemed to retreat prodigiously to the far end of a vastly expanded room. Our wall that was distempered blue and always seemed so familiar and soft had become ugly beneath a coat of coarse brown paint. Without being at all ill-natured, the soldier was shouting at us that we were a bunch of lazy kids and that we would have to make our own beds and be ready in a quarter of an hour if we wanted him to give us any breakfast. After that, he left the room and I began to recall the dreadful trip, discovering that I had become an anonymous little boy, far from his parents, in this shivering dawn, among a crowd of other little boys, all as roughly awakened as I. The soldier hadn't even scolded me as an individual. I had to make my bed, like all the others, and lost my head when I saw the huge bundle of sheets and blankets. At what end should I begin? I never had imagined that I would one day have to make my own bed for that was a woman's job. Almost weeping, I asked my neighbor for help. He was a Mohammedan kid, and just as helpless as I. The paradise that we had expected was turning out to be a boarding school for foundlings and wards of the nation. We were expected, besides, to sweep the dormitories, to help in the kitchen, and to keep our own kit in order. We shared the tasteless chow of the army, with its heavy portions of starches that were either badly prepared or cooked too long, and its gravies of inferior quality.

The only ones who took to this life easily were the kids from public institutions. These I despised and pitied because of their frightful lack of parents, and I feared them because they were so brutal. We never associated with them and they seemed to ignore us too. The very first day, it was explained to me in a whisper:

"They have no parents, and that's why they're like that."

They were indeed different, not like us, nor do I rely, for this, on distorted memories. Each time I have had to do with children from public institutions, I have experienced this same shifty laughter and brutality, these expressions of loneliness and privation. I at least had parents, though I was away from them for the time being. But the mere faculty of being able to reduce the distance between us by thinking of my father, of my mother, of our alley, this gave my heart some security and balance.

Life, in our summer camp, was healthy and simple, but void of any tenderness or friendliness. We were not even subjected to the tyrannous demands of instructors; on the contrary, we were alone, each one of us left to his own resources. The young men who had been assigned to stay with us, as one of the duties of their period of military service, lived among themselves, watching us from afar and approaching us as seldom as possible, for summary and brutal punishments if they found us too troublesome. Once, one of the boys from an institution, whether unintentionally or on purpose, threw a pebble into an open kitchen window. Suddenly there emerged an unusually angry mess sergeant. With oddly brusque gestures he seized the culprit, grasped

him between his knees, tore his pants down and set about
thrashing him with both arms. The child screamed and the
man, made even more angry by these screams, continued to
beat his victim's buttocks, soon red and then bruised, with
all the force of his huge and unrelenting hands. Fascinated,
I watched all of this, my lips tightened with horror, as the
bruised buttocks became purple beneath such an avalanche
of blows. It went on and on, and I felt sick, with a cold
feeling at the roots of my hair and behind my ears, like
when I hear the rasping of broken glass. The boy, after that,
had to be put to bed, and the soldiers nursed him themselves: he became, in all our camp, the only child who was
at all spoiled.

Another time, a sergeant's intrusion in our activities hurt
us cruelly. Mimouni was the son of a street vendor and, as
he received no pocket money from home, had the bright idea
of imitating his father by selling the goodies that came in his
parcels. The news of his initiative spread like wildfire throughout the dormitories, and Mimouni's bed soon became a real
country grocery, while the owner patiently awaited customers. But the sergeant was informed of this by the kids
from the institutions and was horrified. He burst into our
room and struck Mimouni, who was terrified and couldn't
understand how it could be wrong to imitate his own father.
Then the sergeant scolded all of us and, seeing that we
failed to follow his line of argument, became even more
angry. Almost speechless with rage, the soldier finally resorted
to the decisive argument, and that is how, for the first time in
my life, I encountered the device of explaining a defect or
a fault in an individual by referring it back to his Jewish
faith. The furious sergeant revealed to us indeed why this
infamous idea had ever occurred to Mimouni: Mimouni was
a Jew and all Jews are irresistibly drawn toward commerce.
This was my first experience of what was to become a
commonplace, and I thus learned to associate the idea of

being Jewish with the idea of trade, so that I began to resent all Jews who dared engage in business.

In order to avoid any recurrence of this kind of thing, the sergeant decided that all parcels received from home would henceforth be shared in common. As the orphans among us were the majority, our parcels seemed to melt away, leaving the individual receiver a mere biscuit, two candles, or half a chocolate bar. To me, this democratic measure to make us share and share alike was even more hateful. The goodies that we received in our parcels were unaccustomed gifts that we had earned by being far from home, and that was why I never ate them but hoarded them in a tin box, counting them again and again every evening. I got my fill of them by merely looking at them and ate only the broken pieces of candy, when the tin box became too full. In an access of educational or vengeful zeal, the sergeant now made us open all our parcels. His face expressed sheer disgust when he discovered my own sweets, which had begun to melt, all stuck together and their various colors running. He decided that they were not fit to eat, so he ordered me to throw them away. I think I would more gladly have allowed my eyes to be torn out. Fortunately, he was carried away by his own ardor and spared me this martyrdom. His grimy fingers grasped the box as though he were holding some slimy beast, and he hurled the whole mess out of the window, while I felt as though he were tearing open a wound in me. When he went on to my neighbor who was already speechless with fear, I tiptoed out of the dormitory, but my candy had already vanished when I reached the yard.

I soon had to admit to myself that I regretted this trip. My loneliness, the lack of any affection, perhaps also the silence of the forest and the howling of the jackals, the unaccustomed food too—all these weighed on my mind. I hesitated to write to my family and remembered with bitterness how much I had insisted on leaving home. I tried to

maintain my dignity by writing reasonable letters to my
parents, but my unhappiness must have been quite obvious
because, without much skill, they tried, in their replies, to
encourage me to be more patient. When I understood that
they had seen through my defenses, I lost all self-control and
wrote to them about my despair at the mere thought of so
many more days of camp ahead of me. Although I could
easily imagine my life beyond this intervening barrier of
dead time, and although I knew that there was something
after it, a period in which time would regain its accustomed
rhythm and flavor, this yet remained one of my first childish
panics. Deprived of the protection of my parents and of
their physical presence, I found myself, for the first time,
cast alone on the world. Still, I remained sure of one thing:
if I begged him without any pretense, my all-powerful father
would come and help me. This last possibility set a limit to
my despair and gave me enough assurance for me to refrain,
for the time being, from falling back on it.

After attending to the morning's minor chores, after lunch-
ing and then resting for our siesta, we always went out to a
big clearing in the heart of the wood. The place itself was
very beautiful, if I can judge from details that occur to me
even today. The forest guarded it jealously, drawn tight all
around it with wonderful ancient oak trees that rose to
mingle their branches in a vault above us. The light filtered
through the leaves and was scattered in a greenish haze that
shifted gradually to the tender pink of the heather and the
purple of wild mint that grew all over the ground in this
huge natural palace. But even today the tart scent of mint
and the smell of honey and heather still make me feel sick
at my stomach; the mere sight of little boats made of cork
or of wooden canes such as we used to carve all day long,
like invalids or prisoners in institutions, fills me with a sadness
that cuts me off from the world. A wave of anguish sometimes comes over me quite suddenly in the course of conversation with someone who is in other respects quite indif-

ferent to me; then I discover an odor, a color, a fragment
of some object that has reminded me of those hateful afternoons. I developed the habit of secretly wandering away
from my companions and the clearing in the wood. As soon
as I no longer heard their voices clearly, I was even more
lonely, but at last able to weep over my own loneliness. I wept
bitter tears, my breathing interrupted by my gasps as I
allowed myself an orgy of pity for myself and my own
powerlessness.

My Christian companions had at least one event that came
to interrupt the monotony of those days—I mean Sunday
morning mass. I was surprised to note that I no longer knew
the days of the week, though I had been accustomed never
to be wrong on this point. Sunday mass brought order into
the week of the Christians: as early as Saturday night, they
were aroused from their weekday apathy. They had managed
to obtain permission, on that day, to remain in the camp in
order to brush and press their clothes and take their weekly
baths. I envied them their preoccupations, their awareness
of the importance of the moment. The next morning, close
to the dormitory, we watched the believers gather in a small
group. Their hair shiny with lotion, their clean shirts, everything about them conspired to make them at the same time
unusually excited and quiet. On their return from the village
where they attended mass, well after noon, they would
describe to us with interest everything that they had seen.
As for us, our Sunday morning was made different only by
their gaiety.

It was Mimouni who gave me the idea of it, confiding in
me his intention of attending mass. They seemed to be having
fun there, and at least one went through the village on the
way to mass. Although he seemed pretty sure of himself, he
was anxious at heart and asked me to accompany him
because he hoped, thanks to my approval, to gain some
assurance. I hesitated, not that I felt impelled to refuse on
doctrinal grounds, but because his whole proposal struck me

as preposterous. I was associating daily with Christians for the first time in my life, and they aroused in me neither fear nor antagonism; they even enjoyed, in my eyes, the prestige of all Europeans, members of a very powerful sect. But we quite obviously belonged to two entirely different worlds, and nothing could be more alien to me than the idea of entering one of their churches such as I had seen in the course of my Sabbath walks, when I had furtively caught sight of red draperies and of mysterious lights. But Mimouni made fun of my timidity and told me that Christian tourists often visited the old synagogue in his part of town: the faithful always received them well and loaned them caps so that they might enter it without committing any sacrilege. It would only be proper that we be equally well received. I finally yielded, not so much in the face of his arguments as because I felt impelled to bring some interruption to the rhythm of our week. Immediately, I began to await Sunday with impatience.

On the Saturday evening, like all the others, I bathed carefully and got my best clothes ready. The next day, Mimouni and I took our stand in the line, with a reasonable distance between us. The walk, to begin with, was pleasant. The village was at the foot of the mountain, and the road, going all the way downhill, revealed to us, in spite of a ground mist that rose to our shoulders, a valley full of violet-colored rocks that had been scattered by a vast and cataclysmically violent landslide. It both terrified and delighted me. When we reached the church, we were distributed in two pews, with the smaller boys in the front one. I thus found myself quite close to the altar; its magnificence, with painted statues that were so unsophisticated in their expressions, with great festooned candles and the gilded utensils and flowers, all this made a great impression on me. Although a mere country chapel, the whole church struck me as grandiose. I was overcome by a sacred uneasiness that was not new to me because I had once broken the candle at the High Holi-

day. As a Jew pretending to be devout in a Christian house
of worship, I was committing a sacrilege in the eyes of the
God of the Christians. The darkness, the incense, the lights,
the mysteries of the Catholic faith, all these had reduced to
nothing the superficial irony and contempt with which we
always dismissed the aberrations of the idolaters. The God
Jesus must indeed be very powerful to inspire such homage,
and I would perhaps have to suffer His vengeance. Unconsciously, I compared all these riches to the poverty and
nakedness of our synagogue, the bright embroidered vest-
ments of the priests to the sordid everyday habit of our rabbi.
The daring implied by such a comparison disturbed me even
more: I feared and admired the Christians and thereby betrayed my Jewish faith. I was caught between two terrifying
conceptions of what is sacred. Why had I ever left my family?

My position became quite unbearable when I saw the
faithful kneel down. It was indeed impossible for me to bend
down before the altar, out of fear both of the foreign God
and of my own. I tried to spot Mimouni; but only I stood
up in the kneeling crowd, stiff and taut with shame and
anguish. Suddenly I felt, in my back, a powerful blow: I had
forgotten the presence of all the other boys. I scarcely dared
move, but I could perceive, behind me, their shocked expressions, their faces distorted by anger and contempt:

"Down on your knees! Down on your knees," they prompted
me.

But I would almost have preferred to die standing. Another
blow then struck me in the spine. Soon, I was the center of
a silent but methodical aggressive action at the hands of
my neighbors, and the hated cynosure of two whole pews.
From each one of the boys, encouraged by the savage play
of all the others, I received, on my shoulders and my back,
blow after blow, without any respite, until the end of the
service. My whole head hummed, like a beehive.

On our return, I was handed over to the vengeance of
the whole camp; for a while, I was constantly bullied, in-

sulted, and beaten to satisfy their communal anger. Then
they forgot all about me, and I returned to my hideous solitude in an unfeeling crowd. It was quite clear to me that
only my parents really existed in this world, and I again took
to weeping every afternoon.

Finally, I lost all pride and all control of my own feelings.
I decided to expend my last ammunition, to call directly on
my father for help. On a sheet of paper from my copybook,
with my ink-pencil, I wrote him a letter that was intended to
be decisive: it was absolutely necessary that he come at once
and fetch me away. If he left me here, I felt I would soon
die of sorrow. "You must absolutely carry me up," I repeated
five or six times in my short letter, using an idiom that I
translated word for word from our dialect. This somewhat
ridiculous wording expressed clearly my childish despair, but
was subsequently quoted to me often as a joke: "Do you
remember the time when you wrote to us: 'You must absolutely carry me up'?" These jokes contributed to make me
learn, the hard way, how personal one's anguish must always
be, how difficult to communicate at all.

As soon as my appeal had been sent, I became sure of my
imminent rescue. Once solicited, my father couldn't possibly
leave me in this state of despair. Nor did this delay, so full
of hopes that already made me feel less disturbed, last very
long.

Every day we were obliged to rest during a siesta that
lasted from one-thirty until four in the afternoon. We were
expected to sleep at that time, and absolute quiet was
obligatory, though I cannot remember having slept once in
that period. The heat and the crudely bright sunlight
caused adults and all of nature to be overcome by a silent
torpor that was broken only by the shrill chirping of the
cicadas, but all of this had no effect on our vitality. We lay
beneath our blankets, whispering from bed to bed and
swapping well-thumbed comic books. As soon as I ceased to
move, the world was no longer real and, since I could not

exert my body, I began to play with my imagination. The terrifying brightness that confuses all colors in a dazzling white still failed to inspire in me any fear, so that I could abandon myself fully to the magic of light, enjoying to the utmost this invasion in the course of which my body seemed to faint and fail me as I forgot, without any anguish, all of the world that has mass. I gladly stared at the blinding light of the window and soon the stone and the woodwork both vanished, leaving me alone in the midst of the sky, propelling myself with great strokes of the arms in a sea of clouds. Then colors came back to life, long streaks of flickering greens, glistening drops of pink crystal that I found it delightful to turn off and on like lights, with a flicker of my eyelid, and that left behind them, in spite of my efforts, their tracings of darkness.

Suddenly, in the course of this interplanetary trip, I saw my father: his head stood out clearly against one of the panes of the window. This apparition in the general drowsiness of the universe, in the gratuitous world of my joy-riding in the skies, seemed to me quite miraculous, an extraordinary confirmation of his omnipotence. The rules that governed our lives were thereby abolished and I jumped out of my bed. All my anxieties were now but a nightmare, the hostile world around me recovered some of its lost warmth while confidence and security regained control. We kissed each other furtively: in our family, we don't go in much for that sort of thing. I grasped his hand and would not let it go: the order of the universe was thereby assured again. I stared at my father and saw him deformed and glistening through my tears of happiness.

Still, I refused to accompany him into the sergeant's hut. He came out of it at once, with a permit to take me away for the day. Really, all doors opened before him. Then we went into the village. This day that had no name suddenly became a Sunday for me, a Sunday without mass, a holiday without any ballyhoo about it. We sat together in a café, as

we had done in the past. My father offered me what was
left over from his midday meal; he was surprised and alarmed
when he saw me gobble up so gluttonously a huge piece of
makoud (salted egg-cake), a hard-boiled egg, and two cakes
cooked in oil. Food prepared by my mother's hands was
rousing in me the appetite that I had lost. Then he spoke
to me of my last letter, but cautiously, and asked me if I
really wanted to come back home. I had eaten to my heart's
content for the first time in a long while and now felt
reassured by his mere presence, so that my anxieties appeared
to me to be very far away and rather ridiculous. I lowered
my head, not answering him.

"I'll ask the sergeant if it can be arranged," he concluded.

I felt a twinge at my heart. My father had failed to understand me and I had not revealed to him the full extent of
my passionate desire to leave the holiday camp. I lost my
head and all my reticence gave way:

"I want to go back home!"

He placed his hand on my head, as he did when blessing
me and entrusting me to God, so much more powerful than
he. I felt that he was upset. A very painful and utterly disturbing idea entered my mind: perhaps there were things
that my father couldn't achieve for me. Perhaps the sergeant,
with his uniform and his leather puttees, was as powerful as
the policeman! And if the sergeant refused, what would my
father do?

At dusk, we returned to camp. We had gone to the village
cheerfully enough, but we returned now in silence and slowly.
On account of his asthma, which was only beginning at that
time, my father had to stop frequently and would then lean
on my shoulder. In the gathering darkness, with no other
sound around us, his abrupt breathing seemed to resound
throughout the mountain valley. When we got back, he went
and knocked timidly at the sergeant's door and I waited
outside. When he came out again, I guessed at once why his
smile was so constrained and sad:

"My son, you'll have to be reasonable about it. You must stick it out till the end of your holiday."

He didn't add a word, not even one of encouragement. I was too downhearted or perhaps I felt some pity for him and allowed him to leave without witnessing my tears and protestations.

My despair adopted, from then on, a different tone. I was cornered, without any escape, and began to think of death for the first time in my life. Without being at all strange or foreign, this idea of suicide was born within me quite spontaneously and gently, like the world coming to life at dawn. At once, suicide seemed familiar to me, like a release, and I was surprised how convenient and tempting so serious an action could seem. The ultimate solution to my problems was within my own power. In my solitary afternoon retreats, I had discovered a huge depression in the ground that constituted a barrier to my further escape. This ditch that was several meters deep now fascinated me. Full of self-pity and weeping salt tears that dripped into my open mouth, I closed my inflamed eyes and walked ahead, a step at a time, my chest thrust forward, trying hard to abolish all my will power, as when one learns to float on one's back. Often, in a kind of sleepwalking mood, I imagined that I no longer had the solid ground beneath my feet. But no matter how much I kept my eyes closed and tried to forget my own conscience, the reflexes of my body that I allowed to guide me never drove me into the ditch.

I fell into a kind of stupor, lost all appetite, and gave up even my blindman's excursions on the brink of my abyss. Some time after all this, one morning when I woke up, I could no longer get out of bed. In a kind of awakened dream, I heard the voices of my comrades murmuring around me. The sergeant who was on duty was very worried and had me transported on a stretcher to the little mountain dispensary that was far from our camp. My sleepy refusal to live lasted several days, then I developed a fever. As the doctor failed to understand the meaning of it but said he was sure it must be a tropical disease, I was forgotten up there in my infirmary.

That was when I discovered that I had not yet reached the lowest depths of solitude. I was all alone, the only patient in a huge square ward. On the other beds, there weren't even any sheets. Nor was there anything in the room, except the iron bedsteads and the mattresses, to furnish all this bare space. As soon as I was strong enough, I went, on my shaky legs, on a tour of inspection of the infirmary. I met neither patients nor hospital personnel; I seemed to be in a deserted house. The infirmary had been set up in an abandoned old Arab fort, an ancient building of big roughly hewn stones that the weather had stripped of their coating of distemper. The ceilings revealed, in spots, huge scars of mortar from which, every once in a while, there fell a shower of sand. At noon I was visited by a Mohammedan soldier who held a plurality of offices in this infirmary: medical orderly, cook, and watchman. I told him I wanted to go away. He smiled without answering and went his way. I then gave up trying to get away from my bed, besieged by all this emptiness and by the terrifying silence of the mountains.

One day, in that accursed period of my life, I thought that I was about to die of fright. I was awakened by dreadful howls. In a ward close to mine, somebody was beating the door with fists and feet, weeping and crying out aloud, then suddenly silent again, then beginning again frantically, as if all the sufferer's strength were being concentrated in a tempest that could last each time but a moment. Between two waves of this storm, in the pause of calm, I could then hear the serene flight of the cicadas again, as if I had only dreamed it all. I was seized with panic and I jumped out of bed and rushed outside. In the yard, I found the medical orderly, seated on one foot, busy crushing red peppers. My terror could scarcely be reduced to calm by his human

presence. I was still shivering with fright. He smiled and
made up his mind to speak:

"Don't be scared. It's a poor madman. We've locked him
up and he's complaining. Go back to bed if you want to get
better."

I did get better, in order to get away from the howls of
the madman, whose alternating bouts of screaming anger and
of silence gave a rhythm to my suspense until I could leave
the place. When I returned to the summer camp, I no longer
felt like writing to my parents and began to reckon the weeks
that still kept me away from them. I kept but one envelope
for each week, to write to them. All my other envelopes I
swapped against candy and, in my weekly letter, I now
limited myself to a few set phrases, avoiding the tragic tone
of my earlier letters home and asking my parents nothing,
so that they even congratulated me on my having become
reasonable.

When I returned home, my mother found that I had lost
so much weight that she was too surprised to weep with
emotion. I too was unable to weep.

6

BAR MITZVAH

WE MOVED AWAY from Tarfoune Alley the
year of my *bar mitzvah*. For some time my father had been
thinking of renting a larger room if my mother became
pregnant again. The situation was beginning to be critical,
in this respect, when my Uncle Aroun, my mother's eldest
brother, built a tenement house, where we managed to get a
small apartment. My parents then decided to anticipate the
traditional date for my *bar mitzvah* in order to make its
celebration coincide with those of the expected event and of
our housewarming.

Uncle Aroun, in building a tenement house, was indeed
achieving the ambition of all little men who have made good.
In this form, the money he had managed to earn acquired
a material shape, seemed to strike root, and bore fruit. But
all his brothers and sisters asked for permission to move into
the house, which upset his plans considerably, though we all
lived, as I soon had occasion to observe, in a truly tribal
manner. That is why he was unable to reject these applica-
tions. My father, however, was too proud and postponed

applying. When he finally made up his mind to let Mother speak about the matter to her brother, there were no longer any small apartments free in the house. My father immediately took it as an offense. With my Aunt Abbou, who was obviously too poor to afford such a home, we were the only members of all my mother's family not to be living in the new building. Through my mother as his go-between, my father then offered to invest his own meager savings in altering two small laundry-rooms that were on the flat roof terrace so as to make an apartment where we froze in winter and roasted in summer. It is quite probable that my father's asthma became considerably worse as a result of this removal, and that the new premises were also responsible for my mother's rheumatism. But we did at least have a toilet to ourselves, and electric light.

In moving to this new street that we called the Passage, Mother saw an old dream of hers come true. She was now living again with all her family: on the street floor, there were her old paralyzed mother, Uncle Aroun and his wife, fat Aunt Noucha, and her sister Foufa who was always pregnant and looked all the year round like a match that might have swallowed a chick-pea; her brother Filikche the Fool and his wife Menna on the first floor; her sister Maissa, the widow, on the second. All day long, whether for a pinch of pepper or a sprig of parsley, to find out what time it might be or even for no good reason at all, the whole staircase re-echoed with their various names. Actually, they derived comfort and pleasure from constantly finding each other at home, and the other tenants felt like trespassers in this hive of solidarity. After dinner every evening there was a gathering of the clan in Uncle Aroun's flat, where a detailed post-mortem of the day's events would take place, while everyone gossiped and munched squash seeds. Thus, each of us remained completely visible to all the others, and the whole family, by pooling its problems and its hopes, acquired a collective soul. They all looked alike, as a matter of fact:

tall and thin, with their tiny heads thrust forward ahead of their bodies, they had the same general shape. As they sat round Uncle Aroun's table in the evenings, with their heads grouped together above the oilcloth covering, they looked like a litter of animals all eating together. But these animals, so very close to each other in habitat and name, could either be very handsome or very odd in their appearance. Mother, so slim, elegant, and lithe, like a wild filly, was of the same model as Uncle Aroun, who seemed, on the contrary, awkward and disjointed, with cheekbones that jutted out too sharply.

It was in the Passage that I discovered tribal life and learned to hate it. How happy had been the intimacy of our blind alley, now lost for good! As long as I had lived alone, I had lived in peace. In the Passage, I now learned to despise Uncle Aroun who, in spite of his wealth, still lived on a diet of chick-peas, to laugh at Uncle Filikche, poor and prodigal to the point of being a fool, to hate the husband of Aunt Foufa, a stupid brute, to be suspicious of Aunt Noucha's hypocrisy, and to bear with the hysteria of Aunt Maissa. My father hated them, one and all.

He used to mimic, with cruel insights, the tics of each one of them, the terrifying sneezes of Uncle Aroun, the "D'yer get me?" that Chmyane, the half-wit, kept on repeating, or Aunt Abbou's lisp. Not even the children escaped his sarcasm, including Georges whom he so often quoted to us as an example, and whose small head seemed to be melting away as a consequence of his constant work. My mother never accepted my father's jokes about her family, and he never forgave her her constant defense of her family, even when it was in the wrong. This atmosphere of wrangling at home, the pettiness of our tribal community, its futile arguments and treacherous or even friendly gossip, this talk that never ceased but was always untimely, with everybody watched by everyone else, this petty business of petty souls, all of it certainly contributed a lot to the feeling of being

stifled that soon overcame me at home and that I later experienced throughout my native city. To the horror of my
mother and the delight of my father, I rejected with anger
the sickly-sweet advice dispensed to me at our evening sessions around Uncle Aroun's table. It upset me that they
should talk about me, as if it were a violation of my privacy.
My reaction was one of revolt and exasperation, and I earned
the reputation of being heartless and insubordinate. During
those years that we lived in the Passage, I continued to
withdraw into myself, ever more and more, and was finally
so tense that I became a creature of sheer nerves, as unbearable to myself as to others. But my studies and the profound
modification of my stock-in-trade of ideas then established,
once and for all time, a distance between myself and the
tribe, the members of which, on the contrary, had already
found fulfillment in themselves as they were destined eternally
to remain. Eight years after we had moved into the rebuilt
laundry-rooms, they still had, all of them, the same opinions
and the same tics. My cousins, once grown up as young men,
all retained the features of their childhood, scarcely hardened
at all.

   For the time being, the direct access to the terrace seemed
to promise us a magnificent party. All our gatherings, from
now on, would be wonderful, with so much space at our
disposal. On the roof terrace, we were still, to some extent,
at home. Our guests were congratulating us excitedly, and
we gladly accepted their compliments. My imagination was
already aroused more than it should be, and my *bar mitzvah*
thus acquired the importance of an assumption into Heaven.
As an event, it is in any case decisive, consecrating the transition from childhood to adulthood: the boy becomes a new
member of the community, which celebrates his admission
with great sincerity. As hero of the day, he conducts, in the
synagogue and in front of all the faithful, that morning's
service, whereas the profane part of the holiday lasts all
night and the parents, whether rich or poor, have only one

thought, to dazzle their crowded guests. As boys, we used to dream, for years, in anticipation of this triumphant day which set a limit within our lives for all wonderful promises: "After my *bar mitzvah*, I'll do this and that. . . ." In a synthesis of all the wonderful feasts of which I had ever heard, I had imagined that an ox would be sacrificed on our threshold, its blood dripping down the whole staircase, all the poor fed at our expense, lighting so brilliant as to pale the stars, the music of a triumphant procession, an orgy lasting until dawn, all the women and my mother uttering shrill cries of excitement, and the men drunk, happy and grateful. . . . At the mere repetition of all this, dispensed to whoever would listen to me, my chest seemed to swell with pride and joy as if I were already wearing a silken shirt and standing there to dazzle the assembled crowd.

My mother was expected to give birth to the child in April. If luck would have it that she was delivered of a boy, we would kill two birds, even three, with one stone: we would celebrate our housewarming, my *bar mitzvah*, and the circumcision of the newborn son.

To my taste, they all spoke far too much about my potential partner in all this glory. I was jealous of this possible brother who prevented me from being the uncontested hero of a ceremony that would occur only once in my lifetime. I realized that even the date of my *bar mitzvah* had been left undecided, to be determined according to the date of his birth. And so I waited for him. My parents had repeated to me often enough, in spite of all, that I was their first great joy, the only boy and the future head of the family. Now, I learned that I had only just escaped not being what I was. Before me, my parents had had another boy, born with all his fingers joined together, webbed like a duck's foot: "That was a bad omen, but I looked after him well in spite of it all," my mother used to say, "though I knew all the time that something would happen to him." And it did happen, for he died in infancy. On the eve of his death, one of the women next door had heard an owl hoot quite close to our house. As Monsieur Touitou, our teacher, had told us that this superstition was meaningless, I explained firmly to my mother that owls do not kill infants but that the latter die for lack of proper care. The harbinger of death kills nobody; on the contrary, it's a useful bird. That was exactly what Monsieur Touitou had explained to us. My mother was furious and answered me that I was a fool, a very small rat who thought he had a very long tail; and if school taught me only to make fun of my parents, she would prevent my going there. I thus learned to distinguish more clearly what was right and proper at school from what was right and proper at home, though much to the advantage of school; and I acquired the habit of speaking as little as possible to my parents about what I did at school.

Mother was carrying her huge belly ever more uneasily, in spite of her fortitude. She never complained, and she expressed only one longing—to ride in the car of one of our neighbors, which was granted to her at once. But one could distinguish in her vague looks a weariness that weighed on her as she concentrated on this unusual pregnancy, almost unable, it seemed, to attend at the same time to outfitting me for my *bar mitzvah* and preparing for the baby, or the babies, as some women predicted, at the same time. Thus, she attended only to the most urgent things, and set about readying baby clothes. As for me, I had a few ideas of my own about my *bar mitzvah* outfit, and was quite violent in my demands that they become realities. So the purchases were finally entrusted to my Aunt Rbiqua, my father's sister, a tall mummified creature, all wrinkles and shortsightedness, as dry as a grasshopper, who had found herself a husband only late in life and had driven him to despair with her total lack of understanding for the sexual act. (The poor man used to complain bitterly: "I've worn my knees out. . . .") Anyhow, this old mole agreed to take me along to choose an artificial silk shirt, a new cap, and a prayer shawl, a *taleth;* but she

never consulted me once and I remained speechless. She held
my fingers tight in her hand that was hard as wood and
made me trot along beside her too fast, all through the
afternoon, while she went with her own head in the air, far
above mine, peering at the storewindows with her almost
sightless eyes. When I got back home I was tired out, my
nerves on edge, full of disappointment and almost ready to
weep. All the pleasure that I had hoped to derive from the
event was crumbling away bit by bit, and I began to hope
desperately that the baby would turn out to be a girl, as girls
are not entitled to any ceremony and this would make the
whole party mine.

One night, I was suddenly shaken and sent, still almost
asleep, to finish my night's rest on the first floor, in Uncle
Aroun's home. Later, these interruptions of my slumber
became a familiar occurrence. Whenever my mother was
pregnant and I was awakened in the middle of the night,
I guessed, though still half asleep, that she was once more
being delivered of a child. The next morning, the house was
full of busy women, far too many of them wanting to open a
closet door or to empty out one and the same basin, in fact
all squabbling for the sacred honor of serving a woman just
out of childbirth. This time, there had indeed been a girl,
but there had also been a boy. On the door of the bedroom,
the red announcement had been pinned, decorated with a
fish that was intended to protect the young male against the
evil eye. My father was beaming as he served drinks of *raki*
to the guests.

He held the bottle in his hand as he followed our only
glass that went the round of all who were present and had
to be filled again and again. To temper the exquisite burning
of the liquor, he offered, in his other hand, a plateful of
green olives. Birth is a business for grownups, and I couldn't
fully understand their joy. As nobody was paying any attention to me, I pushed the bedroom door open. The heat was
terrific, with two earthenware fire baskets full of glowing

embers to warm the room. My mother was asleep, bloodlessly pale, her brow glazed with sweat, terrifyingly thin. Seeing her in such a state, I began to doubt the sublime quality of the event. Then I noticed the children. I could see, on the divan, two hideous purplish-red babies, all wrapped in cotton wool and apparently of the same thickness from one end to the other, their faces all wrinkled, like caricatures. They were identical and I couldn't distinguish the boy, my inescapable partner in the forthcoming feast day.

I knew that the newborn child had to be circumcised eight days after birth, so that I could celebrate my *bar mitzvah* the following Thursday. The next day, I announced this to all my friends. But a new disappointment awaited me on my return from school: as the twins were too weak, the *mohel* had asked for an additional delay to circumcise the boy. So my *bar mitzvah*, of course, was delayed too, until the child would be stronger. I would gladly have stuck my finger into the eye of this larval being.

Fortunately, the delay was not long, and the great day soon came. Our apartment was already invaded at dawn by all the women of our family and of the building. There was work enough for all: food had to be prepared, furniture moved out, Mother and the babies to be looked after, our terrace to be decorated. But there were too many women around and they all got in each other's way, took nasty cracks at each other, and then sulked, finally uttering sudden cries of joy. I was already aware of my own dignity as a man and despised these women who were all noisy and changing in their moods like children. Their pointless excitement was like that of hens, especially when, looking up and staring straight ahead, with the chin thrust forward, they suddenly uttered long and loud cries of joy in the Oriental manner. At first, I thought of trying to be useful, but they soon steered me away toward the street.

I would never have obeyed them had I really thought that they had come together in my honor. Besides, the presence of all these strangers, busied with tasks that were normally my mother's, irritated me considerably. The comings and goings of aunts, uncles, cousins, and neighbors, through the wide-open door, never ceased. I no longer felt at all at home. Because it was so public, my party seemed no longer to be so much my own.

Toward the beginning of the afternoon, I had to go through the great ritual of washing and dressing. To avoid the expense of the public bath, to which I would have had to invite as my guests all the neighborhood boys, Aunt Noucha had allowed us to use her own bathroom. As none of our families had a private bathroom and none of us had ever seen one before, the mere use of this one gave the occasion a peculiar solemnity. But, to my great disappointment, it was on Aunt Rbiqua that the sacred honor of washing me was conferred, to compensate her never having had any children. I had never stood naked before anybody and now tied a towel securely around my loins while she went down on her knees because her sore back made it difficult for her to bend forward. Then she proceeded to rub my back and chest up and down and down and up with big sweeps of the sponge, as if she were a machine. Finally, she ordered me to remove the towel. I shook my head, without uttering an answer. She failed to understand me at once, lost her temper, mumbled that I was a fool to want to hide such a silly little sliver of meat (which offended me because of her lack of respect for my treasure); she was old enough to be my mother and, if she had been, she would anyhow have brought me up better. The mere idea that she might have been my mother struck me as weird. I held the towel tightly with both hands and stared obstinately at the washbasin, waiting for her to reach the end of her sermon. But she went on mumbling and, retreating from my loins, proceeded to scrub my feet. I had won the battle, relaxed my vigilance, and began to inspect, with admiration, the splendid nickel-plated and enameled gadgets of the bathroom, when her hand suddenly slipped in

between my thighs and began to scrub energetically, but at
random. Wild with anger and shame, I pushed her away so
hard that she fell over backwards against the wall, balanced
as she was somewhat precariously on her pointed old knees.
She stood up again with difficulty, cursing and reviling me,
threw the sponge on the floor, stalked out of the bathroom,
screaming that she was going to complain to my father. She
never returned, so that I was left to finish my bath by
myself.

Once I was clean, the women took me by the hand and
began, with songs and trills of joy and excitement, to dress
me, each one handing me a different garment, as this brought
luck to each in turn. This was the most pleasant moment in
my *bar mitzvah* celebrations, the only one when I was the
actual center of attraction. All the women were crowding
around me, squabbling for the honor of helping me put on
my undershirt, my shirt, or a sock. Though they handled me
and turned me about without much tenderness, I was still
the only object of their thoughts, so I was proud to let them
do as they wished, except when it came to putting on my
drawers.

Dressed in a dark blue suit, with patent-leather shoes on
my feet, I then went to pay a call, accompanied by my
ushers, on each one of my uncles in turn. Tradition required
that they give me presents to thank me for coming. But I
derived no great pleasure from all this. Each one of them,
after kissing me, Uncle Gastoune, Uncle Mirou, Monsieur
Maarek who was Uncle Mirou's partner, and Uncle Aroun,
gave me some money. But money, though it might well be
an indirect way of helping my father, was not of much importance to me, since I knew that I had to turn all of it over
to him. I had hoped very much to get a wrist watch or, in
its stead, a fine fountain pen. Only my Uncle Abbou gave
me, with trembling hands, a small case of worn leather that
I opened as soon as I was out of his house. It contained a
tiny silver cup with a spoon to match. It was an eggcup. I

had never seen one used, and I assumed it was a cup for
drinking, but too small.

When I got back to our Passage, the celebrations had
already begun. I was disappointed, though my pockets were
stuffed with money. Our apartment, emptied of its furniture,
was full of guests who were calling on my mother before
going on to the party on the terrace. Whatever compliments
were made had to be very carefully worded, and many guests
said outright that the twins were a pain in the eye. But they
winked toward my mother while making such statements for
they were merely a trick to fool the Evil Eye. To have two
children at one and the same time might easily arouse murderous envies and the ill will of the demons who had thereby
been defied. The women spat on the floor, assured everyone
loudly that nobody on earth would want to have such little
runts; after which they laughed silently among themselves,
the only human witnesses. As for me, I felt that the babies
really didn't deserve so much attention. They were still as
ugly, red, and round as blood sausages, with mouths that
took up all their gnomelike faces. My mother, unable to control her expressions, didn't seem happy. My father had
refused to ask Uncle Aroun to be the godfather. Uncle Aroun
had already enjoyed the honor of being my own godfather,
but he had failed after that to show any generosity. What
is the use of such a godfather? Offended and especially disappointed at having failed to obtain a blessing that always
brings children to the one who accepts it, my uncle had then
decided not to attend the ceremony. He had gone away, his
head thrust forward, far ahead of him like that of a hasty
giraffe. My mother wept bitter tears as a result of this, and
my father lost his temper once more over his wife's partiality
for her own family.

I could feel jealousy tearing at my heart as I sat and waited
for my share of the congratulations, my hair glued flat with
brilliantine, swarthy and thin and goatlike in my dark suit.
But most of our guests seemed to forget that our party was

in my honor too. Twins are indeed an unusual event. I made
fun of their absurd play in front of the babies as they tried
to make them laugh, rolling their eyes like clowns and grunt-
ing. A few guests remembered me too and uttered some kind
remarks, but I felt, quite unjustly, that they were being
hypocritical or condescending.

So I moved to the terrace where my father and my aunts
took turns, on the threshold, at greeting our guests. An
imaginary line divided into two parts, with all the young
people on one side and their elders on the other, separated
as oddly as too different fluids in one and the same container.
The young people, all thin, stood about, not very firmly
rooted to the ground, and danced according to an exact and
almost mechanical pattern; while their stout elders, on the
other half of the terrace, sat together in a crowd that had no
conventions, eating pickled kidney beans and spitting out
the skins onto the floor, all talking loudly and at the same
time. Nobody paid any attention to me: I belonged to neither
group and understood none of their games. The younger men
had set up a phonograph on a chair and were dancing in a
kind of frenzy, cutting in all the time on the same few girls
and trying to have all the fun they could during the evening.
As for the elders, they sat around some twenty tables that
were grouped close together and, with a kind of slow concentration, ate, drank, and joked. All our guests were thus
occupied, each with his own pleasure. My father and Joseph,
his workman, had set up electric wiring across the terrace,
but what could the poor blinking of these lights do, against
the background of a sky that was too bright, when my
imagination had led me to expect brilliant lighting effects
and fireworks for the occasion? I was bored. Joseph, with a
woman's apron around his loins, kept running between the
kitchen and the tables, a serious expression on his sweating
face. Satisfied with the routine of the party that was going
so perfectly according to plan, my father wandered from one
group of guests to another. True, it was his party too. Two

hundred people, he would say later, and food enough for all and more! Bina, the eldest son of our second-floor neighbors, suddenly found me between two dances and teased me gently: "Don't you want to join us in the dance?"

To his smiling invitation, I gave no reply. Like all the others, he had stolen my own party away from me.

I was unaccustomed to sitting up late and now the night was well advanced. The hour of congratulations was past. I had been warned that our guests, full of food and drunk, would sleep where they happened to be, all over the terrace and our apartment. So I left them my bed and went to sleep at Uncle Aroun's.

7

CHOSEN OUT OF MANY

I WAS EXPECTED to attend. the lycée, the French high school, at the beginning of the school year that followed my *bar mitzvah*. This extraordinary happening was the consequence of an unexpected piece of·luck. The road was straight and easy for sons of the middle class: first junior high school, then senior high school, then the university or their father's business. If they branched off somewhere along the line, it was because they wanted to. But I knew nothing of my own future beyond the school certificate. Not that I had no exact dreams or ambitions but, beyond this certificate, all was still shrouded in darkness.

I wanted very much to become a physician, after having been to the free dispensary at the hospital where we had waited for hours before being admitted finally into the presence of a doctor as distant and sure of his own authority as God Himself. I had been impressed by the prestige of the nurses, the humility of the poor patients. At home, in our eyes, the "Doctor" remained a magician, still inheriting much

73

of the wonder inspired by a sorcerer and having all of the latter's assurance. Often, with a hairpin, I gave imaginary injections to Kalla and Poupeia, the neighbors' daughter, and then bound them up with a handkerchief. When they objected, I gravely reduced them to silence by invoking their inevitable recovery from illness.

But all this was imaginary play. In due time I would realize how impossible it was for me to pursue my studies, and I would probably, like the other boys of my sort, have to bow before the inevitable, without any chance to revolt. After that, as an errand boy or an apprentice in a workshop, all my childhood ambitions would be forgotten.

To encourage us all the better to study, one of my instructors later compared the school system to a series of sieves. In the first, with its coarser-grained holes, a first selection took place; in the second, and finer sieve, a second sorting, and so on. Only the very finest and best elements thus survived the whole screening process. The comparison was good, but unfortunately explains too little. To compete successfully, one needed, in addition to intelligence and the ability to work hard, some financial stability too. But a larger income was required at each test, for it had to make up for the student's lack of any earnings, to counteract the jealousies of relatives, the nagging criticisms of his family, the low morale of the student who grows weary of having too many problems and is soon tempted by the first steady earnings of his former classmates. Nor should one forget school fees, schoolbooks, and clothes. Such, at least, is the problem that arises for students of my social background.

The number of obstacles that ill luck made me contend with was really very considerable. But fate's first gift to me was to open the doors of high school.

I was eleven years old when I was ready to take the examinations for my school certificate, an exceptional age for grade school, which was usually completed at thirteen. Foolishly, we made jokes about the ignorance of the high-school kids who were taking the same examination, but we overlooked the fact that they were much younger than we. Besides, the certificate was not required for them, and whatever backwardness they revealed at the examination was made up for in the course of their seven high-school years. They then came up for their baccalaureate exam at the age of sixteen, whereas the former grade-school pupils could not achieve this before the age of eighteen or nineteen. But I had not yet begun to look so far ahead. I was merely proud of getting into the last year of grade school and of being the youngest in my class. Still, it meant no advantages for me, as the lowest age for admission as a candidate was twelve. Everything was indeed very well worked out. If one of us managed to overcome all these handicaps, it proved that he was really much better than all the sons of middle-class parents. When our instructor, Monsieur Marzouk, drew up the list of official candidates, he was sorry to have to warn me that I had to wait until the next year. For a brief moment, the whole class concentrated its attention on me and I was more proud of it all than disappointed. Nor did I even dream that there was such a thing as an entrance examination for admission to the lowest high-school grade, which one could take at any age and that made the school certificate unnecessary. Who could have informed me? My father, who had attended only a year or two of school, or my mother, who has never learned to read or write any language? Our tribe, too busy with the daily preoccupations of its difficult life, had no knowledge of the passionate discussions of middle-class families concerning the future of their children. My immediate future, in school, was always far too uncertain to allow any long-term planning. So I quietly made the most of this honor of having to mark time for a full year and completed a second year of the same grade, winning all the prizes. These easy prizes indeed had more influence on my future, perhaps, than any precocious success at the school certificate might have had.

Toward the end of my second year, Graziani, our Italian school porter, came into the classroom one day and said to Monsieur Marzouk that the school principal wanted to speak to me. To speak to *me*? Me, of all people? The principal? The school principal was in our eyes a very important person, so majestic and distant that he was almost a legend. His orders were abstract commands, impersonal, communicated to us by signs like the orders of a divinity. But why to me? I could see no connection. On one or two occasions a pupil had had some contact with the principal, but always as the result of a catastrophe or some grave misdeed. The principal had, for instance, broken the news to Nataf Pipo, in the fifth year, of his mother's death, which had occurred suddenly at ten in the morning. And Brami Pinhas, in the third year, had also been summoned to the principal's office, because he had thrown an inkwell against the wall; he had then been expelled and subsequently became insane. My heart beat so violently I could feel it thump beneath my ribs.

The orders of the principal required immediate execution, so I stood up at once and left the room, my knees already weak. I walked across the yard that was strangely empty at this hour, though intensely alive with the concealed presence of a thousand silent children. This magic silence, the unbelievable concentrate of a thousand shouts, was ready, I felt, to explode in all directions as soon as Graziani's bell should ring. But all the demons were still safely bottled up, and only I was free to walk between the two rows of giant eucalyptus trees. A freedom that went to my head, magical, with the whole universe obeying me at that moment; the freedom of the first few days of vacation, or of an adventurer taking off and abandoning his country to its rhythm of everyday life, the office workers at their desk jobs, the workers in their plants, the children in their schools. As I crossed the yard that I had never seen so silent and went by the windows of the classrooms where all my classmates watched me with envy, their arms crossed, I felt privileged indeed, with a great adventure beginning ahead of me.

For the first time in my life, I opened the glass-paneled door of the principal's office and saw him writing at his desk. I was now within the sacred precincts and all my gestures were therefore slow and studied, as if for a ritual. I was careful to close the door and progressed slowly across three platforms or stages, end to end. The desk of Monsieur Louzel was placed at the end of the third, at the far end of the room, against the wall. Three black cabinets, some framed reproductions in black and white, and black curtains. Behind Monsieur Louzel, a bay window revealed a tiny garden that seemed full with a single green banana tree and one aloe tree that somehow tempered the schoollike severity, so solemn and cold, of this room.

With a gesture of his hand, the principal invited me to be seated, then he got up to fetch my file from one of the cabinets. I stole a glance at him, full of admiration. His hair was spotlessly white, of a fine silky white, and gave him a distinguished air. He was, I feel, a bit histrionic, but with sincerity, out of an awareness of his function and his importance in our eyes. He always impressed us because of his perfect diction and polished manners that represented, for us, the real Frenchman from metropolitan France whose prestige remains undiminished.

My various instructors and he too, the principal informed me, had noted my uninterrupted successes and had decided to reward them. So I had been proposed as candidate for the annual school scholarship. It is wrong to think that a child of twelve cannot grasp the importance of a decisive moment in his own life. I remained speechless, so deeply moved that I was overwhelmed. A mass of vague projects, all wonderful, suddenly ceased to be merely imaginary and gained some probability. The prestige of the doctor's white smock at the hospital, the respect that the nurses felt for

him, all this exquisite but serious play, the money earned. . . .
It would now become true, and I would be a physician. I
could hear the word repeated rhythmically in my head:
physician, physician, physician. . . . Monsieur Louzel understood my emotion and my absent-mindedness. He was kind
enough to pretend not to notice it, and set about explaining
to me the ingenious institution of which I was a beneficiary.
Each year the school brought to the attention of the community a brilliant student who needed help. The community
then entrusted him to the care of one of its own former
scholars who now, in turn, paid for the new scholar's studies.
Later, once his studies were completed and his position assured, the new scholar was expected to assume some day the
responsibility for a younger scholar's studies. I found this
idea of a chain that went on forever quite wonderful, and
looked upon the men who had invented· it as benefactors of
mankind.

The principal then paused, with some solemnity. He still
had to ask me my opinion, whether I was prepared to continue my studies. The Jewish community of Tunis, on the
recommendation of the Alliance Israélite Universelle, would
undertake to finance my studies, at first my high-school
years, then the university too. What had I to say? The principal was already asking me what I had to say! Here I was,
already acquiring importance. Did I want to study? Good
God, did I want to continue my studies. . . . "Well," the
principal concluded by himself, "you've agreed. Of course,
we first had to get the approval of your father, and it has
meant his accepting a heavy sacrifice and agreeing to carry
on without any help from you until you have received your
final diplomas." The principal thus revealed to me that my
father had already been consulted several days earlier, and
that nothing had then been said to me, to avoid any possible
disappointment. Only that same morning had my father at
last given a favorable answer. So, my father had accepted!

How could he possibly have said no! I was utterly aghast, full of revolt against the mere possibility of my father's objecting. Obscurely, I imagined an argument with my father, but he never would have been able to prevent me from choosing the path toward glory.

Monsieur Louzel continued to speak in his dictatorial tone, and I continued to remain silent. Still, I had an answer for every question, repartee came spontaneously to my lips, I was bubbling over with promises, gratitude, and dreams. I reacted to every one of his sentences with gestures that were born of my whole body, approving, denying, committing me. There had been some hesitation, Monsieur Louzel confided in me, between choosing Lévy, the son of the widow, and myself. His financial status deserved more consideration, but I was the better student. I nodded, with an expression that wished to convey deep sympathy for Lévy Isidro; but my joy was too great to allow any qualification, except that of retrospective anguish.

"Well, you have deserved your luck," concluded the principal. "Now you must go back to your classroom to fetch your things and go at once to see Monsieur Bismuth, who has been appointed your sponsor. He wants to see you at once, as he has to leave town this afternoon. So, you had better go. . . . But wait, I haven't told you anything about Monsieur Bismuth."

We were already going ahead with the application of our plans and biting into the future. I assumed an attentive and preoccupied look, ready to rush wherever he would send me. Monsieur Bismuth, the well-known druggist, was going to be, it seemed, my paying sponsor. Yes, I knew his drugstore well, though I had never met Monsieur Bismuth: a modern storefront, spacious display windows, with neon lighting at night. A stout thread of gold now bound me to the city. The principal began to speak to me in detail about my sponsor; a son of poor parents, who had been a courageous and hard worker, with the community scholarship coming to bring recognition to his merits, and here he was a wealthy man, an honored member of the community, the owner of the finest drugstore in our part of the country.

"Let him be your inspiration," concluded Monsieur Louzel. "Your destinies have much in common, and I hope, for you, that they'll continue to have as much in common."

Abandoning his histrionic manner to become almost paternal, the principal then asked me:

"What do you want to be?"

"A physician," I answered, without any hesitation.

"Well, if you continue to study as hard as you have been, we'll make a physician of you."

He then dismissed me, and I went again across the three stages, opened the glass-paneled door, closed it carefully. To me, it seemed as if I were awakening from a dream. But unlike those awakenings when one is seized with the irresistible desire to check on the real existence of one's treasure, my own gold was here with me: magically, my dream had acquired a body. The school principal, Monsieur Bismuth, the influential druggist, the Alliance Israélite Universelle, the whole of the Jewish community of Tunis had decided that it must come true.

This was no time for self-satisfied jubilation. My destiny pushed me ahead: I was expected. So I hurried across the yard, without paying any attention to the benevolent eucalyptus trees, to the big bronze bell that waited there, patient and almost motherly, to the sidelong glances of all my classmates indoors. I climbed the old wooden staircase four steps at a time. As I feverishly gathered my things together, I felt on me the gaze of all my classmates. They were perhaps astonished to see me summoned like this by the principal; perhaps Monsieur Marzouk had announced to them my new and sudden glory. But I was sure that they all stared at me. So as not to have to compete against this general lack of concentration in the class, Monsieur Marzouk interrupted his teaching. In the silence that ensued, my heart beat cheerfully, with big, heavy beats, as if it were dancing.

My father's store was not far from my sponsor's office, so I went first to see my father. I showed him, almost without any self-consciousness, how deeply I was moved. He told me all about his talk with the principal that same morning; he had come back from it very proud and convinced that I should continue my studies. The principal had been very complimentary indeed, and this had confirmed my father in his faith in his own intelligence and in that of his offspring. Then I went to the drugstore. Monsieur Bismuth was no longer there, but his clerk reassured me: Monsieur Bismuth had expected me, but now asked me to come back in two weeks. So the various threads were indeed all tied together.

The city's siren that announced noon now rang. I rushed into the street, at last aware of my own appetite, but also because I felt a need to run. I wanted to sing, to announce my unbelievable adventure to everyone, to make polite remarks to utter strangers in the street. Some Moslem laborers were repairing the streetcar tracks, and the sun was glistening on the metal. I shouted out to them:

"May God be with you!"

This is how we greet, in the countryside, laborers whom we do not necessarily know, but merely to reaffirm, in the face of loneliness, the solidarity of all mankind. Now, these men were surprised, because such conventions are generally respected only among believers in their faith; still, they answered me:

"The blessing of Allah be upon you!"

This feeling of communion with all of mankind made me happy. I gave a couple of coins to a Bedouin beggar, now that I would henceforth be so wealthy! An old idea that disappointments had caused to wilt now blossomed again, binding my adolescence that was beginning more closely to my childhood that was gone: I had been chosen among many, ahead of Lévy, who could not be surpassed in mathematics,

ahead of Spinoza, who was Monsieur Marzouk's favorite!
I was surely better than all my classmates, all the students
in the school, perhaps all the students in all the Alliance
schools! Surely, I would go far and be very powerful. True,
I couldn't yet foresee the nature of this power, but it was a
kind of broad movement toward the future, a lunging that
was almost muscular.

Following the advice of my father, who was more aware
of such necessities, my mother began inspecting my wardrobe.

"You know," he explained to her, "only rich men's sons
attend high school, and our boy must be decently dressed,
too."

In their eyes, as in my own, my entering high school
acquired the importance of an introduction into society,
which it actually turned out to be, even more than I had
guessed. Our alley and the Alliance School belonged to one
society, but the European sections of town and the high
school to another. Above all, I was now setting forth on the
adventure that leads to knowledge. I sometimes think back
now, with horror, on the darkness in which I might have
been forced to live, and I then consider the many aspects of
the universe that I might never have come to know. I would
not even have dreamed of their existence, like some deep-sea
fish that remain ignorant of the very existence of light.

Knowledge was the very origin, perhaps, of all the rifts and
frustrations that have become apparent in my life. I might
have been happier as a Jew of the ghetto, still believing confidently in his God and the Sacred Books, devoting his
Sabbaths to the fun of *pilpul* distinctions of Talmudic right
and wrong, flouting tiny details of the sacred edifice of the
Law but never going beyond the approved limits of the game.
But I could only see, in those days, the element of new
adventure, and I approached it violently and full of confidence, sure that I had everything to gain. All my family
difficulties, from now on, took on the appearance of unworthy
worries. I had the whole world to conquer.

A month later, I successfully passed the scholarship examinations that relieved me of almost all the school fees, much to Monsieur Bismuth's satisfaction. The city high school isn't free, which of course reduces one's chances of being admitted to it. I was less brilliant in the exams for the school certificate than had been expected: I was too confident and, carried away by the impetus of my enthusiasm, had already embarked, in my mind at least, on my high school career.

8

THE DRUGGIST

IT WAS ONLY after the summer holidays that Monsieur Bismuth was at last free to see me. I had to wait a long while in the crowd of his customers. The drugstore was luxurious, its windows framed in chromium-plated nickel, the walls painted a light color, the chairs upholstered in leather. On the walls the many framed sheepskins testified to the eminent merits of the owner of the store and to his successes in several pharmaceutical contests. I felt sincerely happy on Monsieur Bismuth's behalf, and somewhat proud too, as if I shared his glory. Wasn't my future henceforth bound, in a way, with that of Monsieur Bismuth and of his achievements? Didn't I now depend to some extent on his prosperity? I gazed in a friendly mood at the faces of his employees, as if I were silently introducing myself: "I'll be coming here often and you'll often see me here again."

One of the pharmacists came into the store by a small door at the back and announced that Monsieur Bismuth was ready to see me. I was deeply moved as I followed him into the endless neon-lit passage that was concealed behind the door. This perspective that suddenly opened out before me, completely unpredictable from the outside, came to me as a surprise. I was fond of rooms that are completely closed off, and the passage, with its walls lined with shelves full of bottles and boxes, was a perfectly isolated corridor where none of the sounds of the city could be heard. The artificial effect of neon lighting, still relatively rare in those days, added to my surprise and my emotion. The pharmacist had meanwhile vanished and, in a silence that seemed heavy, I discovered the open door of Monsieur Bismuth's office.

The druggist was writing, his head bent forward, his hair thin on his scalp that appeared pink beneath the carefully combed strands. His hand shook slightly above the paper. I remained standing in the doorway. At first, he said nothing, as if he hadn't seen me. Then he raised his head and said, in an even voice:

"Ah! Come in!"

But he continued to write and I had not yet learned that businessmen dream up a personality for themselves which they forget to set aside, even when such histrionics are unnecessary. Impressed by the silence, I was embarrassed in this unaccustomed atmosphere of concentration and luxury, and continued to await some further invitation. At long last, Monsieur Bismuth set down his fountain pen, put his papers methodically in order, and asked me to be seated. He called his trembling hands to order by clasping the fingers together very tight. Then he launched forth on a long speech that had perhaps been prepared, all about the need to work uninterruptedly if one wants to succeed in life. He spoke slowly, his voice evenly poised, his words well chosen, with the diction of an intelligent and learned foreigner who has mastered the language through sheer will power. I think he made a great impression on me. He had reverted to the same themes as the school principal, though he avoided the theme of his own life while constantly referring to it indirectly. I had meanwhile had time to inform myself about him; everything that he now said to me was clear and I was able to refer each detail back to his own life story. Though the speech was intended as an exhortation referring to my future, it was actually a summary of his past, too. At least, that is how I understood it, approving and admiring his manner. A man's worth may be weighed according to his degree of success, and he had succeeded. One's background is of little importance: he was the son of a well-known rabbi who had been very poor and who died shortly after begetting him at the age of seventy, leaving a young wife in great indigence. Hard work will overcome, in the long run, all obstacles: as a brilliant student, I too had discovered this truism. Finally, he concluded by affirming outright:

"If you study hard, we'll make a druggist of you."

I revealed no surprise at all, though some muscular contraction of face or of body nearly always betrayed my feelings. Besides, he was not watching me. In the course of his long monologue, he never once tried with his eyes to catch mine. Instead, he seemed to be speaking only for himself. In the seven years of my life when I saw him regularly once a month, we never established any real contact. Never once did I feel current pass between us. His eyes always avoided mine, and I understood later what I had always suggested to him: in me, he recognized his own personal battle, his difficult past, his insecurity.

I lacked the courage to answer that I preferred to study medicine. After all, he was the one who paid, and he added now, with some disdain and the only sign of any real emotion in all our conversation, as if he had already guessed some objection on my part:

"It is absolutely necessary to live on Easy Street. It's very important, and you'll realize it, too."

But for whom this contempt? For those who failed to earn an easy living, or for his own philosophy of profit and earnings? At the time, I seemed to understand that he despised those whose earnings were small; on the whole, I agreed with him. Money was only one aspect of the glory that I hoped to win. In town, people were already complaining that the medical profession was overcrowded and that young doctors found it increasingly difficult to build up a practice. Pharmacies remained, however, an excellent business. Our middle class is too recent to have much respect for professional scales of values or for a disinterested vocation. It still understands only commercial success and, of course, this opinion of our middle class imposes itself on our other classes too.

But even if Monsieur Bismuth was right, he now separated quite brutally two images that I had kept closely connected: the one, of my material success, of my studies, and the other, of myself in a white smock, the lancet in my hand as I accomplished a task that brought health to mankind and earned me its gratitude. At the same time, I was struck by Monsieur Bismuth's happening to agree with my father, who so painfully and disturbingly insisted that one needs to earn as much as possible. I now accepted the advice, in spite of my incipient shame, simply because I felt that my noble mission justified it fully. But if I were to be deprived of the image of the white smock and of the meek and grateful poor, then I would be entirely lost and would find myself facing again my father's bald and unqualified advice: "You have to make money." If I adopted as my own all my father's spoken daydreams, then I was really anxious to become a rich man or rather to break away from our poverty. But I had too closely bound the idea of money together with that of my future, of my most disinterested image of my own self. To my utter surprise, the pure and desirable light that had led me on now seemed to grow dim.

So I was confused, and pushed the whole problem aside. We would see all this later, and I would see it too. But my admiration for my sponsor, spontaneously undivided though it had been, was now less clearly whole, and I began to resent in him this tyranny that annoyed me.

"I'll give you a letter to my bookstore. They'll supply you with your schoolbooks."

After that, the druggist was silent, and the silence at once

regained control of the whole room, as if it were empty. He
stood up and began to walk, so that I was able to see that
he limped painfully, another undeniable proof of his father's
senility. His hip went askew, like a rowboat in a heavy sea,
so that his shoulder and head slumped as if he were about
to fall over backwards. (But the principal had told me to
take him as an example.) With difficulty, he reached toward
a desk drawer, pulled a business card out, and came back,
lifting his twisted foot as if it were a foreign body and
dropping it again heavily, while his whole body was drawn
perilously in its wake. It hurt me to watch him.

Monsieur Bismuth refrained from saying anything more.
I had not opened my mouth, but my mind was all in a
turmoil. In the silence, the telephone rang once, its ringing
like a single pearl. We both stared at it, but it failed to ring
again: it was nothing, the telephone merely dreaming.

But what were Monsieur Bismuth's dreams? Perhaps he
had also hoped to become a physician. I don't know why I
was later convinced that this had been what he was daydreaming about on that occasion of my first visit.

He had now picked up his pen again and was writing on
the card. The trembling of his hands, it seemed, was caused
by the same thing as his limping. He handed me the card
and, without arising from his chair, held out his hand for
me to shake.

I returned along the passage, upset and dissatisfied. All
the noises of the drugstore surged toward me as in a dream,
but even these and the excitement of the many customers
failed to rouse me from my painful thoughts. To the lights
and the luxury of the store, I paid less attention now than
earlier. I might have lacked the material means to continue
my studies. But now, as soon as the means were assured
me, I felt it would be an injustice if I were not granted
freedom to pursue them as best I wished. I was perhaps
irresponsible, but I assumed that my rebelliousness was a
virtue.

As soon as I had left the store, I stared with curiosity at the business card that I carried. It didn't say much: "Please hand to the bearer all schoolbooks required for the sixth-year class." The name of the card's owner was followed by a whole string of titles and honors: Doctorate, master's degree, certificates, but the last line had been crossed out. Still, I was able to decipher it: Vice-President of the Chamber of Commerce.

Would my own success adopt the features of Monsieur Bismuth? A stout man, bald, with a shifty look in his eye, in an oak-paneled office with all the shelves full of leather-bound books? The school principal had been somewhat simple in his approval and admiration of the druggist's successes, and had overlooked the spasms of his hands, his limping, his difficult inner struggle, his accent that he had only just managed to repress, his rejection of his whole identity. The day that I was at last daring enough to denounce the values of the middle class, the violence with which my sponsor defended them revealed to me how incapable he was of ever being a mere representative of this class, one who is undisturbed in his beliefs, through lack of any other awareness.

"Let him be an example for you." Never, I felt it that day, as I slowly walked back to our street, would I be able to be a druggist, to look at all like Monsieur Bismuth. To my pity for his infirmity, for his dreadful limping, there was now added, in spite of myself, some pride and contempt. Both my parents were tall and lithe, both of them of a strong and lively breed; I too, as a mere animal, gave promise of being well proportioned. Men who were small and fat made me laugh.

But why were these unjust demands being made on me? Why was I expected, in exchange for a scholarship that covered the expenses of my studies, to abandon my dream that seemed to me still, at that time, to be so profound, so definitive?

I understood nevertheless the terms of our agreement: if I wanted to become anything worthwhile, I would often have to walk along that silent passage. If I chose that path, I would have to accept . . . or cheat. Because I was being allowed to enter high school, I already thought I had won the battle. But I was beginning to find out, too, that the struggle had only just begun.

PART TWO

Alexandre Mordekhai Benillouche

1

THE CITY

My NAME IS Benillouche, Alexandre Mordekhai.

How galling the smiles of my classmates! In our alley, and at the Alliance School, I hadn't known how ridiculous, how revealing, my name could be. But at the French lycée I became aware of this at once. From then on, the mere sound of my own name humiliated me and made my pulse beat faster.

Alexandre: brassy, glorious, a name given to me by my parents in recognition of the wonderful West and because it seemed to them to express their idea of Europe. My schoolmates sneered and blared "Alexandre" like a trumpet blast: Alexan-ndre! With all my strength, I then hated them and my name. I hated them, but I believed they were right, and I was furious with my parents for having chosen this stupid name for me.

Mordekhai (colloquially, I was called Mridakh) signified my share in the Jewish tradition. It had been the formidable name of a glorious Maccabee and also of my grandfather,

93

a feeble old man who never forgot the terrors of the ghetto.

Call yourself Peter or John, and by simply changing your clothes you can change your apparent status in society. But in this country, Mridakh is as obstinately revealing as if one shouted out: "I'm a Jew!" More precisely: "My home is in the ghetto," "my legal status is native African," "I come from an Oriental background," "I'm poor." But I had learned to reject these four classifications. It would be easy to reproach me for this, and I have not failed to blame myself. But how is it possible not to be ashamed of one's condition when one has experienced scorn, mockery, or sympathy for it since childhood? I had learned to interpret smiles, to understand whispers, to read the thoughts of others in their eyes, to reconstruct the reasoning behind a casual phrase or a chance word. When anyone speaks about me, I feel provoked in advance: my hair stands up on end and I am ready to bite. One can, of course, ultimately learn to accept anything at the cost of an enormous effort and a vast weariness. But, before this happens, one resists and hates oneself; or else, to defy the scorn of others, one asserts one's own ugliness and even exaggerates it so as to grin and bear it.

At the lycée, I very quickly got into the habit of dropping "Mordekhai" from my lesson headings, and before long I forgot the name as if I had shed it like an old skin. Yet it dragged on behind me, holding fast. It was brought back to my attention by all official notices and summonses, by everything that came from beyond the narrow frame of daily routine. When commencement-time came, on the day diplomas were to be awarded, I knew I would be one of the triumphant scholars; in the midst of a nervous crowd, I waited undisturbed, certain of success. When the usher climbed onto a chair, my name was the first to be called out; in the tense silence, the exact order of my legal status was re-established:

"Alexandre, Mordekhai, Benillouche!"

I didn't move. Surprised by the silence, the crowd looked around for the happy candidate, astonished to hear no explosion of joy, no throwing of notebooks into the air; no one was surrounded or kissed by a delighted family. (I never cared to have my parents present at the public events of my life, so they hadn't been told when the diplomas were to be awarded.) I merely smiled to those of my schoolmates who congratulated me with a look; and I was soon forgotten because everyone was concerned with his own fate.

Alexandre, Mordekhai, Benillouche. Benillouche or, in Berber-Arabic dialect, the son of the lamb. From what mountain tribe did my ancestors descend? Who am I, after all?

I sought—in everything from official documents to my own sharply defined features—some thread which might lead me to the knowledge of who I am. For a while, I believed my forebears had been a family of Berber princes converted to Judaism by Kahena, the warrior-queen and founder of a Jewish kingdom in the middle of the Atlas Mountains. It pleased me to think that I came from the very heart of the country. But then, another time, I found I was descended from an Italian Renaissance painter. I tore the article from the big Larousse encyclopedia and displayed reproductions of my ancestor's paintings to all my friends. Philology could explain away what changes the name had undergone, and my friend Sitboun, the star Latin student, backed me up and even discovered that the patron of a Latin poet had had a similar name. But philology is a fragile science, and the past is much too far away. Could I be descended from a Berber tribe when the Berbers themselves failed to recognize me as one of their own? I was Jewish, not Moslem; a townsman, not a highlander. And even if I had borne the painter's name, I would not have been acknowledged by the Italians. No, I'm African, not European. In the long run, I would always be forced to return to Alexandre Mordekhai Benillouche, a native in a colonial country, a Jew in an anti-Semitic universe, an African in a world dominated by Europe.

Had I believed in signs, might I not have said that my name holds all the meaning of life? How is it possible to harmonize so many discords in something as smooth as the sound of a flute?

My native city is after my own image. Through Tarfoune Street, our alley led to the Alliance School; and between home and the schoolyard, the atmosphere remained familiar, all of a piece. We were among Jews of the same class, and we had no painful awareness of our situation, no pretenses. At school, we persisted in speaking our own dialect despite the director's posters which demanded French. Sometimes I crossed a Moslem quarter as if I were fording a river. It was not until I began attending the lycée that I really became acquainted with the city. Until then, I had believed that, by some special privilege, the doors of the world were being opened to me and that I need only walk through them to be greeted with joy. But I discovered I was doomed forever to be an outsider in my own native city. And one's home town can no more be replaced than one's mother.

A man may travel, marvel at the world, change, become a stranger to his relatives and friends, but he will always retain within him the hard kernel of his awareness of belonging to some nameless village. Defeated, blind, his imagination will bring him back to that landmark, for his hands and feet know its contours and his nerves are wonderfully attuned to it. And I—well, I am my city's illegitimate son, the child of a whore of a city whose heart has been divided among all those to whom she has been a slave. And the list of her masters, when I came to know some history, made me giddy: Phoenicians, Romans, Vandals, Byzantine Greeks, Berbers, Arabs, Spaniards, Turks, Italians, French—but I must be forgetting some and confusing others. Walk five hundred steps in my city, and you change civilizations: here is an Arab town, its houses like expressionless faces, its long, silent, shadowed passages leading suddenly to packed crowds. Then, the busy Jewish alleys, so sordid and familiar, lined with deep stalls, shops and eating houses, all shapeless houses piled as best they can fit together. Further on, little Sicily, where abject poverty waits on the doorstep, and then the *fondouks,* the collective tenements of the Maltese, those strange Europeans with an Arab tongue and a British nationality. The Russian Orthodox church too, its illuminations and domes surely conceived in a night of Muscovite dreams; and the clean little electric streetcar line from Belgium, as neat as a Flemish interior. We have Standard Oil buildings too, and an American airport and cemetery, with improved U.S. equipment, jeeps and trucks at the exclusive disposal of the dead; the Shell Company or British Petrol; the residence of Her Britannic Majesty's Ambassadors, and finally the little homes of retired French *rentiers,* cottages with red-tiled roofs and gardens, cabbages—all in a row, just as in French songs.

And within this great variety, where everyone feels at home but no one at ease, each man is shut up in his own neighborhood, in fear, hate, and contempt of his neighbor. Like the filth and untidiness of this stinking city, we've known fear and scorn since the first awakening of our consciousness. To defend or avenge ourselves, we scorned and sneered among ourselves and hoped we would be feared as much as we ourselves experienced fear. This was the atmosphere in which we lived at mealtimes, in school and in the streets. If any youthful ingenuousness or skepticism allowed us still to hope, we were promised nothing but treachery and blood-red dawns. Slowly, as if a poison administered drop by drop had at last had its effect, my sensibility, my sentiments, my entire soul was permeated with it and reshaped; I learned to check the odious inventory of it all. Beyond a ceremonious polite-

ness, everyone remained secretly hostile and was finally horrified by the image of himself that he discovered in the minds
of others.

One can make a mess of one's childhood or of one's whole
life. Slowly, painfully, I understood that I had made a mess
of my own birth by choosing the wrong city.

Bissor was a strong boy, all muscles and big bones, like a
ploughhorse. Healthy as a peasant, robust, vigorous, thickset—
he was a miracle within the ghetto's rotten heart. A mop of
jungle-wild red hair stressed his primitive appearance. Yet,
for all this, he had within him the fears, humiliations, and
resentments of all those born and still living in the ghetto.
At the age of eleven, he had begun to deliver evening
newspapers after school and had thus come to know the city.

I was not self-conscious in his presence, and once I even
told him about my father's terrors and hatreds. But he interrupted me at once:

"Your father's right. You don't yet know what it's like."

His own father's store, he explained, had been burned in
a pogrom, and his old man had then died of grief. Although
Bissor's schooling was paid for by the community, he worried
constantly about his mother and sisters, fearing that they
might not be able to support themselves without his help.
(He was right about this, for even though he left school
before graduating, he was unable to prevent one of his sisters
from becoming a prostitute.) He used to describe to me his
daily rounds: the distrust and innuendoes, the perfect im-
perviousness of others. In Bissor, I caught echoes of my
father's despair, but I still refused to accept it. Constantly,
I heard him talk of his hatred of the city, of his horror of
having been born there, of the impossibility of ever finding
normal opportunities there. I was ironical when the city
seemed to stir but he would then race home, put up a supply
of food, and barricade the doors and windows, terrified by
the unpredictable. Other people's misfortunes could force me

to retreat, but could never convince me; they had bungled
the situation, I thought, through awkwardness or prejudice.
If the same thing happened to me, I was sure I would come
out better.

But I had to confess I was wrong. Sometimes with Bissor—
who was the only one of the lycée boys whose standard of
living was not beyond my own means—I went to the movies
on Saturdays. More than anything else, it was the way we
spent our leisure time that showed up the difference between
ourselves and our schoolmates; we used to go to the Kursaal
which they considered a dive, having never set dainty foot
there. Certainly, they were not altogether wrong. In order
to get in for the three o'clock show, we had to queue up at
one, be jostled and elbowed and attacked by kids of our own
age, older boys, and even adults, until the box office opened.
Often the queue grew too long and dissolved into sudden
confusion; by the time things had straightened out, we had
lost our places. Once, our tickets were torn out of my hand
before I could identify the thief; Bissor in his rage couldn't
refrain from railing at me while I burst into tears. So we
went to complain to the manager and he allowed us into the
theater despite his mistrust.

On one of our movie Saturdays, Bissor was unexpectedly
called in for an additional assignment on his newspaper route.
We decided that I'd go alone to buy the tickets and leave
one with the cashier for Bissor to pick up as soon as he was
free to join me. It was anguish for me to stand in line without
Bissor; I was a weakling, and I don't know how many humiliations his presence saved me.

I got to the Kursaal long before the box office opened,
but there was already a big crowd. To my delight, a policeman was there lording it over the whole square. The Sicilian
laborers who composed our aristocracy, with slicked-down
hair and bright ties; the ragged bootblacks who were its
lowest class and had gathered the price of a ticket by collecting cigarette butts; the fritter-vendors in their greasy

fezzes; the Maltese cabbies with their cap visors coquettishly broken; the porters with professional ropes thrown over their shoulders; all these people, so brutal and dishonest in past weeks, were now miraculously orderly, almost polite, waiting under the eyes of the Mohammedan policeman, an enormous fellow with a pock-marked face and a pointed black mustache. I felt happy being where I was: the façade of the Kursaal, built to look like a dragon's head, spat out its flames; there were colored posters glued to the monster's cheeks, and the crowd itself was disturbing but full of living joy; all this contributed to give me each time the same glow of happiness. On this particular day, there was also the promise of security.

The posters on the dragon's cheeks announced two Tom Mix films and one Rin-Tin-Tin. We were used to this, but we never tired of exulting in the triumphs of our wonderful cowboy. We joined him in his pursuit of the stagecoach that contained the gold and the exquisite blond heroine and was being driven away by bandits. How could one remain a passive spectator when faced with such sublime excitements? We threw ourselves into the scuffles and added to the rhythm of the galloping horses by stamping our feet on the floor; we pulled at the reins with our hero and roared with joy or disappointment. For a few minutes, we all forgot our individual fears and hatreds and became a single unit in the noisy expression of our emotions.

We entered the hall slowly, quietly. I was sorry the policeman had not come in with us, because the crowd's savagery soon revealed itself again. My seat was in the second row and so close to the screen that I would certainly come away with an aching back, a headache, and a stiff neck. The Kursaal, in spite of its majestic name, smelled of wine. But the magic of its silver screen, brightened by a frame of darkness, and the mystery of its little blue lights, even its odor—a special mixture of disinfectant, damp, and human emanations—made me ecstatic.

The impatient audience was already overexcited, stamped rhythmically on the floor and began to whistle. But the projecting staff was used to their outbursts and ignored the cries of: "Come on! Let's go! We want the picture! Give us our money back!" Soon, however, the fiickle occupants of the reserved stalls lost interest in shouting and turned their energy on us, the Jews, who sat crowded together. A shower of beans and gourd seeds began to fall on my head.

Because humiliation was my daily bread, I believed for a long time that all stories which tell of heroic action resulting from humiliation were either exaggerated or completely false. Our skin was thick and, if we weren't stung too deeply, we could bear it: we could manage to continue enjoying ourselves, as people can who are pestered by flies. But, that day the show was delayed and the ingenuity of our tormentors became excessively inventive and went beyond a mere sting. In the gloom, they had the bright idea of striking matches and tossing them over us. Our real fears delighted them and they roared with joy each time they threw a match. Meanwhile, we tried to save ourselves by ducking down in our seats and heard them call: "Kiki! Kiki!"—which is, for them, the nickname of all Jews. Sickened by my own impotence, crushed under the weight of blind and anonymous injustice, I could have burst into tears from disgust and rage.

Then, in the impressive semidarkness of the safety lights, I saw Bissor's square silhouette. Never before had physical strength given me such joy; I stood up and waved to him despite the risk of offering a target for a flaming match. Bissor sat down beside me in very bad spirits because his newspaper route had been reduced by one third since he began his round too late; except on Tuesdays and Thursdays, he could not begin his deliveries before four o'clock. I tried, in spite of the noise, to hear what he was saying. Suddenly, as he spoke, a lighted cigarette butt streaked through the blue air and landed on Bissor's head. I smelled the burning hair and, since he didn't seem quite aware of what was happening, I began to grope for the butt. Then, understanding, he rose with clenched teeth and began looking around for the villain who was easily identified: a Sicilian worker who, with his friends, was shrieking with delight at having hit the jack pot. The Sicilian, ready for battle, shouted:

"*Cosa vole?*" (What do you want?)

Without reply or warning, Bissor lifted his arm and rammed his fist at the man's nose. Blood began to flow over his lips and chin, and there was a moment of stupefaction before the loud and indignant response. No one dared to touch Bissor, but the Sicilians all yelled, surrounded their beaten friend, pushed his head back to stop the blood and, forgetting their pride, argued all at once. Watching them, one might have concluded that we had all been playing a harmless game together and that our side had taken it badly. The rest of the audience was curious, couldn't figure out what had happened, and reacted, as always, by screaming as if a fire had broken out.

The uproar increased and someone went for the policeman who came in at once and saw the injured man, head thrown back, clothes covered with blood. The avenging Sicilians pointed Bissor out to him and the whole audience had risen to its feet and was screaming. The cop felt that no explanation was necessary and moved toward Bissor, who was now returning to his own seat. My heart pounded with fear, as I was terrified of all cops. What was going to happen to Bissor, and perhaps to myself? Grabbing the boy's arm, the officer pushed him toward the exit; I followed them to the door and joined Bissor outside.

"Let's go to the harbor," he said.

That was one of our favorite walks, and although Bissor tried to be bold I knew he was heavyhearted, just as I was. Not only had we lost our money, but we had been cruelly disappointed.

"You see how they hate us?" said Bissor, hopelessly convinced.

They: the young Sicilians, the Arab policeman, the French newspaper owner, our classmates at the lycée, the whole city in fact. And it was true that our native city was as hostile to us as an unnatural mother. We had been disappointed at one blow; it was final and couldn't be healed.

I admired Bissor and often asked myself if his reaction wasn't the best. For a year I forced myself to go along with him and practice boxing in the same gym. I managed to acquire some skill, but I remained weak because I was undernourished. Nor did I ever manage to overcome the nausea that I experienced whenever I struck an opponent's eyes, nose, or mouth. I was already suspicious of my body and disgusted whenever it affirmed its presence, for I knew that no amount of animal self-assertion could ever heal the wound my native city had inflicted on me.

Later, I began to experience a strange new fear whenever I found myself in the bowel-like maze of the covered bazaar. I would feel a sudden nausea and that I must reach an open space as fast as possible, because otherwise I might knock my head against walls that were too close to me.

2

HIGH SCHOOL

CREATED IN THE city's image, the French lycée was peopled so variously that I immediately felt lost. I had French, Tunisian, Italian, Russian, Maltese, even Jewish classmates—but the latter were from a background so different from mine that they were as foreign to me as the others. They were rich Jews and of the second generation of Western culture; like all the others, they too made fun of the nasal ghetto accent which they imitated by confusing the French word *savon* (for soap) and *savant* (for scientist). Ill at ease in their presence, I was furious with them because of the facility with which they rolled the impossible *r* that Paris has imposed on the rest of France. I tried and resolved a thousand times to roll my *r*'s with the proper guttural sound until I found the right tone; but when I watched my speech, I lost the thread of my ideas and, if my thought was difficult to express, I had to leave my tongue in peace while I figured out what I wanted to say; it was then that I reverted to my peculiar speech with its sounds which were as foreign as those of Latin Americans or of exotic films, and deprived all that I said in French of any seriousness. But if I managed to speak as if I were clearing my throat, the others would laugh and imitate me.

"You speak French like a German," they would say, imitating the German accent.

Unfortunately, I spoke like no one on earth. I tried desperately to speak this language which wasn't mine, which perhaps will never be entirely mine, but without which I would never be able to achieve self-realization. Our local dialect was only just able to satisfy the daily needs of eating and drinking. Could I tell my schoolmates that my mother not only spoke no European language at all, but barely managed to carry on in her own dialect? I never told them, or anyone, anything; I hated them, pretended to despise them, made a show of all my own failings, and rolled my *r*'s even louder than before. All the same, I envied them. I'm not trying to give a flattering picture of myself, nor to justify my behavior; I'm trying here to get rid of what's on my stomach and to vomit what I cannot digest and forget. I was jealous, envious, even spiteful, and soon unbearable to all those who were ready to like me. I had every fault that's generally condemned. But could I have been otherwise?

Each morning, my classmates smiled, were confident, smelled of eau de Cologne and of good toilet soaps. I supposed, not without astonishment, that they washed from top to toe every morning. It was only much later that I understood why some people have an unpleasant odor and others no odor at all.

Most frustrating of all, I was completely excluded from their community. Both inside and outside the school, they continued to live as a group, sitting near one another in class, telling stories I couldn't really follow; their tongues glided too rapidly over their words and I often failed to understand them at all. They all belonged to one and the same civilization which remained merely theoretical in my eyes as long as I myself had no share in it. At the school gates, they shook hands cordially and politely, and then began to exchange news about an unknown planet:

"Did you hear Duke Ellington on Monte Carlo at eight-thirty?"

I guessed that this had something to do with the radio, but I would have allowed myself to be killed rather than ask a question. Who was Duke Ellington?

"Did you see the forty-cent Washington? Terrific!"

This had some connection with postage stamps.

"I'm backing Bagheera on Sunday."

Bagheera: yes, race-track talk. Generally, however, their chatter escaped me completely. Social distinctions are as profound as religious differences, and I was not a member of their class. They enjoyed means and luxuries that were far beyond me and of which I had not even heard.

"I'll phone you at four and you can tell me if our home-work is tough."

They dictated whole assignments to each other over the phone and were able to work together while each remained at home. Even the phone, to me, was a princely luxury, and I admired the casual way they said:

"I'll call you."

I could never learn to use the phone. My excitement prevented me from hearing anything and, as I myself screamed and stammered into the receiver, no one could understand me. As for the refrigerator, white and cold and majestic as a medical mystery, I had a very special respect for it. I realized, quite truthfully, that to buy one of them we would have to sell all our furniture, and who, anyway, would want to buy our junk?

So I managed to acquire a kind of practical wisdom. Unable to gain their elegance, their natural ease, their detachment born of excessive wealth, I pretended, at the cost of much self-torture, to be disinterested about the material things of the world. Because I could not afford cakes, I pretended not to like them; I pretended not to enjoy billiards,

going to cafés, horse-racing, collecting stamps, dancing,
dressing with care, chasing after girls. And, up to a point, I
became really austere and modest in my appetites, even something of a moralist, for I was stern in my judgments of the
conduct of others. In brief, I managed to acquire the reputation of being a serious boy. At this game, one can either
diminish oneself or sublimate. I have known boys who have
acquired tearful eyes, a head that always leans or turns to
the side, and the gentleness and politeness of the vanquished.
But I became inflexible in my principles, dogmatic in my
judgments, easily offended, merciless about weakness, whether
my own or that of others, and ambitious to the point of
self-destruction.

More or less consciously, of course, I tried to imitate my
schoolmates. But nothing I did was spontaneous, everything
required effort and calculation. I forced myself to listen to
operas, to follow plays, to note the lives of their authors and
information about the works themselves. I attended gatherings of youth organizations but brought to them so much
tension and gravity of my own that I could never join in
their spontaneity and enthusiasm that was so childish and
thoughtless, but so relaxing. I was one of those rare charac-
ters who reflect on the theory of being a Boy Scout, on the
organization's place in society and its educational value, while
the other boys are living it, singing and playing. It was
impossible for me to forget myself; every once in a while
this was brought to my attention by others. One day, Bouli,
a boy I had begun to like because he was intelligent and
seemed not to be blind to certain distinctions, remarked to
me, much to my humiliation and surprise:

"Why do you dress in such an impossible way? You love
to ridicule the affectations of the overfastidious and yet, at
heart, you have all those of the negligent."

Fortunately, my thick African skin never allows me to
blush. That day Bouli went down several grades in the esteem
and friendship that I had begun to feel for him. I saw

clearly that my cutting myself off entirely from my own original background did not necessarily allow me to enter any other group. Just as I sat on the fence between two civilizations, so would I now find myself between two classes; and I realized that, in trying to sit on several chairs, one generally lands on the floor.

It was then that I discovered a terrible and marvelous secret which might perhaps make my loneliness bearable. To unburden myself of the weight of the world, I began to put everything on paper, and that is how I began to write and to experience the wonderful pleasure of mastering a whole life by recreating it. Of course, this power was as fatal as it was redeeming. To describe people, I had to be an outsider and I could no longer be a part of the world I contemplated. Just as one ceases to live while one watches a play, so did I cease to live and now merely wrote. For my loneliness, it was a balm, but my new loneliness became deeper too because I was more conscious of it and accepted it. In any gathering, I found myself with my back to the wall, an outsider in every respect, alien to the joys of the others as well as to their sorrows. This was a bitter experience, but I still had too much hope to be afraid of my lucid detachment. I was, in fact, arrogantly delighted by its novelty.

Thus began my hand-to-hand struggle with language, if only because my pronunciation of the French *r* and of the nasals was wrong. Dimly, I felt that I would penetrate into the soul of this civilization by mastering its language. I wrote without pause and was never satisfied because I saw that I nearly always worked on the skin of things and failed to reach the flesh. I sometimes asked myself riddles: what is the right word for such and such a thing? It seemed to me that objects would remain foreign to me until I was able to name them correctly. So I often sought a particular word for a long while, questioning everyone around me. When I had found the word, I would repeat it over and over in a loud voice, like an incantation. I had grasped the "thing" and could invoke it at will: a part of the world was subjected to me.

I pretended, however, to reject too pure, too refined a language, one that follows rules that are too strict. It was the meaning that mattered and must by itself dictate the words that would describe this meaning. I would use slang or invent my own words, or put down blatantly incorrect ones if the proper ones seemed ineffective. I no longer know whether I was really sincere. Perhaps I felt that, despite all my efforts, I would never be as adept at the language as my companions whom birth had endowed with an almost perfect linguistic equipment.

The monthly report for Monsieur Bismuth reminded me that my efforts were not entirely for myself. The envious respect of the other students was a source of pleasure for me, and the compliments of my teacher for all my work were a compensation. I saw how the others looked around when I volunteered to recite in class, and how the teacher smiled. In these looks and smiles I could see myself victorious, like a young god. True, I worked like a brute; it was largely for this taste of revenge that I struggled so relentlessly for prizes and honors. But none of the other boys ever suspected what these things meant to me. What I wanted was more than their processed schoolbook learning.

I began to discover the world of books and to catalogue it; I read tons of printed paper, at meals, in the street until the school bell rang, in bed until one in the morning. Sometimes, in my assignments, I would quote an author who was not in our required readings and, in fact, well beyond the normal range of an adolescent. My surprised teachers would then ask me to see them after class; after paying me an initial compliment, they generally tried to discourage me from such precocious readings. Of these meetings, I retained nothing but the attention that had been paid to me and the pleasure given my gratified pride; and I continued to read. In this manner I changed very quickly and began to regain

my self-confidence, but remained all the more easily offended
and hurt, and all the more resentful.

One day I asked for permission to give a report on the
poet Alfred de Vigny and it was granted to me. I admired
Vigny's disillusioned but haughty manliness, his noncompli-
ance. And, of course, I had a weakness for the somber, for
his grandiose sadness. Above all, I was violent in my will to
show and affirm what I was. I took possession of the chair
with aggressive satisfaction. Then, fixing my eyes on my
audience, I began to speak, half-ironically but deeply moved,
without any notes, without any aid, in fact, but from the
poems I quoted. I was sure enough of myself to speak without
a written text, but I wanted above all to prove that one
could do an excellent job while speaking the language of the
street. Unfortunately, my irreverence carried me away, as
always, so that I soon slipped into slang. The teacher suspected an intention to provoke but was held back by my
brutal sincerity; in spite of the outraged class, he allowed
me to talk twenty minutes longer than the allotted time. I
could indeed see his wrinkled brow, the start of a gesture of
anger, and the agitation of the whole class; but I couldn't
stop, could only continue my role in the inarticulate tragedy
I had begun. The other kids were burning with impatience,
waiting for the climax, and approving in advance the inevitable punishment to be meted out to me by the all-
powerful teacher. When I was at last silent, the teacher was
still completely perplexed. He hesitated in the utter silence
of the class and, wishing to be just, not to hurt me excessively
but still to sanction my impertinence and avenge his own
irritation, he said:

"Your report has been most odd. I can add very little to
what you've said about Vigny. But, in order to speak without
notes, which in itself should merit approval, you've allowed
yourself to slip into the language of a street urchin."

I could take it as I pleased. But I saw that the class was
satisfied with the insult; they looked at one another, sneered,

and repeated: "the language of a street urchin." So I chose
to be deeply hurt and, besides, the teacher's reproach had
cut deeper than I myself realized. Despite my efforts and my
superior airs, I knew that what he said was true and, far
worse, that I couldn't expect to speak anything but the
language of an urchin. So, because he had hit my sorest
point, I could only hate him. Returning to my seat, I looked
down into my notebook and did not raise my eyes again in
that room until the end of the hour.

In effect, the language I spoke was an amalgam, a dreadful
mixture of literary or even precious expressions and of idioms
translated word for word from our dialect, of schoolboy
slang and of my own more or less successful inventions. I
tried, for instance, to find names for certain sounds which
had not yet, so far as I knew, been identified either in French
or in our local dialect; or I attempted to create in French
those verbs that existed only in dialect. My language was
thus as wild and turbulent as I was; it had none of the
quality of a clear and placid stream.

Still, I had my successes as well as my failures.

Our physics teacher, hardly out of school himself and not
yet disentangled from his education, added complications to
our textbook by trying to simplify it. Since it was generally
impossible to follow him, we got into the habit of letting
our minds wander out of the classroom or laboratory to our
favorite hobbies and most urgent preoccupations. While he
spoke, I usually worked at my poetry. One afternoon he
had darkened the classroom to prepare an experiment. Usually, this was amusing enough to keep us attentive; but the
teacher, this time, went on so lengthily and pointlessly preparing that the class gradually gave up listening. In the cold
semidarkness of this room that was haunted by appliances,
whisperings, and hysterical laughter, an insistent rhythm
began to beat in my head. I wrote it down; one word evoked
another, and soon the poem seemed to have written itself
on the sheet of paper. I felt that I had locked the rhythm of

life very exactly in those twenty lines and I could hear the pulse of nature beating in them. While our teacher talked and talked and apologized for the slowness of his preparations, I passed my poem down the line to Sitboun and sat back with the pleasurable anticipation of glory. Sitboun, one of the best literature students, always wrote perfectly classical verse: never an error in rhyme or scansion. We often argued together and, although everyone admired his work, I used to tease him about it, complaining that he weakened the content by exaggerating his concern with form.

I saw him read my poem, but he did not at first react. His gaze lingered and, suddenly, he crumpled the paper and threw it away. I couldn't understand why he had done this and signalled to him for an explanation. But we were too far apart and I had to wait until the class was over.

"You slob!" he shouted when I joined him. "It was too damn good!"

I believed I was destined for triumph, and I was never more certain of this than during my years of adolescence when each day represented a discovery of myself and there seemed to me to be no limits to me or to the richness of life.

In the last year before graduation, a man named Marrou, of whom I was very fond and whom I will mention again later, was my French teacher. We were analyzing Racine's *Andromaque* and he was a great enthusiast of the work of this poet; one morning, after we had read the extraordinary scene in which Pyrrhus admits his love, Marrou turned to the class and, in a tired and hopeless voice, asked:

"Which line in this scene is most typical of Racine?"

An embarrassed silence followed; to me, the class did not seem to have quite understood the question. I don't believe I had either, but somehow I felt what he was trying to say. Without raising my hand, I read aloud in the perplexed silence:

"Je ne l'ai point encore embrassé d'aujourd'hui."

Marrou gazed at me with his somewhat heavy look.

"That's right," he said slowly.

My heart cried with joy. I, son of an Italian-Jewish father and a Berber mother, had discovered in Racine's work the line that is most typical of Racine.

Sometimes, at night, in bed, I would weep with joy when, as I read Jean-Jacques Rousseau, for instance, I felt that I could recognize, in his passion and his humble background, his rejection of his own surroundings, my own ambitions and my own future. But I was alone with my book and wept real tears that fell to the pillow, tears of pain and of pride.

3

AT HOME

AFTER SCHOOL, MY classmates scattered throughout the nearby middle-class neighborhoods, and I would find myself alone as soon as I reached the edge of the modern quarters. In the course of these long walks through familiar streets, I made most of my important resolutions, or rather found them already ripe after days and days of unconscious maturing. Despite the number of serious decisions I have made, and even kept with a grim determination, I don't believe I am willful by nature. I think things over at length, and, even after I have made a decision, I continue thinking about it and suffering over it.

How often, as I returned home at five o'clock, with the night already seeping into the narrow streets and the sky a deep blue-black, did I plan to make my peace with my parents and to be a considerate and useful son! I thought I knew the necessary gestures: salted almonds or pistachio nuts for my mother on Friday nights, sympathy for my father over his asthma and a show of interest for his business worries, to offer to run errands, fix the electric iron and the light switches. All these flickers of filial devotion generally sparked up in me after family rows and were the ultimate product of the remorse that I never admitted. I would be touched by the exemplary behavior of famous men who had remained faithful sons throughout their lives. The more the parents lacked understanding for the career, the work, and the ambitions of their sons, the more the latter must have enjoyed the feeling of having done their duty with a model filial piety.

I needed but to cross the threshold of our flat to find again its ambivalent atmosphere so full of bitterness, of slight but constant hostility, of claims on my feelings, all justified up to a point; at once, I became grouchy, deprived of my gratitude, discouraged.

On Friday nights, when dinner had been varied and plentiful, family life was like a cloudless sky. No sooner had the first star appeared than my parents entered upon their day of rest; they would then be in good spirits, ready for a pleasant chat of which I was often the subject:

"Remember what you wrote us from the summer camp: 'You must carry me up! You must!'"

The whole family would laugh and I would try to smile although the story had already been repeated a thousand times. I found it more painful to be reminded now of the nonsense I had written than of my childhood panic. I could spot in their insistence on this little story a reproach that was also a revenge, half-resentful and half-affectionate. In effect, they were saying: "Remember, once you were weak and helpless. You think you are strong now and can do without us. When you needed us, we protected you." I could see their increasing bitterness and disapproval of the turn my life was taking.

It was neither pride nor resentment that separated me from my parents, but a far more penetrating emotion, that of guilt. I had been tutoring other kids ever since my fourth year in high school, so I was almost completely independent—

financially, at least. I never dreamed of reproaching my parents with failing to give me what they had not given me: they had never had anything to give. But they made me feel guilty for what I didn't give to them.

When we moved from our alley, we left our proper social and economic level. Even if people were poor in our new street, they dressed better and patronized more expensive stores. We now had to live above our means and to sacrifice necessities to appearances. As she had in the past, my mother continued to buy remnants and pieces of defective cloth in the covered bazaars; but now, in making our clothes, she had to sew the pieces together into something "stylish." She also started taking cheap permanent waves which reddened her lovely black hair and, for some months, made her head resemble a hideous brown sheep's head. I retained, consequently, a fixed horror of permanents. For the first time in his life, my father now bought a suit of overalls. We had gas and electricity; for her long-term Sabbath cooking, however, my mother reverted to charcoal which was cheaper. Our gas and electricity bills were indeed occasions for collective remorse: "Put out that light! Is it so hard to press a button? It cost us two hundred francs last month!"

I heard those words thousands of times.

My father groaned continuously and made plans to reduce our budget. But he didn't have the severity needed to carry out these plans; besides, we could hardly live on less than we did. In order to pay our higher rent, to buy more conventional clothes and to meet the other indispensable expenses of our new status, we could no longer eat our fill. Besides, our family was always increasing. My father and his friends discussed their common problems at the café, and each passed his own unworkable suggestions on to the next. One evening, my father came home with this scheme:

"There are so many of us that each meal is very expensive. If we cut out only one meal a week we could make a real monthly saving. Of course, this doesn't mean that we go to bed on an empty stomach. That evening, there'll be boiled chick-peas and as much bread as you want." In a firmer tone, he then concluded: "I've decided we're going to follow my plan."

When he announced such a decision, he would wait, in the silence that followed, for some sign of revolt which might enrage him and strengthen his determination. But generally no one even moved, and his beautiful plan would then peter out in bitter words about our indifference to his worries, his troubles, and his health. The younger children continued playing or doing their homework. As for us, the older ones, we either stared into space or appeared to bury ourselves in the books we were reading without being able to understand, for that moment, a single line, a single word. My eyes and body rigid, I was then literally all ears, and this sordid speech seemed to enter deep into my flesh. The book, before my open but blind eyes, ended by changing color. Sometimes, when his words were too pointed, I began to get angry, but then my mother would offer herself as a lightning rod and divert all the blame to herself.

My father had long since come to regret having accepted the proposals of Monsieur Louzel, the principal of the Alliance School. The pleasures of vanity he derived from saying that his son went to the lycée did not compensate his sense of disappointment. My material success seemed too far away to permit him to hope for financial compensation for his loss. All his colleagues had put their eldest sons to work and my father was sorry he hadn't taken me into his store. He would then have been able to lean on me and be assured of his family's fate. It is impossible to deny that I was an outrageous luxury, considering our position. I was no longer dependent on my family as I had been, but I didn't help my father provide for our large family budget. Now, though I had ceased to believe in my parents, I hadn't yet shaken off the values of my community. I hadn't yet realized that I might also refuse to be responsible for my brothers and sisters, for their state of malnutrition, their shabby clothes, the haste with which, one after another, they had to leave school. I needed other ways of breaking with the past and achieving freedom. It was difficult enough for me to find money for my food, the suit I bought at a discount from Uncle Aroun, and a little pocket money. Fortunately, my tuition and school supplies were assured through Monsieur Bismuth. Ever since the fourth year, I had been fortunate enough to have students sent to me for tutoring. A friend's little sister had broken her leg, and I was called upon to keep her Latin from getting rusty. As my schoolmates found it extraordinary that I was willing to have any truck with Latin and French after school hours, I soon acquired a reputation. From that time on, I never stopped tutoring; and I prepared for each hour of it with great care. None too sure of my own knowledge, I would go over my Latin grammar or my literature textbook before visiting my students. So I soon acquired a reputation for competence, confirmed by my own success in school, and was often consulted after discussions. Wealthy students in my grade, or even in the grade above me, sometimes entrusted me with writing whole essays when they were preoccupied with the organization of their leisure, particularly with days at the races. They paid me, of course, my hourly tutoring fee. Once a middle-class boy asked me to do a whole report which had been assigned to him despite his stupidity. I worked ten hours and I was embarrassed to ask for the large sum due me. But my client did not seem to find the price of his freedom at all excessive. Still, I didn't care for that kind of work and I never took it on without feeling ill at ease. I felt we were cheating our teachers. Contrary to school ethics, I refused, without being a sneak, to join my classmates in their solid opposition to the faculty; I somehow failed to feel a community of interests with them. I knew what my pupils thought of me: they despised me. Of course, I despised them, too, for being dumb and for needing me, but my feeling wasn't pure because it was mixed with resent-

ment and envy. They could treat me with indifference, as
the fees they paid me helped them to re-establish a balance
between us. My tutoring brought me into a number of middle-
class homes where badly raised and shamefully spoiled children would be begged by their mothers, with a great display
of hypocritical tears, to submit themselves to education. I
was almost always treated, if not actually in words, like a
kind of intellectual servant; and the worst of it was, despite
my revolts or perhaps because of them, that I felt as if I were
actually wearing livery. Half smiling, I waited patiently for
the poor little rich kid to reach the end of his tantrum.

No one was in a rush to pay me, and it sometimes happened that I wasn't paid at all. The richer my pupils were,
the worse they paid, and the longer I had to wait, and I
never dared press them for fear of seeming to be mercenary
or dependent on their money. Middle-class people, who spent
so much money on their own amusements and vanity, often
felt that what they paid me was excessive and that I was
obligated to them.

Still, if I managed, however barely, to cover my expenses,
I was always left with what I "might have earned." How
stupid it is to take seriously this "might have earned," I
mean the money one might earn had one preferred to work
rather than study or travel or live, had one remained behind
a counter or at a desk. A boy of my age ought to be earning
a certain sum of money. Agreed. Admitted by all. This sum
glittered in my father's eyes, a stopgap, in his imagination,
for the holes in his budget; and it grew more important as
I grew older. His voice was full of regret if he told us how
much money the sons of his colleagues were already earning
for their families. Makil's son was in charge of his father's
shop; the son of Sebah, the forger, was doing twice the work
of an average workman; Bouirou, Aunt Menna's oldest boy,
had been taken on by Uncle Simon and was now earning
three hundred francs; everyone marveled at the courage of
Georges, the youngest of the Abbous, who was now able to

assume all the responsibility of tailoring a jacket. He and his mother, a buttonhole-and-lining specialist, formed an indefatigable team and were bringing prosperity into the Abbou home. A good, good boy! But I felt only contempt for the zeal of Georges Abbou whose whole ambition consisted in tailoring jackets.

"He's exactly your age," insisted my father. "*Ex-act-ly.*" "More-or-less," my mother corrected and began reckoning aloud. "You were born on the third day of the feast of the Maccabees and Georges was born the eighth."

My father threw her a wary, provoked look and continued. What luck it was for my aunt and my poor blind uncle to have such a son! And their other children seemed to be choosing the same path. My father swore that none of my brothers or sisters would stay in school a day longer than was necessary for the school certificate. In the name of justice, they must help him. Besides, modern education didn't lead anywhere; a good artisan is worth more than a scribbler, and business is more certain than a diploma.

Without his having to ask them overtly, the children started quitting school, one after the other, very early. Worn away by my father's daily reminders of their expense, frightened by his asthma attacks, they felt guilty and spontaneously began to want to find a job. When I managed insidiously to persuade them to stay till the sixth year, all they gained thereby was a final examination at the end of the year. Convinced of their failure in spite of the heavy sacrifices already made, they were sure that the struggle was futile, and didn't even dare turn up for the test. But I myself had now gone too far and was too conscious of my own ambition to turn back. On the contrary, the constant aggression, the mournful speeches which ceaselessly strengthened my feelings of guilt, all this gave a considerable importance to my studies. I brought to them a kind of passion, an avidity that my schoolmates could not understand, pleasant amateurs that they were. Like Loriot's chocolates, so expensive for me, I swal-

lowed as much of it all as I could. For whole years, I raced
against time, making each day, each hour of my life count
and conform literally to a strict schedule. I wanted to come
up in the world, to succeed, but succeed at what? I wasn't
sure, but still had to keep going. I set myself provisional goals,
stations on the long road I traveled: to win this prize and
get ahead of that student. Since, at that age, knowledge and
experience are so easily confused, my teachers believed me
very mature and told me so. My major teacher in the third
year noted "an energetic intellect" on my report card at the
end of the year. I had the highest average in the second year
and was probably Marrou's best student in the first. The kids
at school told me, and they would certainly not have made it
up to please me, that Poinsot, our philosophy teacher, had
said: "He's the most intelligent student I've ever had, and
I've been teaching for sixteen years." One day I read that
intellectual and sexual precociousness went together, and
that many famous men had also been sexually very gifted.
After questioning my friends, I came to believe that I was
clearly ahead of them there too. I no longer doubted my
genius and my pride was thereby increased. The apprecia-
tions expressed by my teachers filled my heart with happiness
and made me laugh when I was alone. Sometimes, when I
thought of these compliments as I walked along the street,
I had to clench my teeth until they hurt in order not to
smile like an idiot.

Would I have dared to tell you about all this foolishness
if I had not ultimately realized that intelligence and work
cannot themselves guarantee the happiness or the value of
a man? At that time, however, I believed firmly that they
could; I *had* to believe it. For it was only through my strug-
gles in school that I could triumph, assert myself, and
vindicate myself. The quarterly report cards were my bulletins
of victory. The pleasure and pride I took in them gave me
the greatest satisfactions of my adolescence. They made my
family's sighs and my father's asthma attacks bearable to me.

My homework was done in a room where six children played, shrieked, and argued; sometimes they were joined by little friends and cousins, and by the shrieking, vulgar, and piercing voices of my aunts. I scarcely dared to silence them because they always suspected me of impertinence. Occasionally, I was so exasperated by a difficult assignment in Latin or mathematics that I jumped from my chair and shouted at the children. The hypocritical women then scolded the children gently and pretended to sympathize with me, but calmly went on with the shindy on their own account. The children would remain quiet for a while, but, soon carried away by their games, became as noisy as before; and the noise would go on. Finally, I reached the point where I could read a difficult book on a seat in the street in the midst of clanging streetcars or traffic or the screaming Mediterranean crowds, surely the noisiest in the world. Could I have continued without my fierce will and my ability to ignore my surroundings? Yet, at what nervous cost did I achieve it! With these same efforts, the same passion, I might have become a successful man. You can, of course, succeed in spite of all difficulties, but you must relinquish a piece of fur or of flesh at each contest and more often than not, you die somewhere along the road. Sometimes you end up elsewhere; then you realize that the goal you had set yourself wasn't really so worthwhile after all.

I studied at a little dressing table which I covered with thick layers of newspaper to smooth its broken marble top and to avoid touching the cold stone surface which I detested. Each time I raised my eyes from my notebook, I met my own face in the broken mirror. I can see once more, in the wintry semidarkness, a thin boy with a long neck and hectic black eyes, his hair tousled by his nervous fingers; he had to put two cushions on his low stool in order to reach the high dressing table. I loved to study by myself and to ask the mirror who I was and what my face promised. From having worked before the glass all through my adolescence, much of it has remained vivid in my memory. Night fell early but, for the sake of economy, my mother was always late in lighting the tiny lamp that strained my eyes and made me nearsighted. To this day, I still experience real anguish from that yellow light. When I roam at night in poor neighborhoods and peep indiscreetly through their feebly-lighted windows, I am overcome by the painful memory of a crazily furnished flat with distant corners that the light could never reach.

When my father came home, he noisily threw the big store key on the marble-topped dresser. Then he flung himself heavily on the creaking bed. Climbing the stairs had worn him out. He didn't speak, nor did anyone else dare to speak until his breathing whistled less loudly. Since he never came home for lunch, we managed to forget him during the day; but seeing him each evening like this, glum and broken, was a poignant reminder of how hard his life was. His asthma attacks grew more and more frequent, more and more violent, and the idea of death began to torment him. In silence, we felt guilty as we watched him suffer. He left the house at seven in the morning, winter and summer, and worked without a break until night had fallen. When the days were too short, he managed to work longer by the light of a large oil lamp. The youngest among us always brought my father's lunch to the shop; we had all had our turn at bringing the meal which not only turned cold on the way but arrived—meat, salad, and bread—jolted into one messy dish. We had often suggested he buy a little stove to heat his meal; but he always refused, rejecting any improvement in his life, as if he were too trapped to hope for any relief.

"Rotten day," he said at last. "Not one serious customer. A dumb Bedouin came in this morning with a head as hard as a log and offered me fifty francs for a two-hundred-franc halter. It made my lungs ache to try to explain that I couldn't sell it for less than cost price. He left without buying. Nothing more all afternoon. At five, a European lady came in and made me spend two hours repairing her suitcase, as though I were a luggage-merchant or a leather-worker."

Like most artisans, he hated dealing with anything outside his own craft, and he refused to change a single detail of his technique.

"Then why did you do it?" my mother asked with an interest that was at least partly affected.

"How could I refuse? Besides," he admitted, "if she'd paid me decently, it wouldn't have been so bad. But what could I ask for the job? It takes a long time and isn't worth much. When her suitcase had been new, it wasn't worth two hundred francs. So I said: 'Pay me what you want.' She gave me twenty francs—they're in my pocket. If it goes on like this, I'll close the shop."

He repeated this threat all his life. We didn't more than half-believe him, but that was enough to keep us permanently anxious and unstable. Every time he had an asthma attack he would give us solemn warning that the end had come, that we must now look after ourselves, that, if he recovered, he had made up his mind to give up. Despite the frequency of the attacks, they always impressed us deeply. They might come at any hour of the day or night. At certain seasons, particularly in the fall, the long, hard, strangling cough announcing the attack would awake me every night. Her eyelids heavy, my frightened mother would climb out of bed in her slip and, barefooted, would rush to fix the usual medication. Soon the flat would be smoky with the fumes of the burning Legras powders. We heard my father gasp, choke, call upon death to deliver him. Since we could do nothing for him, we remained under our blankets. The younger children whispered their reassurance to one another through the darkness:

"It's nothing. Dad is having an attack. It'll be over right away."

Only Kalla, because she was too nervous to stay in bed,

got up and went to my father; and when the cough hardened into a threat of convulsions, she would stand beside the bed, motionless and mute as a ghost, her pale delicate face framed by black hair always marvelously supple and wavy. She would stand there and suffer with him. The morning after an attack, my father often rose in a bad temper. His illness was a part of his life and he didn't seem to try to avoid it absolutely. He would sit cross-legged on the bed and, despite the doctor's continually repeated warnings, begin to chain-smoke those horrible cigarettes that are full of straw and bits of wood and that filled the flat with an acrid, stinking fog. He smoked, then coughed, then spat into the yellow pot that was always at the foot of his bed. Afterwards, he would moan and beg God to help him out of this miserable life. Finally, he would dress in the suffocating fumes of the bedroom and go off for a day of ten uninterrupted hours of work.

The younger children had known my father's illness from birth and were not greatly surprised by his sufferings. If he had an unspectacular attack, once the surprise passed, they would return to their games; and my father took bitter note of this. I could never get used to his illness and each attack further convinced me of my selfishness.

At night, I would bury my head in the pillow, trying to stifle the whistling of his anguished chest, his hoarse groans, his appeals to God. I had learned to gauge the gravity of each attack. When he came home on those murderously damp winter evenings and flung himself gasping and with bulging eyes on the bed, I knew the evening would be unpleasant. He would be unable to speak and would wave his hand desperately to my mother who was hurrying to his help. She filled the little fire-yellowed saucer with medicated powder and threw a lighted match into it. My father bent over the smoke, opened his mouth and gasped. At once, he began to cough with all his body and lungs, and the sweat dripped from his face. Sometimes, the cough dragged on and on and never seemed to stop. Caught in the horrible rhythm of his coughs, he became panicky, tried to break out of it, rose suddenly, dropped back onto the bed, and then continued to gasp and cough until, overcome by his anguish, he would thrust his fingers down his own throat. Then, I would pack my notebooks in a briefcase and run from the house, followed a long way down the street by the odor of Legras powder and the sound of my father's cough.

4

UNCLE JOSEPH'S DEATH

HOPING TO CATCH a breath of air, I had opened the door and all the windows of the study hall. The deserted high school was suffocating, paralyzed by the motionless June heat. Blinding white light gushed in from everywhere like a motionless whirlwind, poured through the torn canvas shades with every thread now stiff and dry. Yellow, red, and green flashed from the pages of my book and tortured my tired eyes. I was waiting for the results of the written examinations and every hour was an agonizing battle against the heat and the heaviness of my head. Since the candidates had now been granted the exceptional privilege of using the study hall, I had fled from the gossip of my family at home to spend all my spare time in the school building.

From the other end of the long corridor, I heard the approach of soldierly footsteps resounding in the hot air and easily identified as those of Monsieur Creschi, the Corsican janitor who had once been a top sergeant in the colonial infantry. His approach seemed interminable, till suddenly he appeared in the doorway, a silhouette haloed by a blaze of light. A little boy was waiting for me in the lobby, he said. A little boy? I was in too deep a torpor to feel any curiosity. To hell with all little boys! I could hardly hear Monsieur Creschi, who panted, groaned, and patted his damp forehead. Regretfully, I stood up and pulled the back of my wet and sticky shirt, soaking with sweat, away from my skin.

I found my youngest brother, Birou, in the lobby. He was upset and full of the importance of his errand: Uncle Joseph was dead, my mother wanted me home at once, my father was waiting for me. Birou's excitement amused me.

"Do you know Uncle Joseph?" I asked invidiously.

"Oh, yes!" he said. "I saw him at cousin Louisa's wedding."

"What was he like?"

"He's big and strong. He's nice and has a mustache."

"You're mixing him up with Uncle Binhas. Uncle Joseph is the oldest, the one who sells shoes. Besides, he's not big, he's small."

"Oh, I thought the big one was the oldest. So he's not dead."

Although we lived in the same city, we seldom had any contact with my father's family. I saw Uncle Joseph no more than once or twice a year. To assert a difference from the rest of the tribe in the Passage, my father was always proclaiming the dignity of the Benillouche family and the reserved but real tenderness they felt for each other. This was partly true; but he had actually cut himself off from his own family when he had married my mother, a pretty girl from a humble background. Still, catastrophes and rare occasions of great joy brought the Benillouche clan together again and made them aware of their unity.

Joseph, the eldest of my uncles on my father's side, was the patriarchal head of the family and respect was owed him because he had really been a father to his younger brothers when they had become orphans at a tender age. I refused, however, to accept these old-fashioned hierarchical systems and smiled contemptuously when my father bemoaned the disappearance of an uncle's rights. Had we been on more intimate terms, my uncles would have had the right to box my ears. Still, I would have liked to see one of them try to spank me!

But I knew how irritated my father would be if I failed to come home at once, and how the whole family would be scandalized. If my oral examination hadn't been only two days off, I wouldn't have minded wasting a whole afternoon. But I couldn't afford now to squander precious time on such absurd family obligations; besides, I hardly knew Uncle Joseph at all. I sent Birou away with a vague explanation that I couldn't come now and promised to go home as soon as I was free.

I went back along the warm passage to the study hall and dropped into my uncomfortable wooden seat. I tried to get back into the mood for work. The air moved wearily, but all hope of a breeze vanished when I realized a sirocco was raising and stirring the white dust in the courtyard: it would be wiser now to close the windows. I didn't like thinking about death. It seemed dirty and ugly to me; it stank of sulphur disinfectants and of black draperies that had been badly laundered and were produced hastily out of closets. To me, death was as disgusting as it was frightening.

The mere thought of my scandalized family and of my father's probable anger upset me, and I couldn't settle back to my work. The heat was such that I could scarcely breathe, and I was offered the alternatives of stewing in my own sweat where I was or of swallowing the dust of the yard.

Finally, I decided to interrupt my work long enough for a visit to my Uncle Joseph's home. Why irritate my father unnecessarily? Why not take a little time off to simulate, like all the others? I shut my book and went out into the furnace

of the street where I was attacked by the dry breath of the
sirocco that parched my lips and my eyelids. Somehow, I
still found the energy to run all the way home.

I went first to the Passage. Dressed up and waiting for me,
my mother was prancing about with anxiety and excitement.
Marriage, birth, death, any group event made her feverish
and enthusiastic in exactly the same way; the housekeeping
routine would be interrupted, meals would appear at unlikely
moments, and she would come home at all hours. Called to
greater duties, she seemed to cease to belong to us body and
soul for several days.

She expressed her impatience with me and her displeasure
in a veritable avalanche of scolding: my uncle had been dead
since the evening before and my father was furious that I
hadn't come along sooner. She herself couldn't understand
my negligence; so much trouble simply because I persisted
in spending all my time at school for so-called study, as if
I didn't have a home to work in, and so on, and so on. . . .
Then, without any transition, her scolding gave way to coy
persuasion.

"Let's go. Come with me," she concluded.

She lowered her voice as if revealing a secret in the midst
of a large crowd.

"I know it bores you. I waited for you because I was afraid
you wouldn't come. But it's your father's brother, his oldest
brother—in fact his father! You know how your father hates
to complain, but he's very angry that you didn't come back
at once."

It was a long time now since my mother's simple histrionics
had ceased to amuse or irritate me. I followed her without
a word. The sun was now directly overhead, completely
flooding the streets, and I abandoned all hope of making use
of the fringes of shade. Crushed, I accepted this walk through
hell. Perspiration, as it evaporated, made my shirt cling
unpleasantly to my skin like the coarse linen bandages that
my mother used to put on my childhood boils. My mother,

on the contrary, had kept her race's capacity to withstand
the sun and now walked without any apparent effort, chattering cheerfully and skipping from topic to topic with the
lively grace of the once pretty and lightheaded girl. My
temples throbbed; preoccupied with my worries about the
examination, I was distracted from her babbling and hardly
replied. I admired the way she remained lively and enthusiastic even under the crushing weight of a family of ten. It
frightened me to think how far apart we had grown, how
foreign she was to all that I was becoming. With a simplicity
that tried to be cunning, she attempted to give me some
advice. Really, she'd never seen my father in such a state;
true, Uncle Joseph had given him his education and been
a father to him and such a father had the right to all honors.
So it would be better if I acted as if the deceased were my
own father (God forbid!); then I would show my father how
I would act when his time came too.

As I said nothing, she finally came around to mentioning
what was obviously the most difficult thing: naturally, as a
sign of mourning, I wouldn't shave for a month.

This time I emerged from my torpor and angrily refused.
No, they couldn't count on that. I couldn't go to school
unshaven. She heaved a deep sigh, half-sincere, half-feigned.
My God! What a son she had!

"I can well see," she said bitterly, "how your father and I
will be mourned when we pass on too!"

(I promised myself I would certainly avoid going through
these histrionics when they too passed away!)

The front door of the apartment house was hung with two
black drapes which were powdered with the dry dust from
the street. As we entered the main door, I was struck at once
by the awful odor which, for me, is always linked with
death: that of hot black cloth. I signed my name in the
mourners' book that lay on a table, also draped with a black
cloth. The few hurried passers-by stopped a moment to press
their curious and sullenly solemn noses against the little

funeral notice, black-bordered, that was pasted there to announce the age, profession, and numerous and notable merits of the deceased, and also the immense grief of all the branches of the family, carefully named and listed. Several people took the trouble to go as far as the hallway to sign the register of mourners. This would always give pleasure to the bereaved and put them in the obligation of some day returning the compliment: honor the dead and you will be honored in turn. Well, when I die, I shall be sitting pretty, with a collection of all the city's signatures!

My mother lowered her voice but continued gossiping as we climbed the stairs: "Don't forget to kiss your uncle's wife and your father! Don't leave the funeral service until it's over! Show that you're. . . ." Abruptly, as we reached the threshold of the flat, she rushed in with a frightful wailing, tore with her nails at her cheeks, and collapsed sobbing into a chair. All this lasted only an instant, but it was like a bolt of lightning hurled into the tearful whispering of the women who, all in black, dutifully seated, were ranged in order against the walls of the empty room. My mother had her place in this picture: her handkerchief in her hand, her eyes full of tears, grinding her teeth mournfully. This explosion of grief-stricken cries, this panoply of black, the women's odious ceremony of repeatedly bemoaning their loss, it all made me shiver in spite of myself.

I hesitated and was still standing in the doorway when my mother, apparently in complete control of herself, motioned me to go into the next room where the men were gathered. Had her cheeks not been savagely torn with red scratches, I would have sworn that my mother had played no part in my emotion. I passed along the women and went into the next room where the corpse lay on the floor, covered by a somber red cloth while, on either side of it, a candle flickered its yellow light. The same attendance, but more orderly, more silent. The men, my uncles, cousins, aunts' husbands. This room, where shadows merged, shifted, trembled jerkily at the mercy of the small flames, was also empty of all furniture, sinister. I sat down timidly under everyone's convergent and reproachful gaze. No one was missing; I had really been the only male in the family to fail at this collective duty. My father looked at me angrily, but was so ashamed of me that he said nothing.

Then they began to talk softly; so they had stopped at the sound of our steps. I noticed that most of the men were freshly shaved, and some had obviously just had their hair cut: what an excellent precaution against the month to come when they would no longer be able to go to the barber-shop! They were all, like their wives, dressed in black. The nervousness I had felt gave place to anger. How stupid I was to have turned cold to the roots of my hair, to have allowed myself to be impressed by this parlor game, this collective hypocrisy! From the other room there came the lively chatter of the women, free to talk until the next visitor arrived. On account of the presence of the corpse and their own nature, the men were restrained; though they whispered, they seemed hardly upset. How ridiculous it was, after all, that I had been more deeply upset than they!

An interminable ceremony of several hours then began, and to my great fury, I was trapped. There was no way to escape from this room of naked walls, without corners, where everyone watched all the others. And my oral examination had to wait!

Whenever a step sounded on the landing, the two gatherings immediately became still. Visitors, wrapped in silence, confused before faces closed in uniform mourning, stuttered their condolences, shook countless hands, and disappeared. I pitied them and felt almost guilty to have participated in their discomfort without feeling more afflicted.

My hand was shaken dozens and dozens of times before the hearse finally arrived. The undertakers entered, faceless and insignificant, and we all stood up. When they lifted the limp corpse, it dangled from their arms, and I left the room.

Yes, in spite of everything, I admitted to myself, I was impressed. But why should I be present at such an affair? Barbarous, like all the rest of it! Outside, the luxurious hearse was waiting, all black and silver, surrounded by funerary lamps, drawn by horses caparisoned in black and with black plumes on their heads. This was indeed an expense, which the brothers must have agreed to share, but appearances have to be respected. People would not have understood, had the surviving Benillouche brothers made a mediocre funeral for their senior, their father.

Neighbors and relatives began to cluster around the hearse in the shade, and soon a crowd had gathered. Windows along the street that had been closed for siesta were now flung open, and people leaned out to watch the show. Not knowing who I was, the people around me chatted pleasantly. The funeral had broken up their daily routine and they were, in spite of themselves, in a quietly pleasant mood. Everyone was silent when the coffin appeared; it had been carried with difficulty down the narrow stairwell and now made a hollow sound as they slid it into the hearse.

We, the men, lined up behind the hearse, according to our ages, with the oldest standing at the head. So I found myself next to my cousin, Uncle Gagou's son, who had exactly the same name as I. In the hullabaloo that had begun again, we were able to speak openly to each other. He immediately reproached me bitterly. Why hadn't I come at once? Our widowed aunt had notified all the members of the family, individually and without delay. Uncle Joseph was entitled to all respect. (I was beginning to know this.) My cousin spoke with confidence, sure of his rights; it was also true that we had the same name, the same given and family name, both of us samples of the same job, and the copy could certainly criticize the original or vice versa, for I was deviating from the well-founded rules of religion, custom, and tradition. He was the *real* Alexandre Benillouche, dressed in black and deeply involved in his family's grief for the loss of its head.

The hearse began to move. Howling and shrieking suddenly broke loose from all the windows of the apartment we had just left. The women, forbidden by custom to accompany the corpse to the cemetery, were now bidding Uncle Joseph a last farewell. The crowd below was silenced for a moment by the wailing from above. We began the slow procession across the city. I took advantage of every movement in the flow of the procession to move back slightly, away from my cousin, who kept his place.

Whenever we passed a Jewish shop in the streets, the doors would be slammed hurriedly so that the image of death should not be cast upon its inside walls. Women looked out of windows all along the way. So we took the deceased across the town, passing all the principal thoroughfares before reaching the gates of the city. There the procession broke up and we continued the journey in carriages. Since I was by myself, I was luckily separated from my uncles and cousins.

Our coachman set off at once at a trot behind the hearse which was now moving at a lively pace. This fast driving and the late hour brought a freshness which pleased my companions on this trip. First, they talked about the deceased a bit, then they asked each other for news of themselves and their families; they discussed the hardness of the times, the difficulties of making a living, and finally their business. When they'd told a few amusing stories and had teased each other a bit, they became even more cheerful and were soon joking openly in the well-shut carriage. I was the only one who didn't share their amusement; I, who hadn't shared their grief before.

Our arrival at the cemetery brought all their sad dignity back to my companions. We formed a procession once again and I went back to my place beside my cousin and was not far from my father who stood three rows behind the hearse. The gravediggers were already busy at the grave which was situated between the low monuments of the Jewish graves. This was the first time I had been to the new cemetery. The old one did not impress me; it was in the middle of the city, which had overtaken and surrounded it. Its shattered and abandoned tombs had been invaded by grass and weeds and surely contained by now only scattered and dry bones, disjointed or even turned to dust. But here, we were among fresh corpses and brand-new, well-kept monuments which testified to the increased wealth of the deceased and to the vitality of their heirs: marble sculptured into crowns, birds, and broken columns, wrought-iron gates, golden chains. My God, I said to myself, how ghastly can all this so-called funeral art be! Art, these infamous sandstone vases and odious purple flowers made of celluloid or cloth that became bloated in the rain or shriveled up in the sunlight! But probably it all managed still to arouse some half-religious respect. I was pitiless because I was adolescent and because I was contemptuous of death which seemed too impossible, too inadequate for me.

The rabbi, with his big hairy head doddering above a shapeless and dirty Oriental costume, raced for time against the gravediggers, swallowed half his words, and abridged the formula of the funeral prayers. At a distance, the undertakers talked among themselves. Employed by the community, these businessmen of death, rabbis, gravediggers, undertakers, all betrayed, by their naive indifference, the general hypocrisy. But the rabbi did well to hurry: the heat continued, despite the late hour, and I felt the perspiration drip from my forehead. Fortunately, we had to keep our hats on. At last, the grave was ready and the diggers emerged from the hole and went to fetch the body. They held it a while above the open grave and then slowly lowered it. I knew what was going to happen; I'd been told about it and I didn't want to see. But my curiosity was stronger than my horror, and I couldn't turn my head away. When the body, still strangely alive, was a few inches above the earth, they let it drop and, the moment it hit the bottom, everyone present was supposed, as is prescribed in the ritual, to join in a collective scream in order to stifle all noise. They screamed but imperceptibly too late, and I heard the horrible sound of the body as it fell.

The gravediggers' work was taken up again with their earlier mechanical cadence. Theirs was a practiced skill. To close the grave, they placed flat stones on it. In two minutes, Uncle Joseph had been shut away forever. Afterwards, we went to wash our hands at a consecrated fountain, for the sight of the body was supposed to have soiled us. Why the hands, I asked myself grouchily? Why not take a whole bath? But, like everyone else, I washed my hands. At the cemetery gate, a representative of the community fund waited for our donations. I passed him without giving anything and, as always, tried to make my uneasiness seem like disapproval.

The trip back was even more carefree than the drive out had been. Discreetly encouraged by my companions, our driver slyly tried to pass the carriage in front of ours by going into a canter. The other driver avoided this and forced his nags to race. The passengers became interested in the race and, forgetting all propriety, began to urge their drivers on quite openly. We came back to town with our poor city-horses bulge-eyed from this unfamiliar effort, their manes flying tangled in the wind. The passengers laughed with excitement, as delighted as fans at a football game. Thanks to the crowd, I could avoid the obligatory return to the house of mourning and escape a new session of condolences and handshaking.

It was too late when I got back to school. The sun had gone down and I know the housekeeper wouldn't like the idea of lighting up the study hall for a single student. Besides, I no longer felt like working. Before returning home, I loitered a while, trying to get rid of my bad mood.

But I didn't succeed, and when I got back to the Passage, I was aggressive, ready to give blow for blow. I'd had enough of these histrionics and was ready to say so. I wouldn't wait until they begged me to speak; I'd come right out with the statement that I would never again allow myself to be dragged off to such ceremonies. I knew in advance what I might expect to hear: I would not be mourned properly at my own death. I was little tempted by the thought of being mourned in this ridiculous manner and by these people. I didn't give a damn what would happen to me after I was dead.

But at home, no one said anything to me. In silence, we ate our mourning *couscous,* without meat and badly cooked: my mother had prepared it in a hurry. My father didn't look up from his plate, and my mother and the children were impressed and respected his silence. A sleepless night and a two-day's growth of beard increased the tired sadness of his face. Suddenly, to my stupefaction, he began to sob, a man's sobbing which came from his chest. My mother's eyes filled with tears and she put her hand on his head. This was the only tender gesture she had permitted herself in front of us. It was wonderful to compare her tears to her spectacular explosions in the room of the deceased.

My anger failed me, separated from me like an object, and I was ready to admit my father's ridiculous anguish: the child who has torn out his Teddy bear's eye cries with real grief. My father believed in family hierarchies and perhaps suffered really, in spite of the spectacular show and the rigid ceremonial. He had lost his eldest brother, his foster father, the head of his family according to his faith; now, he saw that I, his oldest son, his heir, would not render to him the last honors due, and would let him die alone. I didn't really understand what dying alone might mean, nor what joy could be derived from the certainty of being buried with all these grotesque and barbaric rites, and of being mourned by one's unshaven son. But I saw that his fear of dying alone, so often affirmed, was not simulated, that his grief was sincere.

In my imagination, I stood up and went to kiss and console him and to promise him everything he wanted. But the self-consciousness of an adolescent is great; besides, my family was never given to kissing and fussing, so that none of us knew the necessary words and gestures. So I remained motionless at the other end of the table, stealthily watching his now silent tears drip into his plate. There was nothing to be heard in the dismal room but the sound of our spoons striking our plates.

5

THE CHALLENGE

I soon understood how ineffectual were my refusals. On the covers of my notebooks, I wrote: "Learn to be silent." I carved "Be silent" into my desk at school. But I rarely obeyed this injunction. Faced with what seemed to be an injustice, an offense against reason, a sly insinuation, I felt my hand tremble as if some piece of machinery inside me had gone into action. Words of justification or revenge crowded into my head and to my lips. At first, I would resist the temptation to utter them and, struggling with my emotion, try to soften my replies. But one word would lead to another, the anger of my opponents would then be aroused and, once openly attacked, I would lose all sense of proportion. I came out of these arguments disgusted with other people and furious with myself. Why, once again, had I failed to remain silent? Because, to be silent, one must be sure of oneself, and I greatly needed reassurances. I was aggressive to justify myself and to legitimatize my stand. But my victories could never be decisive, just as the faces of my opponents could not be identified. I fought anyone, that is to say myself, too.

I believed, for instance, that it was necessary to reject religion. But whom should I attack? What established dogma? The religion of the ghetto does not lend itself to delimitation; it permeates all the gestures of life, as do all other religions in our medieval city. From morning to night, from birth to death, you must pray and thank God. There isn't a gesture or a word that has no sacred significance. Nor is it only a matter of religion. My scorn and my anger were constantly aroused against hypocritical and timorous respectability, against the stupid and tyrannical family, against brutal and unjust authority, against primitive dogma that seemed arbitrary and stifling. Actually, I had to reject everything. Without necessarily being conscious of it, I had to break away from the grasping paws of the monster. To master myself I had to begin by mastering the world, by breaking away from it. Liberation was available, but only at that price, and how expensive!

In our alley, the kerosene lamp had been replaced on Friday nights by Argand lamps which went out only when the olive oil in them was used up. Those little dancing lights, whimsically throwing vividly outlined shadows, contributed greatly to the solemn mystery of the Sabbath. We continued using Argand lamps for some time after we moved to the new Passage. Then electricity triumphed and brought a ridiculous innovation into our home; it was at once the target of my wisecracks. Before the first star appeared, my mother, the high priestess of the lights, switched on at five o'clock the electric bulb in the dining-room and then lit the Roman night lamp in the kitchen. The problem of the night lamp had already been solved by her mother and her grandmother, and my mother knew instinctively the level of oil with extraordinary exactness. The little wick crackled angrily and died a few minutes after the meal. But electricity, too new a gift from civilization, puzzled all the people in our building. How was it possible to prevent the bulb from burning all night and yet avoid committing a sin? Ritual forbade the touching of fire throughout the Sabbath, from Friday evening to Saturday evening. Was turning a little switch the same as handling fire? The rabbis vehemently asserted that it was; some progressive souls claimed it wasn't, but deferred to Rabbinical wisdom. I found the problem void of interest and the discussions absurd. Ostensibly, I shrugged my shoulders and sneered at these controversies which disturbed the tribe; but I had to exhibit my indifference passionately. The more they reflected on the problem, the more I emphasized my scorn and pretended not to understand their sacred difficulties. Finally, their combined wits allowed them to come up with an ingenious solution.

There was one shop, a grocery store, in our building, and Boubaker, the grocer's clerk, a young Negro from the South, slept in the store during the night. It was unanimously agreed to offer Boubaker the job of turning the Sabbath lights off. He accepted, for a small fee and a dish of *couscous*, to make a round of all the flats toward the end of the solemn feast. So everything was saved, modern comfort and the respect due to religion.

For me, this was too fine an opportunity, an additional proof of their hypocrisy and duplicity. With sly jokes or open criticism, I assured them all that, as far as God was concerned, their sin remained as great, whether committed directly or through an intermediary. As a matter of mere dignity, I preferred those who went about their comforts courageously and who chose to turn the lights off themselves. If, however, one wanted to take the old traditions seriously, then one would have to accept discomfort and return to using the Argand lamps. The tribe's irritated anger delighted me; I knew just how to pique their troubled conscience. Unfortunately, however, I didn't know how to accept triumph modestly, and almost no Friday night passed without my making some treacherous remark. How could I tolerate their compromises, I who could never allow myself any?

At one of these bitter Friday evening dinners under the

new light, we were already dozing in the torpor and silence of incipient digestion. I was in revolt against this heaviness of body and mind too, and sighed nostalgically whenever I read the menus advised by health magazines. *Couscous* with meatballs that had been cooked and cooked again in oil, fat marrowbone soup, boiled meat, grilled chick-peas, raw turnip with pickled red peppers. Suddenly, Elisa, my younger sister, burst into sobs. She often did this and began to cry vigorously without any preparation, like a phonograph record turned on in the middle. It was difficult to stop her. We would amuse ourselves by wondering how this swarthy, long-necked, frail, sickly little girl, thin and sullen as a crow, could have such extraordinary vocal powers. She was sobbing and speaking at the same time, and we guessed the usual reason for her despair. She could not manage to swallow her meat and cried for permission to spit out the big colorless cuds. This waste angered my father. In the ghetto, he said, no one ate meat as often as we; he had to work like a dog, despite his illness, to allow Elisa to spit out meat, *her meat!* Crushed and miserable, Elisa cried all the more lustily.

My mother put in her two cents' worth, trying to protect her daughter without further irritating her husband. Elisa had chewed her meat very well: "Didn't you chew it well? Answer me! Didn't you?" Of course, she had extracted all the juice from it, and the juices are the goodness, the soul of the meat! So she had only spat out the waste, the husk! We other children were never fooled by these maternal diversionary tactics which were always a bit too obvious. We protested vehemently that we didn't care a damn whether the crow did or didn't get the juices! But we ourselves were all sick of eating these lukewarm meatballs.

My mother seldom dared to contradict her husband directly and allowed herself to be violent only if my father was being seconded in his views by the rest of us. She accused us of being stupid and wicked, and blasphemous too in daring to disturb the Sabbath peace. My father became surly and silent.

He began all solemn feasts with a glass of fig wine. He was then easily angered, and his moods were heralded by these stormy silences. My mother was aware of how heavy the atmosphere had grown and knew she had to act quickly, so she anticipated the hour when the grocery clerk had to be called and said now to Elisa: "Go tell Boubaker to come up and turn off the light! Go on! Hurry up!" Elisa forgot her tears and began snarling instead. She was always the one, it was always Elisa who was sent on errands! Why couldn't Kalla ever go? Besides, she was cold and sleepy. The raising of Friday night's ticklish question always delighted me. My ironic joy must have been evident as my father said, in a taunting manner:

"Don't go if you're cold, Elisa. Mordekhai will turn the light off, since he's not afraid of committing a sin!"

I hadn't expected this attack. Did he really think I wouldn't dare?

"As you wish," I said drily.

My mother sensed the challenge and wanted to avoid any open conflict between her husband and her son. Brutally, she repeated her order to Elisa; her firm tone put an end to any discussion, and Elisa was so dumfounded that she obeyed without a peep. But the atmosphere was charged, and we finished our chick-peas in a new silence broken only by the rhythmic sound of our chewing. The children were tired and uneasy and didn't want to play games. Kalla was daydreaming. My mother cleared the table of all but the bread and the salt and covered these with another cloth: signs that the Sabbath was among us.

When we were getting ready for bed, my father's repressed anger was still simmering. In a nasty tone, he now forced the issue: "Why did you let Elisa go?"

He thought he'd won. I said nothing, nor did I hesitate very long. I walked over to the switch, turned off the light, and left our flat in utter darkness. The children's surprised voices became more subdued. No one protested. My parents groped around to find their bed. It took me a long time to fall asleep, and them too, for I heard them whispering. When Boubaker knocked at the door, my mother shouted to him, with some embarrassment, that the light was already out.

The next morning, I rose very early, as I always did, and left the house for the school. My family pursued the Saturday tradition of staying in bed until fairly late. My mother had certainly earned these few hours of idleness; all week, she was out of bed at dawn, getting the children off to school and, on Sundays, getting them ready for outings. The children themselves were at home, as they went to the Alliance School that was closed on the Sabbath. My father, of course, didn't go to his store. I was not permitted to light the fire for my breakfast, and Saturday thus preserved its holiday character.

I was the only one of the family who got up early, in the cold semidarkness of dawn, and ate alone in the kitchen and then hurried off to school, the only one in whose eyes Sabbath had therefore lost much of its sanctity and beauty, becoming a day of ordinary routine. But I found all the Sabbath spirit again at noon, when the family came to the table where a vase of fading narcissus stood on the white cloth while the friendly sun poured in. Our clothes were new and the family gathering respected the mood of this special day.

It seemed that last night's incident had been forgotten. Left with my victory and the shame of having acted violently, I now wanted peace. The meal was slow and relaxed. When we reached the dessert, the children began to ask for their week's pocket money, a pleasant little ceremony of ours. After the noon meal, we would thus gather around our father, joke, vie with each other, discuss the events of our week, and joyfully anticipate the film we would see in the afternoon. My father, despite his unwillingness to extract any money from his pocket, enjoyed his momentary importance. Surrounded by the clamoring group, he now pretended to be overwhelmed and began to utter his usual arguments about how hard life was; but there was no bitterness in his voice and no one was fooled. Even my mother, acting like a child, joined in the crowd to claim her share of money.

In spite of myself, I had been left out of this ceremony ever since I had begun earning my own pocket money. In general, I protested and made sarcastic remarks to show my disapproval; because I felt excluded, I became aggressive. Actually, my frustration made me suffer; but so did my independence too. I was proud of my own paradox when I said, as usual, that we seemed to be inspired by a sacred joy to commit a sacrilegious act. Jewish law indeed forbade us to touch money on the Sabbath, and the ghetto was still shocked if anyone did it.

That particular day, however, I said nothing. I lingered at the table, alone and bored as I cut orange skins into geometric shapes, squares, diamonds and rectangles, building orange archtiectural patterns against the white background. The children had cornered my father and compared their ages and respective merits as they protested loudly against the unfairness of their share of the loot. Suddenly noticing that I was alone and struck, it seems, by my exclusion, my father exclaimed perfidiously, as if he had not yet recovered from his anger:

"Everyone wants his Sabbath present except Mordekhai! It's all the same to him, he's not a Jew!"

This rejection hurt me, and something like an uproar was released within me. I wanted to leave the room then and there, but I couldn't bear the idea of being driven out. Did being Jewish consist in adhering to this stupid ritual? I felt I was more Jewish than they, more aware of what being a Jew means both historically and socially. Their Judaism meant having Boubaker turn off the light while they themselves ate *couscous* on Friday night, as if *couscous* were prescribed by the Torah!

"Yes," I snapped back. "Yes, I'm a Jew—but not like you people!"

He didn't understand me and preferred to bring the discussion back to what bothered him.

"If you were alone in the world and had your own home, would you light a fire on the Sabbath?"

There it was! Last night had made no impression upon him. "Of course," I replied defiantly.

The children were silent and listened attentively, trying to clarify problems that were beginning to emerge in their own minds. My mother pouted indignantly. As always, she tried to lessen tension in her husband's reactions by making faces. But I could now feel her disapproval.

"No, no, let him speak," said my father with bitterness. "It's better for you to know what kind of son you have!"

He knew where he stood and wanted only to check once more how far I was ready to go. Perhaps, though I committed monstrosities, I might not be willing to mention them, to utter them. Still, he expected the worst:

"Is there any difference between you and an Arab?"

My irritation grew as he provoked me.

"No," I said. "If there is any, I regret it. I would have preferred it if there were none!"

"Perhaps," he went on hesitantly, "you would even marry a gentile?"

"Maybe . . ."

Actually, at the level of mere speech and challenged as I was, I would have said anything. I couldn't see immediately what this would all imply if acted out in life. Yes, I told them, I rejected everything that anyone wanted to impose upon me gratuitously; the vanity of these practices seemed to me quite obvious. Great problems, true values, and a serious philosophy of life were elsewhere; I found them each day at school, in books, in literature, philosophy, and politics. Were we heading toward a Socialist society? Is poetry rooted in mysticism? Would the machine age bring social justice? Are art and morality bound together? Here were problems that were far more noble than whether one should ride a streetcar on the Sabbath. It exasperated me that I must, in spite of myself, concern myself with absurdly small matters, be involved in sacred triviality.

My mother put her finger to her forehead, rolled her eyes, and simulated intense joy. This signified that I was either joking or insane. That was clear. But it was wrong of me to have carried this thing so far on a Sabbath, especially in front of my father, a good but irritable man.

"Shut up," she said. "You're beginning to get everything mixed up!"

That was her final statement, meaning that I was delirious, that I couldn't distinguish one thing from another, one value from the next. In her hierarchical universe, this was the worst folly. My father hesitated. Should I go on talking? What was there left to lose?

Ignoring my mother's sideplay and her efforts to save the situation, my father brought out his final test:

"I suppose you wouldn't even circumcise your sons!"

I was unable to give tit for tat. I hesitated. Not that I didn't want to shout: yes, yes, yes! But I was impressed by the gravity of their attitudes and an awareness of their horror. Deeply upset, my mother and the children were silent. My father waited, bewildered by the turn in the situation.

"I don't know," I muttered at last.

We stopped there, my father certainly regretting that he had pushed me so far, and I troubled by my temerity and my ambiguous compromise. My mother was relieved that the interlude was over. Nothing could destroy her animal attachment to her children; although she no longer understood me, this did not bother her, no more than if I had been deaf or blind or dumb. She felt I belonged to her as chicks do to the hen: I was an extension of her own body. The anger and sadness of my father were clear-sighted. We had other channels of communication, but he saw that more of them were being condemned each day.

Actually, a time soon came when I could no longer pretend or argue and couldn't care much about appearances either. During discussions in school, I was even surprised to hear myself say, perhaps only to try a new phrase, that there was no God. Often a rhetorical affirmation aided me in the heat of an argument and increased my convictions. Then I took one step further: how could I say that God didn't exist, but still go to the synagogue? What horrible hypocrisy! Gradually, I stopped accompanying my father to temple, even for the High Holidays. Wild horses couldn't have dragged me there. Our local dogma was unbelievably primitive: an incoherent mixture of Berber superstitions, old wives' beliefs, and formal rites that could not satisfy the smallest spiritual need. The rabbis were silly, ignorant, and unprepossessing. Their filthy Oriental robes and faded fezzes were part of the life of sordid neighborhoods that I wanted to forget; their complicity and their resignation, in so many blatant stupidities that stifled me, roused my scorn. Soon, in my indignation, I began to confuse the synagogue with the ghetto.

My overt break, however, was not the most difficult. To save myself internally, I contrived tests. I fought the uneasiness I felt on entering the deeply moving gloom of our old temples, and I walked deliberately up to their damp walls so as to face the mystery of the tabernacle, making wisecracks about the magic of oil lamps and the green light of ancient windows, the oppressive odor of old leather, of parchment and incense. There, I began to reason and to wrestle with myself. The little flames jutting out of the oil lamps are not souls: a ridiculous superstition! Souls are not immortal, heaven and hell do not exist!

I could tell nobody of my difficult struggle with myself for fear of his making a fool of me. So I hesitated between an awareness of ridicule and a heroic satisfaction, between the temptation to deceive myself at small cost and the impossibility of not condemning my failures. You can fool the whole world, but not yourself. To drop the sacred phylacteries that we bind around our foreheads was a horrible sin, to be punished by death. The Law said it, it seems; the rabbis gravely affirmed it; the faithful repeated it with terror. I decided I could; I must cast them aside calmly, I would certainly not die because of it. Still, I didn't do it. And I rationalized beautifully: I had no need of childish demonstrations, it was enough to affirm my own freedom. A free man doesn't have to spend his time being blasphemous to deny God. But I felt my attitude was the least costly; I was ashamed to risk so little. At other times, I went to the point of blasphemy in committing less serious offenses. Bread must not be thrown away or left where it can be stepped on by passers-by; all crumbs must therefore be carefully gathered and left on the windowsill or stuffed into cracks in the wall. So I took whatever bread I didn't eat and made a show of throwing it where it could be stepped on. Of course, I felt ridiculous while doing it, but my very embarrassment seemed a hesitation, a trick of my superstitious fear, and I continued to throw my bread away, in spite of myself. How mixed up I was!

At home, however, my revolt had been completely expressed, and I no longer wisecracked or attacked but merely tried to live apart. Instead of peace, there was only more unpleasantness. When my father put on his cap and picked up his prayerbook to officiate, he seemed to become cramped as if a stranger were staring at him in mockery; and if I too put on a cap and stood up whenever required, I felt that I was watched by him and the rest of the family, as if they unmasked me in spite of my play-acting. It was an intolerable situation. As luck would have it, the younger children began having difficulties similar to mine. Frightened at their own audacity, they would look to me for support; but I refused to give it to them. When they began a destructive argument, they sought my eyes, but I looked away guiltily. My father answered quickly and brutally, not wanting to reopen the burning debates, ashamed before an adversary who was voluntarily silent. We ended by avoiding the ceremonies of minor importance and observed only the most solemn ones.

And, I must admit, as I had nothing to offer in its stead, I was sometimes sorry to have shaken the world of their traditions.

6

THE DANCE

THE WOMEN OF our house had already been living a good week in joyous anticipation of a mystery that made them forget all their dissensions. They tried to remain solemn about it, but were too excited to be able to conceal their wild childish happiness. Actually, they were busy organizing a dance, with Negro musicians and the sacrifice of a live white cock, for the purpose of exorcizing and saving Aunt Maissa.

The poor woman really needed saving. Her brothers had married her off to an old man of sixty who had the reputation of being very rich. The marriage brokers had affirmed that he owned several houses. When they had been questioned, the ignorant tenants of these houses had confirmed the ownership. But the clever old rascal, in spite of his curled up mustache, his upright posture, and the great care he devoted to his dress, was only the rent-collector for an estate-management corporation. His twenty-year-old bride didn't even obtain the standard of living that might have compensated her, by flattering her feminine vanity, for the essential

element of marriage that was lacking, and helped her forget
its absence. Still, her brothers had managed to marry off a
girl who had no dowry, though this is the nightmare of
families like ours. It turned out, nevertheless, to be a bad
deal: she became hysterical and, having soon exhausted her
husband, bounced back on her brothers, a pauper with two
sick children. A sharp word, a mere question as to her right
to hang her laundry across the roof terrace, were enough to
make Aunt Maissa swoon away, collapsing on the ground
and foaming at the mouth while her arms and legs beat the
air like those of a sick mare. When she came to, she uttered
frightful screams that made all the children weep with fear.
Her attacks were becoming more and more frequent, and
Maissa was now falling in the stairway too, rolling down
whole flights of stairs. It was often whispered that she needed
a husband, and a young man this time. But this cure required
such a huge financial sacrifice that her brothers felt it would
not be appropriate: a widowed mother of two children
should devote herself to their upbringing. Besides, no man
would be ready to assume such responsibilities. During the
shameless family discussions held around the table in the
first-floor flat, the poor woman tried to conceal her embarrassment and her hopes beneath an appearance of modest
indifference that was eloquently betrayed by her feverish
glances and her uneasy hands. Men were always right when
it came to money matters. The women, however, fell back
on a more mysterious and less expensive explanation of her
predicament: Aunt Maissa was possessed of spirits.

Those whom we called the "damned" or the "dwellers
beneath the earth," because one should avoid naming the
demons by their real name unless one does it with music and
with offerings, were now becoming particularly obtrusive:
the other evening, they had even left a big bruise on her leg,
which was a warning. They might indeed drive her to in-
sanity, so her sisters and sisters-in-law decided to hold a
meeting on the subject. There, they all spoke at the same

time, in their high-pitched voices, but managed all the same to agree on the urgency of holding a ceremony in honor of the demons that live below. A dance invoking their protection would be a wise thing for the whole house. Noucha, the wife of Uncle Aroun, courageously volunteered to take the matter up with her miser husband, as it involved some expense. Her sisters were suddenly moved to the heart and thanked her with tears in their eyes, like an autumn shower that comes over very suddenly. Then they broke up, all agog and happy at the idea of such wonderful and useful fun.

My mother brought out her wooden box that she hid against the wall beneath the bed. For lack of space in our common closet, that was where she tucked away her own personal treasures. Among broken trinkets, old ribbons, fragments of bridal veils, old purses and baby clothes, she discovered some weird oriental finery, shapeless and gaudy, all orange, yellow, and green, embroidered with beads and sequins. Then she gathered together all the colored scarves and handkerchiefs that she could find throughout the house. Twice, she went busily out to buy, in the covered markets, her share of the incense: a little bit of the kind that is called *ouchak,* some of the *jaoui* kind, and a few sticks of *ned.*

She did everything that could be expected of her as a worthy contribution toward her younger sister's recovery. Still, her joy was very childish and she could scarcely conceal it; it was written all over her face, and she could no longer refrain from anticipating the event by singing snatches of song from time to time. In spite of her protests, we teased her about all this.

On the appointed day, at noon, she was too much intent on preparing for the ceremony to fulfill all her duties as a mother, so that we had to be content with a pot of chickpeas, cooked in water. Whenever it came to the matter of food, we could become really unpleasant with Mother. Quite properly, we blamed the coming ceremony and her for the excessive importance that she seemed to attach to it. Hungry and bad-tempered, we repeated, each of us in turn, the traditional question:

"Is that all there is?"

"Yes, that's all. Father didn't leave me any money this morning, and I'm lucky to have been able to borrow twenty francs from Noucha."

We weren't sure that she was telling us an untruth, but she generally lied with great ease, spontaneously and without much forethought. So we refrained now from believing her wholeheartedly. Her constant and futile untruthfulness exasperated me, and I often felt like accusing her of lying. But I was each time discouraged by the uselessness of being provocative. It would have made her weep, and she would have accused me of being an undutiful son, only to tell another fib an hour later. So I generally had to pocket my ill temper as best I could. In any case, it would have been very ambitious of me to believe that I could monopolize her attention for more than a minute at a time. She was already beginning to live her afternoon of magic, full of Negro music, of bright costumes, and weird gestures. As the whole building now had all its doors open and was agog with crowds of wild-eyed women invading it, I decided to go away. In the general hubbub, I gathered that the ceremony was expected to end around six o'clock.

I had never liked this kind of gathering, even long before I had become fully aware of my reasons for rejecting things. I feared, for instance, the too heavy scent of incense, not so much because it struck me as unpleasant as because it upset me and made me nervous. I associated it, at a very early age, with strange old wives' tales where the hero loses his memory or goes insane after breathing a magical scent, or with the incantations which my mother sang by my sickbed; and that is why they continued to provoke in me some nervous reactions that no reasoning was ever able to dispel. I have now learned, from reliable scientific sources, that *ouchak* and amber have absolutely no mysterious properties at all, but I was still unable to conquer even slightly the feeling of uneasiness that overcame me as soon as I began to inhale their sweetish fumes. For all this somber folklore and its uninnocent myths I felt no sympathy at all. The *Djnoun,* those divinities from beneath the earth's surface, are by no means charming creatures of man's poetic imagination, capable of puckish malice but also of justifiable anger and of love, too. Poor beings exiled in perpetual darkness, they are all vicious and cruel, envious of man's happiness and constantly seeking, on women in childbirth, on healthy babies, and on families blessed with many children, vengeance to compensate some unkown personal sufferings of their own, some life that has been entirely misspent. That is why they like to pierce eyes, to afflict with madness, to twist bones, to paralyze limbs, even to kill. Of course, all this has no meaning at all, except in the minds of crazy old women, but I always avoided returning, if even as a joke, to this world of human miseries and fears. Could I, besides, forget that I too, not so long ago, had been careful to cry out, after spilling water on the floor, to evil spirits: "Excuse me, please excuse me!" and that I had then felt a cold shiver run along my spine?

I decided to return home after six o'clock, and meanwhile sought refuge in Henry's home. I found him by his window that was wide open in the park; he was practicing his violin. Without saying a word, I sat down and waited until he had finished. I was listening to him absent-mindedly, and I think he was reaching the end of a Bach piece. I must admit that Western music rather bored me. As I had not been taught any appreciation of music, I generally had a hard time trying to avoid finding it monotonous and oversophisticated. So I would force myself to follow the development of the harmonies, but it escaped my attention and I would soon be a hundred miles away from the music, dreaming out in the park or worrying over the solution of some problem. If, however, out of sheer obstinacy, I managed to remain aware of my immediate surroundings, then I generally found that the music didn't afford me enough pleasure. My untutored mind enjoyed only those pieces that have a fast rhythm, where the pace is more important than the intellectual content, so that I found myself carried away by the muscular tension. I thus enjoyed music when, far from encouraging me to meditate, it invited me to dance. Still, Henry's violin acted on me as a wise moderator, a mathematician of sounds, the expression of a civilization of men who had become masters of the world; together with Henry's discreet politeness, all this allowed me to relax immediately from the darkness of our Passage, from the dance ceremony dedicated to the *Djnoun,* and from my mother's childish enthusiasm. When Henry at last put down his bow, I already felt much better. So I asked him to allow me to stay, and he granted my request as a matter of course.

We spent the whole afternoon studying; he, his algebra, I, my Latin theme. The air was peaceful and heavy, as before a storm. A few autumn flies, on the verge of dying, insisted on finding some human warmth, in spite of our blows that sometimes managed to crush them. The park was motionless, as if ill at ease, watching out for the storm that threatened. But the storm didn't burst, and the window remained open, while the whole room seemed to be seized by this absolute calm. Soon, it was six o'clock, and I had meanwhile forgotten my problems completely, as always when at work. I then left Henry, who returned to his violin. I was fifteen minutes away from home but in no hurry, and dawdled along the boulevard. Suddenly, night fell prematurely, as if made heavier by the sky that was opaque and nervous, still full of the storm of which it had not yet been delivered.

When I reached the entrance to our street, I noted at once the wild music of tambourines and flutes, which meant that this dreadful ceremony was still in full swing. That was, I felt, too bad; so I climbed the stairs four at a time, rushing past the first floor, where I was met by a violent cacophony of cymbals that sounded strangely explosive in the sudden silence of all the other instruments. I knocked in vain at our own door; the show seemed to have attracted everyone, and the children, I was sure, were now staring wide-eyed at the unwholesome display. To get the key to our door, I would now have to go there myself.

So I went downstairs again. The whole band was in a frenzy, in response to the clashing cymbals that never ceased sounding. The door was literally vibrating as I knocked on it, at first with my fists, then with my feet too. They must all have become quite deaf, if not insane, from this awful music. At last, someone opened the door for me and the din was at once unbelievably louder, swelling to fill the whole staircase, right up to the glass roof at the top. I dived into this weird mixture of hysterical flutes, wild cymbals, tom-tom drums, and *darbouka* bagpipes, all seasoned with the babble of excited women. The air seemed tropical, damp and warm, heavy with human breath and incense. With great difficulty, I forced my way through the throng of women, all of them familiar faces, aunts, cousins, neighbors, but each one of them now a stranger under the spell that had overcome her. They stood there motionless, their hair disheveled, their eyes aglow, rigid as statues, or perhaps like stupid cows that I had to push aside, as if they couldn't understand me. They even seemed not to recognize me.

But I had still not penetrated into the room where the dance was being held, beyond a broad doorway that was cloudy with smoke. To get there, I had to make my way through a tangled throng of women who were watching, some of them standing on chairs, stools, even tables, leaning against the walls, clinging together in clusters, all peering deep into the cloud of smoke. How could they see anything at all? Close to me, I recognized my Aunt Noucha, dressed for the occasion in Bedouin costume. I shouted into her ear:

"Where is Mother?"

When I got no answer, I grasped hold of her arm and

shook it roughly. It was oily and sticky with sweat, and seemed to slither out of my grasp.

"Where is Mother," I shouted again. "I want our keys!"

She smiled absently at me and pointed toward the living-room. The closer I seemed to get to the heart of all this mysterious din, the more crowded it was. The women who were watching were treading on each other's feet, almost melting into a mass of compact flesh. I had to be really rough to reach the blue-gray cloud that was so thick that I could scarcely distinguish, through the smoke, the red embers of an earthenware brazier, like a shepherd's fire in a fog. My eyes smarted from the smoke and became clouded with soothing tears. The noise was so loud, so full, that I seemed no longer to hear anything at all. One moment, I felt I was in sheer void, with no shapes or sounds around me any longer. Then my eyes grew accustomed to it and began to distinguish with difficulty what was going on. Above the red point of the brazier, the heavy smoke of the incense rose; beyond it, I saw the strange creature that haunted this place. A woman, dressed in gaudy veils, was dancing wildly, throwing out her arms, jerking her head back and forth with so violent a motion that it hurt my neck to watch her. She turned her back to us and I could see her long loose hair cast wildly around her like tangled black serpents. Right at the back of the room and seated on the floor, the terrifying Negro musicians were playing. There they are, I thought, the demons! But this was only a half-hearted joke. The man who played the bagpipes, with his eyes bulging out of his head, two white spots against a coal-black background, his cheeks ready to burst, blew hard into his goatskin instrument. The tambourine-player was drunk, had reached a peak of frenzy, and kept on throwing his instrument in the air, catching it again and screaming all the time, without ceasing meanwhile to thump on the taut skin with all his strength. The cymbal player, punch-drunk, hypnotized, shook his head with the epileptic rhythm of his four metal plates. These men, I was sure, were no simulators; possessed by ancestral rhythms, they were repeating gestures and ritual that, in their childhood or in their distant homeland, had left deep marks upon them, scars on their cheeks that had been incised to impose on them, for all time, a hideous grimace. Nor would it be play when they would tear apart with their hands the live white cock, splashing the bird's warm blood all over themselves.

Nor was the woman dancing a simulator. That the musicians should be possessed in this manner was far from surprising: they were from some tribe of the deep South, a strange offshoot of Negro Africa sent out toward the Mediterranean. But the woman was a sensible housewife, with children who went to school; did she deserve my anger or my contempt for allowing herself to become hysterical, limp as a rag, a jointless doll tossed back and forth, without any conscience, in this manner?

The cymbals and the bagpipes were suddenly silent and gave precedence to the tom-tom drum that began, at first in a solo, to send forth grave, slow, evenly spaced sounds that seemed to be muffled, as if rising from the ground. The dancer followed this rhythm and became more calm; she allowed her arms to fall to her sides, relaxed her legs, seized by an occasional tremor that followed the drum's play as it urged her to leap in a single mass from the ground to the sky. The silence of the other instruments, subjected to the strenuous authority of the drum, seemed to crush the crowded women, who were silent now and gathered together in a single moody mass. I could distinguish them more clearly. There were women everywhere, clustered together, seated, standing, on the floor, literally lining the whole room. Their anxious motionlessness, repeated everywhere, disarmed me, in spite of my ironical nature, and prevented me from flying into a rage. Suddenly, as the cymbals clashed again, together with all the other instruments now released in a frenzy of revolt, the confusion became general. The tom-tom seemed to go insane, beating ever faster, struggling against time; the

flock of women was seized by nervous spasms, and the dancer
was again overcome by her seizures that seemed to tear her
apart. Her arms and legs and head, each one moving in a
different direction, appeared to respond to contradictory im-
pulses, going off madly at cross purposes, as if trying to tear
themselves away from the body. I could almost hear and feel
the flesh torn in its dreadful struggle against rhythm, against
the demons, when suddenly the crazy dancer turned toward
me—my mother, she was my own mother! My contempt and
disgust and shame now became clearer, more concentrated.
Instead of running away, I stayed there, crushed by the
crowd of women pressing against my back. Was this really
my mother's face, this primitive mask, glazed with sweat, with
its disheveled hair, eyes tightly closed, lips all bloodless? I
recognized the tawdry finery that she had unpacked from her
wooden boxes, the orange-colored *djebbah* gown strewn with
red and green sequins, the artificial silk *fouta* veil, brilliantly
colored and gaudy, orange, yellow, green, and red, and the
green and yellow scarf decorated with Fatma's hand and a
fish. To myself, I kept on saying: "She's my mother, my
mother," as if these mere words could re-establish the lost
contact and express all the affection that they should contain.
But the words refused to adapt themselves to the barbaric
apparition in its strange costume. And this woman who was
dancing before me, with her breasts barely covered, abandoning herself unconsciously to magical contortions, suggested to me nothing that was familiar or that I could
understand. In the books that I had read, the mother was
always somebody more soft and human than all others, a
symbol of devotion and of intuitive intelligence. How her
children must be grateful and happy, proud of having such
a mother! As for my own mother, here she was: this wretched
moron, with a spell cast on her by the dreadful music, by
these savage musicians, themselves under the spell of their
dark and obscure beliefs. My mother? Well, here she was. . . .
But why am I seized by this obscure emotion that is so

closely allied to panic? My God, my God, I'm afraid even
of my own mother, even my mother has ceased to seem
familiar and understandable to me! This must be what a man
feels when he awakes at dawn and sees beside him the face
of an unknown woman, sealed within her dreams that he
can never penetrate, the face of an unknown woman by
whose side he has chanced to sleep. She was a stranger to
me now, my mother, a part of myself become alien to me
and thrust into the heart of a primitive continent. Still, it
was she who had given birth to me. What somber ties still
bound me to this ghost, and how shall I ever manage to
return from the abyss into which she is now dragging me?

But here the musicians are slowing down again, the tom-
tom is silent, yielding to the shrill bagpipes, insidious in their
tone, that seem to trace brief arabesques of sound which my
mother follows obediently, her body swaying as if boneless
in the slow dance of the charmed serpent. Her disheveled
hair falls over her face that is distorted by pain and feebly
lit by the embers dying in this fog of smoke; like black serpents beneath a spell, her locks seem to follow her movements. Faithfully, my mother obeys the rhythm, or is it the
rhythm that rules her from within? She must have lost, long
ago, all awareness of her surroundings. The musicians then
begin to accelerate their pace, driven by some mysterious
force. Their eyes bulge out of their faces, veins swell in their
foreheads, their hideously incised faces grimace like magical
masks that suddenly come to life. As for the dancer, she
seems to explode, torn apart as her limbs begin to cast themselves wildly all around her.

But how is one to stop this collective seizure of epilepsy?
I felt like shouting insults at them, like beating them, beating
with all my strength these women and musicians. But I was
paralyzed, as if watching all of this through a glass pane.
How could I communicate with these people? Perhaps I too
should dance until I became giddy, until I lost consciousness
after accepting these rhythms and beating my own head

again and again with disjointed gestures, repeated until it
continued to shake all by itself, as empty as a doll's head
that moves as it follows its leaded pendulum, until my whole
body became dislocated in all its joints, so that no longer a
single bone, not a muscle, remained in its proper place, with
all my consciousness vanished and my body disintegrated
while I allowed the bagpipes to seize my nerves, the tom-tom
to rule the beating of my heart and blood, and the cymbals
to tear my limbs apart and scatter them north, south, east,
and west, throughout the sky and the earth? Would I then
manage in turn to get through to the other side of this pane
of glass?

I felt almost delirious. Suddenly, the music stopped on a
single beat, leaving behind it a silence that was heavy and
painful. Like a puppet when the thread that guides it breaks,
my mother now collapsed, abandoned by the music, limp as
a rag, motionless. Why, at this point, such a nauseous pity
within me? My heart followed her to the floor and suffered
from the sound of her heavy fall on the woven straw mat.
Meanwhile, the other women continued their movements.
Fat old Khmeissa, our neighbor from across the hallway,
seemed to be suffering as she bent forward, with her head
and her heavy breasts over my inanimate mother and, forcing
her spine so that her buttocks protruded like something
monumental, managed at last to place her mouth close to
my mother's ear. The women whispered among themselves
in a moment of relative peace. Khmeissa then placed her ear
close to my mother and seemed to be listening attentively for
a long while. Suddenly, she shouted:

"They have spoken! They have said: a red scarf and a
white cock!"

So the *Djnoun* spirits had answered! They had expressed
their desires to the dancer in her seizure! But what could you
really hear, you crazy old witch, from the lips of this poor
woman in her coma? Still, Khmeissa may not have been
lying that day, perhaps she really heard the voice of her own

imagination, educated to this end and convinced of its truth ever since childhood.

The babbling of the relaxed women now spread like water boiling over. The compact crowd gave birth to sudden movements as the individual women decided to change their positions, to climb down from a chair, to rise from the floor, and they all laughed, rushed off to find red scarves, to add incense to the burners. The musicians also seemed to shake their limbs like snorting horses, laughing among themselves with all their teeth showing white and yellow in their black faces. One could hear their guttural voices against a background of shrill gossip. The drummer heated and gently beat above the fire the skin of his instrument, the cymbal-player checked the leather thongs that bound the metal to his hands. Then, like flames, the red scarves were handed above the heads of the crowd, from woman to woman, to the heart of this gay, happy, and relaxed gathering, where my mother, still in her seizure, still lay on the floor, all by herself, in the indifferent gathering of her sisters and of all these other women. When at last the cock was brought in and the musicians got ready to start again, I had to admit that I was entirely helpless and took to flight.

I ran down the stairs, rudely pushed aside anyone who was in my way, and was out of the house before the music had started again. In the cool evening air I shivered and then noticed for the first time that I was in a sweat. Unconsciously, I thought of going back, to avoid catching cold: this too had been taught me since childhood, not to leave a warm room without first drinking a glass of water, then to go out by degrees, breathing the colder air in small doses. But I no longer wanted to do anything that I had been taught to do. From now on, I'll stare straight at the moon, though I've been taught that it may strike one blind; when I cut my nails, I'll throw the parings away anywhere, without fearing that I'll have to return every night, after my death, in order to find them, by the light of my own ten fingers flaming like torches, throughout all the dust and mud of the whole world; and I'll no longer whisper to the *Djnoun* spirits, before throwing out water: "Excuse me, please excuse me!"

So I rushed out of our Passage with my teeth already chattering from the drafts of the windy street. I walked fast to keep warm, and the exercise reduced my anxiety, which at the same time depressed me. Once more I felt that my revolt against all this was useless and made no sense. With whom was I really annoyed?

Avoiding the well-lit streets, I reached Henry's house. His window was still open and the light that shone out of his room pierced a hole in the darkness of the park. Henry was still practicing his music. I didn't dare, or didn't really want, to disturb him, so I let myself collapse onto a park seat. Was I only angry, or was my anger tempered with anxiety? Had I really escaped, will I ever manage to escape, from all these sounds and rhythms that live in the depths of my being and can immediately gain mastery over the beating of the blood in my arteries? After fifteen whole years of exposure to Western culture, of which ten were filled with conscious rejection of Africa, must I now accept this self-evident truth, that all these ancient and monotonous melodies move me far more deeply than all the great music of Europe?

Henry was still playing and came close to the window, standing out against the rectangle of light and casting his shadow clearly on the trees of the park. The music he was playing continued according to an exact scheme, always sure of itself, transparently clear, while at the same time full and heavy, with the weight of rock crystal and the rigorous structure of something mathematical.

Yes, I suppose I am an incurable barbarian!

7

THE KOUTTAB SCHOOL

IN MY EFFORT to break the mythical ties that I feared while believing that I merely despised them, I used to experience transitory moments of happiness as well as sudden defeats. Any chance scene witnessed in the street would at once make me feel the old and familiar uneasiness, so that I would doubt, all of a sudden, that I had achieved any progress.

One day, for instance, I had boarded the streetcar that passed by the high school. As it made no better time than I did on foot, I practically never took it, except when, as this morning, it happened to be raining. Each new passenger who boarded the car arrived among us wet and covered with mud, hurriedly slamming the sliding door behind him. The car itself, all warm from its human load and saturated with the steam of our breath, was acquiring an odd kind of intimacy as the passengers felt drawn together by a common feeling of well-being that contrasted with the storm beating against the windows. A mysterious sense of communion was thus born among us. All the races of our city were represented there. Sicilian workers in patched blue overalls, with their tools at their feet, were arguing noisily; a French housewife, conscious of her own dignity, was on her way to the market; in front of me a Mohammedan sat with his son, a tiny little boy wearing a miniature fez and with his hands all stained with henna; to my left, a Djerban grocer from the South, off to restock his store, with his basket between his legs and a pencil over his ear. The rain was sweeping against the panes of the car, opaque with steam, and the drops of water fell against them like the blows of a whip. The Djerban, under the influence of the warmth and the calm of the car, became restless. He smiled at the little boy, whose eyes twinkled as he turned to look at his father. The latter, flattered by this attention and grateful, reassured the child and smiled at the Djerban.

"How old are you?" the grocer asked the boy.

"Two and a half years old," the father replied.

"Did the cat gobble it up?" the grocer asked the child.

"No," the father answered. "He isn't circumcised yet, but some day soon. . . ."

"Ah, ah!"

The grocer had indeed found a theme which was rich in conversational possibilities with the child.

"Will you sell me your tiny little animal?"

"No!" the child replied with horror.

Quite obviously, the boy knew this whole routine and had already heard the same proposition before. I too, knew it all, and had myself played the game some years ago, attacked by other aggressors and feeling the same emotions of shame, curiosity, and complicity. The child's eyes sparkled with the pleasure of his awareness of his own growing virility, and with the shock of his revolt against such an unwarranted attack. He looked toward his father, but the latter only smiled: this was an accepted game. All our neighbors in the car took a friendly interest in the scene which was traditional and earned their approval. In this warm and human car, pro-

tected as we were against nature's aggressiveness, we were
like one happy family.

"I offer you ten francs for it," the Djerban proposed.

"No!" the child protested.

A Bedouin pushed the sliding door open and hesitated as
he entered. The stink of a stable and of stale cooking fats
spread throughout the car, as well as of something else that
I was unable to identify. Through the still open door an unpleasant draft reached us.

"Close the door!" the Sicilian masons shouted, though
apparently without any hostility or clannish animosity.

The Mohammedans in the car all pricked their ears up.
For a while, the little game stopped. But the Sicilians had
really intended no harm and we were quite clearly, one and
all, a big family of Mediterraneans. One of the Mohammedans, to show that he appreciated it, even decided to join
in the fun:

"Close that door! Don't they have doors, back home on
your mountainside?"

The Bedouin smiled foolishly and, without giving an
answer, finally closed the door before sitting down heavily
beside the French lady who, without making any display of
it, grew tense and pulled herself together. She didn't actually
move, but my own antennae had already detected a violent
disturbance in her magnetic equilibrium. The third odor of
the Bedouin now became more recognizable in the closed
car: the bitter and penetrating smell of burned charcoal.

"Come on! Sell me your little tail," the Djerban began
again.

The child's attention had wandered, and he now started.

"No! No!"

"I'll give you fifty francs for it."

"No!"

"One hundred francs!"

"No!"

"Ah, you're a tough number! Two hundred!"

"No!"

"Well, I'll go all the way: a thousand francs!"

"No!"

The eyes of the Djerban tried to express greed.

"And I'll throw in a bag of candy too!"

"No! No!"

"So it's no deal? Is that your last word?" shouted the Djerban, pretending now to be angry. "Repeat it once more: is it still no?"

"No!"

Then, suddenly, the Djerban threw himself on the child, pulling a terrifying face, and grabbed roughly at the boy's fly. The child defended himself with his fists, shrieking in terror that was no longer a pretense, tore the fez off his aggressor's head and began to pull at his hair. In the end, the Djerban, almost blinded and his face already bruised by the tiny hands, let go of the tiny little animal. The boy's father was laughing out loud, the Djerban was doubled up with nervous laughter, and all our neighbors were smiling broadly. Even the lady who sat beside the Bedouin must have found it, deep inside her, quite funny. At last the child, still pale and distrustful, decided to smile at his partner in the game.

Can I ever forget the Orient? It is deeply rooted in my flesh and blood, and I need but touch my own body to feel how I have been marked for all time by it. As though it were all a mere matter of cultures and of elective affinities! When the boy in the streetcar screamed with fear, I felt my own sexual organs quiver as if in response to a scream that reached me suddenly from the depths of my own childhood. Throughout this little byplay, I had looked up at the roof, like a man who pretends to have better manners and doesn't want to seem to mind the business of his fellow-passengers.

But my whole body followed the game with great attention and shared in the disgust of the child and the complicity of the crowd.

Yes, I know well that unpleasant but voluptuous tremor. Before going to grade school, I used to go to the *kouttab*, the Hebrew *cheder* school in our neighborhood, where every morning the rabbi used to make us repeat aloud and in chorus the prayers of the Jewish faith. We used to make a fine noise, which any surprised wanderer in our part of town may yet hear if he goes into the heart of the ghetto. Out of the windows of the *chedarim* the voices escape toward freedom, a cacophony of the tones of fifty children of all ages as they repeat constantly, in every kind of nasal singsong, a mysterious text that is meaningless to the listener outside and, it would seem, to the children themselves. One morning, as he had to go away, the rabbi entrusted the supervision of the class to the oldest among the boys, who submissively promised to watch us carefully: "Yes, Rabbi, yes . . .," repeating this after each one of the rabbi's remarks, so that our collective recitation continued: "Yes, Rabbi . . .," without being interrupted once until he returned, "Yes, Rabbi . . ."; only the smaller boys were to be allowed to leave the room to go to the toilet, the older boys only in extremely urgent cases; nothing in the old synagogue that served us as a *kouttab* was to be touched; our new supervisor would be allowed to report to the rabbi all those among us who were guilty of breaking any rule, and they would be punished with ten strokes of the cane on the soles of the feet—"Yes, Rabbi. Yes, Rabbi. Yes, Rabbi. . . ."

We all listened carefully, sneaking glances of complicity at one another and anticipation for the gala of wild jubilation that we would soon be celebrating. The rabbi's gouty foot may still have been on the last step of the narrow and steep stone staircase that twisted and turned before leading straight into the street downstairs, when a wild clamor rose throughout the *cheder*. We jumped up so hastily from our

wooden seats that they toppled over onto our heels. Those of
us who were seated on the floor on esparto-grass mats climbed
in turn onto the benches and chairs. We all began to shout
as if only to prove to ourselves that our voices were still
capable of producing other euphonic sounds besides the
monotonous singing of the prayers we were there to learn.
Never had the old synagogue's walls resounded to such a
collective hymn of joy. But it didn't seem to stir up a crowd
in the neighborhood, where the senses of most people had
probably become blunted to any musical charm in the usual
singsongs of *kouttab* schools. Once we had had our fill of
screaming, gesticulating, climbing onto the benches, rolling
ourselves on the grass mats and saying anything that went
through our heads without even trying to be at all understandable, merely for the joy of shouting all together at the
tops of our voices in this place of prayer and of contemplation, we then began to wonder what we might organize in
the way of fun. As soon as all the anarchic fantasies that
suggested themselves to our minds had been acted out, we
felt that we needed one another and discovered that we were
a crowd. How were we going to organize ourselves? The
older boys were more experienced and more daring, strong
enough, too, to impose their points of view. They soon
agreed to return to ancestral traditions and decided to play,
like adults, at circumcision.

The crowd at large began to express some uneasiness, then
a mitigated enthusiasm as we screamed and clapped hands.
We all felt attracted toward this mystery in which each of
us had taken part, against his will and in the unconsciousness
of his first days of life; it was indeed the act that bound us
within the great and sacred chain which, throughout the
centuries, went all the way back to God. The extraordinary
promise of consecration contained within this mystery ap-
pealed to us and disturbed us because the covenant with God
was of a sexual nature; at the same time, it terrified us
because it imposed itself on us like a fatal necessity in which

we saw, each day, our younger brothers and neighbors, soon after their birth, also involved.

Our enthusiasm was soon followed by a silence full of mystical terror when it came to the problem of choosing the victim, the baby to be circumcised. But were we still at play? The older boys began to examine the younger, who included me, with the sadistic calm of executioners. I was absolutely terrified of being chosen. Besides, I was quite unusually shy, and could already feel myself turn pale with shame at the mere idea of having my pants torn off me in front of everybody. For some time now, I had been concealing myself from my mother whenever I had to change my shorts, and for anybody to touch me would make me feel that I had been violently raped. So I retreated against the distempered wall and felt the blisters in the distemper break as I pressed against them. Even the big boys seemed to be impressed by the general silence and began to whisper among themselves, like men who are about to perform a sacrifice that involves terrifying responsibilities. When they at last approached our group, where the smallest boys were gathered together, I closed my eyes and my lips and prayed to God to save me. I would never have been able to defend myself, and my disorganized movements would have only served to encourage my aggressors. On other occasions, I had learned at great cost that it is always wiser, with grownups and with a crowd, to play possum, as if beneath the snout of a fierce animal. I was about to be seized by a hundred hands, brutalized, stripped of my pants, subjected to the touch of these other boys. In my distraction, I began, with my eyes closed, to whisper to myself the *Sh'mah Yizroel,* the prayer for the dead, until the shouts of the crowd made me realize that I was at last free from this unbearable suspense: the victim had been chosen, and I was not to be sacrificed.

But the mere threat had bound me closely to the victim and made me feel all the terrors of a real calvary. I could feel the anguish of the small boy who, all trembling, was now being carried, like the sacrificial lamb, on the shoulders of our supervisor. How would I ever be able to forget his distraught eyes and rejoice now with all the other boys? The procession began to form and, in the greenish light of the dark old synagogue, behind our improvised high priest who was bearing the live offering up to the altar, a most unusual line was already marching past. In single file, with serious expressions on their faces, the children went slowly, raising their faces as if in ecstasy toward the tabernacle that contained the sacred scrolls. The tiny blinking lights of the mortuary lamps hung close together all along the walls and surrounded the procession with a solemn lighting that gave it the same shadows as all the ceremonies of our elders. The children might indeed be playing, but their shadows were the same as all those of their fathers and their ancestors. Surely, the old synagogue was being deceived and was vesting in them all the solemnity of which it was capable.

My heart beat faster, under the pressure of fear and confused emotion. What was going to happen to the poor child, my God, what was going to happen to him? Were they really going to cut off his penis? The mere thought of it gave me a vague but not unpleasant pain in my own loins. My body, as usual, was going ahead of me, already in tune with the ceremony.

The older boys began to sing the ritual for circumcision while the rest of the crowd, in unison, repeated it. The younger kids were singing, with their shrill voices, in tones of respect, but quite calmly and without being exaggeratedly abject. The chant offered to the Lord Jehovah the new sacrificial offering that we bore, and reminded him, on this occasion, of the Covenant and of His own duties towards His people. They all smiled with a certain dignity, raising their heads whenever this was required, lowering their gaze whenever the text ordered it. This was exactly as our fathers did it, and we were all rehearsing our own future parts. But I was both ashamed and scared, as I have said, and even today

I'm to a great extent disgusted and horrified, but I still cannot manage to feel entirely alien to this procession, not in any way accessory to this sacrifice that is constantly repeated.

Slowly, the procession passed twice along the walls of the synagogue, then went up to the high chair of the priest on the dais. The crowd was silent while our supervisor, still conscious of his responsibilities, climbed onto the heavy wooden chair that was carved with sacred texts. His aides then placed the boy on the High Priest's knees, lying face upwards, after which, sharing in the traditional honor, they climbed onto the steps at the back of the throne. In the middle of the watchful group of his torturers, the victim waited, not daring to move or to say a word. His skinny little legs were folded, drawn up over his body, stiff as the legs of a cataleptic chicken. One could hear the breathing of the crowd watchful in its suspense, and the dry sputtering of the flames in the little lamps.

The High Priest then drew out his blade and solemnly, with broad gestures, reached out toward the child's crotch. I felt that I could not bear the sight of what was about to happen. All my groin ached as if the knife were about to wound me too. But why, in spite of this, was I unable to look away, why did my eyes remain glued to the boy's tiny white penis that I could discern from afar in the light that came down from the air vents which had become green with all the mold of the years? An intolerable fear kept me close to the wall, a feeling of shame before this nakedness; all this was mingled with a feeling too that I shall never forget, a pleasure at being accessory to the ceremony, accepting it all. Within my own penis, I felt the pleasure of fear transformed into tremors like those of an electric shock. How shall I ever forget my complicity? Yes, I was playing my part in the ceremony, in the ancestral and collective ritual that was food for the mind.

It was physically intolerable, and I felt truly faint when the High Priest's right hand, armed with a razor, came slowly down toward the tiny bit of white flesh that rose between the index and the second finger of his left hand.

But my sense of having been liberated was sudden, and all my fear vanished explosively, together with my shame, my pleasure, my disgust, and the unbearable tension that was born of the anguished silence of all of us: unable to stand it any longer, the victim had just burst into tears.

What did the crowd do now? What did we do? For a fraction of a second we all hesitated in silence and surprise, then burst out laughing, began to roll on the floor, all of us, big and small in a tangle, beating one another with our fists, climbing onto the benches, upsetting them, in an uproar of shouts and insults, insulting the victim too, still pale as he was from fear as he smiled and trembled in a corner of the synagogue, his eyes glistening with tears. The stupid urchin had really taken the whole farce seriously and been afraid of a mere piece of tin! A good joke indeed, and what fun it was to play at being grownups!

8

GINOU

MATURE WOMEN HAD no place in my world
of feminine ideals, and the girls that peopled it could be
divided into two categories: those that I dreamed of at night,
wishing I could approach them but believing them to be
inaccessible, and those that I knew well, who might have
accepted me but who left me cold. It would have been
impossible for me to kiss a girl from my own background.
All my neighbors and relatives made themselves up badly,
using too much rouge; their hair was reddish from cheap
permanents, and they wore dresses that were poorly cut,
always longer at the front than at the back, with gaudy
colors and too many ornaments, pleats and frills and fur-
belows; most of the time they looked as if they had been
bundled into their clothes and tied together carelessly. The
mere thought of them and their very presence failed to inspire
in me the tender and exquisite emotion that made my heart
beat faster. No matter how much I found excuses for them
and pitied them, their company bored me. They were females
destined only to be housewives, so ignorant and lacking in

any culture that they were completely cut off from me. As for the other women, those who used lipstick with discretion, whose perfume was enchantingly light, whose flesh was clean and fresh, who flirted in a manner that I found, deep within me, quite wonderful, well, these girls all come from middle-class homes and I believed I was cut off from them just as definitely, but by my own poverty.

The absence of any feminine companionship was not the least of the reasons that made my adolescence quite morbidly austere, with a stifling quality about it of which I was actually rather proud. As a matter of fact, I never did anything for the mere pleasure of relaxation. Every one of my gestures had a purpose that was calculated in terms of what it was worth. I studied because I wanted to assure myself of fame in the future, or I worked to make money. When at last I was too tired and allowed myself to write or to devote some of my time to social life, which was also work in my eyes, I brought to either of these occupations the same kind of earnestness. I was really a very serious young man.

But I managed, in spite of all this, to experience the kind of adventure that is unique and entirely wonderful. One of the girls of the kind that I admired and believed to be quite inaccessible accepted my admiration and even encouraged me. Now, I can understand it better: she fell in love with my earnestness. But here, at last, I was tasting of happiness. As an adolescent, I was never very happy nor very unhappy. I had no time for such states of being; on the contrary, I was always busy learning, changing, being active. In the light of individual incidents of this constant struggle, I was also indignant, revolted, or exultant. But my adventure with Ginou revealed to me that, although I had been unfortunate enough to be born into an impossible moment of history, life could still leave a taste of honey in my mouth.

One day, I was playing volleyball in the sun, wearing only my bathing trunks, with Mina, a scout-mistress. The sky was a pale blue, all of one spotless color, above a sea that was exquisitely warm and green. While she was busy throwing and catching the ball across a low breakwater that lay between us, Mina continued to tell me, with much sarcastic humor, details of their last summer camp. I was rather fond of Mina because of her very realistic views about other girls. She was the daughter of a tradesman who had made good, but she could still remember what life had been like before her father had struck it rich, and she now observed her new social background with a very lucid mind. Her sarcasm was pitiless but always smiling, and her own rather sickly health was certainly at the root of much of her bitterness. Her rather pleasant venom may also have acted upon me as a revenge for some of my own jealousy that I was never ready to confess.

"By the way," she suddenly confided rather knowingly, "let me congratulate you. It's the first time I've ever heard Ginou talk like that about any boy. She's a reasonable girl, and one who is well aware of her own charm. That's why she never does anything silly. Well, she mentioned your name to me six times in six days of summer camp, and even told me all about how she had dreamed about you. I think she would be ready to allow you to sit in the front row, just beyond the footlights of the stage where she gives her personal appearances."

I knew how much Mina enjoyed all kinds of go-between business. It gave her a chance to exercise her catty tongue and her foxy mind. That was why everyone was a bit scared of her but quite willing to use her services once in a while. So although I only shrugged my shoulders, I decided that she couldn't be inventing all of it. True, she helped people to fall into each other's arms, but she never brought couples together at random. Anyhow, I was too much interested and flattered by what she hinted at, and that alone excited me, though I tried to force myself to act as if I didn't care much. So I threw the ball back toward her, carelessly at that, so that it fell without much of a splash on the crest of a lazy wave, borne almost to the shore, and then immediately lost again in the light foam. The sea was like us, content to play languidly with the tips of its fingers. But Mina insisted:

"Still, Ginou's a wonderful kid. You know, she's my best friend, and she really dreamed about you."

Ginou, also called Jeannette, was playing ball over the breakwater just beyond ours; she was the only girl there, in a crowd of five boys. She was petite, plump, as perfectly proportioned as if an artist had created her, bursting with health, her cheeks rosy, her lips red, eyes blue, almost like a celluloid doll. Whenever she won a point in the game, she shouted out her joy; but when her opponent scored she threw the ball right at his head, splashed around in the water, clapped her hands, put on a real three-ring circus with all her excitement and byplay, a show indeed for the boys who were with her.

"She's a bit of a minx," added Mina. "Watch her now! You had better be careful, boy. Anyhow, good luck!"

I pretended to be surprised and annoyed:

"What on earth do you think you're talking about? You're even crazier than usual."

But I felt grateful to Ginou who was always so charming and flirtatious, because she had chosen to dream about me, of all people. I was ready to believe Mina's story, and there probably existed, between Ginou and myself, points of contact that had never occurred to me but that she had discovered. Moreover, I was ready to develop a crush on any one of these girls, leaving it to circumstances to decide why it should be one rather than another. Of course, I would never have dared to approach Ginou on my own, but she had now opened the way and I was already upset and grateful. All the desperate tenderness that I had repressed in my heart was concentrated on her. Within a couple of days, without my having said another word to her, she already began to assume, in my eyes, all the qualities of a great love.

Still, I had to undertake some kind of courtship, though it might be much easier than I feared. After all, she had more or less taken the first step when she had dreamed of me and mentioned me to Mina. These arguments served to give me the necessary courage and made it all the more easy for me. Besides, it was summer, the season that was in every way most appropriate for this kind of situation. Two days later, as I was swimming beside her, I suggested to Ginou that we take a walk together along the beach at five o'clock that afternoon. Her eyes glistened with sea water as she expressed some surprise, perhaps candidly, but in any case already disarming as far as I was concerned.

"Why don't you suggest that the others come along too?"

I mumbled: "I thought it would be more fun if we were alone."

"O.K., if you say so," she concluded.

She spoke as if she were merely yielding to some fancy of mine. I would have preferred it if she had shown some emotion about accepting my proposal, as if she were trying to conceal her pleasure. Still, she did grant me an awareness of complicity; she assured me she would tell nobody that we were going out together, all by ourselves. I was too glad to be at long last able to enjoy the business of being in love, and too proud to be going out with her, elegant and lovely and popular as she was, so I wasted no time quarreling about shades of meaning. I knew that all the other boys surely envied me my luck, now that I had caught up with them and was even well ahead. Yes, I of all people, the boy whom they all found too serious and a bit of a prig, as they said. I was stupid enough to believe that I had been deprived of these pleasures which, I thought, were exclusively reserved for the rich, I mean the business of pretending to be in love. Still, I'm not unattractive, I found, and, as a matter of fact, better looking than most of them. I began to look at my own reflection in mirrors and rather enjoyed being able to rediscover myself in this manner. My nose, it's true, might be a

bit long, but only a trifle. I found I had a good profile, firm
features, good strong teeth set in even rows, the high forehead
of an intellectual and curly black hair. Be that as it may, I
had been chosen among many, and by Ginou of all people!

The very first time we went out together, I was clumsy
enough to talk to Ginou about what worried me most, about
myself, my ambitions, what I felt sure of achieving in life.
Being a woman, she listened to me with interest and kindness and asked questions and gave me advice. She was herself more interested in fashions, tennis, cooking, and music
than in her actual classwork, but she held my successes in
high regard. All the others, for that matter, showed me the
same respect, which didn't help me much. My vanity might
be satisfied by it, which I would never admit to myself, but
I would have preferred a warmer sense of equality rather
than this intellectual esteem that set me apart without accepting me. Ginou's admiration for my achievements never seemed
to me to be the essential factor in our friendship. Now that
I could see her being so full of attentions for me, I soon
became convinced that she felt as much tenderness for me
as I for her. As for myself, it had become quite clear that
my tenderness for her was tremendous, clear as daylight. I
still didn't dare to use the word "love," for it seemed to me
too vast, too magical, too rich in literary implications. On
the contrary, I was rather proud of being a realist and I knew
that Ginou too was not of a romantic nature. Hers were the
very soundest middle-class virtues: a practical common sense,
good judgment, an avoidance of any exaggeration. I, on the
other hand, was always too impulsive and excited, so that I
really needed a more balanced, realistically inclined, and
sane woman. So I soon began to think of marriage, for all
this, of course, could lead only to marriage. I respected Ginou
too highly, and there were other things in life besides mere
fun. I never forgot to think of my own future in constructive
terms.

But I still didn't dare to propose to her quite openly.

Instead, I described to her what kind of wife I hoped to marry, and the portrait that I drew was as realistic as a good photograph of Ginou. I would always insist that I hoped to do everything in my power to make my wife happy, and she modestly pretended not to understand what I was after as she discussed my views and argued with me in the name of all womankind. I could see that she got my meaning, and I used to dream of her every evening as I fell asleep, repeating her name to myself: Ginou, Ginou. The "ou" in her name seemed to me to express some particularly sweet harmony as it melted in my mouth. . . .

I even tried, for her, to achieve things that had never particularly interested me. Mina realized now what she had started and how difficult it all was; that was why she watched us so closely, as if stimulated by everything that seemed to defy fate in this situation. I allowed her to check my progress and swallowed my pride. I learned, for instance, with some displeasure that I shaved badly and not often enough and that people made remarks, behind my back, about how carelessly I dressed, about my noticeably North-African accent when I spoke French, and about the violence of my language. So Mina assumed the task of educating me. She was quite pitiless about it and pointed out to me each time there was a trace of tattletale gray about my collar, or a button missing from my jacket, or any stain that should be removed, or a tear that needed mending. At any other moment, I would have answered that my appearance didn't matter to me, which wasn't really true, and I would have demanded the right to be free in my violent criticism of the histrionics and the bowing and curtseying that characterized most of my friends. But Ginou was worth all this discipline to me. She was a middle-class girl, Mina would remind me, each time I feebly protested.

I grumbled, but I still accepted the idea that Ginou was a kind of lofty mountain peak that I had to conquer. Never, in all my life, have I been as humble, with a humility that lacked all bitterness. The unbelievable luck of being Ginou's official boy friend cost me untold sacrifices. I had to explain to my mother how to starch a shirt collar, though she was never able to learn the trick. I tried to learn how to be more gallant, but I was never spontaneous enough to be the first boy to think of what should be said or done. The other boys always quickly showed me what I might have done only after considerable forethought. If a flower-vendor passed us in the street, all the girls would be wearing, in a twinkling, corsages or necklaces of blue jasmine, and they were always served ice cream or peanuts or cookies before I had even delved into my pocket for the necessary cash. Of course, it wasn't easy for me to pay; instead of making one seem more noble, poverty actually makes one petty. In many respects, I was a rather stingy beau: I asked nobody for anything, but I also hated to give. My pocket money had cost me too much hard work and I always had too many better uses for it. So our outings always left me some bitterness, more disappointed by myself than by Ginou and the others. As soon as we were together in a crowd, Ginou no longer paid any attention to me but returned at once to her flirtatious manner, her teasing and her constant references to the details of middle-class life that transformed her, in my eyes, into a stranger. I would then feel alienated from her and her friends and often began to wonder how it could be possible for me to court a girl who had so little in common with me and so much in common with the others.

Still, we happened to be alone, on this specific occasion, by the breakwater, playing ball together. I was quite obviously her favorite companion. It was five in the afternoon and we had been on the seashore in the sunshine since morning. Between two swims, we had lunched off sandwiches on the beach. Now the violet-colored hills seemed peaceful on the other side of the bay; the seagulls hovered dreamily, almost motionless, in the air, and we were all drowsy, weary of so much light and heat, our skins caked with salt from the sea.

The water was warm, lazy; it cast up on the sand short and foamy waves which blended the pale pink of the setting sun, the yellowish green of the sea water itself, and the pale blue-violet of the sky. Suddenly, I was seized with so unbelievable a happiness and could feel so fully the richness of the whole universe that I almost wanted to weep.

After an initial failure in her exams, Ginou had made up her mind to come up again for the baccalaureate in October. She pretended to be very serious about it and I offered to coach her in literature, which she accepted vaguely, always postponing any action till the following week. As for me, I was beginning to be sick of all this comedy of hints and double meanings. Quite obviously, I was marking time, and I began to feel a bit foolish too, almost guilty about never having dared a more direct approach. All my classmates constantly talked of petting, of kissing, and even of other things that I disapproved of. Ginou, in my eyes, was more than a mere crush that one has to make the most of while it lasts. I respected her and I owed her a certain gratitude, though I might be able to allow myself more daring liberties within the framework of this respect. The very health of my love for her demanded more. Perhaps, after all, her new swim suit, a silver-colored knitwear model with red dots that revealed every contour of her exquisite figure, had something to do with it all. On one or two occasions, I had been ashamed of my own excitement and been forced to dive immediately under water in order to conceal my very obvious emotion. But now that I had decided to follow this line of action I couldn't rest until I had worked out a plan. The most difficult step would be to get Ginou to agree that we be left alone together in a room, behind a closed door. On Saturday afternoons, my parents generally left our overheated apartment for a neighborhood beach. It never occurred to me that Ginou, too, had thought seriously of what I was about to propose to her.

I can still remember every detail of that day and of the

whole scene, though our days at the beach were so much alike
that they now all melt into a single image in my memory.
Ever since the morning, I had repeatedly failed in my attempts to drag her away from the rest of the crowd. Then
the others all agreed to rent a rowboat, but Ginou felt tired
and refused to join them. So we stayed alone, a real treat to
be by ourselves. We lay together, face to face, on our
stomachs in the sand. Ginou's face seemed to fill the whole
landscape ahead of me, spreading beyond the sky line of the
hills, filling the whole sky, while the sunlight, reflected off
her tousled hair, seemed to form a halo around her. I chose
my words carefully as I suggested to her that she come and
prepare her French literature exams with me at home; my
excuse was that I would have all my books there. We would
be all by ourselves in peace and quiet. This last I stressed
carefully.

I was so upset that I could scarcely pretend that all this
was only normal, and I would have made a fool of myself
with endless apologies if she had merely frowned. But Ginou
answered my hesitant invitation quite simply:

"Yes! O.K., for Saturday."

My heart beat so fast that I felt I might faint. I stared
tenderly in her direction and tried to find, in her own eyes,
some inkling of her complicity. But she evaded my appeal or
failed to understand what I was after. Still, I was so happy!
I might have dared to kiss her then and there, not out of
sensuality but out of sheer affection. So I took my fill of the
sight of her, of the sky, the hills, the Mediterranean sea that
seemed to love us. I felt that Ginou and the whole universe
had signified their acceptance of me, their full confidence.
I left her there and went off to swim all by myself, going
against the waves with clean strokes of my arms, thrusting
my chest forward and head on.

The following Saturday, I could scarcely conceal my impatience to see my parents leave. The long Sabbath lunch
seemed to me to be literally endless, and I could barely stand

it as I watched the kids receiving their weekly pocket money. As for Aunt Maissa who had come with her sad nun's face to swell the crowd, she drove me nearly insane. Finally, however, the house was silent. Once the door had closed on the last of them all, I leaped from the couch where I lay trying to read, and feverishly began to do my best to make our dining-room tidy. Actually, I limited my efforts to kicking all stray shoes beneath the furniture and stuffing the clothes just anyhow into the sideboard. On the table, I spread again our Friday night's white tablecloth and set two chairs side by side. Then I left the door ajar, so that Ginou need not wait till I came and opened it, thus she would avoid being seen by any of the neighbors. But it was still too early and I was so impatient that the time seemed to·go by very slowly. So I went back to the couch and again tried to read, but in vain for my eyes somehow failed to come to grips with the text. All the joys that I was anticipating were too illicit, too new, too mysterious, too rich in promises.

Furtively, she knocked twice on our door, then understood and walked in without further ado. I rushed to meet her and found her already in our foyer. So I closed the door, slamming it as if to cut us off from the world. Nobody would be able to know that we were there together, just the two of us. She carried in her hand a notebook, all wrinkled from being rolled tightly, and she now put it on the table. As soon as she noticed the two chairs, she sat down hurriedly. So I said, without waiting any longer, without even stopping to greet her:

"Let's get down to work!"

I sat down on the other chair, as if our job were an urgent one, as if our unaccustomed presence here required immediate justification. All our comradeship that we had experienced in the sunlight and that had always been so uncomplicated had now vanished. It was indeed as if we were meeting for the first time. As I undertook to explain to her the main themes of Racine's tragedy, *Phèdre,* I could hear my own voice in a key that was several tones lower than usual, a baritone that sounded almost husky. Meanwhile, she remained silent, trying to take notes with a bit of a pencil that had a copper ring around it and badly needed sharpening, the wood almost completely covering the lead. As for me, I kept staring at this pencil with which she wrote so uneasily, and at the finger that pressed on it, her ɪorefiɴ.ᵤer with a small piece of lint bandage tied around it for luck. I scarcely dared look at her, and my embarrassed voice went on talking all on its own, turning out its remarks on *Phèdre*, stuff that had all been said a hundred times before. My eyes kept on seeing her page of paper that seemed to refuse to be anything but white, her dimpled fingers like those of a baby, her finger that looked like a doll with a ribbon tied round it; and my mind, as I stared at all this, stubbornly and jerkily repeated to me in an insistent manner: "You must dare, dare, dare. . . ."

My thoughts re-echoed inside me, as in a hollow, a desert that was quite alien to me. I scarcely dared obey such an imperative and, as soon as the rough wooden edge of the worn pencil began to rub against the paper as she wrote, I felt that I had to put an end to this unpleasant sound. To achieve it, I had to touch her hand with my own while she tried to trace heavy childish letters, but something had to be done to stop the noise that was so irritating in the otherwise silent room. After my discovery of this important fact, whole centuries seemed to go by. At long last, I plucked up enough courage to act: my hand moved, grasped her own, which stopped still, tense in mine that held it. Everything seemed to stop and I no longer even felt that I existed. Our noisy family apartment was capable, it seemed, of breeding unbelievable silence too. Then, all by itself, my heart began to beat, like a gong. This lasted, lasted, until she suddenly shook time to its very foundations, literally upset it whereas it had seemed to curdle, transforming us into statues. She spoke:

"Don't you want to let me write?"

She had said it in such a friendly and even tender tone. She was far less disturbed than I, it seemed to me. I raised my eyes at last and stared into her face that I had forgotten so long ago in all this excitement. She was smiling and her hair fell over her forehead and one third of her face, following that year's hair style; her lips were tinted with a deep-rose lipstick that suited her perfectly. No, she was not in the least bit shocked. She smiled and, little by little, I regained control over myself. Something must be done now, something must be done now, in order to behave really like a man in love. I lowered my eyes and very suddenly, with the motion of an automaton, placed my left arm around her neck. Again, for centuries it seemed, silence settled down on us and we were way out of this world. Finally, I said to myself:

"You must kiss her, you must kiss her, now's the time."

But I had no desire to kiss her. Sexually, I seemed to have been completely neutralized and only conventional thoughts rattled through my body that had lost all power of motion. Still, these thoughts knew what was expected of them and followed certain directives: the moment had been reached when a kiss was due. All the boasting reports made by my schoolmates had convinced me of this, so I remained with my right hand tightly grasping hers that held the pencil and my left hand around her neck. But our chairs were too far apart, though I would never have had the courage to draw them closer. In this rigid position, and from such an absurd distance, I thrust my head forward toward her mouth. I had almost reached her lips when she moved suddenly and withdrew her head, so that my lips met her cheek.

This left me free; she had put an end to all of it, setting distinct limits to what she was ready to permit for this one day. Of course, I would never have taken such liberties had I not thought. . . . I would never force her. . . . Meanwhile, I had recovered some mastery over my own body and could control my thoughts again. I withdrew my right hand, then my left arm too. I rose from my chair and walked across the room. As if the electric current that fed it had been cut, I suddenly recovered from the tremor that had overpowered me ever since she had entered the room, though I had noticed it only now. I was back in the ordered world of everyday events, with my classmate Ginou.

I had almost forgotten that Ginou had to be coached in composition. Walking up and down the room, I now began to explain things to her as one might to an audience of strangers in a lecture hall. Meanwhile, she took notes very actively and her pencil no longer scraped against the paper I made a few wisecracks about that dumb cluck Hippolytus and his horrified surprise when his stepmother propositioned him, but otherwise we studied seriously and with great concentration. When we had finished the job, she asked me not to accompany her downstairs and I heard her footfalls grow fainter and fainter as she went down the stairs and left me alone. I was calm, but as if I had just recovered from a moment of drunkenness, of happy drunkenness that left me no hangover and no headache.

"It's the first time I have ever touched a girl," I repeated to myself, "the first time, a girl. . . ."

I felt proud of myself, as if this had all been some kind of promotion or of admission into a world of initiates, and I came to a clear conclusion, that Ginou's answer could only be interpreted as an admission of her love.

But she seemed, when I next saw her, to have already forgotten the fabulous experience that we shared in common. All my references to it called forth no response, and my enthusiasm remained fruitless, matched by no admission, on her part, of any complicity or of any tenderness. At all of our meetings that followed, I scarcely dared remind her of our wonderful Saturday, and I had to return to my old devices and random hints.

One day, we had reached the end of a long walk in a public park. It had been raining, and the autumn shower had summoned forth heavy and deeply moving scents from the damp earth. I love the smell of the afternoon, the damp breath of plants, the leaves shining with drops of rain that quiver, the flowers that are ready to droop. We had been very talkative about everything except what mattered to me, and I at last broached this subject too, affirming, though in an abstract manner, as usual:

"If only a girl would really trust me, I would be ready to do anything for her!"

Without any hesitation, she answered me:

"Well, you can count on me, for always!"

She had come to this decision reasonably and was expressing her consent: we would now be able to marry.

But I remained speechless with surprise, though I had prepared everything and had long been expecting this confirmation. Ginou was ready to accept me as her husband! I scarcely knew what to do, what to say, how to express my joy.

"And to think that you waited until now to say so," I remarked reproachfully. "We have been together for the past two hours. Don't you think it was selfish of you to deprive me of two hours of sheer happiness?"

She smiled with great tenderness as we reached the gate of the park. The tall trees at the entrance bore mauve-colored blossoms, like flowers pinned in a girl's hair. We were no longer by ourselves for there were other people around us. I was so happy and excited that I wanted to have her all to myself, to hold her tight in my arms. So I suggested that we turn back into the park. No, she felt it was too late; we ought to be more reasonable, she thought, and refused. I barely touched her cheek as I kissed her, but still she withdrew. I knew how worried she always was about her own reputation, so I didn't insist now and walked her home. All the while, she spoke in an even voice, very reasonably, in the tones of a housewife organizing her household chores. She asked me not to mention anything yet to anyone, not a word of our secret. We would have to wait until I had been admitted to the medical profession as her parents would never accept a son-in-law who had neither job nor profession. So I promised her everything she asked for and would have been ready to promise her, had she wanted it, the moon too.

All the same, I rushed to Henry's place as I had to share my happiness with someone. On the way there, without any loss of enthusiasm, I began to think too that I would have to make a lot of money. Ginou was accustomed to certain luxuries, but one more element in my defiance of fate no longer scared me at all and I was sure I would be successful. When I got to Henry's, I found him fixing his bicycle. Every Saturday evening, he cycled fifty kilometers to go and whistle a serenade beneath his girl friend's window. I told him my whole story at once and he congratulated me:

"She's a very attractive girl."

Then he added, jokingly:

"But what the hell, is it you or the physician that she wants as a husband?"

I answered quite seriously that she was right and that her decision proved that she had sound common sense. She was the kind of wife I wanted. But I was disappointed when I saw that Henry failed to appreciate the full extent of my happiness. I decided that great joys, like great losses, can never be shared.

9

THE PARTY

OUR MEMORIES OF things impose some order on the past and give it its meaning. As I grew older, it thus seemed to me that my whole life had been but a series of breaks and interruptions, each one in turn more serious and definitive. Still, I had long continued to hope that some harmony might be achieved, and had even thought that I might be able to impose on myself and my relationships with the outside world some kind of order, if only by using my own will power and my ability to choose. I thought I would end up as a member of the middle class, not so much because belonging to this class was a kind of ideal as because my education, the tastes that I was discovering, and my concern with the arts, in fact all my future position in life, were already forcing me into this position. Still, I continued not to like the middle class, though I was forced to admit that I really felt at ease only in its midst. They were the only people to read books, to understand my preoccupations, to enjoy and practice poetry and the arts. One day, however, I became brutally aware of the fact that I was not a member of the middle class and could never become one.

All my childhood friends were now becoming tailor's apprentices, their shoulders rounded by their work, their whole appearance weak and sickly in their black waistcoats; or else, grocery clerks, pale from working in the shade of the covered bazaars; or office workers who were already becoming flabby, with yellowish fat. We scarcely even greeted each other any longer; they were ashamed of their own condition and respectful towards me, and I was full of feelings of guilt, though God knows why. Only Levi, an orphan who was a baker's assistant and rode a tricycle for the deliveries remained quite spontaneous in his manner and always shouted, the moment he spotted me in the street:

"Shalom, Mordekhai!"

Such a public utterance of my name that smacked of the ghetto displeased me considerably, but I was afraid of hurting his feelings if I asked him to be more discreet about it. So I suffered each time I saw him emerge on the horizon, dancing like a puppet on his wheel.

As for the middle-class boys who were now my classmates, they had become my equals and my everyday companions. In spite of myself, I respected their new suits that were so elegantly cut, their high-quality school equipment, and their healthy appearance. I even envied them their being able to refer without any hesitation to their parents and their social background. I, on the contrary, always had to be careful and watch my step when it came to admitting anything about myself or my family. If anyone asked me about it, I always said that my father was "in the leather business." Yes, up to his elbows in leather, I would add mentally. In the same manner, I blew up to unnatural proportions my Uncle Aroun's business and, in spite of my distaste for him, often boasted about it. About my mother, I avoided speaking as there was nothing much I could find to say about her. Without ever admitting it, I would have been ready to pay dearly for the privilege of being a middle-class boy, born and bred in the leather or grocery business.

In spite of the friendships that I made in school, I never really managed to penetrate the social life of my schoolmates. They probably felt that I was too sarcastic and too severe in my judgments, perhaps even rather unpleasant. I was proud and easily hurt, so that I took no steps at all to suggest that they might invite me. I would have had to return any invitations, and it was impossible for me to entertain any guests at home. So it was Henry, who was not one of my classmates in high school, who brought me out socially. He introduced me to a group of scout leaders who were looking for an instructor for the Jewish part of their educational program. As I was still quite undiscriminating in my intellectual appetites and ready for anything, I happened also to attend some Hebrew night classes that had been organized by the Zionists. In an audience from the ghetto, I was thus one of the few high-school boys to have acquired both kinds of culture. The middle-class boys in secondary school were sarcastic about such an amateurish and hit-and-miss manner of teaching, being quite blind to its historical significance. Although their position made it clear that they would one day be the leaders of the community, they had lost all interest in the social problems of its daily life. Because their own future seemed to pose them no problems, they could only be flippant on every political issue, which shocked me deeply.

I was fond of Henry, but even he was but charmingly whimsical when it came to any matter that deserved serious attention. He was the son of a French mother and of an Italian-Jewish father; himself a British subject because his father came originally from Malta, he belonged nowhere. There was too great a diversity about him and he felt no urge to solve any particular problem. When his parents began to quarrel and finally separated, it left him free to lead an utterly airy life, without roots of any kind. I tried several times to convert him, in turn, to each one of my successive views; but politics left him cold and he slithered between my fingers, so to speak, and answered my arguments with talk about his guitar, about painting, about summer camps. In the Italian high school where he studied, Fascism discouraged, in those years, all serious thought and was producing a whole generation of lightheaded boys who actually knew nothing thoroughly, only a smattering of mathematics, of doctored history, and a lot of poetry, music, drama, and drawing. So I ended up by accepting Henry just as he was, enjoying in his presence, as if by a clear spring of water, a kind of repose that did me good. It helped me relax and I would then allow him to dream away as I listened to him grow enthusiastic about imaginary projects: miraculous fishing expeditions off the shores of Southern Tunisia, with millions to be made there, or the building of a monstrous theater in the ruins of the ancient one in Carthage. Then he would vanish for a couple of weeks and, when he reappeared to meet me at the gates of our high school, all absent-minded and with his hair ruffled, he would already have forgotten his theater project in favor of a fabulous voyage to the South Sea Isles. I was fond of Henry because life, in his company, seemed less drearily serious, and I have often wished it were indeed less serious!

But my classmates were no innocent poets. On the contrary, they were all quite satisfied with themselves and their social background, with their parents and little celebrations and annual charities, and knew all the rules of their own mediocre little game. As for me, I was disappointed by their meetings, which struck me as quite futile. They constituted a kind of miniature society, with its gossip, its flirtations, and its worries, but everything there was playful and childish. Their parents footed the bill for their parties, gave them the use of the apartment, with cakes too that their mothers had baked. In my own family circle, everyone systematically distrusted any youth group, expecting only trouble, as was repeatedly said, to come of them. The less privileged young Jews, it is true, were all drifting into Zionism or Communism. But the middle-class boys and girls made fun of the tragic

and austere expressions of the youth of the ghetto and
affected, on the contrary, a pleasant and sociable manner.
Quite satisfied, they were harmless and enjoyed the blessing
of their parents. They had all been scouts as children and
were still active in the movement as scoutmasters or as
patrons; in addition, they organized themselves in little
groups of amateur actors, musicians, or collectors. This allowed them somehow to continue their childish games they
had learned as scouts, and they still practiced their scout
cries, imitating toads or cocks and calling each other by
animal names and still reading pathfinder literature. But I
never managed to be able to laugh at their constant jokes
and puns and witticisms, though they were very sharp at
seeing the funny side of things and of people. The world
had been theirs from the day of their birth, much to their
satisfaction. As for me, I felt that everything was still to be
conquered and the struggle ahead of me gave me no reason
to laugh. Besides, I hated everything funny. The instruction
in Hebrew and in Jewish social matters that they had asked
me to organize for them had its place, in their scheme of
things, alongside courses on how to tie knots in ropes. This
gave me an additional reason to despise them.

But I was all the more anxious to approach them because
they refused to consider me as one of their crowd, and I was
really quite gratified when Henry transmitted to me their
first invitation. They were planning a reception in honor of
their national chief, who was coming to Tunis from Paris.
The party was to take place in the home of Michel, the son
of a lawyer who had agreed to evacuate the apartment, with
all the rest of his family, to allow the reception more
freedom.

On the appointed evening, I demanded of my mother that
she supply me with a spotlessly white shirt, a symbol of all
that is both solemn and clean. I made her iron it a second
time beneath my very eyes as all our linen, crowded in
drawers that were too full, always had a crumpled appear-

ance. Before dressing, I put brilliantine on my hair but was then obliged to clean it off with a rag, a tuft of hair at a time, because I had put too much on. As always when the occasion warranted, I wore my sweater beneath my shirt, under the impression that a shirt front looked more dressy. Besides, none of my sweaters really matched my suit, so I had no real choice. Finally, I turned my overcoat inside out and folded it over my arm: it was too worn for me to be able to think of wearing it. I couldn't yet afford an overcoat every year as I could a new suit or a new pair of shoes, so I simply had to go without an overcoat on special occasions like this one.

When I reached my destination, I found the downstairs lobby in our host's house completely dark. I fumbled a while along the walls, trying to find the light switch, but soon had to give up. So I went ahead in the darkness, hoping to be able to guide myself by the streaks of light that appeared beneath the doors or the light of the glass roof above the stairwell. But the passage soon followed a bend and I then found myself in absolutely unmitigated darkness, as if I had closed my eyes. I was shortsighted by nature and had developed a kind of carelessness about looking, often trusting to my sense of touch. So I now tried to find the wall, then clung to it with one hand, and began to go ahead, for a while, hesitant and full of misgivings, until my hand felt a curve. I followed it and finally reached what I supposed to be a stair rail: I was saved! One step at a time, I then began to climb, being careful to feel my way at the edge of each step with the tip of my toes, as a precaution. But it all took a long time. I followed a first turn, then a second one, till my shoe at last met nothing ahead of it and came down again unpleasantly to the same level. I then guessed I had reached the first floor, but Michael lived on the second, so I followed the stair rail, without letting go of it, all the way round the landing until my foot bumped again against a step, the first one of the second flight of stairs, after which I began to go up. I was still in total darkness, as if I were buried in the heart of something solid and opaque. Nowhere did my eyes detect any light that could guide me at all. Again, I was able to conclude, from the way my foot had fallen a second time without having met a step, that I had reached another landing, the second floor. The stair rail was really an excellent guide in my ascension, though no longer of much use to me. I figured out that I should try to reach the wall opposite the stair rail and follow it, which would inevitably lead me to a door. So I regained some of my assurance, especially when my hand found its way quite easily to the wall and I was then able to move ahead towards the left, however slowly. Following the stone wall, I then turned a first time, then a second, in gentle curves. How odd that there should not yet be any doors! I began to feel annoyed by this business of creeping around in the silent darkness. I must have already spent a full quarter of an hour of my young life in this hole! Perhaps I exaggerated the time this adventure had lasted, but I had climbed up the stairs at a snail's pace and was now moving along a passage that seemed to have no end. Where was I? The wall followed another turn, this time at a right angle, but where was it leading me? There must have been some other wall opposite: I felt my way and found it. So I left the first wall for the second, which may have been a mistake, and began again to go ahead. At long last, my hand felt the framework of a door. I knocked, without hesitating; if it was the wrong door, I would apologize, but there came no reply, there was nobody there. A really stupid anger came over me: what on earth was I up to in this place, chasing around after a party that was none of my business and where I would feel an utter stranger? To hell with all middle-class snobs with their huge empty houses! In any case, it was wiser now to go back into the street and to wait there for another guest to arrive and show me the way. Or even to go home, and that would be all. But how was I now to find my way downstairs again?

My only contact with the world was by means of a wall that I could never see. My eyes and ears seemed to have become useless, and I was reduced now to my sense of feeling. I tried to find the wall opposite and to go back the way I had come. I let go of my support and stretched out my arm toward the left, but met no resistance there and went a few steps on my own. Nothing, only emptiness and darkness. So here I now was, adrift and with nothing to anchor me anywhere, an invisible man in an invisible world, reduced to mere thought. Suddenly, I was scared, with a regression toward all my childhood panics. I realized all at once that I happened to be some thirty feet above the ground, and that one more step might be enough to plunge me headlong down the stairs. I no longer dared go forward or retreat, terrified of my own excessive freedom as a prisoner of sheer void. The floor, beneath my feet, acquired an unbelievable importance as the only fixed point of which I was aware. In my state of absurd frustration and defeat, I wanted to feel assured at least of this foundation beneath me; so I folded my overcoat in four, placed it on the floor, and sat on it, calmly waiting for another guest to come to my rescue.

Fortunately, I was spared having to wait long. There was suddenly light, unexpectedly brilliant, recreating the whole universe around me. I saw that I was seated in the middle of a landing between two floors, and Jean-Jean, a huge boy whose nickname was Hippo, was slowly and heavily climbing the stairs, carrying a bottle in either hand. With him, I entered Michel's apartment, as disturbed as if I had been visited by signs and portents.

I spotted Ginou at once. She had a crowd of boys around her and was beaming with pleasure, her cheeks already flushed with happiness. I took my fill of her vitality, till my eyes and heart were satiated with the bursting health of her complexion, the delicacy of her hair, the dappled colors of her dress, all green and purple. Nearly all the boys had already arrived, but there were still only a few girls at the party. Mina seemed pale from her constant coughing; she threw me a knowing glance that made me ill at ease. Most of the boys were expensively dressed, with custom-made suits of imported English cloth and silk shirts and smart sport shoes; they were already surprisingly like their own parents. Their very natural ease, in such fine clothes, made a deep impression on me, and I felt stiff and solemn in my only good suit. But there was Pinhas too, the leader of the working-class scout outfit! I didn't know why, but I didn't like meeting him here. His suit had certainly seen better days too and suffered worse treatment than my own overcoat: his wasn't even a once-a-year suit. But what was he doing here, so much out of place and so badly dressed? The scout movement, in order to make a show of its interest in ghetto affairs, and also to satisfy some of its own scruples, now wanted to organize a working-class scout group and had asked Pinhas to take charge of it. This whole business, to me, seemed hateful and absurd. Was it at all possible to bring rich men's boys, well dressed, with their pockets full of petty cash, accustomed to spending enough pocket money on a single outing to feed a whole family on a holiday, together with undernourished urchins dressed in rags?

Now the girls who had chosen to come late were arriving too, always two at a time and laden with cakes that they themselves had baked. The boys pretended to be enraptured by the contents of these sumptuous packages and uttered cries of affected admiration. The scout movement didn't encourage flirting and courtship, so that it was not permitted to make gallant remarks about the appearance of the girls, though most of them were exquisite, and exquisitely dressed. The living-room where we happened to be meeting struck me as unusually big, with space enough for a public gathering. I made a round of the other rooms in the apartment for all the doors were open. I counted nine rooms, or perhaps ten, all of them very spacious and some of them larger by themselves than our whole flat. I was unable to understand how one could need so much space. Besides, these rooms were sparsely furnished and I felt, on the whole, that they did not give one an impression of intimacy at all.

Suddenly, all the gossiping stopped and the crowd gathered together according to a preconceived plan and began to sing in chorus. The National Commissioner had just arrived, accompanied by our local Commissioner. Standing to attention in the doorway, they joined in our song. I think the song was about our chief being like the Iroquois who is noble and virtuous, with a piercing gaze, a fleet foot, a lion's heart, the faithfulness of the dove, and the wisdom of the Almighty. I have always, I admit, admired them for this: they could sing perfectly, these scouts, without a false note, but each one of them according to his own voice and in his own tone. The National Commissioner was singing with a convinced expression, his face lowered and thrust forward by his effort, his mouth open, as if he were drinking, whenever he reached the deep and graver notes. He was very thin and tall, his shoulders hunched beneath the weight of his bony build, his heavy and angular head somehow, so it seemed to me, like that of a prehistoric animal. Furtively, I glanced at Ginou, who was singing too and gazing earnestly at our chief.

The song stopped dead, on a single collective cry, so perfectly timed and attuned that it sounded like a single voice. Then, for a second, complete silence, but followed at once, as suddenly as earlier, by an explosion of strange and childish sounds that I have never been able to utter with the rest of them, being always struck dumb by a sense of the absurdity of it all. These tall young men were already adults as far as their social sophistication and cynicism were concerned, but here they all were uttering catcalls and other animal cries like children. This cacophony of theirs even had a special name of its own and was known as "the firemen's cheer," unless I'm mistaken. But the ice was now broken and they abandoned their stance at attention; the tone of the gather-

ing became more familiar and the National Commissioner
left the doorway and entered the room while someone closed
the door behind him. His muscular face relaxed into a kind
of fixed half-smile that beamed kindness ("A pathfinder must
always be good-tempered," as the *Pathfinder's Code* asserts).
Then our local Commissioner began to introduce us all:
"Owl, Deer, Rhinoceros, Gazelle, Hippopotamus, Caribou,
Willow tree, Forget-me-not, Apple. . . ." The National Commissioner, himself known as Gray Wolf, shook our left hands
and, in front of each in turn, raised his right forearm with a
quick gesture. At the same time, he folded his fingers in such
a way that his thumb was against his little finger. This was
all according to the Scout Ritual. In front of me, the local
Commissioner uttered my real given name:

"Alexandre, Alex."

This seemed to elicit utter surprise:

"How come, Alexandre? Not yet initiated?" The National
Commissioner asked me.

No, I had not yet been initiated, had not yet been given
an animal name in the course of any special totem ceremony.

"No," the local Commissioner apologized on my behalf,
"he's a Pale-face," which meant that I was an outsider, not
a scout, "and we have asked him to organize our Hebrew
classes for us."

"Well," the National Commissioner said as if with regret,
"I hope you will soon decide to join us too."

His face had resumed its calculated smile, though he quite
obviously disapproved of the presence of strangers in the
group. A stranger is always a problem, destroying the harmony of the gathering so that the rest no longer feel really
at ease. For instance, I had failed to answer his greeting
properly, with the appropriate gesture of the right arm. I
admit that I had somehow felt like doing it but had refrained, being ashamed.

Once everyone had been introduced, we formed a circle
round the old Commissioner who gave us a speech about the

uniform. He insisted on the necessity of keeping one's unit always smartly dressed: it was a matter of principle and of efficiency, a means of influencing the children as well as their parents. This was greeted with another cheer of applause, the one that they call, if I remember right, "the swallow's cheer," with imitations of that bird's song. After that, there was some discussion, but rather vague as they had all been in agreement with these principles ever since the beginning. Still, Pinhas objected timidly, as I had expected, by making some reference to the difficulties encountered by him in his working-class units, which were certainly a mere matter of money. Gray Wolf then returned to his argument: a smart appearance was even more necessary in the working-class units in order to resist the temptation of sloppiness; something had to be done to combat the influence of the homes there. Yes, one must actually make even greater demands. Of course, the problem of funds existed too, but there again he proposed a very simple solution: the wealthier units would help the poorer ones. At this point, Pinhas mumbled something or other and no longer made any comment. To me, the whole idea seemed quite hateful. I wondered what the attitude of the poorer scouts would be in a common gathering of rich and poor. How odd that these middle-class people failed to understand these matters! Gray Wolf then ended his speech by formulating a twofold wish: that we should all be, for life, perfect scouts, and that the whole universe should, in the long run, be like the scout society, loyal and cheerful. This was followed by a final cheer: "the swallow's cheer," imitating the cries of these birds as well as the rustling of their wings, the sure and swift movement in flight. After that, the more profane part of the party, if I may say so, began.

The girls retired into the kitchen to play at being housewives. At home they all had servants, so they found it entertaining to wait on the boys every once in a while. Besides, they did it with far more grace and efficiency than our

ghetto housewives who spend their lives in the kitchen. My
mother, my sisters, and my cousins were all kept too busy by
immediate necessities, so that they were always in a hurry
and had no skill at any activity that could be considered a
luxury. My mother's cakes, for instance, I mean her *makroud*
and *dibla,* were always hard and not very sweet. Our girl
guides, however, had prepared sandwiches and cakes that
could vie with those of any of the city's pastry-shops! They
followed the recipes of women's magazines and swapped
unpublished recipes for unusual menus that they cooked as
surprises for their gatherings. While the girls were at work in
the kitchen, the Commissioner taught us a new boys' game.
On their travels, commissioners always demonstrate some
new games or songs, which help make their visit a success
and increase their prestige. Legend would then go: "Do you
remember? I mean the game that Gray Wolf taught us way
back in 19. . . ."

I joined the girls in the kitchen and offered to help them,
but they all laughed and chased me away. Mina, in particular, marked her disapproval:

"So you're the serious one again. Well, go away and play
with the others now. . . ."

I protested that I had already played and won.

"We don't want you here," she insisted. "The kitchen is
no place for a boy."

The evening progressed, from game to game, and with
songs between games. We danced a bit, not too much so as
to remain proper, that is to say mainly folk dances and turn-
of-the-century numbers, all considered, I gather, less lascivious
than modern dancing. A lot of wit was wasted all around.
In spite of my willingness and my promises, I found it impossible to feel that I was really a participant in any of the
fun. I was always alien, a critical and bad-tempered stranger,
and this business of remaining a spectator at a party gave
me an unpleasant feeling of watching myself too. Would I
ever become an actor? Certainly not, come what may, with-

out some seriousness and bitterness. Meanwhile, I ate and drank a lot, and animal living, as often in my life, prevented me from losing face. All this lasted until after they all had their fill of food; dazzled by the lights and their own sleepiness, exhausted from so much collective excitement, they then decided, as the rhythm of the party had visibly slowed down, to call it a day. It was indeed late, and we decided on the spot which boy would take each girl home. Mina made me her choice, with somewhat of a show of authority, and appointed me to wait on her and on Ginou, like a knight in ancient times. The National Commissioner then gathered us together in a circle for the last time and we sang one more song in four parts, all about the brotherhood of the scouts. Once the last note had ceased to ring, in the silence that was still charged with emotion, the old scoutmaster uttered one last sentence, in a tone of severity, like a command:

"Pathfinders, forever. . . ."

"Ready!" the others all answered, in a single voice.

But I had not joined in the cry. The Commissioner, after that, became familiar again and shook us all by the hand, the left one, raising each time the right forearm with the fingers stiff in the scouts' grip. As he stopped before me, he smiled rather pointedly, with an air of complicity: I should remember the advice he had given me.

"Pathfinders, forever ready!" But ready for what? They were ready, and that was all. But they knew nothing about the ghetto and all its wretchedness. Or rather, yes, they thought about it once a year when, at Purim, they organized a lunch for all its ragged kids and then took them along to the movies. From this party, they came home later with a full load of funny stories about the voracious appetites and the filth and the brutal manners of the ghetto kids. Besides, it was true that these kids stole from their own parents and took things from the girl guide chiefs who did social work among them, and that they generally spent on that one day, on firecrackers and sweets, all the money that they had

managed to collect, instead of saving it up for useful purchases; true, too, that their parents were careless and that
the clothes given to the kids were in rags only a few weeks
later. All this was true, but there was nothing there to laugh
about. As for the rich kids, their annual *couscous* dinner for
the poor, at Purim, followed by the movie party, allowed
them to ignore the problem that was at the root of the
matter.

On the way home, Ginou was resolutely silent while Mina
unloaded all her criticisms on me:

"You acted again, all evening, like a mortician's assistant!
Can't you be natural? Like all the rest of us?"

I felt like telling her to go jump into the lagoon, but she
had trained me, by now, to suffer in silence. Besides, Ginou
was listening, and I would have been incapable of explaining
to either of them what I really felt. So I protested lamely:
yes, I had had plenty of fun, after my fashion, but I was
quite incapable of showing it any more than I had. Mina, as
intolerant as ever, refused to believe me and insisted that I
was a liar and a clumsy one at that. Mina's father's house
was in an outer suburb and we had to stop, on the way there,
at Ginou's home. Generally, we agreed tacitly to bring Mina
home first and then come back together alone, the two of us.
But Ginou now protested that it was late and that she was
tired. I didn't insist and stayed alone with Mina. The one
who had originally been our go-between now explained to
me that I was not following the right path to win Ginou for
good. Ginou would prefer it if I were less complicated, more
cheerful, in fact a bit more like the rest of our crowd. I had
no desire to argue, so I let Mina chatter away. Finally, my
silence seemed to be catching and, when we reached her
home, we had both been speechless for some time. On her
doorstep, as she shook my hand, Mina gave vent to one of
her extraordinary intuitions:

"Poor old Alexandre! They're all like that, even Ginou!
You're in love with her, and you must be ready to pay the

price!" Slowly, I made my way home to our Passage. To reach our hallway door, I had to chase away the flock of night-prowling cats that fed out of our ashcans. Not in the least scared, they waited a few feet away, their eyes bright in the darkness. Late though it was, I couldn't sleep. One more road that I was closing, that closed itself ahead of me. Had I really wanted very deep in me to become a middle-class bourgeois? I wasn't one and no longer wanted to be one. How could I ever be like Jean-Jean, like the Gazelle, like Michel, like the Commissioner? Polished as pebbles picked up on the seashore, they had no memory. Would I ever be able to forget Pinhas and the others who are like him, merely to save myself? How had I ever been able to believe that I would be able to lead a futile and self-satisfied existence? That evening, perhaps, I caught a glimpse of what their life really is.

But that was also the time when I thought I had discovered in myself the signs of a calling, to teach philosophy. The bohemian manner of Poinsot, my admiration for him, the satisfactions that my successes in philosophy classes assured me, all this made me feel that teaching was an intellectual profession that was not committed to middle-class values and that maintained its independence as far as prejudices and earnings are concerned. It was also about that time that I began to develop the habit of going on long walks, all by myself, in the poorer districts of the city.

10

COMMENCEMENT DAY

JUST ONE MONTH before our final examinations, I learned by the high-school grapevine that my name had been proposed for the philosophy prize, an honor that was awarded every year to the one student in the whole country who had maintained the highest average in his grades. It thus came as a final reward at the end of a successful school career. And now an official and public recognition would consecrate my own past efforts and talents. Well-informed classmates added, however, that the discussion for the choice of the prize-winner was going to be difficult. Though I was heartily seconded by Poinsot, my philosophy instructor, I was opposed by others, particularly our chemistry instructor. These classmates quoted remarks that had been made in the heat of the debate as well as details of the discussions, as though they had actually been present. I pretended to disdain all this idle gossip, but listened all the more intently as I knew how surprisingly reliable were their sources of information. The parents of many of these boys often invited our instructors as guests to their homes, and these teachers, flattered at finding themselves in the homes of the wealthier middle class, often confided details of school administration to their hosts. Nor were they to be blamed, their sole motive was to assume an appearance of power.

I happened to hate our chemistry instructor, and the science that he taught us suffered as a consequence. Foolishly, I felt that he gave tuition to too many private pupils and had thus transformed our noble profession, already his and some day to be mine, into a trade. This indignation of mine was inspired by a prejudice that I shared with the middle classes. Why shouldn't a teacher make the most of his profession, just like a doctor or a lawyer? But I had reasons of my own, better ones, in fact the only ones: I despised money-makers, one and all. My history instructor, on the other hand, was not prepared to forgive my political aggressiveness. The prize that was about to be awarded required an exemplary conduct. But I had shouted so often, in front of the whole class, my admiration for Robespierre and my respect for Saint-Just, or my indignation against the injustices of the nobility and the treason of the higher clergy, that I could no longer claim to have behaved with decorum.

In the end, my supporters won the day and, one afternoon, as we sat in class listening to a lecture on astronomy, our little supervisor, Dubois, came in, his red nose stuck out ahead of him and his eyes glistening with tears of timidity. He then handed our instructor my summons to the commencement ceremony where the prizes would be announced, and ran off. Our mathematics instructor, a heavy Alsatian who constantly reminded us of his Germanic background, as opposed to the softness of Africa, and who therefore affected a Prussian crew-cut and a brutal manner, now read the message aloud, carefully pronouncing each word. In the silence that had come over the expectant class, my glory was becoming a reality under the very eyes of my classmates as they all stared at me. I lowered my own gaze, overcome by pride, in spite of my desire to appear detached. I could no longer feel the existence of my own body. I seemed to be only the hard beating of my own heart as it struck like a bell in the air. Again, I began to feel the burning heat in my cheeks, and I was called back to reality when Sitboun, who sat next to me, remarked:

"Say, you swine. . . ."

This consecration of my glory made all my desires crystallize. I would make a career of philosophy, a daily business of it. My present prominence and the envious admiration of my classmates would then be permanent. Before the results of our written examinations and especially of the one in philosophy had been announced, my classmates had stared at me; when my name was announced again and again, they shrugged their shoulders and returned to their own business of scrambling for the next best places after me.

The ceremony was to take place the next day, a Thursday, at five o'clock. I still had to announce my triumph to Monsieur Bismuth before going to the assembly hall. I went all the way to the drugstore with my shoulders proudly thrown back and, as on the day of my *bar mitzvah,* all the way back home from the synagogue, people in the street turned around to stare at me as they had on that previous occasion too, when I went by in my new blue suit, followed by my ushers. Now I could hear their voices and I was anxious to see the people stare at me as before. I felt lightfooted as an angel and my head seemed to be up among the little white clouds in the sky that is always blue when I have triumphed. For the first time, I would see Monsieur Bismuth without feeling ill at ease. Now that I had managed to obtain recognition as the best pupil in the school system of my whole country, I had certainly proved myself worthy of the opportunity that had been granted me. I had justified all the hopes that had been vested in me by the Alliance Israélite Universelle, by the community and by Monsieur Bismuth. I had never admitted to anyone the nature of my relationship with Monsieur Bismuth, not even to Bissor, who was also the beneficiary of a grant. It had all remained a secret, reassuring to me but also humiliating. When I told Ginou that I would one day be a physician, my hopes were always firmly founded on this financial security. But all my dearest hopes were also intermingled with a secret shame. My great success now left me the same delicious taste as suddenly finding myself free of a bothersome debt.

Monsieur Bismuth's pharmacists always treated me with a condescending manner. They identified themselves with the store, and I was somehow sure that they said to themselves: "There's the kid whose studies *we* pay for. . . ." Whenever I went to the store, I simply put in an appearance and waited until someone decided to attend to me. Generally, they served several customers before announcing me. But I was in a hurry, that day, and swollen too with legitimate pride as I had to be on time for the announcements of the prizes. So I refrained from waiting for one of the pharmacists to be kind enough to attend to me; instead, I interrupted one at his work, told him my business was urgent and asked him to announce me without further delay. Miraculous though it might seem, he smiled and complied, and Monsieur Bismuth immediately sent back a reply to the effect that he would see me at once. So I sat down beside some waiting customers. I pitied these anxious, resigned, and suffering people from the bottom of my heart, for it was brimful with the noble and generous feelings that characterize men who are happy. There was much coming and going, there was a screeching sound whenever the glass panel of a display case was slid open, and the reflections of the neon lights varied constantly as the mirrors and glass panes and shining metal fixtures moved. Customers whispered and the cash register noisily made us aware of its presence; it was indeed an essential fixture, enthroned there regally and constantly working beneath the self-satisfied fingers of the owner's niece. One touch, two touches, three, then a bell rang and the cash drawer opened. A veritable shower of money seemed to pour. The drugstore owner was really making a lot of money, and that was why the general con sensus considered him a success. I smiled as I thought of my own secret ambition: no, I was too noble in my own eyes too disinterested for a profession like this. I was made to live and to promote ideas (which was a slogan I had learned in my philosophy class), to experience the true and the beautiful. Official recognition of this had only just been granted to me. No, I would never allow myself to become a mere cash register. How vulgar! Monsieur Bismuth, former President of the Chamber of Commerce. How odd that some people take pride in having devoted their whole life to money-making!

But time was going by, the appointed hour for the ceremony was approaching, and I had still not been summoned to the office of my benefactor. I asked the pharmacist whether Monsieur Bismuth might not have forgotten that I was waiting. And I suggested that he might make the trip along the corridor to the office again, but he pretended not to understand me and made a vague effort to reassure me.

A minute later, he went back through the little door, apparently in order to fetch something from the storeroom. I hoped my benefactor would be too busy and would now ask me to come back another day. Wearily, however, the pharmacist returned to tell me that my benefactor was going to see me, that he even wanted to see me and had important matters to discuss with me. This was an untimely development; it had been a foolish idea of mine to come on this visit just before the scheduled ceremony. But I would never have dared disturb the pharmacist and my benefactor a third time; so, to overcome my impatience, I began to think of the ceremony and of how, in a short while, I would answer the principal of our high school and perhaps even our Director of Public Education. They would both congratulate me in public, that was certain. But was I expected to reply to them and to express my thanks? Yes, I would have to do it,

I would utter a few words before the assembled crowd of
parents and representatives of the press. I supposed there
would be journalists present, so I made up a nice emphatic-
sounding statement that would be impressive and subtle, full
of various meanings, promising that this prize, a landmark
in my life, would also mark the end of the first stage in my
pursuit along the road that leads to wisdom. The whole
crowded hall would then applaud while I went up to collect
my prize on the platform, where all the official personalities
sat. The principal and the Director of Public Education
would shake my hand, but I would be in no hurry, no longer
paralyzed by my own timidity, since all of this was really
owed me. So I tried to formulate my brief reply and to give
it the proper rhythm, but my anxiety, as time went by and
the customers of the store constantly came and went, prevented me from remaining among the rosy-colored clouds
of my imagined triumph. Finally I came to a heroic decision
and approached the pharmacist as he was gluing a label
onto a bottle; I asked him to express my apologies to Monsieur Bismuth because I had to leave at once, but that I
would be able to come back later in the evening, around
six o'clock, or the following morning at eleven. He stared at
me, obviously surprised by my nervousness and annoyed at
having been disturbed so frequently as well as by my apparently independent attitude toward his boss. I mumbled that
I had very important business, was in a great hurry to be
present for the awarding of prizes, for the honor prize; I
absolutely had to be there and it was now already five minutes past five. He hadn't answered me yet when we heard
Monsieur Bismuth's clubfoot at the end of the long passage
that led to his den. The pharmacist then opened the little
door ahead of me and I saw the druggist coming slowly
toward us, his hip swerving out of joint at each step. He
saw me too, waved to me to come along, and went back to
his chair.

It was the last time that I ever went along the tunnel with

its walls lined with boxes and bottles from floor to ceiling. With a gesture of his hand Monsieur Bismuth invited me to be seated. It was also the only occasion, I think, when he did not put on a show for me and continue, for a while, to write. As usual, he was the first to speak and, as long as he still spoke, I said nothing; still, he spoke simply and clearly. If his attitude was at all calculated, then it was rather one of indifference. In a carefree manner that seemed to me to be affected, he announced that I was no longer to expect any help from him. It had become impossible for him to continue to bear the expenses of my studies, especially those for higher education. As for me, I was stunned by this decision that allowed no appeal, contradicting as it did all my dreams and everything that had ever seemed certain to me. It was as if I felt a chill, while he continued to speak with poise, in studied tones. Business, he said, was bad, much worse than it had been, and he was the father of two little girls and had to think of their future too. Behind him, hanging on the wall, there was his portrait, the same one I had seen seven years earlier, when I had come for the first time to see him and had left him with the feeling that the whole world lay open ahead of me and that I only needed to deserve it. How ridiculously self-complacent one can be! Fancy hanging one's own picture on one's wall! As soon as one looks at all older, everyone notices it. In the past seven years, Monsieur Bismuth had indeed aged a lot. He now spoke, still giving me advice, as I recall, directives for the future. He seemed to forget that our only link was that of financial assistance and that, once he ceased to give me any, we automatically became strangers again. Out of sheer habit, he continued to give me instructions:

"You will study pharmacy all the same. You can do some tutoring and live in one of the dormitories of the Cité Universitaire in Paris. Come back and see me before you leave town and I'll give you a letter of introduction to the director of the Spanish House there. He's a good friend of mine."

But my future was no longer any of Monsieur Bismuth's business, and this alone was a good enough reason for me to dare at last to express to him an objection.

"I was planning to study philosophy," I said.

His gesture expressed only contempt. "To become a teacher? A civil servant? You'll never earn a living that way."

He had overridden my argument, just as he had before when he decided that I must study pharmacy instead of medicine.

"No, go ahead now and study pharmacy, or medicine, if you prefer the latter."

Now that he was no longer paying for my studies, two extra years didn't upset him at all. He offered me his hand, without rising from his chair.

"If you ever need any advice, or a recommendation, don't hesitate to come along to the store."

So I went down the passage again, and remembered only then that I had forgotten to explain to him the purpose of my visit, the Prize! But I was surely very late as it was, so I hurried along the bridgelike passage that led from the office to the store. Why should I go back and tell him now? How could it interest him at all? It no longer concerned anybody but me. My crowning success thus coincided with my achieving responsibility for my own decisions. He was leaving me to my own devices! Once my surprise was over, I tried to feel anger or indignation. I kept repeating to myself: "He's giving me up, the skunk!" But I could feel no real anger, only a sensation of being at last free from my state of financial dependence, which, for the past seven years, had been like slavery. I tried to walk fast through the crowded streets of the central food markets: a huge conglomeration of trucks, horse-drawn carriages, wooden boxes, mountains of vegetables, bright fruit of all colors, thrown there on the ground, among all the rotting refuse. But no, his behavior was almost what I should have expected. I protested against everything that I saw all around me, against my parents, these tradesmen, this city that is torn apart in separate communities that hate each other, against all their ways of thinking. I wanted to study philosophy, perhaps a strange idea in the eyes of all these people, but I refused to be a money-earner, and even this was being refused me. Well, I would study all the same, and I found again, deep within myself, some violent emotion to confirm me in this decision. They would all see whether, yes or no, I would manage to study what I wanted, not what Monsieur Bismuth wanted! I would indeed study philosophy, instead of pharmacy or medicine. It never even occurred to me that any difficulties might arise in my path. I felt too much vigor in me, too much momentum carrying me ahead.

Today, without any useless pride, I can really admit that I have sometimes regretted not having studied medicine. I chose, instead, this terrifying and exhausting search for one's real identity that philosophy implies, and also the ceaseless attempt to master the universe that is the writer's fate. But are these preferable, I mean this proud choice, the constant anxiety, the look in one's eyes that is always restless, are these better than stability, security, no matter how mediocre? I might even have forgotten philosophy and remembered it only as a boyhood love, nostalgic and yet ridiculous. As a physician, however, I would have preserved the somewhat simple complacency and intellectual security and pride of one of those petty-bourgeois representatives of culture. On that day, however, when Monsieur Bismuth informed me that he was withdrawing his financial support, I saw it as but one more obstacle to surmount. I no longer had anybody on whom I could rely. This was one more rope that had once guaranteed my security and that had now broken and failed me. I was not afraid, I only felt that it would mean all the more glory if I made a success of my life, battling my way ahead by the sheer strength of my own wrists. I contemplated myself with some emotion and self-complacency: Alexandre Benillouche, professor of philosophy! To me, it seemed prodigious, so full of promise. For this wonderful goal remained, after all, only one of many stages on my way. As a physician, I had no chance of fame; nor could I have remained content with a profession that clearly imposed on me such intolerable limitations. As a philosopher and writer, I would be able to taste every experience and seize at every kind of glory. At that time, I never stopped to count the cost, in blood and sweat, of these experiences, nor had it yet occurred to me that, without assistance, without advice, above all spending my gifts profusely, I might collapse out of sheer exhaustion.

I reached the Parents' Association Hall in a sweat, and the crowd was already streaming out of it as I ran up the four steps to the entrance. In the middle of the hall, the long table, still littered with glasses and bottles, had been abandoned. The celebration was over and only a few small groups, probably parents of those who had won prizes, were still gossiping, with all sorts of polite intonations in their voices and gestures of their hands, of their whole plump little bodies that seemed to be brimful of foolish happiness and pride. Nobody has ever come along with me, I said to myself, but I've always managed to come out ahead of their children. Now, I hesitated in the doorway, not knowing a soul in the hall. By failing to appear on time, I had missed celebrity and now stood there in an undeserved and insuperable incognito, with nobody to recognize me. Still, I couldn't call out to them: "Hi, there! I'm the honors prize-winner, the boy whose name you heard called out, with all his credits, a little while ago!" In a corner, I spotted our school principal, his hair carefully trimmed in a crew-cut, but his pants too short as always, surrounded by parents who were all putting on an act for him. Theirs were indeed the grace and the lightness of a dancing bear. Devoid of any hope, I circled this fort that was being besieged, hoping to catch his eye, though effectively barred by the backs of the crowd. At long last, he caught sight of me and beckoned me to come closer:

"Ah, there's Benillouche, our honors prize-winner!"

A wave of happiness came over me as all these people whom I despised now turned to stare at me, perhaps with indifference or even jealousy. The principal was talking to a little man I had failed to notice because he was concealed by the crowd. His glasses framed in black, like those of a comic actor, were the only element of self-affirmation in his otherwise sickly body, modest appearance and characterless clothes.

"Come, come here, Benillouche," insisted the principal.

He then introduced me to the little man, who—none other than the Chief of Public Education for Tunisia—held out his hand and smiled in a friendly manner. I felt very guilty about being late and mumbled that I had been prevented from coming earlier, which seemed to interest nobody at all.

"What are your plans for the coming school year?" the Chief asked me politely.

"I want to study philosophy," I answered with assurance.

By affirming it now in public, I gave myself the impression that all discussion of the matter, within myself, was now closed. My own answer did me good and reassured me.

"That's perfect," he replied. "We need teachers. Study hard and we can give you a job."

His promise was vague and concerned a very distant future, but still justified my decision. It made me feel joyously confident. But the attention of the principal and the Chief of Education was again demanded by the aggressive parents circling around them. I was cast out of the group by a movement like that of an amoeba ejecting a foreign body.

11

THE CHOICE

In the decision that I reached by myself at the time I graduated from high school, two men, probably played a decisive part. Marrou, who taught me French in my last year there, and Poinsot, who taught me philosophy, both acted as midwives in helping me to give birth to the man I was destined, for better or for worse, to become.

In Marrou, himself a Berber by birth and family background, though a Christian as a consequence of his upbringing, I thought I had discovered a symbol of my salvation. He proved that it was really possible to come into the world poor and an African and yet become a man of culture, well dressed, and smoking expensive cigarettes. I always admired his long and carefully manicured fingers, stained yellow at the tips, between the index and the middle finger, from the Turkish tobacco that perfumed his classroom. He had published two slim volumes of verse of a beauty that, to me, seemed quite disconcerting; this alone showed me that it is possible to achieve a true mastery of a language that is not one's mother tongue. Marrou, however, was not very pop-

ular. Our other teachers made no bones about proclaiming
their opinions on his vanity and his pretentiousness. As for
my classmates, they made fun of his elegant way of dressing
and rather theatrical manner, his majestic gait as he walked
with slow movements but a springy step, which they all suspected, perhaps quite rightly, of being affected. It was
whispered that he could be violent and brutal, that he had
been divorced, and that his wife, a Frenchwoman, had no
longer been able to bear his violent rages. It was even insinu-
ated that he had struck her, and they then pretended to
blame her for having had the strange idea of marrying outside her race. That was where all mixed marriages are
bound to lead!

Perhaps this very hostility aroused in me a greater sympathy for my French instructor. I could sense all the conflicts
within him and his struggle to achieve calm and become an
example of civilization. His continual play was but a sign
of how he constantly repressed his passions. I felt a violent
urge to communicate with him, transgressing all those conventional distances that exist between an instructor and his
pupil, and to ask for his help in solving my own similar
problems, even to offer him, in all simplicity, my assistance.
But he was too preoccupied with himself and did not immediately understand me.

To please him and attract his attention, I saw to it that
all my compositions were well prepared, properly thought
out, and carefully written. As he was a poet and an artist,
I would do my best to surprise him. Unfortunately, I was
never able to get into the front row among the best students
in his class. Because he himself was both impulsive and passionate, Marrou could accept only the kind of art that is
perfectly controlled. He used to declare with passion, allowing no contradiction, that there can be no such thing as an
art that is not classical, and he even managed to force us to
share his contempt for all Romantic makeshifts. But my own
compositions, though they may well have been richer in

content than most written by his class, were always defeated, in the matter of literary form, by the compositions handed in by a young Frenchman who had a natural felicity of expression and easy style. This made me feel angrily that Marrou's obsession with form prevented him from discovering my talent, and I became even more attentive and eager, always at his elbow. On one or two occasions, when I thought that I had managed to attract his attention and that communication between us had been established, my heart beat faster out of sheer joy. I awaited a friendly word, only a veiled expression of comradeship, a mere allusion. I would have comprehended all, divined everything. But his heavy-lidded eyes, that expressed only contempt and sadness, never rested anywhere for very long. When one day, as I have already told, Marrou asked us which line of the poet Racine in the celebrated passage from his tragedy *Andromaque* was most typical of his art and I gave him at once the right answer, I felt sure that our minds were about to meet. He must then have understood, at last, that I was the only boy in the class to follow his thought and that I was not a student like the rest of them. He was desperately trying to reveal to us the beauty of texts that he admired because he too was a poet. Had I not done my best to prove to him that I knew he was no ordinary teacher and that I did not view our work in common as mere classroom drudgery? But, here again, his silence and his gaze were perhaps more pointedly impersonal, and he seemed to refuse to go beyond this.

What was developing within me into affection then turned to spite, so that I unconsciously began to resort to aggressiveness. My compositions, which had always been very serious when the topic was one that pleased me, now became exaggeratedly bad when I had to make an effort. Why should I take any pains for this man who remained blind? I often gave vent to such obvious ill-humor that he was at last forced to express his reproaches openly. This only egged me on and I criticized him in front of the whole class, though with a sarcasm that was too heavy and forced. I knew his tastes and began to defend all that he disliked, systematically making out a case for content against form, a generous abundance of the whole as opposed to the dull and pompous artifice of the desiccated classics. He had experienced, until then, only the discouraging indifference of my classmates, but our little duels of words exasperated us both, without bringing us any nearer each other. I was still looking for a chance for a showdown, and I found it one morning, when I least expected it.

He admired the prose of Pascal very much and, in spite of our curriculum and the fact that little time was left before our baccalaureate exams and that my classmates were all impatient and concerned only with these tests, he seemed to us to be wasting valuable time as he tried vainly to communicate to us a taste for the anguish that is contained in Pascal's thought. That day, he was in a bad mood; we were not responding, our minds all preoccupied with a history composition for the following hour. In bitter tones, holding his head high, he expressed his contempt for us and reproached us with being morons. The whole class was hurt and pretended, for a while, to be interested in the tragic situation of a man who is situated exactly between the two infinites. To me, Marrou's insults seemed particularly pointed. If he was incapable of recognizing his true disciples, then he had no reason to complain. So I chose the moment when he thought he had his class in hand to attack him again. Swinging backward and forward in my seat so that the steel framework strained and grated, I very ostentatiously sighed with boredom and stared at the ceiling, pretending to sympathize with all his misery. My mimicry was so obvious and so full of histrionics that it pierced his customary indifference to all such behavior. He stopped talking. One of his habits was to play around with a piece of chalk, throwing it up in the air gently and catching it again with a regular and unhurried motion. He had managed to bring the rhythm of

this play into harmony with his own gait as he walked, so
that he moved effortlessly, the one rhythm helping the other.
Now, he stopped dead, but his hand continued its play.

"What's going on there?"

I expressed in my answer as much irony and indifference
as I could:

"Nothing," I said. "But it's impossible for me to scare up
any interest in all this nonsense."

This time, however, Marrou's piece of chalk fell and remained motionless in his hand. He stared at me, then turned
without a word toward the blackboard. His arm rose slowly
to write, but hesitated before he turned toward us again.
The whole class was waiting, utterly silent, as it watched his
face for any sign that my aggression had hit home. His prestige was at stake. Now, either exemplary punishment had to
be meted out to me, or one of those particularly bitter sar-
casms of his that would crush me and all my pride and
re-establish his own superiority in the face of my impertinence. Marrou, by the way, was a master at this kind of
crack. But I was not afraid as I had been too anxious for a
showdown to be unwilling now to pay the price. Still, I
trembled for the affection that I still felt for him. Good God,
if he would only understand, at last! He stared at me, his
face expressionless, as he dryly ordered:

"You will see me after class!"

Such solemn meetings were generally followed by catastrophe and Marrou had perhaps convinced the rest of the
class that his reaction in my case would be terrible in its
consequences. But I was sure that, this time, he had understood me. I would not have been able to say why, but I was
quite sure of it. So I waited till the end of the class, my face
buried in my notebook, pretending to be taking notes though
I was quite unable to write a word. I was disturbed and
ashamed, as though I had made an emotional declaration of
friendship.

From then on, he often spoke at length with me, gave me

advice that made me really very happy, and confided in me
his own difficulties. He was proud and ambitious, and he
lived, among the instructors and pupils, in utter solitude. In
the eyes of his colleagues, it was an unpardonable scandal
for this alien to handle the French language better than
many native sons. Their sarcastic remarks and defamations,
their repeated hostility, all these made it quite clear to him
though he was clumsy enough to encourage them with his
own sarcastic replies and his pompous attitude. As I listened
to his difficulties, I found some consolation for my own. One
day, I had enough courage to show him a short story I had
written. He gave it back to me the next morning and expressed a severe criticism:

"Only the structure is acceptable. As for the style, it should
be entirely rewritten."

The first part of his criticism gave me pleasure. Well, I
would work at the form, I would rewrite my story sentence
by sentence, a word at a time. My admiration for Marrou
gave me some reassurance concerning my own future. He
had made a go of it, I felt, and I was his double.

It was only later, too late, that I understood that he had
never managed to solve his own problems and that mine
would probably break me too. For the time being, however,
I was no longer entirely alone, since others seemed to live
in the same kind of loneliness.

Marrou helped me understand what kind of an individual
I am and gave me reason to hope, but Poinsot taught me
self-confidence and the joys of knowledge. He was my philosophy instructor, as I have already said, and taught me how
to think. I wanted him, besides, to be my confessor and my
ideal as a human being. Nearly every day I used to wait for
him at the gate of the lycée and, as I walked him all the
way to his home on the hill to the east, beyond the city
limits, I would express all my ideas and hesitations and test
on him the effect of the impulsive decisions I had taken.
Only in his presence did I drop my uncompromisingly dog-

matic attitudes, for I knew that he was extremely well inten-
tioned. Whenever I called on Marrou, I listened to him
because he spoke both of himself and of me. With Poinsot,
however, I generally did more of the talking, though he was
my instructor. And he would listen to me, smoking his pipe
and smiling. Through his teeth, stained yellow from tobacco,
that tightly gripped the stem of his pipe, he would mumble:
"Yes, of course, of course, I guess that's reasonable. . . ."

I do not know how he managed to reconcile this unlimited
approval with his merciless critical intelligence that was unbelievably sure in its judgments. Because he viewed the world
with an open mind, everything seemed clear and translucent
to him. Mysteries, complexes, and difficulties all resolved
themselves, in his presence, into clear notions that one could
grasp and analyze with wondrous facility. That is how I
learned to see conventions, habits, and prejudices clearly, so
that I was no longer scared of them. After his last morning
class, when he was weary of answering the questions of the
students, he would beckon me with his hand. The rest of the
class had finally admitted that this was my privilege. We
would leave the school building together, walking slowly in
the sun as he smoked and I thought aloud, reporting to him
all the latest news of my intellectual progress. I was straight-
ening out everything between myself and my surroundings.
Certainly, one's social duty should also imply some personal
freedom, otherwise it becomes mere tyranny devoid of any
ethical value; naturally, tradition must be examined anew
and either rejected or accepted, and a revival of mysticism
implies, of course, the bankruptcy of philosophical specula-
tion in a society that has succumbed to sickness. I was proud
to discover that I was in agreement with all the great thinkers
he quoted to me as references in order to supply my stammering discoveries with the right foundations. He had read
everything, thought of everything, understood everything,
and I could come to him for assistance in any field of human
knowledge. He knew more about Judaism, for instance, than

any Jewish scholar, and about Islam than any student of
Mohammedanism. All national, religious, and colonial bar-
riers collapsed before him when he smiled with benevolence
and irony. In his presence, I forgot to defend bitterly all
the obviously lost causes and to praise all that clearly deserved no praise. Yes, he helped me place things in their
right context, because it had never occurred to him to be
unjust. I thus felt strong, with the strength that comes of a
mind that is serene, as I walked beside him. And when I
was weary, scared, and ready to let myself be submerged,
I would leave our Passage, go through the suburban neighborhood, and climb the eastern hill that was covered with
flowers all the year round. There I would find him in his
study, the window open on the garden, surrounded by his
books and his furniture made of light-colored wood, with
his numerous pipes beside him, his two cats and his pet
chameleon. Flowers and green ferns grew right up to the sill
of the open French door, and sunlight dappled the tiles on
the floor. He would come toward me, barefooted in his
Moroccan slippers, small and almost lost in his ink-stained
bathrobe, his hair badly combed, often unshaven. I compared
his careless appearance to the perfect elegance of Marrou
and I saw that Poinsot needed nothing to reassure him, that
he knew exactly where he stood. In such moments, I felt
surprise at having managed to leave behind me, down at the
bottom of the hill, the narrow street where I lived, the dark
and steep staircases, the whole sordid city.

Marrou knew Poinsot well and often spoke to me of him.
He envied Poinsot's ability to live at ease under any sky, to
hate'nothing and to bear everything with ease. As soon as
his first volume of verse had been greeted with some praise
by Paris critics, Marrou had decided to go and live in the
capital. But there, he was soon homesick for the Mediterranean and he returned to Tunis six months later. He understood that his own instability and Poinsot's total ease were
the ineradicable marks of two entirely different situations,

each one complete in itself. Poinsot's mere presence had a liberating effect on me, while Marrou made no attempt to help me. On the contrary, he openly doubted the outcome of his own situation and cultivated in me an anxiety akin to his own.

At that time I had no clear notion of what these two men actually meant to me. Once in a while, a sign, a mere comparison, gave me a foreboding of it. I had long felt, for instance, a strange desire to bring Poinsot home to meet my family. Unconsciously, I wanted to make him face the facts of my life, to make him see and feel my study table in the midst of all the furnishings of our home, my few books, my couple of shelves of plain wood, roughly carpentered and painted, held to the wall by heavy iron hooks placed in badly fixed brackets.

I had not been able to see him, one day, at noon; so I waited to join him after the late afternoon classes. The afternoon had been surly, and the sky was like a blanket, weighing heavily on the damp air. When he saw me turn up, as always, little Poinsot beckoned gently. He was very absent-minded and always allowed me to decide on our itinerary, following me without making a remark on the way I chose to go. On an impulse, I decided this time to take a short cut, going by our Passage, though I still had no idea how I would be able to prevail on him to enter our home. We had barely left the middle-class downtown area when it began to rain, a sudden shower with drops as big as peanuts. The crowds scattered like a flock of sparrows; in an instant, the street was deserted. I grabbed Poinsot by the sleeve and forced him to hurry.

"We're not very far from my home," I shouted to him in the hurried tattoo of the rain splashing on the ground. "If you'd like, we can find shelter there. . . ."

So I dragged him home. It would have been wiser to have waited in a doorway until the shower was over, an autumn shower that was very heavy but brief. Still, I had

the opportunity now, and we got home quite breathless and
drenched by the time we reached our staircase. After the
odor of warm earth in the rain, we suddenly encountered
the usual stench of cat excrement on our stairs. Habit had
made me ignore this detail that I was now sharply aware of
again. Still, I was glad to find none of my brothers or sisters
at home, all, it appeared, had been delayed by the rain.
When I heard my mother busying herself in the kitchen, I
decided to introduce her to Poinsot. I felt that I must reveal
to him this other side of my life. I was not only his disciple
in philosophy, a brilliant student, I was also the son of this
woman. While he cast an absent-minded glance at my book-
shelves, I went to fetch my mother. She smoothed her henna-
reddened hair with the palms of her hands, adjusted her
apron, and followed me.

I said to Poinsot:

"This is my mother."

And to my mother, who could understand no French, I
said in our dialect:

"He's one of my teachers, the most intelligent among them
all."

Poinsot held out a kindly hand and said:

"How do you do, madame."

Mother was not accustomed to shaking hands and caught
hold of Poinsot's fingers, much as one grasps a kitchen utensil.

But she had understood his greeting and replied in the
same words:

"How do you do?"

They were both smiling, my mother with curiosity, Poinsot
with embarrassment. As the silence that ensued seemed in-
finite to me because there was no hope of its being filled
from either side, I hastened to throw a bridge across it.

"You see," I said to Poinsot, looking toward my mother
so as to keep her interested, through my gestures, in what I
was saying, "She's still young, isn't she? But she has already
had eight children."

"Yes, it's rather surprising," Poinsot replied as he looked her over.

In dialect, I added hastily, for my mother's benefit:

"Monsieur Poinsot thinks you look very young."

At least this flattered her vanity. She gave him a look of gratitude and answered:

"He looks like a nice man, your teacher."

I translated this comment at once for Poinsot. After that, they both remained silent and waited again. I was trying to find some other verbal link between them when I suddenly felt with real anguish how impossible any communication would be. It was like an access of vertigo. When I find myself at the foot of a wall and look up at the top and see it rising above me endlessly toward the sky, I feel this same vertigo, as if the sky had suddenly become an abyss. The two parts of my being spoke two different languages and would never understand each other.

Thus, I allowed the conversation to die. My mother retired into her kitchen, accustomed to being excluded.

Poinsot calmly filled his pipe and waited for the end of the storm, without asking me any questions about my nervousness and my sudden silence. It had always been his habit to wait for me to reveal my preoccupations to him. But an explanation, this time, was beyond me. I felt as if walled in. Besides, he would interpret my explanations as useless histrionics, believing that the obstacle could be overcome if one found out first what the whole problem really was. But would I ever be strong enough to survive this split in my being? I was beginning to understand that, however much I might want to become a second Poinsot, the chances were stronger that I would become but another Marrou. Faced with the impossible problem of joining the two parts of myself, I made up my mind to choose one of them. Between the East and the West, between African superstitions and philosophy, between our dialect and the French language, I now had to choose. And it was Poinsot whom I chose passionately, with all the strength of my being. One day, as I entered a café, I suddenly saw myself in a mirror and was terribly scared. I was both myself and a stranger. The mirror ahead of me covered the whole wall, so completely that I could see no frame. Each day, I thus became more alien to myself. I had to stop watching myself, I had to step out of this mirror.

Toward the end of my high-school years, I began to know what I did not want to become and, if only in a confused manner, what I wanted. I did not want to be Alexandre Mordekhai Benillouche, I wanted to escape from myself and go out toward the others. I was not going to remain a Jew, an Oriental, a pauper; I belonged neither to my family nor to my religious community; I was a new being, utterly transparent, ready to be completely remade into a philosophy instructor. It had to be done, and I would reconstruct the whole universe, with simple and clear elements, like all the philosophers who were my masters, and as Poinsot too had done.

It would be a tough struggle, though I felt that no struggle could really be too tough for me. I exaggerated the difficulties that lay ahead of me, but this was only to enhance my own heroic attitude. I organized my life accordingly, working out several basic plans, then developing the individual details, as do all great builders. In this manner, my first efforts were soon crowned with success. I filed an application for a job as supervisor of studies in a high-school dormitory for resident students. Our principal remembered his promise and, within a week, I received my appointment. I then wrote a letter to the Head of the Philosophy Department in Algiers, which was the nearest university, asking him in all simplicity for some assistance. Though a professor on a university faculty was, in my eyes, a very important person indeed, he wrote me a reply that was full of encouragement; he even promised to look over my essays.

My life as a poor student was divided between my work

as a supervisor, monotonous and bothersome, and my own
studies that were difficult enough, for lack of any advice
other than this irregular checking of my philosophical compositions. My time was broken up, even my thoughts interrupted, by my constantly having to watch what was going
on in passages and staircases, by my having to be present
whenever the students moved from one class to the next,
and by my having to attend to endless administrative details.
Every hour on the hour, as soon as the bell rang, I had to
put on my jacket and rush out of my room. Once the rhythm
of my studies had thus been interrupted, it was difficult for
me to return to the concentration and the flow of thought
that are necessary for any productive work. I made up for
all this, however, by making increasingly heavy demands on
myself and by becoming even more austere. I no longer
allowed myself any outings, stopped going to the movies,
and added several more hours to my schedule of studies so
as to make up in quantity what I had lost in quality of concentration. The study plan that I worked out for myself was
calculated on the basis of periods of fifteen minutes, not only
from day to day but for several months ahead, and I then
forced my body and my mind to comply with this schedule
that fitted me like a tight corset. I got up at dawn, my eyes
still smarting from sleeplessness, and I went to bed again in
the evening only when I began to fall asleep over a difficult
textbook. But all this made me somehow aware of my own
superiority.

There can be no question about it, I had really taken
myself in hand, achieved financial independence and managed to study a subject that I had picked out for myself. In
the high school where I had to live, everything was old and
familiar to me. I was entitled to a room that I had to share
with a colleague, and to the same food as the pupils who
boarded there. Everyone complained of this diet that was
heavy and monotonous. Though I never dared say it, I was
delighted with the sheer size of our portions. All these dried

vegetables and spaghetti and potatoes were very much like the food I was used to at home. But here, every meal included meat without fail, so that this particular monotony of our diet was a blessing to me. Whenever the students grumbled and my colleagues wisecracked about our food, I once more measured the distance that still separated me from them; what they despised gave me pleasure. My new bed also gave me as much joy as our diet, and I slept at home only when it was unavoidable, and chiefly because of the bedbugs. On the rare occasions when I did use my divan-bed, the starved bugs ravenously attacked me. I would wake up, after the first heavy sleep, with my neck itching like mad and my hands covered with heavy red swellings. No matter how heavy my eyes, I could not fall asleep again. My shoulders, armpits, ankles, and hands itched unbearably and I scratched myself desperately and had to bathe the irritated skin with vinegar. My battle against these dreadful insects would continue all night, while the room reeked with their sickly odor. Often a single massacre was not enough, and I would be attacked again and again. Sometimes, in the dark, I thought I could feel their horrible little legs crawling over my body. At once I would turn on the light and suddenly throw off the blankets and strip myself naked, only to find it had been a false alarm. But I would go ahead and make a new inspection of all my bedding and my clothing. In the middle of the night, with silence all around me and the electric light making my tired eyes smart, I worked furiously and methodically in an attempt to exterminate my enemy. At long last, I had to give it up and decided to spend all my nights in the high school dormitory, even when I had a twenty-four hour pass. My colleagues were surprised at this, for in their eyes a night away from the dormitory was a great relief.

Actually, there was another reason that made it unpleasant for me to stay at home. The children there didn't have enough to eat and were growing up all bones, with big heads and long knotty legs. My little cousins, however, unlike my brothers and sisters, were all soft and flabby, rather too fat, with the unhealthy fat one gets from eating too many starches. They seemed to suffer from a dyspeptic appetite and they constantly asked for food. Nothing was more unbearable for me than the exasperated voice of my widowed aunt grumbling all day long after her children:

"May the Red Death carry you off! You're eating too much! I've nothing left to give you!"

All this made me feel ashamed of the luxurious diet I enjoyed at school, and I tried to ignore the guilt-feelings I felt. Most of my joys were indeed spoiled for me in this manner, though I had learned to drive out of my mind all disquieting thoughts. At least, I had a room where I could live protected from all this, so I moved all my belongings and my books there. For a while I even thought I would be able to build myself, within the sphere of philosophy, a sort of private garden, fenced off with little columns on which would be placed the busts of Aristotle and Plato, Descartes, Kant and Hegel. Of course, I no longer wanted to live alone, but it was good too to have a place where I could withdraw and feel at peace with myself. It was in this period that I began to keep a diary, which contributed not a little toward giving me a taste for certain other adventures. At least it seems significant to me that I adopted this habit of careful written introspection exactly at the time when I had decided to abandon my reclusion and face the outside world.

But this new organization of my life failed to obtain the approval of two people, Ginou and my father. Ginou was disappointed at seeing me give up the plan to study medicine, and I was disappointed and annoyed to see how little she understood me. I tried to explain to her, rather emphatically, how important philosophy had become in my life, though I avoided referring, at the time, to the financial difficulties I would have encountered if I had chosen to pursue my studies in any other field. Finally, I shrank from telling her that my future wife should not think so much of money matters, though I realized that this was what preoccupied her. With my father, on the other hand, I did not have to beat about the bush in this manner. In his case, money matters were discussed at once and we quarreled in the most spectacular manner. At that time, he was beginning to take to drink and we had already, for some time, been trying to find an excuse for a fight. He used to come home rather unsteady on his feet, his eyes popping out of his head, and ready for a fight. Behind his back, my mother would gesture to me, urging me to be respectful with him and not too demanding. I think he could sense her gestures and, far from getting angry, even seemed to find them a flattering recognition of his all-powerful status as head of the family. But I was exasperated by this very connivance between my parents, and refused to follow my mother's urging. When I announced to my father my decision, he said to me:

"How about us?"

That was the best way to make me angry. I already felt all too guilty about not helping them, and his insistence on this duty seemed utterly hateful to me. Had I not been so torn by contradictory emotions, I might have tried to reason with him, perhaps even have suggested to him that he would be getting a better deal in the long run if he only remained patient for a while, since I would be earning much more once my studies were completed. But I no longer even thought of justifying myself, and my decision had not been taken in the light of any such considerations. On the contrary, I was anxious to break away from this unbelievable tyranny of the family, and I found nothing to say to him that would not hurt him. I therefore answered that I was not bound to work for him or for these children that I had not begotten; besides, money was the least of my considerations. So we returned to our endless arguments:

"Money? I couldn't care less. . . ."

"Money's everything. If I had money now, I wouldn't have asthma. If I had money, I wouldn't have had to work twelve hours a day in the heat or in the cold, slowly killing myself. Instead, I would be respected now, in fact loved and admired by all and sundry. I wouldn't have to beg my suppliers for a little bit of extra leather or a few cartons of nails. . . ."

I was thus made to understand that, if he was to go on suffering all his life and coughing and experiencing humiliations as now, well, it was I who was to blame.

"This morning," he continued, "I went to see Marsal, who supplies me with leather. It was a cold day and my eyes were running so that Marsal thought I was weeping because I was desperate. So he looked at me and said: 'Come on, Benillouche, come on.' Then he told his salesman Giovan to give me some leather. I had already taken all that I was entitled to and was coming now for the lining material, but I understood, and so I let him think I was crying. And that is what one has to do when one has no money!"

I hated these appeals for pity because, in spite of myself, I actually felt it, and also because I was ashamed on his behalf and could well visualize the whole scene he described. So I began to shout at him and he too began to shout. He told me I was selfish, and this hurt me for I had already reproached myself with being selfish. Finally, he demanded of me simply that I balance my accounts with him:

"I paid for your food and your clothes, and I permitted you to go ahead and study when the sons of all my colleagues were already working in their father's shops and getting calloused fingers from handling the leather."

He could not pretend that he was paying for my studies and that he lacked this last argument made him all the more angry. But he was claiming returns now for all the years I had failed to earn my own living and for my childhood too. This made me so furious that I could find no reply. He was handing me the check, that was all:

"Who was responsible for your upbringing?"

"Yes, you were," I admitted. "But your father was responsible for yours, and you had a debt to pay. I'll bring up my own kids in turn, and then I'll be quits."

For a long while we refused to speak to each other, and it did not cause me much unhappiness, I admit. Had it taken such a quarrel to terminate this whole chapter of my life?

PART THREE

The World

1

THE RED-LIGHT DISTRICT

THE MEREST GLIMPSE of a woman's skin upset me. An uncovered knee or an open blouse caused me such embarrassment that I was forced to look away. But my embarrassment itself was so obvious, and my efforts to keep from looking so violent, that they made the women far more self-conscious than if I had insistently stared. Their quick defensive gestures of pulling down a skirt or fixing a blouse told me that my involuntary aggressiveness had been perfectly well noticed. This left me feeling miserably guilty, so that I found it painful to approach any woman.

I had never been able to participate in the sexual games of boys. When I was told that one of the older pupils offered to caress, with enough skill to cause an orgasm, anyone who wished, I refused with scorn and horror. My comrades organized these parties of collective pleasure out on a vacant lot not far from the school. Apparently, they all lined up with their back to the wall and Giacomo passed up the row one by one. I was the only one in the boarding-school common room not to talk of my adventures or to describe with delectation the sexual attributes of men and women a thousand times a day. To me, such promiscuity was repulsive; besides, what had I to tell? Nevertheless, shy though I was, I was forced to admit that my sexual and general isolation were becoming unbearable and that my secret demanded to be shared with another.

The narrow alleys of the red-light district bordered immediately on the open ghetto and nothing particular distinguished them from other streets. Impatient men waited at the little doors of the cells only ten yards away from the ragged children playing marbles in the cracks in the uneven pavement. The first shops on these streets were still occupied by second-hand dealers. The topography of the place suited me perfectly, for I could wander around as though I were passing there by accident or looking for something. But I could not prevent myself from walking too fast and too stiffly, with a false air of preoccupation. My quick searching glances into the main street, vaulted like a covered bazaar, never went beyond the dealers, and I avoided their eyes and those of passers-by as though I would find in them some sort of ironical accusation; so I hurried past. But even if I were to cross into the zone of public shame, how could I ever accost the women I saw there, sitting on their doorsteps? That seemed an insurmountable trial. And there was another frightening obstacle. I knew, from having often heard our school supervisors say so, that one should never go there without a condom. I had already seen comrades of mine, pale and proud, with rings around their eyes and an awkward gait, announce with affected nonchalance that they had caught gonorrhea, as though that were a proof of their virility. The others, who knew most of the prostitutes by name, would nod knowingly.

"Never go to Lola without a condom. Fontana caught this from her."

I listened with intense curiosity, also with some anxiety and an affectation of indifference. As virginity was considered a joke, I had to avoid being suspected of it, so I discouraged their jokes by pretending to be as calm as an old roué. But how could I possibly walk into a drugstore and, in a loud voice, in front of everybody, perhaps even women, ask for a rubber? I might just as well announce solemnly to all and sundry: "I'm on my way to a brothel." So I would walk up and down in front of a store until the druggist's worried attention was attracted, and then I would flee down the street while he stared suspiciously after me. When I had enough courage for another attempt, I would choose a different part of town, and eventually I eliminated half the drugstores in the city this way. Sometimes, I would pluck up enough courage to face the druggist, or at least I thought I had, but then the presence of customers would prevent me from going in and, however long I waited outside, the shop would never empty. My torture lasted until the day I finally admitted to myself that I would never get to the streets of love alone, nor even to the drugstore. I needed a mediator between my sexual isolation and women. It did not take me long to choose one; of all the more experienced boys, Bissor was the only one who would not cruelly humiliate me. This certainty calmed me for a while and even made me less impatient.

One Friday afternoon, I set to work at my uncomfortably high chest of drawers, with its cold slab of marble broken in three places. I could not concentrate and, at first, blamed the objects around me. As usual, I had carefully placed four newspapers under the marble to even it and a cushion on the chair to raise my own level. But no position was comfortable. First, I sat on my left leg, then on the other; then I was uncomfortably warm and removed the cushion. Finally, I recognized the old turmoil within me that I knew so well. Without thinking twice, since the idea was now well rooted within me, I quickly got up and, with trembling hands, stuffed my books and papers into my briefcase. I never left any of my things lying around because of the children who tore up everything. I had often run, in imagination, this errand to Bissor's house, so my legs now carried me there without any hesitation, while my brain stood still. Bissor was just home from his tiring evening paper round. I knew his schedule. As I had hoped, he made no joke, but simply took on an older brother's manner for which I was almost grateful.

Outside the drugstore he asked me for the price of the rubber. As I seemed to intend to wait for him, he took me gently by the arm and said: "No, you must get used to doing this yourself." In a clear voice, perhaps slightly histrionic, or at any rate so it seemed to me, he asked for a prophylactic—surely it was not necessary to speak so loud. I watched the druggist, small and bald and drowned in a great white overall, with his face hidden behind the thick lenses of his spectacles; but he didn't even look up, handed the little package at arm's length, and vanished behind the cash desk which rang a bell.

Until we got to the labyrinth that led to the red-light district, we spoke of all sorts of other things while my heart thumped away. By the time we reached the first shop under the old green vault and crossed this passage beyond which I had never dared venture by myself, my heart beat so hard that I could no longer hear what Bissor was still saying in the same tone of voice. At the other end of the tunnel-like passage, I could see the women standing in their doorways.

Bissor slowed down and walked nonchalantly, still talking as we approached, with me close to him like an animal, silent and distracted by the emotion in my dry throat. I looked straight ahead, like a horse with blinkers, and passed among all the women whose presence I merely guessed. But soon I felt all the promises held in the scattered crowd around me. The little cells were close by each other and seemed no wider than their doors; in very little space, there seemed to be lots of women. Some were Europeans in shorts and blouses, of all ages, of all nationalities, of all colors, with their hair bound up. There were blondes—whether real or not, I could not tell—and Sicilian brunettes in bathrobes cut out of blankets; Spanish women who stressed their type by displaying the appropriate high combs, black shawls, and beauty spots; Moslems and Jewesses with flowers behind their ears, shaven eyebrows replaced by thick streams of black makeup, and even some Negresses with wiry hair and scarlet or bright blue petticoats. I no longer knew where to look. I was stunned by so much opulence and upset by all this offered flesh which I could see and even touch if I wished or dared. After all, my wildest dreams had never gone beyond trying to give shape to vague memories of a street encounter or to give life to an illustration. I was frightened now at having come so far, so close at last to the mysteries I had secretly dreamed of and which morality forbade. I no longer knew whether I stood on the verge of a scandal or a wonderful adventure.

There were as yet but few customers. The women chatted among themselves like housewives on their doorsteps. Some smiled at us, perhaps because we were so young and so obviously embarrassed. Like in a novel, a big brunette said, and I am sure it was to me, a phrase I knew well and was at last really hearing: "Won't you come in, darling?" Enchanted and petrified, I hardly dared look at her and, unable to smile, I went by obediently at the same pace as Bissor. Bissor had a plan. He stopped in front of a plump little woman with a pleasant face and a pointed nose. She was dressed in a short blue frock with big celluloid buttons well spaced out all the way down the front. They smiled and greeted each other: "I've brought you a friend. Be kind to him, he's nice." She turned to go into her cell. She had said not a word to me, hardly looked at me. I did not, of course, expect her to welcome me in and shake hands formally. Still, I was taken aback. In any case I had expected nothing, and anything would have surprised me as much. I hesitated in the doorway, daring neither to enter nor to leave and awaiting God only knows what. Bissor gave me a push in the back, and I found myself inside a tiny rectangular room, as narrow

as a corridor, so narrow that the sparse furniture had had
to be placed along the two walls. She had just finished putting
a sheet of rubber cloth on the iron bed. She came back to
shut the door and, as there was not room enough for two
between the bed and the wall, she pushed me with her hand
against the little table, covered with a newspaper, on which
were crowded all sorts of combs and creams and women's
magazines. The mere contact of her hand, of the body I was
about to possess, upset me. This pressure already seemed
familiar and promising to me, and I tried to catch her eye
to express to her my budding tenderness. But her back was
turned and she was preparing herself.

She poured two measures of water into an enamel basin
which she then placed on top of the earthenware jar that was
also against the wall. Thus crowned, with its long neck and
its narrow hips, the jug looked like a water-carrier, but was
all sticky with filth. Both the furniture and the room were
extremely poor and evidently of no interest to their owner,
for her only effort at decoration were a few pictures on the
walls, women naked or in their underclothes. These pictures
filled me with shame, for their obscenity spoiled what I insisted on considering pure. All around them, the damp reddish
distemper was dropping off in scales, letting the sand and
plaster run through. The bed was sway-backed in the middle,
and the table, of ordinary unpainted white wood, was black
with dirt. But I forgave and accepted all this; I was alone
in a room with a woman, and she was undressing for me.

I felt grateful to her and was moved by what was about
to happen to me, by the extraordinary gift she was about to
make. She shut the door and, in the intimate darkness, one
single slanting ray of light descended from the shutters onto
the bed. Then she unbuttoned her dress from top to bottom
and was naked. So that was all she was wearing! I did not
know what to look at in this body, so rich and so real. Here
were the shoulders, the legs, the stomach, the loins, and the

breasts, all in one and alive, all of which I had so often tried to imagine separately.

I was not so much surprised as overcome and satisfied. I had already seen naked women in drawings and films and dreams. But I stood in a daze and watched her move. When I saw her at last naked, I feverishly undressed very quickly. I had developed a special technique for the nights when I was in a hurry to get to sleep. In one movement, I took off my pullover with my shirt and undershirt; with one more, my pants and drawers. When she saw that I had stripped she made a gesture of displeasure.

"There was no need to take off your shirt," she said.

It pained me that I had displeased her, as though I had done something tactless, and I picked up my heap of clothes.

"I can put them on again, if you want."

"No, never mind, now."

She was saying *"tu"* to me. I knew that it was the custom to use familiar forms of speech with prostitutes—my friends and books had taught me that. But I was unable to utter them, the instant was too solemn. So I waited, self-consciously. She adjusted the rubber sheet on the bed and lay down on her back.

"Come on," she said.

I lay down alongside her body. She fixed the hard horsehair pillow beneath her head, threw back her arms, and was motionless. So much passivity, such an absent manner, disconcerted me indeed. Vaguely, I had rather expected some sort of gentle communion, a game we would play together. I tried to catch her eye, but she was staring at the ceiling. Fortunately, I had prepared myself for this meeting, I had thought about it and had heard accounts of similar ones. I knew what I had to do and, whatever my shyness, it had to be done. I began by stroking her shoulders. After a while her very coldness gave me courage, and my desire, needing no such subtleties, became manifest. Slowly, I was spontaneous again. As she remained with her face to the ceiling, my hand became a little more daring and slipped down to her bosom. Without a word, but firmly, she removed my hand. I understood that I had reached an area that was out of bounds. Submissively and afraid to hurt her feelings, I kept away from it, skipped the breasts and descended further, with no more embarrassment than if I had been alone. Soon I had almost forgotten her existence and was in a suave solitary dream when, far too soon for my liking, she guessed I was ready and, in a blank voice, ordered: "Come on, now."

Obediently I let go of her. Without looking or changing position, she stretched her hand toward the table and soaked her fingers in a glass of olive oil, which I recognized by its odor. She rubbed some between her thighs, while I furtively looked on, in spite of myself and my shame. The mystery which had, in my dreams, been so disturbing, was really a little disgusting in its biological reality and its vulgar animality. Then, as I hesitated, she must have realized that I was inexperienced. She drew me toward her, and like a child, I clumsily let myself be guided.

To be joined in this manner to her flesh along the whole length of my own body now maddened me, and when her grasp became more specific, I could wait no longer. This angered her, and she grunted as she hurriedly guided me. I had already nearly finished, and left the matter at that. My pleasure had been too hasty and left me all tense; I found it much less satisfying than self-abuse. Because I had depended on someone else, my enjoyment had been meager.

She pushed me over to one side, slapped her hand between her legs, and went and sat on the basin. I also got up and stood there with my loins all tense and sticky. I wondered what I was supposed to do. I could not put my clothes on over this mess. Meanwhile, she was quickly washing herself with careful movements that splashed the water from the basin all over the red distemper of the walls.

But even as she went through her usual toilet, a thousand

times repeated, with her legs spread apart over the old basin, its blots of rust where the enamel had worn away and the soapy water dripping off her thighs, she became less terrifying to me, also a little despicable, as were all prostitutes in the eyes of my schoolmates. But I also felt that my disgust and scorn were to some extent also for myself. She emptied the basin out into a little gutter that led to a hole under the door where I could see daylight. She then filled the basin again and handed it to me. As I did not immediately grasp what she intended, she looked at me as though I were quite stupid and said: "Here, catch!"

She put it in my hands, pushed my wrists down to the proper level, and started soaping my body over the basin. It was hard for me to hold the basin straight, for I was so unsatisfied and tense, and, at the same time, so close to more unbearable pleasure. As her fingers soaped and rinsed and soaped again with the same dexterity as on her own body, I watched, as I would have watched any artisan working away in his shop, had he asked me, a curious passer-by, for a helping hand. I might have been a complete stranger to what she was doing to me had it not been for the nagging and painful sensation of pleasure caused by her fingers, and for the effort of not moving, as well as for the humiliating feeling of being so completely dependent and childishly ineffective. At last, with a sharp movement she tore some toilet paper off a roll hanging from a crooked nail in the wall and wiped me. Then she put on her blue dress again, turned her back on me and, in front of the mirror by the little table, got herself ready for the next customer. I dressed too fast and got my feet caught in my shorts and trousers. All I had to do now was pay her. But now that she was dressed again, she was a woman once more and full of mystery. I found her as terrifying as before. I had put the necessary sum in a separate pocket. I did as I had read in novels, and placed the money on the table without looking at her. She did not wait for me to be gone, but picked it up and put it away in a cigar box. As she moved to the door I realized that it was all over, that I had nothing more to expect, and that I had finished the chapter about initiation to love. I did not want it to end thus, with so little ceremony. I would have liked to make the moment last, to make it memorable for her and for me. My emotion rose again, and I tried to feel some surprise at having changed my condition, at having slept at last with a woman. I wanted to tell her of my gratitude, of the kind of tenderness which, in spite of my disappointment, I thought I felt for her, and for all women; rather, that I wished to feel, for I could not accept the fact that love was so unimportant a matter.

"Thank you, madam," I said, "You've been . . . ever so kind."

She stared at me, surprised by the madam, by the thanks, so unusual in that part of town, and by the muffled emotion in my voice. I saw her hesitation and decided to surprise her even more, to overcome her indifference, to discover even the smallest spark of communion so that this meeting would really put an end to my loneliness.

"You know . . . you're the first woman. . . ."

For the first time, she smiled faintly. Then, as she had to open the door, she turned her back on me and let in the violent daylight.

Bissor was waiting for me with his back to the wall as he eyed a little blonde in pink rayon panties. She was smiling broadly at him, and all her teeth that were mounted on a metal setting turned her mouth into an inhuman machine.

"Well, how was it?" asked Bissor.

"O.K.," I answered sadly.

It was getting late, and the first wave of customers, all white-collar workers, was closed behind the doors of the more presentable girls. Those that we saw now seemed to be the ugliest. As the narrow alleys had been heated by the sun all through the afternoon, I now began to discover the smell that dominated the reserved quarter. The water streamed from under the closed doors in little spurts and wet our shoes, flowing into a gutter in the middle of the street and forming there a kind of blackish mud which smelled penetratingly of sperm, piss, and sweat. I had noticed none of this when we had arrived. To keep up an artificial enthusiasm, I kept repeating to myself: "It's the first time I've seen a woman naked; it's a historic moment." I wanted to feel enriched and more manly.

But, I was ashamed; I felt dirty and cheap, as though I had been an accomplice in all this wretchedness and collective scorn. I was disappointed, unsatisfied, and disgusted; all this stuck in my throat and made me want to cry. Fortunately, Bissor was silent. The poor girls without customers sat on their doorsteps and invited us in, with forced smiles and languid looks. I was not even afraid any more. The last ones we saw, the women I had not even dared look at earlier, were hideous and fat, with withered skin and flabby jowls, with oily hair and thick makeup, like eczema scabs. Most of them were collapsed on the stone steps of their doorways to rest their thick, varicose legs.

"They're for the old guys," Bissor explained.

Before we left the district, he made me piss in a corner against a leaning buttressed wall, all damp and sticky with a yellow pool that stank of ammonia at its base. It was necessary, he said, to avoid catching clap.

I returned for a time to my sexual loneliness and to my attempts to imagine one of the neighborhood girls in the nude or to give consistency and life to pin-up photographs. My attempt to escape from my aloneness had only forced me back on myself, all the poorer for the loss of my illusions. How I envied Sitboun, who dreamed at night of the girls he had noticed the day before! But I had reached a stage in my life when I was no longer satisfied with myself. As I got over the bitterness I felt after my first adventure and as my memories of it became blurred, there remained only the

ghost of a woman whose pubes or breasts I still tried to
recall. Then, driven by a new urge, I returned to the narrow
alley of the red-light district. I was no less disappointed, but
I was less surprised about it. I realized that this is all there
is to physical love and that it always leaves one unassuaged.
I did not return to search for rarer pleasures, but for something else which was not to be found. So I stayed away again
for a while, but naturally came back again, each time promising myself never to return to the filth and disappointment
and bitterness and loss of self-respect I experienced after
each visit. Besides it was expensive, and I had to be careful.

Thereafter, my sex-life, like all the rest of my life, went
from one extreme to the other, from attempts at communion
with others to hasty and nauseated retreats into despair. My
disappointments were not merely physical, as a result of the
hurried and indifferent behavior of the girls. I had not found
what I was looking for and had hoped for so long: to make
love to a human being. The girls' faces remained blank and
impersonal. One of them smoked, and another gossiped while
I had my fun alone. Once, someone came along and banged
on the door just as I was reaching the moment, so brief,
when a man forgets where he is and with whom. Sometimes,
the next customer standing outside would express his impatience, and I would try to take no more notice of it than
of the other noises in the street. For some reason, the girl,
on one such occasion, lost her temper and started to hurl
insults at the waiting man. He replied in kind, and this vile
dialogue continued across my body.

The loneliness of sex in a brothel! So that was why my
classmates talked so much about it among themselves: they
had to rid themselves of the solitude they experienced each
time they faced a woman. An adolescent who is in the least
bit shy, as I was, finds sex wretched and shameful. One day,
I almost discovered intimacy. I had come during a busy
period, and I had always refused to wait in line, for I needed
to maintain the illusion that I was the only lover of a willing

woman. After the disgusting promenade along the closed doors all besieged by waiting men, I was finally taken in by a thin little redhead with a sharp profile and enormous freckles all over her face. Nobody seemed to want her. I was often attracted, in spite of their ugliness, to women who had been ignored, for their expression of sadness made them seem less frightening and more attentive. She welcomed me joyfully and fussed over me and, for some unknown reason, called me her little pinhead. I was almost happy.

The next time I came to the district, I made at once for her crib. My hesitant steps found it automatically. She recognized me, called me her little pinhead again, stroked my hair, and made no attempt to hurry me. Afterward, as she was not expecting many customers, we rested alongside each other on the couch. It was winter and the rain was falling outside. She had lit a brazier over which the water from her basin slowly rose in steam. The little room was comfortably warm and we were both nude. Such confident relaxation, only a yard away from the cold and the rain that beat against the door, added to my poise and happiness. She babbled all the while and kept asking questions, ordinary ones as well as some indiscreet ones. I lied a good deal, but answered willingly enough. Physically, I felt satisfied, not having been hurried, I had almost had time to exhaust the unbearable and painful tension with which all other girls had left me. It really was quite something to be chatting away with a woman, both of us nude, and the word "nude," which I repeated over and over again to myself, seemed full of confused meanings. She took an interest in my life and seemed to admire me, and I had, at last, a feeling of sexual communion and of sharing my secret.

She got up and asked if I were in a hurry. No, I was not; I felt at ease. So she started washing herself from top to toe with the water in her little basin, which rapidly became a mouselike gray. But still she went on soaking her sponge in it and rubbing herself down with the dirty suds. She was so accustomed to the presence of men that she had lost all self-consciousness, and she washed every part of her body with the same thoroughness. When I bashfully asked if I could leave, she said that she would catch cold if she opened the door now, but that she would soon be finished. When she finally decided that she was clean, she picked up a razor blade between her thumb and her index finger and went through the routine of trying to shave her legs. After each stroke over her skin, she dipped the blade sticky with hairs in the blackish water. It made me sick at my stomach to watch it. When the blade ran over her protruding shin, she cut herself; and the little red stream of blood was certainly the least repulsive thing that I saw.

2

THE OTHERS

AT LONG LAST we removed the iron bars and came out of our barricaded houses. The streets were somnolent after our sleepless nights, the air tasted of ash, and a weird yellow light flashed through purple clouds and lit up our tired faces. A few useless and indifferent patrols of Negro soldiers ambled around. Occasionally, the police also showed up—when everything was over. Our main thirst was easily quenched as uncertain and contradictory bits of news poured in. Bissor was among the dead. About the corpses there could be no doubt. There was no possible mistake: Bissor was dead, and all his family had been murdered, except the prostitute sister who had been lucky enough to be away in Marseille. I am sure that Bissor had fought back wildly with his big hard fists. As for the rest, will we ever be able to understand? It was said that the Moslem infantry had been called to the front and that, before being shipped off to slaughter, they had felt, as warriors for whom all is right, that they could get away with anything. Tradition ad-

253

mitted that they could rob, rape, or kill as they pleased. Of course, they chose to descend on the Jewish quarter. Others maintained that the pogrom had been fomented by the government, as a trick to divert attention from its political difficulties, and that all the Jewish soldiers had received orders to remain in their barracks. The coincidence indeed seemed incredible. Perhaps the disaster, after all, had started in some silly way, with a quarrel between a Jewish shopkeeper and an Arab customer in a town of the South; it had then led to a fight between the Moslems of the neighborhood and any passing Jews, and had spread from there to neighboring towns, finally setting the whole country ablaze.

Without knowing why, the city had been simmering for several days. We avoided leaving our own street, and all intercourse was reduced to a cautious politeness. Each little group kept to itself. At home, we were worried, but we insisted on believing that times had changed as we repeated old tales—not so old after all—about Jews having their throats cut by nearby wells, being walled up alive by princely creditors, or sadistically raped. Little by little, in spite of ourselves, we regressed into the historical darkness of bygone ages, of blind brutality. When the storm broke out we were already certain of our inevitable fate.

At eleven in the morning, my father rushed home in spite of his asthma, carrying an armful of provisions, including meats and sugar. Usually, he lunched in his store, but it was said that fights had already started not far from the ghetto. My mother ran to the grocer's just as the store was closing down. Then we barricaded our doors and windows, the front door with two bars of wrought iron. After that, we sat and listened for any unusual sounds. But we were far from the ghetto and could only study the deathly silence of our own neighborhood, periodically broken by the rattling noise of empty streetcars. My father had an occupation for such stay-in periods: he then made heavy canvas feed bags for horses.

From time to time, he dropped his work and rushed to the window. As he grew paler, I recognized on his face the marks of the terror which he had transmitted to me in my earliest childhood. Will I ever be able to rid myself of that cold clamminess at the back of my neck, and of the absurd feeling of being paralyzed and disarmed in the face of a humiliating death?

It was in high school that I discovered how painful it is to be a Jew. Until then, the world had been alien to me, hostile of course, but no more so than anything unknown. I was not the cause of my own suffering, I did not feel alien to myself as I do today. Can I make myself more clear? Anti-Semitism seemed to be a characteristic of the others, much as they might have a way of speaking or of dressing. They were not Jews, as I was, so they were anti-Semites. Naturally, it was not very pleasant, but no less so than the brutality of Sicilians or the prerogatives of the French. It did not fit any particular characteristic of my own, for I did not feel Jewish in any way that might provoke anti-Semitism. In short, I felt neither accused nor guilty.

In high school, I began to suffer because they forced me to ask myself what I was. This problem never could have arisen at the Alliance School where we had all been Jews, all but a tiny minority which had soon been reduced to discretion. But in high school a constant flow of remarks made me ponder the problem of the ideal Jew and forced me to study myself in order to discover in me the typical characteristics. Such introspection calls up ghosts, and through sheer rebelliousness, I defended my own ghosts and thus assured them an existence of their own. I, an artisan's son and poor, defended merchants and financiers in the presence of non-Jews, trying to explain historically why some Jews went into trade as though I had personally been responsible for Jewish trade and believed that non-Jewish trades were indeed more acceptable. As I condemned Jewish trade, I attacked it in the face of Jews, too, but far more virulently than the anti-Semites did and more openly.

This insidious and argumentative form of racial prejudice, disguised as objectivity, was tolerated by my upper-middle-class Jewish classmates. It is true that they were spared certain humiliations. They were assured that such criticism did not apply to them. Anyway, doesn't every human community have its faults? Apparently, I was too touchy and saw anti-Semitism everywhere. But the point was that my classmates did not suffer enough from it in material terms. There were, of course, little annoyances sometimes in the street. On a peaceful day, for instance, a drunkard might shout: "Death to the Jews!" Or the ticket-collector, harassed by the crowd, might say: "These Jews are all alike." Or inscriptions might be scrawled every once in a while on the walls of the old cemetery: "Down with the Jews!" Or again, uncomplimentary references might appear in the press, and one would then have to face smiling and unexpected remarks such as: "Really, you must admit that. . . ." But as, in the long run, the families of my classmates were allowed to go about their own business, they were convinced they were on the winning side. They did not even seem to experience any spiritual anxiety. They were of European culture, going back at least one generation, and the nearness of Europe and the apparent solidarity of the modern world comforted them; several times a year, they went abroad, pampered their digestive systems in various spas, and did most of their business with European firms. It is only fair to add that the Western world really did mean something to them. To us, the pauper Jews, it had brought the end of feudalism as well as movies and cars and doctors; but it also meant that small hucksters were chased around by cops and humiliated each time they came into contact with the authorities. Pogroms never swept so far as the residential sections where Jewish, Moslem, and Christian homes stood side by side; but our huge ghetto, neglected by the anti-Semites because of its sordid misery, was always in mortal danger. Any battered-in door might reveal Jews behind it. We had never been away from the southern shore of the Mediterranean, and we felt cut off from the rest of the world, abandoned to all the local catastrophes.

I was neither as polite nor as secure as my middle-class brethren. I was impulsive and badly behaved, and allowed neither jokes nor mealy-mouthed insinuations to be made. I am willing to admit that my anxiety often increased my suspicion, and I frequently suspected people of meaning more than they said; but what they said was quite unbearable enough for any ordinary pride, and I had the greatest contempt for my Jewish classmates, for their tolerance and so-called fair play, as if fair play did not imply equality for both players.

One day, and I recall it with terror, my exasperation almost made me lose my head. We were climbing the steps to the new science wing in our school. Behind me, I could hear a political discussion between Dunand, one of the few French Socialists in our class, and Papachino, a French boy of Italian origin. Those whose naturalization is recent or whose family background is vague are always more involved in race prejudice and more nationalistic than others. I detested Papachino, with his head that leaned over on one shoulder, and his yellow face full of a snarling craftiness. Although the discussion was violent, I was not paying much attention to it, until suddenly the word Jew struck my ear. I might be anywhere in the world, surrounded by respect and confidence and enjoying every honor, but the slippery sound of the word would still make me prick up my ears and listen. Papachino's bitter, whining voice concluded:

"It is they who are ruining France."

In a second, I had whipped around and grabbed him by the neck with my tense fingers. I was two steps above him, and my rigid fist forced him to look up as I strangled him in his own shirt collar:

"Repeat that! Repeat it, and I'll throw you over the railing."

He hesitated, wondering whether to take it as a joke or to be angry.

"Say it again," I repeated, furious.

Around us, everything had stopped. The look on my face could not have been very reassuring. From above, I could see Papachino's eyes rolling in his motionless face as he tried to measure the fall in the stairwell. He must also have felt the trembling of my hand around his neck, as I could too, and he muttered:

"You're mad . . . you're mad. . . ."

I let go, suddenly afraid myself; my fear was greater than my anger. Dunand had said nothing during all this scene. I only noticed the color come back to his cheeks as he smiled and said, at last:

"Chicken shit!"

Papachino was stammering, trying to explain what he had meant and what he had not. I turned my back on him and went on up the stairs, without quite understanding my sudden exasperation.

But I could not be continually defending myself against the constant hostility and slyness, the very atmosphere of the place. Every time a native, whether Jewish or Moslem, said something silly, our mathematics teacher, a fat and placid Alsatian, would declare in a radio-announcer's voice: "This is the Voice of Africa calling!" He thought he was funny, and the Europeans laughed noisily while the others smiled to show their willingness to play the game. We would then stare at each other and swallow our pride.

The history teacher, a retired lieutenant with a wooden left leg which thumped on the floor with a martial sound, would slyly imply: "The destruction of French hierarchy and of its traditional values." I did not even quite know what he meant, but he managed to make us Africans loathe all hierarchies and their values. Every morning he would force us to stand at attention and to say: "His Majesty the King of England," or "His Royal Highness the Prince of Wales," which made me link race prejudice with authority in my aversions.

Several of my history instructors were at the same time anti-Semitic, anti-Arab, and politically reactionary, so that I learned to identify anti-Semitism with prejudice and with reactionary political opinions. The school forced this conclusion on me: that no Jew, unless it be as a result of blindness or of the lowest kind of false self-interest, can ever be a reactionary, and that this attitude is forced on us by our situation and not by choice.

The fact that the same contempt was felt for Mohammedans made me feel a sense of community with them. Anxiously, my eyes would sometimes scan the class for allies and would catch the gaze of a young Moslem bourgeois by the name of Ben Smaan. But I felt that such a gulf separated us Jewish boys from our Moslem classmates and that the impetus that bore me toward the West was so strong that these encounters could be but accidents. I believed, firmly but not very clearly, that our future lay with Europe. Two inconceivable acts of treachery on the part of the West were necessary before I ceased to associate my life too closely with it. By then, however, I had already broken with the East too.

Life in school slowly taught me my exact position, making the picture clearer each year. Our Alsatian teacher was an example of ordinary anti-Semitism arising from incompatibility. As a man of the North, he disliked living on the Mediterranean, and he reproached us with liking all the things he detested, such as speaking loud, or living on the streets, or being sunburnt, whereas his complexion was milky-white. Then there was the traditional and stupid race prejudice of Naud, the retired lieutenant with the missing leg who taught us history. Another historian also tried to give race prejudice a scientific basis. What complexes drove him to devote his doctrinal dissertation and many years of his life to nonsensical gossip? He forced himself to demonstrate his theories calmly, without ever raising his voice. Years later, he was to betray his secret violence when, with unexpected audacity in such a silent man, soft and almost an invalid, he became a leader in Franco-Nazi collaboration.

But his classes were carefully prepared and intelligent, so that they did me more harm than any stupid or aggressive jokes. I respected all that seemed scientifically accurate, and because I found no immediate reply to his arguments, they troubled me and made me feel guilty. To combat this, I threw myself into studies of Judaism and became intellectually aware of our own Hebrew spiritual tradition. For a few years I enthusiastically attended any lecture or meeting which could help me in these investigations; then firmly entrenched within my new knowledge, I tried to undermine as best I could the teachings of this doctrinaire racial theorist in the minds of my school-fellows. But they all laughed at my discoveries, much as they also derided what our teacher said. So I resorted to my usual vengeance. As he had at least the tact to allow us to express contrary views, whether he liked it or not, I was his best pupil, and I remember well writing angry sixteen-page compositions for him.

But this was impossible with Murat, whom we nicknamed the sprinkler because he constantly spat as he spoke. He was an old crank who was a good example of the kind of anti-Semitism that is bred of stupidity. His mere physical appearance repelled me, with his rotting and uneven yellow teeth, the deposit of thick foaming saliva in the corners of his mouth, his colorless and lifeless hair, and the eternal moist cigarette stub which made him blink with its smoke. He allowed no discussion and, being mean and grumpy, took petty revenge on any obstinate contradictors, that is on the few pupils who thought at all. The others laughed at him and teased him with excessive humility, and this seemed to flatter him. When he was exasperated he would relieve himself by insulting them grossly. On the whole, however, they got on well together. On days when his temper was good he would leave his desk and, putting his left foot up on a bench, would rest his chin on his hand and his elbow on his knee; it was time for a more intimate exchange of views. As he spat over the more unfortunate pupils who sat in the front row, he would ask seemingly innocent questions which were intended to make us reveal our most secret faults. Why was it that, in this country, the Jews always mentioned the profession of the deceased in death notices? He pretended not to know the reason, but he smiled knowingly: simply because Jews make the most—even of death—to advertise! But his stupidity went hand in hand with his greed, and my comrades learned to play the dirty trick of giving him presents. He was so grateful, it seemed, that he would even go so far as to hint at the subject of our next composition, without compromising himself, of course, but with much winking and subtle smiling:

"You would do well to work on Louis XIV. Most important, Louis XIV, most important!"

But all this was superfluous, for in Murat's class, we copied our compositions quite shamelessly out of books. Still, it made a good story for us to tell the rest of the school. I was incapable of such tricks and, though I despised Murat, I hated those who bowed and scraped and bought him off, even if they hit at him afterwards behind his back. I could never speak to an enemy without showing my teeth. I was indeed a wild man, and my comrades who bribed Murat certainly had the cleverer and the better vengeance, whereas I could only talk of my disgust and thus make more enemies.

Murat used the same tactics against the Moslems, and my year in his class really brought me together with Ben Smaan. Murat maintained that Moslems have a particular smell of their own, and he explained it by saying that it came from the sweat caused by eating too much rancid mutton fat. Then he would direct the discussion toward the second statement which, he hoped, would make us forget the first. He was so clever! And the same pupils laughed, and the same ones were angry, all behaving like good sports. Every dog had his day, fair and fair enough. The day Ben Smaan asked if it was true that the Chinese think that Europeans stink, I seconded him.

Politically, Murat was naturally a legitimist Royalist. It is odd how many history teachers are Royalists, as though their studies commit them to a past world. Being a Royalist seemed to me to be the height of anachronistic absurdity. Ben Smaan was the son of a merchant who had been accidentally killed by a bullet in one of the periodic riots which upset our country, yet he was one of the few Moslems to attend Socialist youth meetings. In his composition on the consequences of the Revolution of 1789, he had dared to approve the Revolution itself. Murat gave him D, and in his report on it later in front of a silent class, told him his essay had been full of as much nonsense as its author. Ben Smaan was a fat boy who moved awkwardly, and he proceeded to take this very badly and to interrupt the solemn routine of this session by protesting that his grade was unjustified and that he had not written nonsense; if he had, it would interest him to hear more specifically what was wrong. . . . The class was always on the lookout for a row and now began to shout: "The nonsense! The nonsense!" to the popular tune of "To the Lamppost!"

Murat became irritated, fussed through the essay, and at last found what had made him angry enough to grade it so low. Ben Smaan had written of the "admirable" Robespierre and the "Age of the Enlightenment" when the one was branded in our class as the most bloodthirsty of tyrants and the other as the darkest period in the history of France. This quarrel did not concern me personally; but Murat's injustice and the solidarity that I wished to express toward Ben Smaan as well as the huge admiration I felt for the French Revolution, perhaps also the expectation that I too would get an unfair grade, made me intervene impulsively and brutally, as always when justice seemed to me in danger.

"A gang of degenerate bandits, and the most shameful period in the history of France," Murat repeated firmly.

"The most generous and the most honorable!" I shouted.

My voice came from the back of the classroom and was veiled with emotion in spite of myself.

"Who shouted?" he asked, surprised and angry.

"I did!" I replied in the same passionate tone that revealed that I was ready for anything. My intention to provoke him was obviously insolent. Usually, the pupils took advantage of the slightest chance to laugh and imitate animal cries. Murat would then treat them as idiots and pretend to be angry while the class laughed all the more at his tenderness toward his pupils. This time, however, they all felt that something uncommon had occurred and, in their surprise, were silent. Murat, for once, was up against a real show of fervor and no longer knew what to answer. He merely muttered:

"All right, all right, shut up!"

He then quickly went on to criticize the next composition.

Ben Smaan smiled at me and waved his plump hand. I realized I had been fortunate. Murat had not insisted. Had he not retreated, I would never have been able to control myself.

During the recess, Ben Smaan joined me and said he wished to talk with me alone. I said I was prepared to listen, but he frowned with his eyes almost closed in his broad face and said mysteriously that he would rather we went some-where out of the way. So we made a date to meet in town. He then told me he was the local secretary of a political youth movement composed only of native Africans and asked me to join it. I was delighted but a little embarrassed. Of course, I suffered from my growing awareness that I was alien in the eyes of Europeans, but it had not yet occurred to me to make a move toward the Moslems for I thought of this road as closed.

"Precisely," said Ben Smaan, "that is something new in our program: we would like to have some Jews too, so as to express the aspirations of the whole Tunisian nation."

"But are we a part of the nation?"

"Of course you are! Where was your father born? And your grandfather? Have you ever had any other nationality in the last few centuries? No! There you are!"

"It's true," I said, "that I was born here, like my father and all my ancestors, and I've never been out of this country since my birth. You consider that we belong to the same nation, but what about the others, Ben Smaan, what about the others? I'm afraid that, to them, we may still be foreigners."

"Maybe the times have changed. But there's a job for those of us who know how to speak and explain and convince. We must promote unity among all the native sons of the country and make them act according to their own conscience. Why should we do without the help of the Jews who are an important part of the population and a particularly active, clever, and powerful one?"

The last part of this sentence did not please me. What could he mean by "clever and powerful"? I preferred to think that his words had been tactlessly chosen.

"I can only agree, but I must admit that I am a pessimist. One cannot force oneself to be accepted as a relative or even a neighbor. That is the opinion of many Jews for whom the only solution is Zionism."

He stopped me with both hands and a scornful expression on his mouth that was as small as his eyes; he curled his lips to express his indignation and disagreement.

"Zionism! Leave that alone! It's a utopia and one that will arouse the whole Arab world. What could a handful of madmen do against the whole Arab world? No, let us put aside what would split us apart and look only to what can bring us together."

I did not know then what to think of Zionism, but such a rapid condemnation hurt me, and the implied threat particularly shocked me. Nevertheless, I felt that Ben Smaan's advances and generosity were sincere. His contact with the Socialist youth movement had given him a broad-minded humanism and the idea of the necessity of a social as well as a political liberation. He realized that the local middle-class had exactly the same appetites as all others of its kind and that there would come a day when it would have to be fought too. He had left the Socialists now that he saw that the local groups of the European parties could find neither response nor roots in the native population. The people of Tunisia needed their own party to fight for them and to express their own aspirations. Ben Smaan spoke with a confident faith in his mission that I envied. He knew the sufferings of his people and was working to alleviate them. He seemed to be in the right and his task was obvious. But what was my people? And what did it want? My violence in the discussion and my resistance melted to indecision and a feeling of not belonging anywhere when it came to actions.

"You know what you are and what you want. You're lucky. If you were asked point-blank what your main political aim is, you would say the withdrawal of the European colonials or at any rate their neutralization. But I have to stop and think. You very much want a return to the culture and language of the Arabs, but I now belong to Western culture and would be incapable of writing or expressing myself satisfactorily in Arabic. Still, the injustices and refusals of the West. . . ."

"But that only makes our task more urgent," Ben Smaan insisted. "The more time we let pass, the more unlike ourselves we become. We must pull ourselves together and clearly define our program."

I was too shy to add that Moslem hostility would have to be dispelled and that there was also the hostility of the Jews who had been driven behind thick walls by centuries of fear. This reminded me of my never-concluded argument with my father:

"They don't like us," he would say bitterly.

"And do you like them?"

"Why should I like people who hate me?"

"Well, someone has to start. . . ."

My father would shrug his shoulders.

I promised Ben Smaan now that I would think all this over. I talked to Bissor about it, hoping that he would come with me, but I only met with an immediate and obstinate refusal.

"You don't know them," he said. "Ben Smaan represents nothing. Go to the Arab part of town and mix with those blindly fanatical crowds. Then come back and tell me if you still think one can work with them."

He reminded me of his own father's death and of their shop that had been looted and burned. The whole of Bissor's face, his hard and energetic jaw and his big and bright hazel-nut eyes expressed complete refusal and an incomprehension that was almost despair.

"We would only be polite to each other until the day when they will inevitably fall upon us again. I cannot forget it," he said darkly.

Yet it was necessary to forget and to pull down those old walls. I too knew some nasty tales and had even had one or two experiences of my own. One day, in Tarfoune Street, in the middle of a game, a little Jewish boy had caught at a Moslem girl's earring. The violence of the children's movements had caused the jewel to split the lobe of her ear. For three days the street had been in an uproar while the Moslems besieged the Jewish home, refusing all offers of a money indemnity and demanding that the little boy be handed over so that his ear could be torn off.

Another time, after a quarrel between the local Jewish carpenter and a Moslem customer, the latter, having exhausted all his patience, had thrown the carpenter flat on the floor and tried to saw his throat. The victim had been saved only thanks to the screams of his womenfolk, all crazed with fear.

But one had to forget and act. Only action could deliver both sides from their mutual isolation.

It was then only a few weeks before our school certificate examinations, and soon we would be distracted from these problems by reviewing. Ben Smaan was again on duty with me as a boarding-school prefect. I decided to go with him the day Poinsot, in his endless curiosity, wanted to find out the difference between a Jew and a non-Jew. He thought he had found the answer, but his curiosity made me angry. I had too much confidence in his intelligence and, as Poinsot was well-meaning and incapable of prejudice, there surely existed a gulf between us, if he saw one.

There were not many of us at these secret meetings, and we felt strongly even if we had no very definite ideas. But I always left this Arab house filled with warmth and a feeling of generosity. The communion which ten of us could achieve was of good augury for the rest of the city. I smiled at the little street vendors and was amiable to the ticket collector in the streetcar; when two women began to argue, I sided with the Moslem one. But the vendors did not understand my smiles, the ticket-collector hardly returned my politeness, and the Moslem women formed such a solid bloc in their opposition to the Jewess that I ended up by feeling sorry for her as the victim. Perhaps, I thought, if they only knew that I had just left an Arab home in the middle of the Halfaouine section, with a fig tree growing in the middle of the patio, and that I had just drunk tea there with Ben Smaan and the others, if only they knew that I was working for them, who I was and what I thought. . . . But I had to overcome the hostility of the ticket-collector and teach the shopkeepers not to insult Jewish housewives by calling them bitches, and I had to send Jewish and Moslem girls to the same schools.

Our success depended on our work and patience and on time.

Naturally, I had my ups and my downs. When I was discouraged, I thought of the sufferings of the Jews, of their despair in the ghetto: "They will never never like us!" I thought also of the utter misery which so blinded the Moslems. How could one cut a path through such tangled darkness? Then again, when I was strong enough to view it all with the calm of a Spinoza and to recover from my own nervousness, I seemed to see the solution clearly, and this vision gave me a certain serenity and a philosopher's joy. In action, I felt happy and optimistic. For a while, I thought I could discover salvation through trying to save others.

After the pogrom, however, as soon as it was again possible to move around, Ben Smaan came to see me. We went for a long walk all around the old ramparts, with me slowing my impatient gait to keep pace with his small unsteady steps. He talked a lot, perhaps to hide his own embarrassment and emotion, and I said almost nothing, not knowing what to say. He had worried about my personal safety but, even more, he admitted, about what I might think, and he now apologized for his doubts. He was sure that I had realized that it had all been cooked up. Yes, I had. It must be explained to all in our respective religious communities. Yes, certainly. (Would mine believe me, I wondered?) It was more than ever necessary to be united. Yes, it was. (I was sick of those nightmarish nights!) He was preparing a petition. Yes, I would sign it.

Bissor was dead: what was I to do about this death? Whether it was a miserable European diversionary move or a spontaneous and blind mob action, no amount of research into responsibilities would ever bring him back to life. Ben Smaan was right: one had to educate the mob, unmask those who fooled it, and draw attention to the real problems. But I was tired and the results were too far off. For the moment I stood between two walls: how was I to choose between repulsive hypocritical anti-Semitism, which had probably been the instigator of the massacre, and these murderous explosions which, like letting blood, periodically relieved the pressure of so much accumulated hatred?

How vain and futile are all theoretical and philosophical constructions of the mind when compared to the brutal realities of the world of men! The European philosophers build the most rigorous and virtuous moral codes, and their politicians, brought up by these teachers, foment murders as a means of government. After how bitter a struggle had I chosen the West and not the East! And now I was beginning to listen to the reasonings of Jewish nationalists when the war came to fill up our lives and postpone any solution to these problems.

3

THE WAR

In order to emerge from my solitude, as I have already said, I tried making advances to the outside world. I did not have to do it for long; suddenly, the world flooded my life and dragged me in its wake with so much violence that I hardly knew what was happening to me. We had become accustomed to the idea of war; for a long time it had been a far-off and inoffensive affair, but then suddenly it was present, exploding between our walls.

In the first days after the declaration of war, a few Italian planes flew so high above the city that they could not be seen, and they dropped some light bombs at random on the countryside. Although the first bursts of antiaircraft gunfire frightened us, the apparent inefficiency of the aggressor soon allayed our fears. Jokes were made about the poor Italians who were more afraid of our antiaircraft fire than we were of their bombs! For a while, we continued to use the trenches in the middle of the street, and I got into the habit of taking with me a book on psychology. Before long we were using them as refuse dumps, and the children took possession of them for their games. Besides, this war meant nothing to us, nor any other war, for that matter. Not since any man or community could remember had we ever been involved in an armed conflict; those were European games and disasters, and we bore the consequences of them because our fate was linked with that of Europe, but neither our minds nor our hearts were preoccupied. When the Italians finally stopped their timid flying expeditions, the war ceased to have anything to do with our everyday life. Even the pogrom which today seems to me so significant was only an accident, a part of our way of life.

And then, all of a sudden, one day we found ourselves right in the middle of the tragedy. When I think how little I foresaw at the time what was about to come and actually did come, how politically ignorant I was, I cannot understand why I still suffer such confused remorse, so much repressed self-criticism and dissatisfaction with myself. Perhaps because I might have acted more wisely, perhaps because the acute self-awareness that I have since contracted like a disease does not allow me now to recognize the young man that I was at that time. My whole conduct was based on impulse. I lived through that period like any mediocre imbecile, stunned by hunger and exhaustion, believing any piece of gossip and reacting exactly like all the others. Or is it simply that I feel indebted to my age for not having been carted off to hell or had my nails torn out of my fingers or lost a leg or an arm in a slave-labor camp? This is required by the times, whether one be the hangman or the victim. I don't feel victimized enough, and it tortures my conscience.

Historians today tell how, one afternoon, as the red and purple dusk lingered on, the big Junker planes of the Nazis started landing on El-Aouina Airfield. I did not see the aircraft, and nobody told me about it. I believe that I was reading my newspaper that evening, just as I am today. Later, I learned that a few wise people had left the country in time; the army, it seems, had arranged a train service for those wishing to join the Allied Forces. I never had any connections in the army and was living in the closed world of the Jewish artisans. But even if I had known of the Junkers' landing, I would not have realized the necessity of escaping.

In fact, I understood so little that I was convinced that, between the Jews, the Germans, and the French, it was all a matter of pride. When Pétain came to power in France, the new anti-Semitic laws were applied to us but with some delay. When the decrees were published, I was not so much struck by the material side of the catastrophe as disappointed and angry. It was the painful and astounding treason, vaguely expected but so brutally confirmed, of a civilization in which I had placed all my hopes and which I so ardently admired. With a crash, the reassuring idea that colonial Frenchmen and those from metropolitan France were not the same was now demolished. The whole of Europe had revealed its basic injustice. I was all the more hurt in my pride because I had been so uncautious in my complete surrender to my faith in Europe.

I reacted impetuously and without a moment's thought. I did not wait to find out how the new laws were to be applied. Instantly I wrote a letter of resignation which I handed to the principal of the school. I have no idea what he thought of the young man who was handing in his resignation from a so unimportant post with the grandest of manners. I still felt a pupil's respect for him, and my indignation and the difficulty of explaining myself all gave me an appearance of great solemnity. In any case, he played the part I expected of him perfectly. This retired commander of a Spahi regiment, tall and straight in spite of his age, impressed us by his physical presence and his firm and elegant muscles which he carefully kept in condition on the tennis courts.

He accepted my letter, adding that he approved of my gesture and would have done the same himself. I was proud and moved that I had had the courage to do what my school principal himself would have done, and I left his office feeling quits with the persecutors of Vichy. I had hit back, blow for blow. Of course, I had lost my job. But my reputation, both as a serious pupil and as a student, assured me many requests for private lessons. When they had encroached on my rigid schedule, I had refused them; now I would accept them. Even when the universities were closed to Jews I was not alarmed. Having no money, I could not attend them anyway. But we did have the right to continue to the end of the school year. The war was not real enough for me to imagine how long it might last. On the contrary, my own near future seemed so promising that in my own mind I just ignored this obstacle.

Immediately, with the arrival of the Germans, came disaster. No longer did I have the leisure to meditate; we were hurled into such a whirlwind that we only started breathing again after they left. Disaster certainly makes one less lucid. The first morning after that sinister evening when the German authorities settled in the dark city, the Kommandatur took its first anti-Jewish steps. Armed with well-prepared lists and accompanied, as was fitting, by their French colleagues, the German police went out to collect several hundred hostages. It was announced that, at the slightest opposition, they would all be shot. Then came requisitions and exactions and murders. Now that we have news from the rest of the world, I know that we did not reach the bottom of the abyss. We had no gas chambers or crematoria. Those of us who were deported to Germany probably went through all that, but we did not know about it at the time. We were saved from despair by our ignorance and our lack of understanding concerning all that was upsetting our daily routine. I found out all about it later, and I know now what risks we ran and might still have run. That is why I want to deal quickly with this part of my story. We certainly had our share of misery, however meager compared to that of others.

We also had our victims, executed for fun or as punishment or by mistake, our women raped and our homes plundered. The Germans fired into windows to enforce the curfew, they said, but they did it preferably when they saw somebody there, and only in Jewish homes. The next day, we were told the name of the victim. German lorries would draw up in front of a building occupied by Jews; soldiers would get out and, blocking the exits, summon all the inhabitants to leave immediately. Without quite knowing what was happening, the poor people suddenly found themselves in the street, as destitute as the day they were born, the women and childrer weeping. We only heard about rapes indirectly for the victims preferred to remain silent. The impression of being wide-awake in a nightmare was reinforced by the more and more violent bombings, day and night, ever more frequent and terrifying, which upset all our sense of time. We lived and slept as best we could.

Soon, however, disorder and fear became familiar, and we adapted ourselves to it. As soon as we tried to react, we realized how weak and isolated we were. The Moslems did not wish to take sides in a war between Europeans. Indeed, it was a miracle, and one must do them justice, that the whole Moslem population did not go over to the Nazis. Nothing had been neglected: promises of complete independence, Arab broadcasts from Berlin, and reminders of Kaiser Wilhelm II's Islamic sympathies.

The Italians, undermined by Fascist propaganda, by free distributions of black shirts and magnificent balls, thought they were living in the Golden Age of ancient Rome or of a Greater Italy. Many Frenchmen, reactionary by necessity or taste, found at last the regime of their dreams. The others, disconcerted and under surveillance, retired into silence. We were really alone, and far more dangerously isolated than in any other country. No disguise was possible as each group or individual could be perfectly identified. This, of course, did not occur to us since we could get no outside information; but any sort of resistance was inconceivable. The least move would have caused a huge massacre, amidst the indifference or the rejoicings of the others. It is only now that I can draw up this disastrously clear balance-sheet. At that time I fortunately did not realize how isolated we were. On the eighth day, after they had taken all their precautions, the Germans ordered all Jewish men between the ages of eighteen and forty to assemble to be sent off to forced-labor camps. Our immediate reaction was to ask the French Residency for its protection. To our amazement, our delegates were thrown out.

"Gentlemen," was the reply of the Resident General, "I too must carry out the orders of the Germans."

For the first time our community had been failed when it turned to our French trustee for protection. Bewildered, unprepared to undertake responsibility, it had to decide its own fate.

Nevertheless, like a tracked animal, I thought first of saving my own skin. I relied on what connections I had among the French and on my admiration for France. It is not easy to believe in the betrayal of a myth. First, I put my papers in order and hid some vaguely political writings in the laundry-room; then I piously buried in Henry's garden a number of poems that were almost finished and many more drafts. I'm not quite sure what it was I most feared, whether the bombings, the inquisitive hands of the children, or German police-raids. Not once did it occur to me that I might never come back. Then I started to move. I went to all the people I could count on. Luckily, at the head of my list was one of the highest French dignitaries in the country. Until the eve of the German invasion, I had been his son's tutor. An incident to which I had not given its full meaning now came back to me. One day, quite recently, he had sent for me in his office. I had gone full of respect and proud to be able to tell the guard on duty that I had an appointment with His Excellency. He was an aristocrat in the diplomatic service of the Republic, tall, dry, theatrical, with white hair, fine features, and a discreet voice and gestures which greatly impressed me. I myself was incapable of speaking without becoming excited and of expressing myself without movements of my whole body, so that I admired men who could be brief and speak with no agitation. He wanted to know about his son's work. At the end of our talk, he thanked me and said I could come and see him if ever I needed him. At the time, I did not realize the importance of these words. I was grateful that so important a personality should allow me to have recourse to his influence on my behalf, and the simplicity of his manner had impressed me.

On another occasion, I had been received by his wife. I had never approached a woman of such high rank. I left full of wonder for the perfect balance between her simplicity and dignity, for her elocution, her manner, her reserve, her blond hair, her fine features and hands, and for Heaven knows what else. It seemed that the splendid idea I had of French culture was all contained in one exalted individual.

So I went first to their magnificent government villa. The footman recognized me and I asked to see the Administrator. He disappeared and returned to ask me what might be the motive of my visit, which rather embarrassed me; as usual, I had acted too fast and had not foreseen this move. I could not bring myself to tell the servant what his master should have understood at once. Again, he disappeared with a confused message. I waited in the hall, miserable that my request should have such a bad start and already sorry I had come. The staircase which rose from the middle of the hall turned in front of the rooms of the first floor, so that the occupants could see the visitors waiting below. Suddenly, a door opened and a disheveled woman in a negligee appeared: it was his wife.

She placed both hands on the banisters and started screaming. I could not clearly understand what she was saying, and caught only bits of sentences which poured like a hailstorm from the gallery: ". . . bothering people . . .

thinking only of your own little person . . . rudeness . . .
selfishness, etc., etc. . . ." I was amazed that my request should
have made her so angry and could find nothing to say;
besides, it was uncomfortable to speak from one floor to the
next. In any case, I was not given time to think: she had
said what she wanted to say and had slammed the door shut.
I pushed the heavy Arab door open and was once again in
the silence of the gardens.

My plans were going badly: I had just lost my trump card
and an illusion. I had been childishly disappointed and was
sad that I had seen my symbol of dignity and politeness turn
into a Fury. Besides, my disappointment seemed to me absurd.
I had made myself an ideal of this woman and was now
surprised that she had not lived up to it.

I went off in the direction of Poinsot's villa. He was not
on my list, but I needed to talk to straighten out my ideas.
I carefully avoided the main streets for fear of police drag-
nets; the Germans had not waited for the deadline for the
community's reply and had begun raiding the streets. It took
me a long time, in my panic, to climb the hill I had so often
climbed full of hope. Following the instructions of the Civilian
Defense Authorities, the Poinsots had abandoned their house
to live in the cellar. I found Poinsot all bewildered and lost
without his books, quite at sea among the absurd wooden
props which were supposed to sustain the ceiling in case of
a bomb hit. I told him about the requisition orders; he had
already heard and seemed overwhelmed. I told him the
latest news and of the panic of our community, which was
so unused to this sort of warfare. I also reported to him the
arrest of some of his former pupils and my own decision to
stay in hiding and await developments. Was I right or wrong
to try to save only myself? I was doing nobody any harm,
neither could I be of much help. Besides, my health would
not be able to withstand the camps. The inspecting doctor
of the school, Dr. Nunez, whom I still saw, had warned me
that I had an infected spot on one of my lungs.

Poinsot said nothing, nor did he smoke; he seemed to be

in a cage behind the wooden beams. He and his wife exchanged glances, communicating with each other in silence. At last, she spoke:

"You know, I'm terribly sorry we can't offer to hide you here. It seems the Germans search French homes too."

I reassured her: I had not come for that. I could say this without any effort as I was not lying. But the suggestion instantly seemed to me reasonable; I could certainly have hidden there. The Germans apparently wished to conciliate the French. I was suddenly very embarrassed at having to explain why I was not asking such a service of them. Their villa, I suggested, was too exposed and would be most dangerous; I would surely be spotted there at once.

Between Poinsot and me, silence was meaningful too. I felt sorry for him, so silent and so powerless in the cold cellar. He had put up the collar of his dressing gown and was huddled up on a wooden bench against a bundle of linen. Madame Poinsot was more at ease and said she was going to fetch some wood for a fire. But I did not want to be left alone with him and at once took my leave.

I then gave up my list of friends and my attempts to save myself. If Poinsot did not want to help me, no other Frenchman would. Furthermore, it was more and more dangerous to go out. As the community was taking its time with its reply, the raids in the streets were becoming more and more frequent and efficient. The German police were being helped by the French: unpleasant mistakes had to be avoided. So we retreated into our homes and closed our shops. The ghetto became like a desert. But the police knew the Jewish homes. Through habit and a certain respect for formalities, they still knocked on the doors and cried "Police!" The Germans then followed or simply waited in the street near their big closed vans.

I was still indignant enough to want to reject this new image of France. After all, were not the policemen just as French as Racine and Descartes? I was out when they raided our Passage. Our neighbor had been dragged out of his bed in the middle of a fit of malaria and had continued to rave in delirium in the stairway. When he saw the uniforms, he began to sing the "Marseillaise"; the policemen were annoyed because they thought he was being sarcastic and began to beat him up while he stood stiffly at attention.

The situation was becoming disastrous. The raiders carried off all men indiscriminately, the old and the young, the healthy and the sick. A few young girls disappeared. The families of the hostages begged and prayed and wept. Something had to be done about those who were already in the camps. When they saw that no help would come from anywhere and that ostrich tactics led only to disaster, the leaders of the community got in touch with the Germans. Later, they were violently criticized for this; at the time, however, we heaved a sigh of relief. I have enough other reasons to feel strongly against our middle class and can dare to say this. The ghetto was there, easy to cut off and surround with a handful of men, and open to any attack. The Germans could kill, rape, and loot as they pleased. Those who protest today are the ones who found refuge in homes in the European quarters, but could one hope to hide the whole ghetto? The little hucksters, saddlers, tailors, bakers, and cobblers had no connections. Something had to be done. The Germans agreed to stop the raids and to allow us to organize a medical service that would exempt the sick and the aged from labor camps. In exchange, the leaders had to supply a given contingent of workers. At last we thought we would be able to leave our anguished seclusion. I must admit that, at the time, we found this arrangement preferable to the day-to-day terror of random police raids.

What really convinced me was probably the fact that the medical commission declared me unsuitable for work. When I received my summons I went again to see my doctor. He certified that he had given me medical treatment for a lung infection. What with his certificate, the limited staff, the

superficial character of mass examinations, and probably
some implicit directives, I was hardly examined at all by a
young doctor who was in a hurry and not very sure of himself. I was put into one of the already overstaffed offices of
the new community organization. For once, I blessed my
physical disability, which indeed I no longer felt. The graver
dangers I was now exposed to even made my temperature
subside.

But I could not be satisfied with merely saving myself. As
soon as I had done it, I was ashamed. Reports from the
camps were very bad. As they had never had any experience
of war, or of natural or historical disasters, my brethren—all
city-dwellers, artisans, office-workers, salesmen, and petty
traders, with a skin that was too white and flabby stomach
muscles—lost all appearance of being human after only a
few days of camp life. They neither washed nor shaved any
more, were covered with lice, and just gave up, in spite of
the efforts of the braver young men who tried to help them.
The best of them, those who in a moment of revolt tried to
escape, had to cross hostile country and were quickly caught
and shot or deported to Germany. Those who came home,
wounded, sick, or on leave, were so thin, dazed, & aggressive
in their filthy rags all caked with mud, that we were ashamed
to look at them. The Germans, following a plan which we
could not guess, grew more and more demanding and vicious.
They shot the stragglers and the sick. They multiplied their
demands and became increasingly difficult to satisfy. After
they had taken all the men younger than thirty-five years of
age, they demanded those aged forty, and then those aged
forty-five. We began to realize that if the German occupation
were to last much longer we would be completely lost, for
the Germans had time on their side and would eventually
exhaust us. It was no longer possible to answer their summonses, and the community could no longer furnish the
required monthly quota of men, so the raids began again.

Our anxiety of the first days gripped us again, but this

time we were angry and disturbed, like hunted down beasts. We could not sleep any more. The German air force was busy elsewhere, so we spent our nights, which were nothing but one long alarm, standing half-asleep in trenches, with our backs against the damp earth. In the daytime we skirted the walls as we hurried to find some bread or to get news of our loved ones, safe at most for an hour or so. The women were hysterical, not knowing whom to blame, and not daring to accuse the Germans, they invaded the community offices and demanded their brothers, husbands, and sons, screaming insults at our overwhelmed department heads, spitting in their faces, and rolling on the floor. In order to make the President of our community understand what her only son was suffering one woman emptied a box of live lice on his head. Another, whose son had been killed and his corpse half-charred, tried to set fire to the office. What could one do? What could we do for all these men who were suffering and dying in camps, and for those who were half-crazed? By now I was far from thinking only of myself, as I had at the beginning of this adventure. I could no longer bear to stay behind my desk filling out forms all day. Every day we had a procession of women, weeping or fierce. When one of them once went into a fit of hysterics and I clumsily tried to comfort her, she screamed at me and asked what I was doing safe in an office while her son was in a camp. Again, I thought of trying to find some hiding-place in the town, but I had seen too much. I no longer felt I had the right to run away from the catastrophe. What demoralized me completely was my finding out the real reason why I had been spared. In the offices I learned that the middle class had assumed these responsibilities to save themselves and their children. Rich men's sons were everywhere in the auxiliary offices: food supplies, ambulances, transport and medical services. But they had also decided that certain categories of men were to be spared, for instance the intellectuals. So I had been granted the advantage of the undeserved privilege of a group. It was because I was a student, not because of my lungs, that I had been saved. Now I understood the hurried medical examination much better. "We wanted to save the elite of the community," explained one of our leaders without even smiling.

By some stroke of luck, as it turned out, most of the intellectuals were of the middle class. So the intellectual and the economic elites were confused. It seemed to the middle class only fair, since they had to pay the heavy cost of the camps, that their own sons should be exempted. But I could not forget that I was poor, nor accept this ambiguous situation.

How was it possible to stay in the offices while all those young Jews were being beaten, humiliated, and killed in the camps? To the astonishment of our directors and the half-ironic surprise and respect of my colleagues, I asked to be allowed to join the camp workers. I am not trying to pride myself on my decision, and perhaps I behaved like a fool. But I do not remember the details of my argument. I only know that the action I took seemed necessary to me, and I refuse to discuss the matter today. I asked to go because it seemed intolerable to stay. Painfully but definitely, I was discovering that others really existed, and moreover that I would never be content merely with my own happiness. I was simple enough to think that I could be of help to them. I was fortunate to enjoy some culture and a few ideas; I would go to the camps to help the others live. I believe that, in the midst of the despair of those days, my move was optimistic. I wanted to go out toward men and thought I could help them. For myself, my decision was certainly a happy one: I immediately felt better.

4

THE CAMP

ALL THROUGH THE long day's journey the
worn-out springs of the old truck passed on to us the smallest
bumps in the road. We had left Tunis almost gaily at dawn,
with rucksacks on our backs, which reminded us of our youth
movement excursions. The sharp air and the warm sun were
just as promising then, and when one of us burst into a
marching song we all joined in. I was lighthearted as I left,
for I had left nothing behind me. The evening before, Ginou
had yielded to the last of my arguments and admitted that
we were not made for each other. I must confess that I had
indulged in some histrionics for a quarter of an hour as I
tried to find in my heart a pain that was not there. But I
had to leave her hurriedly in order to pack my bag and had
no time to think more of it. Ten minutes after our departure,
I was already singing with the others, standing in the wind,
full of the healthy impression of having volunteered for a
great adventure.

At the first alarm, however, we stopped singing. Aircraft
appeared suddenly from behind the hills and crossed the road

in a streak firing their machine guns, sometimes quite insistently. Lying in a ditch we waited for them to be gone
before we resumed our uncomfortable positions, tightly
packed against each other. The men joked and bragged to
hide the anxiety which grew in us as we moved further south.
The landscape became more and more rugged with eroded
purple rocks, thorny vegetation and cactus, and the atmosphere of a silent Western movie. At last the truck entered
the bed of a dried-up *oued* and jogged and bounded over
the white stones of the river bed.

At the far end of the *oued,* the camp appeared in the
middle of a circle of chalk cliffs, like a big white hole surrounded by red bushes. Above, on the ridges, there were a
few meager bushes with tiny mauve blossoms. A long line of
men stood waiting by the kitchen, and the cook was filling
each bowl in turn like an automaton. There were tents of
coarse canvas all around the edge. With difficulty, the truck
climbed into the hollow and stopped.

The men looked at us and, when they saw we were only
a new contingent of workers, took no further notice of us.
Dusty, silent, and motionless on the parched earth, they
looked like hungry locusts. My companions no longer had
the courage even to pretend and were silent. I jumped from
the truck and limbered up my legs. Suddenly, for no apparent reason, two men from the line were at one another's
throats, rolling on the ground and hitting out blindly, hin-
dered by their rags. They were brutally and unhurriedly
separated by the others while the soldiers looked on indif-
ferently.

The degradation of my new companions was so complete
that the idea of the job I had set myself gave me anguish.
I caught myself swearing inwardly to myself that I would
never fight for a bowl of soup, and found that, whether I
liked it or not, I was already prepared to run away.

Fresh work crews arrived, followed at a distance by soldiers
who chattered among themselves. The men were visibly ex-

hausted and never made a move that was useless but took
only enough time to lay down their tools, fetch their bowls,
and rejoin their line. They looked at us briefly and without
curiosity. Those who had already received their portion sat
on the ground in groups of two or three to eat. We looked
on, in front of our truck, disconcerted.

I had come to the work-camp of my own accord, and I
fully realized it when I saw that my presence could be of no
help to these men. I am not trying to justify myself, I am
only relating what I believe I must say. I had been simple
enough to think I could help the others, but in fact I could
neither break through the massive suspiciousness caused by
their suffering, nor get them to accept me. Maybe I lacked
love, maybe I was too feeble for such a struggle which was
mostly a struggle against myself. To help them rediscover
and keep their dignity, I had to fight the danger of losing
my own. It was at the camp, in my daily life with them, that
I came to realize how far my studies and my high-school
education had removed me from any possible communion
with my own people. When I slid under the tent where the
head of the camp had assigned me a place, I thought I
would never get used to the stifling animal stench that rose
from the stale straw. Jute sacks and rags showed that all the
places on either side of the doors were occupied. Courage
failed me and I was unable to make up my mind to return
to this lair the first night; I left the tent with my bag on my
back.

When somebody called my name and got up from a little
group, I felt very great pleasure, as though I had been lost
in a hostile crowd. In a shapeless hairy *gandourah,* patched
but clean, I recognized a boy I had met at scout meetings.
He led me toward his companions, all members of the same
movement, so I felt relatively at home. Here there was a
little oasis of affection in the middle of the silent suspicion
of the others. They told me they had a small tent which they
disciplined themselves to keep tidy and clean. The five of

them were, as a matter of fact, fairly well shaven, and their metal bowls seemed well scrubbed with sand. They offered me a place in their tent, which I spontaneously and effusively accepted.

But I was immediately ashamed of my joy. I felt that I should have made the effort to live in an ordinary tent in the rotten straw and the stench of human beasts, for there I would be among workers, and it was for them I thought I had come. But I did not have the courage to do this. The devil whispered all sorts of excuses: would I be better equipped in such filth? Would I not, on the contrary, ruin what was left of my health? Perhaps a certain distance between us would give me more authority? Surely it was better to avoid the excessive familiarity which the promiscuity of sleeping and waking together would breed.

In short, I brought my bag over to the scouts, and thus began a retreat which was to have important consequences. The distinction between the middle class and the ghetto population continued within the camp. Of course, the soldiers made no distinctions and manhandled and degraded all the workers alike. But the men grinned when they saw a middle-class son arrive, caught in a raid or requested by name by the Germans, for they were sure he would not stay long. Nor were they wrong: as soon as he had been forgotten by the Germans, the middle-class boy went home in the convoys of the sick and the fathers of large families, or became a driver or nurse who, one day, on a trip to town, just disappeared. I found that the scouts, who slept apart, were also left outside all the little intrigues of the camp. Besides, the rejection was mutual. When they started confiding in me, they admitted they had invited me so as to avoid a disaster: the head of the camp had asked them to take one or two more men in their tent, but they had feared they would not be able to command the same cleanliness and discipline in the others. It was certainly too late now for me to indulge in remorse.

All through the long monotonous days in the camp, I still tried to force the confidence of the men. Today, the spring that drove me is broken and I'm amazed at my decision to go to camp and at my naivete, as though they were foreign to me. What innocence, what fervor, but also what self-sufficiency I must have had to believe I would be welcomed by the others merely because I had gone to them, full of faith and goodwill! In spite of the difficulties, I thought I was succeeding. The men, covered with lice, no longer fought disease. I discovered a barber among the workers. He had brought his tools with him, but he was called upon only on the eve of a day of leave. Together, we organized a little plot which would also be profitable for him. The following Sunday, rather ostentatiously, in the middle of the camp, I had my whole head shaved. After a few ironic comments, a few men followed my example when I explained that this would help protect me from lice. After that, the barber held his sessions every Sunday.

I even became almost popular when I succeeded in obtaining an extra day of rest through a new system of rotation in our duties. A Jewish doctor had been specially appointed to the camps and came around once a week. We also had a permanent nurse, a former pharmacist who had no medical training. Only the more clever had managed so far to be reported sick. I persuaded the doctor, who pretended he was happy to speak at last to an intellectual, that it was necessary to grant a rest to those men who threatened to break down. Many had given up all hope and withdrawn into a mute stupor, and the unexpected rest certainly helped to save some of them. I remember with emotion the extraordinary scene when poor Basmouth, who had become a sort of hairy animal clothed in rags, spent his day off feverishly washing himself, as though he were afraid the day would end before he had managed to get clean.

I triumphed the day two men came and asked me timidly if I could organize a Sabbath service. In other circumstances,

I would have refused vehemently. For years I had not even been inside a synagogue. But they were asking for what seemed most important to them, so I joyfully accepted. I soon saw what use I could make of such meetings. Through the group chiefs I requested permission of the military authorities to hold a strictly religious service. My excuse was that the men's morale must be improved, which was true, and that, in consequence, they would work better, which was doubtful. My reasoning seemed valid, and permission was granted. As I could not undertake the religious part, rather because of my ignorance than of any scruple, I found an assistant capable of saying the prayers—they were all capable of this—and kept for myself the sermon, which mattered more to me. It worried me to have to trick my own people like the enemy. But if religion could help me save these men and give them a collective consciousness which would keep them sane, I would use their religion. They did not, however, all have confidence in me, and the more suspicious were among the most faithful. Some welcomed the idea of keeping up religious education, others demanded a rabbi. On Wednesdays and Thursdays the coming ceremony was the center of discussion, and often silence fell as I approached. To add to the solemnity of the occasion, I induced the kitchens, which were supplied by the community, to make a special effort. I prepared my program with great care. The rest was a question of propaganda, and in this I was greatly helped by the scouts and a few men who had understood my ultimate aim.

On Friday evenings when they returned from work, several of the workers would go to the stream, in spite of the cold, to take an extra wash. They put on their least tattered clothes and slowly came back to the middle of the camp. I too had dressed up and awaited them with a few determined helpers, the group captains, and the scouts. We had agreed to stay at equal distances from each other and to form a circle. The men hesitated as they approached, argued among themselves and, in their minds, drew an imaginary circumference. At last they were all still. The moment I was about to open my mouth, a difficulty I had neglected occurred to me: although I had prepared my subject and even words which would be understood without awakening the suspicions of the guards who were looking on, I realized only now that I should speak in dialect.

I think in French, and my interior monologues had for a long time been in French. When it happens that I speak to myself in dialect, I always have the strange impression, not so much of using a foreign language, as of hearing an obscure and obsolete part of myself, so forgotten that it is no longer native to me. I do not feel this strangeness when speaking to others, it is rather like playing on a musical instrument. But I did not know enough words of Judeo-Arabic to convey my whole meaning to them. I can express myself well enough in Arabic for concrete everyday purposes, but I have always used French in social and intellectual exchanges and the expression of ideas. I would have liked to speak at length to the men and, above all, convey to them certain things under the very noses of the guards. For that, certain subtleties which only French allowed me were necessary, but unfortunately their knowledge of French was deficient. In the last resort, I decided to attempt the experiment in French, although I realized how much closer I would have been to them and how much more intimate had I spoken their own tongue.

I did my best, avoiding abstract terms and using comparisons with events in their own lives. The pivot, I think, of my sermon was dignity and one's duty to preserve it. I linked dignity with hygiene. I gave them hope, promising they would soon be home, and warning them of the memories they would then retain of themselves; I quoted Ecclesiastes to prove that nothing ever lasts, and insisted on courage and morale in the fight against our vices and weaknesses. When all seemed lost and the enemy invincible, obstinate courage would triumph. I ended with the example of the glorious Maccabees whose courage had not been merely of the spirit. The men followed me attentively, and I could see in their sparkling eyes that they had difficulty in repressing their reaction. They were evidently enjoying our complicity very much, only a few yards from the guards.

Sooner or later, we had to come to that part of the ceremony which was our excuse for holding it. I made a gesture to signify that it was time to start the ritual. It turned out to be even more painful than I had expected. I had quite forgotten the ritual words and gestures; not only did I have to simulate fervor, but also to watch my neighbors and copy their gestures, sway to and fro, nod my head, mutter and answer at the right moment. I would be lost if the men guessed my ignorance. But the last Amen of the service delivered me from this unbearable situation.

I had expected a great show at the end, but before parting, I suggested we all sing the *Hatikvah,* the old Jewish national hymn. Although it was little known, there was a danger that the hymn might be recognized by our guards, but even such a risk would be useful in consolidating the effect. I called the congregation to attention in Hebrew. The word itself is a modern creation of the Zionists but, for every believing Jew, Hebrew remains a sacred language. The men stared at each other, then slowly obeyed like inefficient and ungainly automatons, every inch of their body hesitating. As soon as they were in position, they stiffened, staring into space. I counted "one, two, three" in Hebrew, then gave the signal, and their discordant, wholehearted voices burst into song with such conviction that I stopped watching them and also turned to stare at the sky. It was almost dark, and all the light was concentrated in the distant flickering stars. In moments like this, in spite of my shyness and my complexes, I caught glimpses of what being saved through others might be. But these moments were scarce, unfortunately, and almost immediately followed by doubts.

The next morning our guards informed us that all such meetings would henceforth be forbidden, which did not surprise me. I had gone ahead too fast, instead of first lulling them into inattention by a few strictly religious gatherings. Under our little tent, we held a conference with the scouts and a few group captains. The five scouts felt doubtful about the results of my enterprise, though it broke the monotony of camp life for them. As for my decision to join the workers voluntarily, they had found it comical and had judiciously advised me not to let it be known; the men would have been suspicious of me, they said. Finally, we decided to start a study group where we could, ostensibly, interpret and discuss the Bible.

We now had even greater difficulties. There was little leisure, we had no books, and the men were of a very low cultural level. They knew the Bible and the Talmud only superficially, but had no knowledge at all of science, politics, or modern history. My own education was too recently acquired for me to be able to adapt it or to make it other than dogmatic. The others annoyed me with their objections to every detail, their constant mingling of legends and superstitions. This was no time for slow demonstrations, though I did not want to shock them in any way. So I continued the same comedy and accepted the role of a learned and progressive rabbi, giving answers as best I could even to questions of religious orthodoxy. An expected consequence of these sessions was that the men regained an awareness of a renewed faith. The rediscovery of the Biblical belief that misfortune is the just punishment of sin gave them the impetus to live more purely. On Friday evenings and Saturdays they refrained from lighting any new fires and tolerated no smokers; they even forced our cooks to prepare the three Sabbath meals in advance and, if our little lamps went out, went to bed in the tents in the dark. I thought I did well to approve all such behavior.

What discouraged me most, however, was the impossibility

of becoming really intimate with the men. They never quite considered me as one of them. They could not see why I stayed in the camp when all the other intellectuals and middle-class men managed, in the long run, to get themselves evacuated. When, of an evening, I would slip into one of their tents where they were still awake around a carefully camouflaged light, they would make room for me and often give me the place of honor, but they changed the topic of their conversation at once and became self-conscious. They avoided, for instance, all trivialities. I told them my father was an artisan, but they did not believe me. Those who did had more respect for me: a son of the people who has worked his way up is more to be admired than a middle-class boy. As for me, must I confess that I never really felt at ease among them? I wanted to love them, and I fear I managed only to be sorry for them. I reproached myself for this pity because I so much wanted to be one of them! In spite of myself, I watched myself and played a part. Perhaps, as is so natural to me, I exaggerate my guilt; had I been one of them, I could not have helped them. But what I did not see clearly at the time was that I was seeking in the camp and in the approbation of others only my own self-respect; after a few months, I was sure I had failed. It seemed clear to me that the men respected or distrusted me but that they would never adopt me.

I saw this well one evening. As we had returned too late from work to eat by daylight, we had retired to our tents to sit around the lamps. I had left the scouts to join one of the other groups. We had started eating when one of the workers had such a violent fit of vomiting that he had no time to leave our little circle of light. The others noisily protested and insulted him. He got up with difficulty, went over to the second pole, and leaned against it; there, with his hands in the air and his head hanging, he went on throwing up spasmodically. Finally, he tottered to the door and, no sooner had he passed it than he doubled up, hugged his

stomach, and fell howling to the ground, clawing at the earth
in his pain. In the half-light on the parched grass, he was
like a big animal struggling in the grip of an unknown
disease. How could one relieve such an attack of appendicitis
in a work-camp? Maddened by the pain, the sick man had
become a child again and was calling his mother. I knelt
beside him and tried to touch his stomach, but he pushed
me away so brutally that I got up, disconcerted by his violent
refusal. All the workers left their tents and stood helplessly
around him. At last the camp tailor, an elderly man who
had been forgotten here in spite of his large family, took him
gently on his knees and nursed him like a child. The patient
calmed down and I stood there, useless and humiliated,
watching what I could not do myself, I mean take one of
them in my arms and nurse and comfort him.

Soon the others recovered their spirits and decided to
cover his stomach with hot ashes and oil, believing that he
must be suffering from intestinal trouble. I came out of my
·dream and protested, trying to explain that what he needed
was ice and that they might kill him by treating appendicitis
with heat. They would not believe me and · insisted on the
virtues of their traditional remedy which they had already
applied, they said, most successfully. Too energetically, I
answered that they had always been wrong, which angered
them so that they decided to take no more notice of me. The
moment was too grave for their usual show of superficial
politeness toward me. I gave up the argument and went
back to the tent where the scouts, their curiosity satisfied,
had now settled down again. They spared me their irony,
but their faces were eloquent and, as the sick man could no
longer be heard and was no doubt soothed, they tried to
while away the evening with part singing.

Gradually the vanity of my presence in the camp dawned
on me, as well as an awareness of how simple-minded I had
been, so that the decision to escape slowly began to mature.
Perhaps the monotony contributed more to this than the

constant anxiety and sudden dangers. I kept a diary regularly, and it filled three books, but if I were to try to sum up this period today I would not be able to do it. Naturally, there were the few episodes of sheer horror that I can never forget. The vision, for instance, of a comrade who, stripped to the waist and attached to a wrecked tank, had become delirious in the middle of the night. And the sight too of the two machine gun volleys at night, one of which killed a wretched escaping worker while the other killed poor Basmouth in his own excrement because he had dared to leave his tent during curfew. Then there was also the stupid allied Spitfire attack which, having spared the guards, left two perfectly silent corpses in the middle of the deathly consternation of the landscape; and a few other incidents besides. But on the whole, this period remains a solid and alien block within my memory.

Events helped to speed my decision. The Germans were yielding ground every day with their backs to the sea, and the camps accordingly retreated northwards. In two months we moved five times and were obviously becoming useless. Rumor had it, and this was confirmed by discreet information in letters we received, that we were to be shipped to Germany. We dared not consider the more probable alternative of extermination on the spot, but we were reminded of it by a Czech noncommissioned officer in a German uniform whose *Volkswagen* we retrieved from a ditch. He confirmed the signs of the coming Nazi collapse and the preparations for a retreat. The Germans no longer had enough ships and would certainly not set us free. We should therefore expect the worst and escape immediately.

One morning, we thought the hour for our mass executions had struck. The whistle which usually roused us at dawn failed to sound. From habit we awoke at the same hour, surprised at such a respite. Soon the camp began to buzz, but no one moved, of course, so as to avoid the beginning of work. We formulated hundreds of suppositions as to the cause of our luck: our whistling guard had had a stroke, Germany had been defeated, the Nazis had suddenly become humanitarian, our guards had all gone out of their minds together. . . . We joked as though we were in a holiday camp, and we had difficulty in refraining from pillow fights. At last, as time passed, we risked a few steps outside the tents. Our new camp was on a bare slope with an open horizon at the bottom of the valley. The army huts had been built a few yards higher up; to get out of their field of vision and escape being shot, one would have to run for several miles. Up there, nothing had moved. We washed and ate without hurrying and settled down peacefully to tasks like letter-writing and sewing. I was signing my last letter when one of the scouts came in, alarmed. Above us, between their huts, the soldiers were carrying out strange operations. Wearing battledress and hideous oilskin overalls striped green, yellow, and brown, they had lined up at fixed intervals and were fixing their machine guns on pivots. The mechanical slowness of their movements made the scene all the more solemn and sinister. When they stopped moving, we found we were in the center of a semicircular firing line from which escape was impossible. We would be mown down like rabbits. I smiled to my companions and tried to lie all the same.

"It's only a maneuver."

But I could see that our death was being planned. That day, however, it was only a rehearsal. It was time to escape and, a week later, there came a chance.

5

ESCAPE

WE WERE STILL at work when the clear and bright-eyed night fell on us. Our guards were as bad-tempered as we were tired. In the last fortnight, the Germans had handed us over to an elegant Italian lieutenant who kept perfecting this strip of road to avoid being sent to the front. He went to and fro nervously, whipping his shiny fascist boots with a swagger stick as slim and black as his own mustache. At last, his thin lips condescended to smile. He had overworked us to make us appreciate an extraordinary gift: tomorrow there would be no work.

But fate would not let us enjoy so unexpected a holiday. We had hardly gone a mile toward the camp, chattering cheerfully and already feeling less tired at the prospect of a full day's rest, when we came upon preparations for an approaching battle. Carefully and without hurry, German artillery men were setting up their short and dwarflike guns, bigmouthed as bulldogs, right across the road. A sort of sergeant, with a face like a cook and no cap or tunic, was rolling up his shirt sleeves with a greedy look. Our Italian guards came together to argue excitedly without concealing their fears. We waited and watched, worried and intrigued, our ears cocked to hear what they were saying, but they grew ashamed, and roughly ordered us to get back. We had to break ranks to pass between the guns, with the screaming Italians behind us. Further on, we met a stationary German truck full of silent men packed against each other and carrying the full weight of their imminent death.

The contrast between the calm despair of the Germans and the excitement of the Italians sent us into a flurry as soon as we were inside the camp; the soldiers ran about and pushed each other around as they undid the tents and prepared to load their equipment. The exhausts of the noisy Faravelli trucks sputtered as they stood awaiting the orders which were finally brought by the lieutenant. We had to evacuate and all men were to be placed at the disposal of the Nazi command.

At any moment the whole region was about to become a battlefield. The lieutenant decided that his men would have to abandon their personal belongings so as to save the equipment. The maddened workers then threw themselves on the meager belongings of the furious soldiers and there was almost a fight as they stuffed lamps, clothes, and utensils into their bags and even loaded whole sacks onto their backs.

Then the lieutenant took care of us. We would leave first, on foot, naturally, and alone; it was impossible for us to disappear on account of all the troop concentrations in the region. We had to go as far as we could, in our own interest. Otherwise, we would be caught between two firing lines. These explanations cooled down our joy at being avenged. The situation also had its disadvantages: we might get killed on the same battlefield as our bewildered oppressors.

We returned along the same road that passed through our place of work, which was deserted. Again, we met the German artillery men and their sergeant with a cook's face. They had finished their work and were now seated on the ground,

quite unconcerned. Further on, Italians were being loaded
into the first convoy of trucks as they swore at fate and the
Madonna to relieve their anxiety. Each time they saw our
column, they were upset again. Ironically, we reassured them,
but quickly, for fear of a sudden volley:

"*Lavoratori!* Workers!"

As long as we were neither "Inglesi" nor "Americani". . . .

At one of these encounters, some soldier was struck by
the idea we so dreaded and had avoided:

"Why haven't they all been shot."

We went forward, close together, without lingering among
the long rows of Faravelli trucks. A car with three wheels
passed us, stopped, and awaited the first men of our column.
The big red head of the Neapolitan sergeant showed itself
and sang out the one syllable "Stop!" Then he stuck his
head out and, with much gesturing, explained the direction
we were to follow by order of the lieutenant. Ten miles
ahead, the road branched in two: to the left, it went straight
to Tunis and, to the right, through Bir-Halima, our last
camp but one, before it also reached Tunis by a roundabout
way. Of course, we were to take the right and stop at Bir-
Halima. The sergeant concluded by furiously screaming:
"*Non è finita, la guerra!*"

After having let us go, the lieutenant had regained control
of himself. But the men's hopes had risen too high and too
fast to let resignation replace their thwarted joy. As soon as
we had left our guards, we had all immediately thought of
the road to the left at the other end of which were our
families and friends. But the three-wheeled car now carried
the bust of the sergeant away and our grumbling column
pulled itself together. None of us objected or even considered
the risk. We had to hurry, so we started a race against time
and against our clogs and empty stomachs and the heavy
sacks of loot that we did not want to abandon. We had
already trudged six hours of forced marching, after twelve
hours of road work. Loaded down but sustained by hope,

the men still found the strength to joke and show their high spirits:

"Aren't they going to have a surprise when they see us!"

"And how about Lieutenant Liquorice [that was his nickname because he was thin and long, and his skin, mustache, hair, and boots were all black] when he doesn't see us at all!"

After that, only silence could help us economize our energies. For a long time we marched to the dull thud of our wooden clogs. When we passed through Pont-du-Fahs in Indian file, the night was already dissolving. The village was deserted and sinister, with great black wounds on the houses where the doors and windows had been torn out. Solitude is more oppressive in places abandoned by men than in the middle of the wildest desert. After the bewildered crowds of the Italian sector, we were, in this deserted village, rather like the survivors of a huge catastrophe which had emptied the world of its inhabitants. We had to walk round great shell craters in the road. At long last, after Pont-du-Fahs, we came to the expected fork in the road. There were two green signposts with black lettering. To the left: *Nach Tunis.* To the right: *Nach Bir-Halima.* It was here that the first men let themselves fall into the ditch, weighed down by the bags they had not the courage to unfasten. We were still in a group and, without protesting, we lay down by the hedges. I then felt my own weariness, which was no longer muscular but nervous, and which no short pause could cure. Then men said nothing this time and did not joke. When the more impatient ones got up, two men just removed their straps and lay down again.

"The grace of God be with us," they decided. "If we survive, we will continue on our way, but we can go no further now."

The group leader, a little redhead who was silent and tenacious when it came to the execution of an idea though he himself was incapable of ever formulating one, swore copiously at them and at their mothers and grandmothers and said they would not be alive long if they stayed where they were.

"It is no use," said Picchonero, the little shoemaker with feverish eyes and a bloodless face. "In five minutes, their trucks can cover the distance that we take an hour to go."

But the men obeyed, glad to be led by someone. We set forth again, our clogs dragging along the tar-surfaced road, stiff with exhaustion, each body a painful heavy mass that passively obeyed. In my empty head, a last obsessive relic of thought beat to the rhythm of my blood: "I want to get home, I want to get home, I want to get home. . . ." It was like a hard little stone, condensing all my will power, with no possible answer: "I want to get home."

We took the road to the left, *Nach Tunis.* One man stopped, tore off his shoulder straps, and let his sack fall.

Then, without looking back, without a word, he lightly quickened his step. Five others did the same, and the little group soon outstripped us. I had neither the courage nor the weakness to follow their example. In my haversack I had, among other things, an annotated Bible, my diary, and some letters. I would have been ashamed, besides, to leave the long column which still clung together.

At one turning we came upon a German antiaircraft battery, camouflaged under palms and reeds.

"*Arbeiter!* Workers."

They asked no more questions, but warned us we were going toward the front. We could now imagine the plan of battle. They were still fighting on the wings of an arc, and the retreat had been ordered in the center. We knew that the Germans shot any civilians found in the battle zone. Whatever the price, and in spite of the Italian danger, we had to turn back. With a quick thought for the six men who had vanished ahead of us, we retraced our steps.

But we were lost in any case. If, by luck, we escaped the gunfire, we would certainly be recaptured by the Italians even sooner than we thought, for we could hear voices like

hallucinations in the pale unborn dawn. Had it been worth
so much trouble and pain? It did not occur to us to run or
to fight. Heavy as oxen, unable to move swiftly, we stopped
and awaited our pursuers.

But our mistake was full of pleasant surprises: the voices
were only those of our comrades on their way back from the
danger zone. In spite of our dejection, a ray of joy pierced
our armor of fatigue. We congratulated each other; the idea
that they had been lost and found again made them dearer
to us, each one of them more vividly present as a member
of the group, reducing for a moment each man's growing
sense of loneliness. I suggested to the leader that we stop
this exhausting march which only led us back to the Italians.
We should hide in the bushes of the countryside and let two
men watch on the road for a ride:

"If our guards arrive before they hitch a ride, our friends
can then lie and say they have left us and are alone. If
something comes along before the Italians, they will get a
ride to Tunis and come back with one of our community
trucks."

He thought this over at length and finally agreed. The men
disappeared behind the thorny Arabian acacia bushes that
lined the road, while Picchonero and I sat on the ground
and awaited any vehicle that might show up.

"I warn you," said the little shoemaker, "if I get there
I'm not coming back. You don't need me to recognize the
spot."

We waited at least half an hour before the first car turned
up. As the day advanced there began to appear, from the
other direction, an occasional big munitions truck marked
with the yellow flag: explosives, danger.

The Germans evidently intended to stop the Allies somewhere nearby. In a few hours we would be in the middle of
the fight. At last, there came a truck bound for Tunis. We
rushed for it, as fast as our stiff legs permitted; but the
driver hardly even looked at us. It would be better to stand

on the edge of the road, so we decided to take turns at this so as to be visible from a distance. Time passed. I was tense, my head empty, with one arm stiffly held in the hitchhiker's gesture. The few drivers who were going toward Tunis stared curiously at us but did not answer our signals that grew more and more frantic. A caterpillar car drew up in a clatter of chains, like a huge beast. I tried to run, but my joints were stiff. Picchonero rose too, but when the German driver understood what we wanted, he cursed us and started off again.

We jumped, for the first bursts of gunfire were very close, leaving trails of motionless smoke in the sky to our left. I had enough experience to realize that it was just a beginning; the reply, more dangerous for us, would not be long in coming. We had to formulate other plans, so we now joined the other men. I was surprised to find them talking, lying on their backs with their heads on their bags, in a mood of cheerfulness again. They had slept, eaten, and drunk a little; perhaps they had not quite understood the situation. I was vaguely angry with them for being so relaxed and carefree. Then I blamed myself; had I not fasted for the last twenty-four hours, and had I too rested for a while, I might also have been more cheerful.

The firing was now going strong. We had to leave and go forward to get out of the range of the artillery on the opposite side. It was difficult to go faster with our feet as wounded as they were after twenty-five hours of being chafed by the clogs we wore. My big toe felt as though there was a big cut right across it. The men got up reluctantly. Through the whole of this adventure, not once did I feel so far from them as at this moment, when they stretched and yawned.

A gentle yellowish day had driven away every trace of the cold white dawn. We set off again. All along the road, there were burnt and broken skeletons of trucks; some, put out of action by machine-gun fire, were like insects bitten by a spider, motionless and apparently intact. The first volleys of machine-gun fire stopped us and we hesitated. From where were they being fired? In what direction? In our complete ignorance of the situation, we did not know whether each step might not be leading us headlong to death, and this worried me as though I had suddenly been struck blind. I tried to master my brain that was so weary that it ached behind my painful forehead. So we were in the center of a semicircle and there was fighting on both flanks. But how far from the center were we? With daylight, aircraft would sweep over the interior of the arc. The firing grew louder, accompanied by the intermittent choking of machine guns. Suddenly, from behind the hills, two British fighter planes came flying low over the fields to attack a farm which, to us, looked like a doll's house. A German antiaircraft gun, hidden in the hills, reacted violently and dryly like a piece of cloth being ripped.

Swift and elegant, the steel-gray pursuit plane rose and then, as if unaware of the antiaircraft barrage, swooped down on the road. We threw ourselves into the ditches just as a terrifying din burst out. I lay with my face to the ground, beneath the weight of my haversack, and was only aware of the mauve thistle that was scratching my face. I supposed that, seen from above, the red, green, and blue Bedouin blankets in which our kits were rolled on our backs must form a colorful ribbon. Automatically, I slipped my blanket beneath me. In the general noise, a hurrah came from the men. I looked to the side: a little cart, madly drawn by a galloping donkey, tore down the road. I joined in the shouting too when, with my shortsighted eyes, I made out Picchonero, oblivious to the bombing, gesticulating on the seat by the driver.

"I'll send you help from Tunis! I'll send. . . ."

So he disappeared. Across the road, from the depths of their ditches on either side, the men lay flat on the ground and made joyous signs to each other. If Picchonero was not killed on the way, we could hope for a truck in a few hours.

Silence followed the uproar. We were all alive, not quite

knowing whether we had been aimed at, but our new hope
reviving all our last and most selfish energies. We took to
the road again in small and scattered groups, linked only
loosely by our ebbing strength. The first group disappeared
far ahead, and the last straggled to the rear. Each one wanted
to exploit to the full his last chance, and the redhead no
longer tried to regroup us. Nor did I have any more suggestions to make. Maybe he was right, and it was better to
save a few than lose the lot. I hid my precious papers, some
sugar, and a piece of bread in my pockets, and threw away
my haversack.

The road grew narrower, constrained between tall wall-
like hedges of cactus. At the entrance to an Arab farm, we
saw two charred and disemboweled mules.

We had had nothing to drink since the distant and vague
time of our work at the quarries. We ran to the well of the
deserted farm, and took turns drinking from a bucket an
opaque and salty liquid, the mere sight of which made us
drool.

Some men lay down in the shade of the narrow shapeless
buildings and refused to move any more, so we went on
without them. Discussion implies at least a minimum of contact and it had long since died between us. We regretfully left
the wretched farm, which still had something human about
it, for the wild, hostile countryside where we had no compass
to guide us in our wanderings.

Outside, horror had taken on the quiet and sinister disguise of a machine. Regular and even flights of bombers
came over us in waves, dropped their bombs on the hills,
and flew off again. During all this relay race, the machine
guns kept quiet and there were no accessory noises. Death,
at this stage, seemed to neglect all the smaller means that
were at its disposal. I had not tried to eat since our last
departure, so I now put a piece of sugar in my mouth, but
sucking it was so painful that I soon spat it out.

Was it a mirage? A dirty yellow jalopy, crudely painted

with a red cross, rattled around an elbow in the road; it was
the community ambulance! The men yelled, threw themselves
forward in an effort to run, and waved their thin arms. In
my tired head, another useless question had formed: how
had Picchonero arrived so soon? How much time had gone
by? I found it unpleasant to feel that I had lost all concep-
tion of time. The men surrounded the prehistoric vehicle
deliriously; with their stiff hands they touched it and groped
for the door handle, found it, and dived inside. They climbed
into it with their knees and chests and elbows and heads
banging against each other, pushing, squeezing, piling up,
disappearing in the dark as fast as possible. This took as
long as was necessary for the driver and the guide, who was
not Picchonero, to set the brakes, open the doors, leave their
seats, and appear smiling and shy. They gazed at the over-
flowing truck with its wide-open doors, covered with men
hanging onto the windows and standing on the step. Unfortunately, they explained, they had precise orders, and first
they must. . . . The others, their arms hanging and silent,
stared vacantly at their lost hope.

"Who is the group leader?" the driver asked timidly.

Nobody answered. The redhead was certainly buried in
the dark belly of the ambulance.

"We'll come back and fetch you," he shamefully went on.
"The community could find no other transport. We'll be
back as fast as we can."

The driver and his guide hesitated, waited in vain for a
reply, and got back into their seats. With great difficulty, the
truck turned round, jumped, and slowly started on its way.
With its doors open on both sides, it looked like a great
beetle, too heavy for its wings, with masses of little fleas on
its back.

We were once more alone with the war, which was steadily
catching up with our torn feet. Now that the bombers had
made sure of the silence of their former objectives, they
were aiming closer to us on the left. Clouds of thick gray

smoke slowly rose and hung in the air, and the whims of the wind brought us the acid smell of bomb explosions.

The fighter planes! We forced our swollen feet to run and threw ourselves into the ditches. Intelligently and diabolically, the planes passed over us, changed their minds, came back, then swooped and fired wherever they saw any sign of life. A German courier was racing past on his motorcycle, both he and his machine wrapped in striped oilskin camouflage like a fabulous caparisoned beast, when suddenly a Spitfire dived and flew low, riddling him with bullets till it rose again and left behind a flaming human torch. I closed my eyes. But there were neither screams nor spectacular convulsions. The machine silently went on, left the road, cut straight across a field, then lay down on its side, still burning. So the war had caught up with us; any encounter now was dangerous.

Outside Bir M'Cherga there was again some traffic. Without quite losing sight of it, we left the road and cut across country. Armored cars, tanks, and trucks formed an endless procession. The bombers resumed their relays. At each alarm, the drivers and their assistants left their vehicles and dashed for the ditches. We threw ourselves flat on the earth which shook hard beneath us. When it was over, each of us glanced at the others to count the survivors, and we then set forth again, uncuriously following the road. Vehicles were burning, and soldiers were trying to save them. I can no longer recall each attack separately: the roar of motors, the screams of warning of the men, their flight, and the silent anxiety as death took its pick, then the thuds of the bombs that shook the ground beneath us, the din of explosions, and again silence, with a gun still rumbling in the distance, and our departure once more. I was no longer surprised to find myself still alive, and the fear of death was no longer so acute. My mind was detached from my body, which lived on and automatically looked after itself.

Evening fell before I expected it. Night imposed silence

on the cannon and machine guns and engines all along the hills and within the arc of the front. But this sudden peace seemed to me so false and so heavy that I regretted the daylight. It was wiser to stop, and we also badly needed a little sleep after these past forty hours of being awake, which included twelve hours of shoveling, and twenty-six of forced marching on an empty stomach. We entered a field of ripe wheat which nobody dared pick. We arranged to take turns at standing watch and hid ourselves in the wheat. I was still chewing a thistle stem which was sour in my mouth when the war, for a moment silenced by the night, started again, more cynical and terrible than ever. A magnificent fireworks began: magnesium flares blindingly white, yellow, and then red, like dying stars; straight bright red streaks of machine-gun fire; elegant and clear lines of bullets traced like fugitive neon lights; and scarlet, sinister rugged patches from anti-aircraft artillery. Then the noise: after the solemn, promising silence of the flares came the mad disorderly reaction of the inhabitants of the earth to the regular, obstinate sounds of the invisible motors in the sky.

The airplanes replied to the nervous coughing of the machine guns with great battering blows that shook the earth. It was a celebration in honor of death. On the other side of the road a tribe of Bedouins rose from the middle of a field like a flight of partridge whose nest has been wrecked by a storm. These fugitives were perfectly silhouetted against the intermittent and richly colored flashes of light, until they disappeared, pursued by their fate, chanting monotonous prayers. This vision taught us a useful lesson: it was best to stay where we were.

I dozed, then came my turn to watch, and when I was relieved I dozed off again. I closed my eyes, but for a long time I followed the lights and colors from under my eyelids. Three bombs dropped so close that we were showered with sulphur. At last, as the tired night receded, the war again became wary and silent. We made the best of the truce and marched on. I did not feel rested. Sleep, which had not for a moment been deep, only reduced my weariness to a general torpor; in the same way, dawn veiled the landscape and obliterated the contours of hills and the ragged olive trees, softened the harsh brown earth and the dry green of the cactus hedges. We trudged silently ahead step by step, for centuries, it seemed. I have no recollection of this dead and shapeless time when nothing existed but the monotonous and independent movement of our clogs. Nothing, I imagine, could have made me more tired, and I no longer had either memory or desire. But I stopped once more to drink. Beside the road, a clay-red stream wound along the bottom of an eroded bed, and I rediscovered my thirst which made my tongue cling to my palate. The water was muddy and tasted of iron.

The early morning did not bring the violence of the day before. The front seemed to have become stabilized. The traffic started again, calm and scattered. If the front moved back a little, hitchhiking would become possible again. The men took to the fields again, and four of us stayed by the road to watch for a ride. Without moving, we let two German armored cars go past, only too relieved not to be questioned. We waved down a big truck driven by a civilian. He slowed down, rolled by, and stopped. We ran after him, an Italian civilian, probably a paid volunteer. We started vaguely explaining to him and ended up by being more explicit. Yes, he would take us, but he risked getting himself into a great deal of trouble, a great deal. . . . We wasted no breath. Among Mediterraneans there was no need to beat about the bush—with a German we would never have dared— how much? He hesitated. We proposed five hundred francs. He accepted, protesting with his hand that it was not the money that influenced him; he would get into trouble any- way. As soon as we had struck the bargain we yelled with all our might, as much to show our joy as to call the others.

They were not far off and were inside the truck as soon as we were.

Never has a machine seemed more miraculous to me. In less than an hour we had left an unreal world and entered a familiar one. Now the men re-enacted their outward journey, but their painful memories were tinged with joy.

"Look," one of them said to me, "see that big building there. That was where they held a thousand of us. They kept us there three days without letting us go out or even leave the straw on which we slept. . . ."

"The smell was something. . . ."

They were almost proud of their stories and were already reconstructing their memories.

"Look, that must be where poor Berdah. . . ."

Silence fell. It was a mistake to recall this detail. There were no traces of the machine-gun murder of poor Berdah, the clubfoot who straggled behind. All intent on the joy of returning to town, the men did not want to be reminded of things they could not joke about. Instead, they told me at length of the group-leader's protest to the German officer who would not permit more than one man to go to the toilets at a time. The leader had proved, with figures in hand, that going there in turns would mean that each man could relieve himself only once every five days. Thus Jewish logic had triumphed over German force, they concluded.

It was broad daylight when we reached the Roman aqueduct. As we passed under the enormous antique stone arches which cut across the same blue sky that its ancient builders had seen, I thought I was still dreaming. The men never stopped chattering. Again, they felt a group loyalty and that they were bound to each other by ties of affection. To me, however, they remained as alien as this historical monument. We stopped at the outskirts of the city. The driver could go no further. We paid him and walked toward the first houses. The city was motionless. We hesitated: how would we find it after our long separation? A door opened and a woman emerged with a can of milk. Everything was still in its place. One of the men rediscovered his tongue and his long frustrated desires.

"Oh, a woman," he exclaimed.

After that, I went into hiding and thought only of saving my own skin. And I was fortunate, for I survived the raids and bombings until the final German collapse.

6

THE INVENTORY

AFTER I HAD been back for a week, I noticed that I was running a fever, low, but regular and persistent. It was a few tenths of a degree above normal in the mornings, and then rose enough in the evenings to give me a disagreeable impression of heat around my cheekbones. In the dangers and preoccupations of the camp, I had forgotten to worry about my health. Now that I could nurse my toe and my wounded feet, could sleep in a bed and feel all my pains, I realized how wrecked my whole body was. The failure of my naive adventure in search of others brought me back to myself. Besides, the curfew and my illegal position should have been enough. As the Germans came to feel that all was lost, they multiplied their raids. When the bombings were particularly violent, I ran to the trenches of the old cemetery. But the German military police, with their tagged dog collars, were sometimes already in the shelters. It was wiser not to go out at all, and so there was nothing to distract my attention from myself.

I could not even think seriously of looking after myself.

To be on the safe side and as a mere matter of routine, I went to see Dr. Nunez. He greeted me severely. He had been expecting my visit and knew all about my expedition. He said that he disapproved entirely, medically speaking, at any rate, and my visit confirmed his fears. On purpose, he exaggerated the severity of his tone. When I told him of my temperature, he immediately pushed me into the icy X-ray room. The sound common sense of doctors, which gives them their reputation for wisdom, is barely shaken by the intuition of a move they cannot understand. He was clumsy in speech, like most physicians, and fumbled for words. Finally, he decided I had been too "sentimental." If the men suffered, there was nothing I could do about it, and to suffer with them and lose my own health would certainly not help matters. I got undressed as I listened without answering and pretended to be more obstinate than I really felt. He finally said no more, for he was not really sure he was right, and the rest of his argument trailed off in bad-tempered grunts. Finally, he put out the lights and the darkness isolated us from each other. I shivered when he pressed the cold screen against my chest. Then he made me turn around, breathe, and cough. He growled: "You may dress again." Finally he decided to satisfy my suppressed impatience and he spoke triumphantly: I had been insane to leave. The X-ray gave him a considerably stronger position, and he forgot all his doubts. The healed spot on my lung was again an active focus and had spread. Had we been living in normal times, he would have ordered me to a sanatorium. Meanwhile, I was not to tire myself and must eat plentifully if not well.

I did not tell my parents of my condition, for they would have lost their heads and worried me without being able to help. I preferred to keep it to myself. Maybe this was motivated as much by shyness as by the futility of telling anyone. Why should I admit that my health was wrecked? But perhaps my reserve was not so pure. Without admitting it to myself, I was giving in to one of the ridiculous prejudices of my education: tuberculosis, the "bad disease," was considered shameful. I could not ask to have more to eat without depriving others. But I could rest, physically at least. This was possible as long as I did not have to run to the trenches and climb stairs twenty times a day. With the excuse that I was exhausted from camp life, I managed to be left in peace in my bedroom with the door shut. All day I dozed on a sofa, my cheeks feverish. For the first time in my life, I had nothing to do. My only occupation was to take my temperature three times a day, and sometimes more, out of curiosity or anxiety. When I had taken it once I took it again, with the excuse that I had to check it because I had been too impatient or had taken it too soon. In spite of my refusal to take myself seriously, I was in fact far more worried than I admitted, and the rhythm of my daily life was determined by the thermometer. I tried to work in spite of the doctor's advice, but within a few minutes, my eyes would burn, my head grew heavy, and I would feel exhausted. I had always worked too much, but I now knew that it would be unbearable if I were not able to.

I could no longer think of anything but myself and the balance-sheet of my life that I was now forced to examine. In the past, some urgent task had fortunately always required attention, and I had only stopped once in a while to ponder the meaning of my life. But I was now locked up with myself by war and sickness, with no possible diversion. The worst part of being sick, I found, was this concentration on one's self and the tyranny of the self. Perhaps others who live more extrovertedly find this profitable. But for those who tend to be introspective, sickness is stark solitude, the worst of all possible conditions.

For several weeks I had not been able to make entries in my diary. I now returned to my scrupulous and methodical habits, but my point of view had changed. Before, it had been metaphysical and impersonal, scrutinizing the world passionately to understand it. Now I became the only center of my own preoccupations. Who was I? What were the results of my long struggle ever since my childhood? In the confusion of my buzzing ears and burning cheeks and feverish brain, I was certain only of the need to come to a conclusion. Would I have the courage to go on living in so unstable an equilibrium?

But once more my balance-sheet was almost forgotten. The collapse of the Germans was as sudden as the arrival of their Junker transports full of troops had been, at least to me. One afternoon, probably at about five, I had just taken my temperature when shots rang out in the streets. As we always expected the worst, we started to put up barricades, before we caught sight of the first American tanks. For several days we gave ourselves up to delirious joy. Miraculously, our anxiety was gone, and here again were freedom and abundance. The German planes soon disappeared and our nights ceased to be nightmares, we devoured endless cans of meat, and spoke loudly in the streets to relieve ourselves. It was more than peace: it was a party. Then we had to start everyday life again. I realized that the historical change in our situation required a new kind of behavior. (But I wonder whether the gravest problems are not less painful than having to face one's own self.)

This was certainly one of the most terrible periods of my life. Again I was forced to choose, and my weariness made the least effort exhausting. But this time the choice would not be personal; it required an urgent, definite, and public solution. When war had been declared, a spontaneous movement had caused all native-born Jews to sign up. At the Liberation, not one of them volunteered. The instinct of human groups is usually sound. The war had taught us our real place in the mind of the West. Each time we had needed the West it had ignored us. The news that now reached us from the rest of the world confirmed this selfishness of the West: the desperate appeals of the Warsaw ghetto, the

silence of the West's religious authorities, and its abandon-
ment of most of the Jewish minorities to the Germans. As
soon as the Germans left Tunis, our ghetto decided for itself
that the war was over. For me, it could not be so simple.
Once I had overcome my rage against Vichy, the *numerus
clausus,* and the Fascist Legion, I began to doubt the treason
of France. To accept it would indeed have been unbearable.
All my ambitions, my studies, and my life were founded on
this choice. How much would I have to uproot in myself now?
What would be left me? It was in this dreadful moment that
I finally caught a glimpse of my ruin. If I rejected what I
was becoming would I be able to return to what I had been?

I hung around the deserted recruiting offices without being
able to make up my mind. One of my motives was to end
this constant brooding and to do anything so as to be done
with it. But a new phenomenon appeared in my life: I developed insomnia. Until then, no noise or irritation had been
able to provoke this, and I could have been carried around,
fast asleep, without being awakened. I now started to have
nightmares and it took me so long to fall asleep that, the
next day, my features were drawn and my head empty. One
night I had such a terrible dream that I awoke in anguish
and leaped out of bed. I no longer remember the details,
which I was anxious to chase out of my mind, but I still
have with me the curious and horrible impression that it left.
It was about a replica of myself, dead and stretched out on
the floor, while my mother inhumanly forced me, with a
cruel hand, to stare in its face. Alive, I still felt that I was
dead and that I had to live and accept and put up with my
own death. I jumped out of bed and ran to open the window
to let some fresh air into the room. My hand trembled on
the window latch and I had to walk up and down to calm
myself. That was what I was suffering from, far more than
my lungs. I stood before myself as before a deforming mirror; something strange had slipped into the core of my life.

Travel if you wish, taste strange dishes, gather experience in dangerous adventures, but see that your soul remains your own. Do not become a stranger to yourself, for you are lost from that day on; you will have no peace if there is not, somewhere within you, a corner of certainty, calm waters where you can take refuge in sleep.

During all this period, Henry was an admirable example of calm, of smiling serenity. He had no ties that he felt he needed to break, and he saw and acted directly, without suffering. Although I was too agitated to listen to him properly, he reduced my scruples by teasing me. Do others have scruples about us? He had turned a part of his room into a workshop where he manufactured toys. He invented new toys and he carved and painted wood with great skill and taste; it was the only useful thing he had learned in his Italian school, he said. The merchants of the city had long been short of goods and they paid him whatever he asked. This source of income allowed him to break with his father for longer periods and his independence made him happy. I used to stretch out on his couch and watch him at work. As his paintbrush moved over a panel of plywood, he would talk away about his latest daydream, with great precision and carefully collected details. In his generosity, he included me in his plans. This time, he had found he had an uncle who was a planter in Argentina, a new country full of possibilities. Europe was ruined and would need everything. We would go to Argentina and carry on his uncle's flourishing business, even extend it and plant more and more to supply Europe. Soon we would be powerful and perhaps famous in Argentina, where cultured and educated men must be relatively scarce. Henry was a practical dreamer and quoted figures as well as the promises of his uncle who had answered his questions through his daughter. He even showed me some letters! I did not take him seriously, any more than when he had planned a fishing business on the desert coasts of the South. Did the uncle really exist? But I liked Henry's daydreams. They were a relief for me from the insoluble problems that entangled me. With a single stroke of his brush, an eye appeared; another, and there was the bear's snout too. Henry would then stop and judge the whole.

"How d'you like it?" he would ask.

I emerged from my silence.

"And what about the war, Henry?"

He was in the middle of his dream and could not free himself so easily from it. He thought I was alluding to the dangers of the sea voyage.

"The Germans are finished in the Mediterranean."

"That's not what I mean. Can we really stay out of this war?"

He exploded.

"So you think we haven't paid a high enough price already? The truth is that you are speaking for yourself and that you are terrified of being accused of fright. Besides, damn it, first of all they should want to have us. They don't want our help because they don't want to grant us our rights. Our dignity now requires that we all volunteer together; if they want us, they must take the lot of us."

Unfortunately, it was too late for anything but individual solutions. The French were now sure of victory and refused to make any postwar promises, so the traumatized Jewish masses withdrew to themselves again. But I could not hope for any peace without having first tried everything. Why has nothing ever been simple for me? I envied any young Frenchman who had just received his orders to join the army. If he delayed answering the call, the military police came and fetched him. My ex-comrades in the camps had a freer conscience. They felt that they paid their tribute to a war in which they did not believe and which would change nothing for them. I alone had no idea what to do because I was too free, with the too perfect freedom of a seed which seeks a place to settle. Freedom is one aspect of solitude, and my solitude was too painful for me to enjoy the full weight of my freedom.

The rumor got around, however, that the Free French Forces were more liberal than the regular army which accepted only conscripts. When the Gaullists opened their first recruiting office in a tailor's shop, I went there with Henry, who was sarcastic but always willing to follow me. A Free French lieutenant with a blue cap and red lapels awaited his clients behind a huge counter. He rose exuberantly:

"So you want to fight?"

"Yes," I said.

He pointed to an open register which was the only object on the counter and, indeed, in the shop.

"Here, fill in your name, address, age. . . ."

It was still the first page, almost blank: I counted three names. The lieutenant followed my eyes.

"It's true, your compatriots don't seem very enthusiastic," he said cheerfully.

Henry and I looked at each other. It would take too long and be too difficult to explain, and it might hurt his feelings. Why should they be enthusiastic? What had they to defend or to hope for? I did not answer. Jumping from column to column, I carefully wrote down my name, address, age, nationality, and profession. The last column was headed: "Reasons for which you are not already in the army." I wrote: not subject to conscription.

From the other side of the counter, the lieutenant read it upside down.

"Please give details," he said. "Why can't you be conscripted? Are you a foreigner, or exempted, or rejected. . . ."

"Foreign," I said. "Well, not exactly; native African Jew."

"Ah, then wait," he said hurriedly, "wait, don't write anything. It's that . . . er. . . . Would you mind enlisting under another name?"

"But. . . ."

"Of course," he quickly added, "it's simply a formality. We are very happy to have you; it's just to avoid . . . you know, politics. . . ." he stammered. Out of pity, I helped him.

"You don't want any Jews?"

"Oh, not us. You know, we already have lots. They're good fighters and good comrades at arms. That's why General Giraud's men say that the Gaullists are mostly Jews, which isn't true and does us a great deal of harm; so, for the moment, well. . . ."

The demonstration was painful, so he shifted to safer grounds, those of his own enthusiasm.

"The important thing is to fight, isn't it? I mean the pleasure of smashing the Krauts! You know, when we took Bizerte, I wept tears of joy. . . ."

He tried to warm himself and us with the memory of his emotions. My face must have been fairly impassive. He shut up. Henry smiled pleasantly, as though he had a great liking for the lieutenant and perfectly understood his difficulties. But I knew his face too well.

The poor officer glanced at the register again.

"I'm so glad you're a student. I too was a student, in pharmacy. You must understand, politics has nothing to do with. . . ."

He lied clumsily. He must have known that I too wanted to fight my own war, and not just any war. War is either a personal affair or a swindle.

His face lit up, and he seemed to have found an idea:

"Look, leave your name and just add 'Mohammed.' There is no difficulty for Moslems."

He had spoken alone all the time.

"I'm going to think this over," I said at length.

I looked at the register and at my name which was only the fourth: Alexandre Benillouche. As usual, I had forgotten to write Mordekhai.

Benillouche could well be a Moslem name, since "Ben" is

a prefix common to both Jews and Moslems. But why should the Moslems fight? In any case, I wanted to avoid any misunderstanding.

Mordekhai, I was certainly Mordekhai Benillouche. Before leaving, I picked up the pen again and, without looking at the lieutenant, added "Mordekhai" in brackets. Fortunately, Henry was silent about his triumph.

For a while, I tried to be calm and to reason. These refusals might well revolt me, but they also gave fresh strength to the arguments of wisdom. I kept telling myself that a medical examination would have exempted me and that my zeal was excessive. Any man who was liable to be conscripted and who happened to have a spot on one of his lungs could permit himself to be rejected with a peaceful conscience. Wasn't Henry right? Wasn't my insistence undignified? Had I a right to try to solve the problem individually instead of waiting for a collective decision?

It may seem immodest not to mention as well the simple fear I had of the war. Not that I never thought of it. But the idea of death had so often been with me beside my bed, obscurely tempting but rejected, that the anguish of battle could not be much worse.

Meanwhile, I wrote also to the Military Commander of the city and waited a long time for his answer, which said that nothing had been planned for people in my category.

Finally, after much reasoning I admitted what the masses had immediately felt intuitively. I could only be a victim of this war; never would I be accepted as one of the victors. In the end this side of the question was cleared up completely. A member of the Chamber of Deputies demanded the mobilization of native Africans, but the Algerian Assembly refused. From a distance, we followed the disappointing debate. The heads of our community then proposed, of their own accord, that the Jews be conscripted. That too was refused. Such a collective measure would evidently have meant extending the rights and advantages of servicemen to their families, and that was out of the question. There was no longer any reason to doubt; for the second time, the West had rejected and betrayed us. The first time, I had been able to find an excuse for it: the Vichy government was much criticized by the Western powers. This time, however, there could no longer be any doubt. Some time later it was rumored that one could join the Second Gaullist Armored Division in Tripoli. Apparently, they did not dare send back those who had traveled so far to enlist. But I did not make any further moves.

I would never be a Westerner. I rejected the West. Still, my ideas were too confused and my heart too passionately involved in all that happened, so that I could not fully realize my position or draw practical conclusions from it. I had rejected the East and had been rejected by the West. What would I ever become? What was my future? Again, I fell prey to harassing doubts, utterly overwhelmed. At least there were now few air raids, and I could rest better. So I spent most of my afternoons with Henry. For hours, I would listen to him dreaming about wealth in Argentina and the wonderful life out in the open, on horseback, in boots and sombreros. I did not argue about the war any more. He had included it in his plans, which became more complex. First, we would go to England and join the British forces which were less difficult than the French. He had found out that British R.A.F. pilots were being trained in America. We might do a little fighting, to satisfy me. Afterwards, as the war drew to a close, we could get ourselves demobilized in America. From there, we could get to Argentina.

Once again, I was exhausted by the effort to escape from myself. The usual cycle was completed and I was incapable of taking an interest in the world or of coming to a decision. To me, the war was far off and of no importance. I listened to Henry as he spoke with precision and conviction. I knew too well how deceptively rational and clear his dreams could seem. Anyone else, seeing us there, with me so attentive and him so bright-eyed and talkative, would never have guessed that he was only daydreaming.

I borrowed some books from the public library and tried to do some studying again. It was my old means of protection against the world and against myself, in fact against anything that happened. At this time the temporary Algiers government announced by proclamation that we were reinstated in the university and that exams were to be held within two months. This forced my decision: perhaps it was wiser to continue my studies and become a professor of philosophy, as I had always so much wanted, and to bother less about others.

Unfortunately, this time the way back was full of pitfalls. If I wished and, indeed, was forced to break with the West, could I peacefully keep its values and philosophy and become one of its officials? Actually, I got caught up once more in the fever of preparing for the exams and avoided my self-questioning. But I soon realized how impossible it all was.

7

EXAMINATION

I HAVE NOW come to the point where I
began my narrative. Here I am in the examination hall, in
the huge university library. All around me, as far as the
distant shelves on the walls, my comrades are feverishly at
work. The early morning sun begins to warm us through the
stained glass. The first beads of sweat are tickling my forehead and forming heavy drops in my eyebrows. On my desk
there are a thermos flask, a package of sandwiches, cigarettes, and a bottle of ink, as on all the other desks.

*But as I face these white sheets of paper and long hours
that call for an effort, I must admit at last how impossible
my whole life has become.*

*The buzzing in my ears has started again these last few
days. At first, I tried to ignore it: it was nothing but a slight
fatigue that would leave me after the exams. But now it
sounds like the incessant ringing of a bell. Come, it's high
time! My chest aches too; to tell the truth, it has always
ached, but I would not let it worry me. Now I cannot but
admit it: my ears are buzzing and my chest is aching. I*

might uncork the flask full of such strong coffee and it would bring the dead back to life, and drink a cupful and perhaps even finish this paper. But again I have to admit that I can work only with lots of coffee, while my hands tremble and my heart beats fast. The truth is that I am a wreck. I have wasted too much energy and for too long. I paid a far higher price than the others for my smallest success because I always had to fight under impossible conditions. It is now time to put an end to this disastrous business. I am beaten.

In any case, had I been capable of continuing, I did not want to. How could I go on taking seriously this little world of conventions, of arbitrary values, of exams and their little emotions, together with the absurd administrative hierarchies? The sheet of paper before me waits for me to tell the examiners what I think of John Stuart Mill and of Condillac. What do I think? Precisely, today I am incapable of thinking about anything but my own ideas and what I am.

I look at my comrades around me. With their pale heads bent over their work and their nervous hands in their tousled hair, they know exactly what they want.

They can work themselves into a frenzy over something that is not themselves. What is required of us? That we express the balanced opinions of our examiners and the impersonal ideas of the university concerning John Stuart Mill and Condillac? They would then be able to choose the twenty essays that are most alike because they reflect most slavishly the university's ideal version. I am no longer able to forget myself and to think of something else. Nothing can distract me now from this basic quest. Anything else would be a luxury. As if my life were on the same pattern as all the others, clear and comfortable and without any mystery or contradiction, I tried to organize it quietly on the same model as any other man. I am poor; so I shall get a lucrative job and forget all my humiliations. I cannot pay for my studies; so I will coach other students and work my way through school, studying only in the evenings. My memory is full of superstitions and *Djnouns* and strange anxieties; so I vigorously opt for Western culture and try to ignore all that is barbarian. I saw, of course, that I was simplifying a great deal and that I would have to hack my way with an ax; still, I believed that it was only a matter of effort and will power.

But my life has again risen like a vomit in my throat; I cannot be simplified. Every event proves this, every move brings me back to myself. Perhaps I would not give up if I still had some strength. I have already proved myself, but I have now come to the end of my tether. Perhaps it is best as it is.

I have already told how I came up for these finals. The official decree which announced that exams would be held again and the Vichy laws would be repealed had suddenly put an end to my hesitation. My decision to resume my studies had been but a personal refuge from my insoluble problems and, in this manner, had acquired an objective basis, so that it became unequivocally serious. I quickly wrote to the university, prepared my transcript files, and was impatient to return to my job in school, as though I wanted to put an end to a period when all my convictions and hopes had been subjected to questioning. I was thus going to pick up the brutally broken thread of my life, which would acquire again its initial purpose once so convincing to me. The world I had doubted was going to resume its real course and signify to me that its rejection of me had only been a passing error which it would now be ungracious of me not to want to forget. When everything would once more be in its place there would only remain the memories of a few private nightmares. So these days of rushing around asking for interviews, going to school, and writing quick joyful letters had given me far more happiness than those of the military liberation of Tunis. I again felt I had an open future ahead of me.

In a gesture of good will designed to efface somehow the humiliations recently inflicted on us, the administration offered to consider valid all the time that we had lost. To take advantage of this new measure, one had to go back to work immediately. The faculty had organized special courses to prepare us quickly for our exams, so I decided to go to Algiers and wrote a long letter to the Board of Education requesting an interview. Like everybody else, I wanted to take advantage of my years of seniority, and above all, I requested an exemption from returning to my teaching job. I argued that I wished to leave the city solely in order to improve my professional training. I thought that, in the general atmosphere of good will, this could not be refused me. My request was submitted in the most favorable circumstances. Luck had it that my former principal, Monsieur Marouzeau, was now chief of secondary education. Although he had absolutely no ambitions, he had been appointed to the job because there were no other candidates and because he had a right to the job. At school the decision was taken unjustly as a surprise and his friendly and informal manners and his shorts were ridiculed, but for me, it was an unhoped-for blessing. My imagination went to work and I began to plan far ahead. Soon I would return from the university; I would then need, to start with, a job as a teacher. My former principal had often promised me his support.

I got back to work while I waited to learn when my interview would take place. With difficulty I got together a few books and I made up for the lack of textbooks that were out of print by studying more collateral readings and other compilations. In order not to be distracted during study, I gave up taking my temperature. It was a good idea: soon I experienced once more a long-forgotten happiness. With delight, I discovered that my mind had not gone to seed, in fact this period of lying fallow had done it good. When I tired of taking notes, I rushed around town to prepare for my trip. Owing to the confusion in government agencies and the suspicions that were a hangover from the state of siege, it was difficult to get travel orders. But I was optimistic and resolute. I experienced such a pleasure in wandering freely in the liberated city, without always having to fear a German dragnet, that I even discovered a liking for purposeless roaming, as though I were renewing acquaintance with my own city. In short, I was a new man.

On the appointed day I was ushered into a big office, rather like a government department. The desk stood in the middle of a carpet of thick blue wool with black squares. Behind the desk, on this magnificent Gabes rug, was my little principal. The heads of Oriental agencies take great care to stage a princely setting and I was accustomed to this. But the frail silhouette of Monsieur Marouzeau, with his sparse short-cropped hair and his pants too short above his socks, seated here in the proud surroundings of his predecessor, this was indeed very funny.

When he saw me, he rose in a very friendly manner and greeted me without any ceremony.

"Good morning, Benillouche, take a chair. . . ."

He had read my letter. So I was resuming my studies! Very good! I was wise to do it immediately, and he could but encourage me heartily. He had always known I would succeed. Besides, he would help me as much as he could.

I was grateful to him for his simplicity in still treating me as a former pupil; this allowed me more freedom. As he chattered on without coming to the object of my visit, I reminded him of it.

"Ah, yes! You've made a fine mess of it, you know. I'm told that you're no longer a government employee."

I did not quite see what he meant. I felt only that very bad news was coming.

"You might have obtained the delay you asked for, and I would have helped you. But when I was shown that letter of yours I could obviously do nothing. The chief of personnel was final about it: you resigned and you were not thrown out like the rest of your colleagues. As a point of law. . . ."

I suddenly remembered. I had completely forgotten my resignation and, not prepared for this objection, no longer knew what to reply.

"But," I stammered, "you remember that they asked us to sign a circular swearing that we were neither Socialists, nor Communists, nor Freemasons, nor Jews. I couldn't sign that kind of paper. . . ."

"You were not obliged to. . . ."

"And so they would have fired me!"

"But that was only to be expected, like all the others."

"But it was under the Vichy government and I thought. . . ."

"Look here, Benillouche, the administration may change, but your file remains."

I felt within me a surge of unreasonable anger, one of those sudden bursts of anger that made me say anything in front of anybody.

"It was a question of dignity! I'm glad I didn't stop to think, like the government! Such petty calculations don't even interest me!"

The principal was a decent guy. He hesitated, shrugged his shoulders, and rose from his seat, the carpet muffling all sound.

"Come now, you made a mistake, that's all," he said in a fatherly tone. "After all, it's no tragedy. You've lost your seniority, but you're not an old man and can start again. Pass your exams first and then come back and see me; we'll try and get you a job here if you want one."

Monsieur Marouzeau seemed so kindly, as he turned in embarrassment around his desk, with his socks showing in the sandals that he wore all the year round—since he was in the "colonies"; and my fury dropped immediately, blown away by the feeling of futility and the emptiness of the future which was oppressing me more and more. This was probably the precise moment when I ceased to care about the university and my studies, but I was not clearly conscious of it. In spite of my spasmodic rages, I was accustomed to injustice and to the natural inequalities among men.

Monsieur Marouzeau had convinced me and sat down again. Daydreaming is contagious, so he started dreaming out aloud: everybody has his own difficulties and he too had been harmed by the war and had seen neither his family nor his country for five years, and it pained him. Yes, he had the impression of living on borrowed time.

To live on borrowed time. That's an eloquent expression. But I had never lived on anything but borrowed time and I had been waiting to live, God knows how long. I can see now that I was already condemned.

"Well," my good principal concluded with much originality, "such is life, Benillouche, such is life!"

He took me to the door and we shook hands cordially. I went down the great marble staircase and found myself outside, outside in the cold, out of the educational system. It was my own fault, Marouzeau had said. No, I did not feel I had made a mistake, and I would have done the same again. No, that had probably not been the right place for me either. How odd was the feeling of relief that came after each break! Had the principal said yes and reinstated me without discussion, had I been granted my leave of absence as I requested, would I really have been glad to go back to the civil service? Would I not, sooner or later, have realized my mistake in choosing this path and trying to be what, within me, deep down within me, I was not? And if I had obstinately insisted on not realizing it others would have forced me. This refusal was a warning. It was my fate to be always breaking with something, but without ever being able to retrace my steps for my past always slammed the door in my face. If my nose had been too long that might have been fixed in a couple of weeks in a clinic, or a gangrenous arm could be amputated, but I had a heart that was defective.

My misfortunes were never chance encounters, and I could not easily avoid them. The more I get to know myself, the more aware I become of this. To put an end to this state of affairs would mean putting an end to myself, to die or to go mad. My principal's temporary appointment would end one day, but I would never find the solution to my problem because I am that problem.

I was no longer in a hurry as I left the Board of Education. Where would I go now? I followed the old ramparts with their white battlements that cut the sky in equal slices of blue. Then I went through the great green door with its useless rusty gates. The setting is unreal and absurd, like pasteboard in a provincial theater. I went into the covered bazaars, between rows of low houses leaning against and climbing over each other. This was the architecture of my native country. Would I agree to live in one of these houses, without water or light, in these muddy streets? Could I bring myself to return to live in the Middle Ages?

But how could I ever have become a professor of philosophy and dedicated myself to the play of well-defined ideas, teaching the young my phony solutions to phony problems, with all the imaginary psychology of university textbooks? One has to teach calmly, with peace of mind and a pipe in one's mouth like Poinsot; to walk to and fro in the classroom and puff away before answering a question with conviction, with conviction and irony, in fact with complete detachment. How wonderfully transparent was Poinsot! He walked around with tiny steps, one hand in his pocket, the other at his pipe, his eyes vague. In the middle of a sentence, halfway between his desk and the window, he would stop and take off in a quick reverie, while we waited respectfully. There was only the puffing of his pipe to disturb the silence; then, after a moment, he would deliver his precise and methodical conclusions. What could I be sure of? Before one scoffs at national pride and the fatherland, at wealth and good manners, love of one's country, family, and traditions, one must have arrived at a proper evaluation of one's country, have had enough to eat, and have received a good education. Then one can look on from afar and make wisecracks. But I have no sense of humor and not enough courage to be cynical.

I would have had to rediscover everything for myself, build it all up again, and reconsider every proposition. Is it possible to build with anger and passion, indignation and envy, shame and a sense of being alien? If my principal had only known how I envied him! This average Frenchman from Burgundy, with his old culture and good background, a university man and a Republican of good family, suffered because he was in a foreign land! I am ill at ease in my own land and I know of no other. My culture is borrowed and I speak my mother tongue haltingly. I have neither religious beliefs nor tradition, and am ashamed of whatever particle of them has survived deep within me. To try to explain what I am, I would need an intelligent audience and much time: I am a Tunisian but of French culture. ("You know, the art of Racine, an art that is perfectly French, is accessible only to the French. . . .") I am Tunisian, but Jewish, which means that I am politically and socially an outcast. I speak the language of the country with a particular accent and emotionally I have nothing in common with Moslems. I am a Jew who has broken with the Jewish religion and the ghetto, is ignorant of Jewish culture and detests the middle class because it is phony. I am poor but desperately anxious not to be poor, and at the same time, I refuse to take the necessary steps to avoid poverty.

But in spite of this interview with the principal, I did not realize how close at hand was utter despair. I went on getting my papers in order for my departure. The momentum of the old machine still carried me ahead. The situation in the city, at this time, was still disturbing. At the victory parade, an onlooker who was pushed around by a policeman had answered too violently. There was much loud talk about the new Rights of Man saved from barbarism, and the man had let himself go too far. But the policeman had been more influenced by racial propaganda, so he fired on the onlooker and killed him. As the victim was a Jew, the murderer was acquitted. The indignant Jews inferred that nothing had changed. The Moslems too, as a matter of fact, for not longer after this, their nationalist leaders were arrested. Some thought that order was being restored. Lastly, the French Constituent Assembly definitely rejected the law on conscription. Things got organized, merchants started going back to business as usual, and the politicians returned to cheating. In short, all was once more in hand.

After all, I too had gone back to normal, I believed. I decided to resume my interrupted studies again and even thought I had once more found the rhythm and the pleasure of productive work. The French *Revue de Philosophie* appeared again in Algiers, the temporary capital, and I sent in my subscription. I bought new notebooks and went back to keeping a diary. Six weeks before the exams, I turned up in Algiers, like every other serious student, to verify my transcripts, sit in on a few lectures, and get inside dope by means of the grapevine.

This morning I got up before the alarm clock rang. I washed my face with cold water and bathed my smarting eyes in my cupped hands. When I finished dressing, the window was still dark. I was well ahead of the first streetcar, with its load of sleepy grocers on their way to market. In the examination hall I took the seat that was marked with my name and made the acquaintance of my neighbors. The boy to my left is small and dark with black eyes under heavy brows; his name is Bounin. On my right, my neighbor's name is Ducamps. When the supervisors with their expressionless faces and ritual gestures deposited the examination papers on the end of the table, I read the little square of yellow paper like the others. Soon silence reigned. Not a breath in the vast hall with its hundreds of students. Each has identified

himself with his work, each is alone for the next seven hours.
It is then that it dawns on me, with the white paper in front
of me, that all this no longer concerns me at all.

This time the spring within me is quite broken; my strength
and my will power fail me now. I might have stopped before
leaving Tunis, or at the customs, or in a railroad station on
my way, or at the entrance to the college. But I stopped in
the examination room. It really is the end: I shall never be
a professor.

8

DEPARTURE

It was on the interminable return trip, during the twenty-six hours in the train, that I decided to leave Tunis with Henry. As a matter of fact, I do not quite see what else I might have done, except let myself die here. Every morning, fits of coughing exasperate me and send the blood rushing to my head, like an echo of my father's spells of asthma. I used to be so full of disgust and pity for this ritual of pain, and here am I already aping him. It is high time for me to leave or to complete my ruin.

It was a very tiring night. The wooden railroad car bumped us about on the seats and against the walls. My companions had shut the door and the window of our compartment. Soon the air became stifling and my temples and neck were sticky with sweat and soot. Once, I almost fell asleep, but the suitcase that was on my knees and on which I rested my arms and head was jerked away. Outside the compartment, the cold made me cough violently, but at least I could think.

Once I had thrown up the sponge in the exam, I never entered the college again. But I did not wish to leave Algiers before having set the whole matter straight; after that, I was face to face with myself. If I now remain alive, I'll never forget this extraordinary meeting and the strange way I came up against myself.

So I have progressed from crisis to crisis, each time finding a new equilibrium, though a bit more precariously; still, there was always something left that could be destroyed. This time, the accounts are balanced: at last nothing shields me from myself. I made my break with our blind alley because it was but a childish dream, then with my father and my mother when I grew ashamed of them, with values of our community because they were obsolete, with ambition and the middle-class world because they are unjust and their ideals all questionable, with the city because it still lives in Oriental medievalism and has no love for me, with the West because it lies and is selfish. Each time, a part of me has disintegrated. I thought of death, of leaving the world. But never has the idea of death been so familiar and so present, like a ripe decision.

I am amazed at not being afraid; but habit gives one courage, and I have actually watched for my self-discovery for a long while: I am dying through having turned back to look at my own self. It is forbidden to see oneself, and I have reached the end of discovering myself. God turned Lot's wife into a pillar of salt—is it possible for me to survive my contemplation of myself?

I did not kill myself because I remembered the ditch in summer camp where I used to go and weep every afternoon, and because I refuse to allow myself any compromises. I am leaving now with Henry to give what is left of my life its last chance. Here, there's no solution; whatever my choice, I would have suffered. If the world is everywhere such a tissue of lies and hatred as here, then life is but endless despair. Perhaps I owe it to myself to cross the ocean first. Perhaps elsewhere I will be taken for a man of good will with a simple case history and simple feelings. Perhaps my body and my soul will recover there. If ever I get cured of my tuberculosis and of my life which I should never have known, I will then have all of my life ahead of me. The secret of living must be simple, since all men live. If I die, at least my apprenticeship will have been thorough. With all my heart, I hope what I have learned can be of help to others.

Our train reached Tunis at eleven in the morning. The city was full of soldiers of all kinds and all races, and they seemed foreign to me. The unusual and limitless nonchalance of the crowd gave one the erroneous impression of a fair. The merchants had organized their business accordingly, with English inscriptions and banners across the streets and exhibits of the most heterogeneous wares. The soldiers were buying as souvenirs all the junk that had not been sold for years. So it was time for me to get out of this dry rot too.

In our Passage, the children were playing on the sidewalk as they waited for lunch. On the stairs, I met my mother, who kissed me joyfully, as usual. I was surprised to find her all made up at this hour, her eyelids black with kohl and her lips blood-red. She was also wearing a new apron. Did I want something to eat? No, I would rather sleep. Not even an egg? No, not even an egg. I was very tired. She asked if I would mind sleeping at Uncle Aroun's; it had all been arranged with him. Before I could inquire into these new arrangements, she excitedly told me she was serving meals to soldiers, in partnership with the second-floor neighbors who had a large flat. The neighbors had put all their beds in one room, and since our own flat was smaller it was used as a pantry and kitchen. Proudly, she announced that in this way she earned more than my father and the shop. She seemed so happy and so sure that she deserved my admiration that I dared say nothing. My legs were giving way and, in spite of myself, I could not hear her chattering away. I left her and knocked at the door on the first floor. Kalla opened it and blurted out that she had been expecting me. I noticed now that she had our mother's thin lips, bloodless and tight

when she was sad or angry. She was angry and ashamed of
Mother's commercial enterprise and was now living with our
uncle:

"And you don't know the latest invention of the neighbors'
son? He mixes wine and bitter almond syrup and sells it at
a huge price as a special local beverage."

A month earlier, I would have joined forces with my
sister in disapproving of these scandalous goings on. Now, I
only saw in her my own ridiculous and irritating simple-
mindedness. I vaguely promised Kalla I would look into
this business and, without taking further notice of her disappointment, went to bed.

When I awoke, it was striking five but the sun was still
warm. I had slept perfectly, for four hours in a deep sleep
such as I had not known for a very long time. Kalla had
disappeared, but on the table I found some letters addressed
to me. Although they had been there for days, I did not open
them immediately with my usual impatience. Who could still
hold me in this city? Only a printed letter from the Community Treasurer attracted my attention. I had expected it
and I knew what it contained. Indeed, it was to tell me I
could come and collect my salary as a forced laborer. I
dressed and went at once to the cashier, who was just closing
shop. The sum was fairly big and very welcome, for my stay
in Algiers had emptied my pockets. I divided my money in
two sums, put the smaller one in my wallet and the other
in my pocket within easy reach of my hand.

Night fell suddenly while I was still on my way home. In
the Passage, the heat had driven all the tenants out of their
flats. In summer, after gulping down their dinner, they usually put chairs out on the sidewalk and chatted until it got
cool. In the silence of the night, they formed an island of
sound. This reminded me of our well-hidden clubroom in our
old blind alley, where we had sat in the cool when it was so
hot outside. All this chattering with loud calls and exclama-
tions from sidewalk to sidewalk now seemed unbearably vulgar to me. The blind alley had never really existed; my

heart had only been more peaceful before I had come to understand.

My father was still upstairs, so I went into the apartment. I pulled out the larger part of my earnings and gave it to him. "I've collected my pay," I explained, "you know, my worker's pay."

He stammered, embarrassed by his obvious pleasure.

"All that! Have you any left for yourself, at least?"

"Yes, yes, quite enough."

Then I went to get some food in the kitchen. Never had it been so plentiful. I settled at one of the tables of our temporary restaurant and read as I ate. I heard my father dressing slowly. I was certain he would never say more of this. In fact, after having puttered around and hesitated, he went and joined the others in the street. But it did not last long. Our usual intermediary, my mother, came up. She bustled around in the rooms, moved a few chairs, finally came closer, put her hands on the table, and said confidentially:

"Your father blesses you. He is very moved, you know. It's not so much the money, but the thought behind it that has moved him."

I smiled vaguely and pretended to be busy with my book. She did not insist and disappeared. It was not a question of money! I cannot even be angry with them; there can be neither judge nor accused. So this is what is required of the elder son, feared and respected even by his father: to bring home money and assume the authority that this confers, even at the expense of his own individual existence and significance.

I did not have to hurry to get to Henry's, for the heat kept the whole city awake. His mother did not seem at all surprised as she opened the door. She was a tall, thin woman with a far-away look in her eyes, a chain-smoker. In spite of thirty years in this country, she had never become a part of it; she lived alone, silent and reserved even with her own son. Before I had time to open my mouth, she pointed

toward the upstairs rooms with her cigarette. Henry was
certainly in his converted laundry on the roof. I climbed
the stairs in the semidarkness and suddenly came into the
light of the moon on the flat white terrace. Night, in our
country, is no real night, and in the daytime, all color dis-
appears in the violent light. The penthouse laundries, huddled together, stood out like chiseled panels of light and
shade on the roof.

With the door and windows wide open, Henry was writing
by the light of a symbolical candle. The doorway framed the
swollen orange moon and the bluish light in the room melted
on Henry's head and shoulders, as in a cheap chromo-
lithograph that had miraculously come to life.

Henry said: "I've finished. Sit down, and in a moment,
I'll read you my prose."

Without thinking, I closed the door before sitting down.
The multicolored sheaf of light was sharply decapitated and
the candlelight, winking and absurd, dominated the room.

"Why have you closed the door?" asked Henry.

"Because of. . . ."

My sentence remained unfinished. I had been about to say:
"Because of moonstrokes." Instinctively, I had wanted to protect him against this evil light. That is how I became eman-
cipated. I had been told that moonstroke made the eyes pop
out of the head, caused huge bumps that are soft as a baby's
skull, and brought about death by violent madness. One
must cover one's head in bright moonlight as well as in
sunlight. I would never rid myself of those pictures of men
who, having slept bareheaded in the moonlight, woke up
blind and mad and then ran howling through the night.
Can one live with such endless distrust and refusal of oneself,
with this doubting that is nevertheless so necessary?

"Leave the door alone and listen to this," said Henry.

He then read me a very funny description of life at the
Italian school. I tried to be attentive and complimented him.
Then we turned to Argentina. I had been afraid he might
have already forgotten this last plan of his. It had, in any

case, probably been only a fantasy. As soon as I spoke of it, however, it again assumed reality in Henry's eyes. He told me he had definitely decided to leave.

"Well, I'm delighted," he concluded. "You'll see how rich we'll become."

Henry, who was disinterested and both lavish and a little miserly, often spoke of fabulous deals and wealth. Financial power was a compensation for him and fed his imagination:

"It is not wealth that attracts me," I said.

"Then why are you leaving?"

"Just like that."

"Ah? And why follow me to Argentina, of all places?"

I was trapped. I realized too late that I should never have started this discussion. An explanation seemed unbearable. What could I say, and how could I make myself clear? I had no intention of telling Henry about my health. Impulsively, however, I chose this alternative as the lesser evil. So I told him how necessary my departure was because of the climate, as though this was the real reason for my decision.

He was the only person I had ever trusted with this secret. Sometimes I have childishly regretted it. Perhaps I did not derive from my illness all the attention and affection it generally warrants. Perhaps I revealed it to Henry, in spite of myself, to compensate for this. Well, I achieved my little success. Henry, who had his back turned, whirled around suddenly and, with real friendship, put his arm around my shoulders. He even used a few Italian expressions while his free hand gesticulated.

But there was not the slightest trace of emotion in me. I was ashamed at cheating him like this, with such an obviously emotional excuse. My physical catastrophe was the least of my misfortunes.

Henry told me that his sister too was "stricken": he could not pronounce the word tubercular. She was living in Switzerland and was slowly getting better. It's not as dangerous as it used to be, he assured me, and one gets over it very

well. I would quickly get well with the will to do so, and I
was sensible to come with him to live in Argentina, in the
fresh air.

For a second, I was tempted to confide in Henry and tell
him all the truth. Did I still feel like living? But my courage
failed. I confirmed him in his opinions and vaguely assured
him that I very much wanted to get well. He let himself be
persuaded, and I unjustly reflected that no one can put himself in the place of another.

He took a new copybook and, on its cover, wrote: "Argentina." He listed first the indispensable things that still had
to be done and divided the work between us. He was very
busy when I left.

It was late, and I could not hope to sleep after so long a
nap. When I reached our Passage, seats and benches were
being noisily moved. For all these beings with regular and
unconscious lives each hour had its meaning. To avoid useless
questions, I sought refuge on the terrace. The moon had
risen high and it would have been easy to read. I leaned on
the white railing. The scent of the night was forever marked
with the sulfurous odor of bombs. Of the eight buildings in
the Passage—four to the left and four to the right—three had
been hit. The last one to the right was a spectacular ruin,
cut in two as by a knife, with a piece of wall hanging from
the third floor by its iron supports, motionless above sheer
void. Fifteen yards from the ground, the tiles of an open
kitchen reflected the blue light. Hard and perpendicular in
the Passage, the moonlight flooded the smallest detail. Soon
the last sounds died out; a dreaming baby screamed and went
back to sleep.

Complete silence. The chime of a Westminster clock broke
it, and then the hoarse spasms of my father's fit of coughing
seemed to wrench the night air, drowning the elegant chimes,
then becoming fainter as the music gained the upper hand,
delicate as a thin spiral of smoke that a sudden wind had
scattered for an instant. I tried to count the strokes, in spite
of the blanks that the cough had blotted out: three . . . five

. . . six . . . eight . . . ten, eleven. Eleven or twelve? How can I find out? The world is dead and I have no watch.

For once, Henry planned efficiently and he soon had our passage booked. We were to sail in five days' time. I used these days to do my share of the preparations and make a few calls. After much hesitation I went to see Poinsot. I had not seen him since the beginning of the German occupation, after the incident I have described. I did not find him at home. Because of a slight nervous depression, he had gone back to France for treatment. Why did this give me a certain strange pleasure? It was as though it excused Poinsot. Even such clear certainties, it seemed, could save nobody, and Poinsot's piercing vision could also get blurred. There was also a touch of childish regret: he would not give me the last piece of advice for which I had perhaps unconsciously come.

Why did I put it off so long? I only told my parents of my departure the day before I left—to make things easier, or as a last expression of filial pity? My father did not insist much and my mother understood nothing and cried up to the last minute. Before leaving the house I destroyed my diary. There were already eight big notebooks, and I was taking only a bag on my back, like when I left home for the labor camp. Besides, books are my only possession and they weigh too much.

We should have sailed at five o'clock, but the job of loading the ship seemed interminable and we weighed anchor only at sunset. As soon as we came out of the channel that leads into the harbor of Tunis, Henry was sick and went to lie down. I stayed on deck till we were out at sea, leaning on the rail. I lost sight of the coastline as night descended on the ship. It seemed to ooze from the holds, to fill the hatch, and to stain the blue sky with gray. First one star shone, then a second, then thousands. I grew uneasy gazing at the violet sea which attracted me like a sorceress while it heaved and settled, so I went down to the hold to sleep.